when it Rains

By
Lisa De Jong

ISBN-13: 978-1492784180
ISBN-10: 1492784184

Edited by Jessica Carnes and Jennifer Roberts-Hall
Cover by Mae I Design

Contents

"Love is the flower you've got to let grow."
-John Lennon

Prologue

WHEN YOU LIVE IN A SMALL TOWN, there's not much to do on a Friday night after a football game. When the season started, some of the seniors at my high school decided that we should all get together and have a bonfire after each game. It was really just an excuse to drink and hook-up: two things I wasn't interested in, but I always went to hang out with my friends anyway.

That's where I was that night.

The night I retreated into darkness, where my night sky had no stars, my days had no sun, and all hope was drained from my body.

It was the night my life ended.

Beau Bennett wasn't there. If he had been, he would've saved me, just like he always did. He was grounded that night for staying out past curfew the Friday before; in fact, it's the only weekend I remember Beau ever being grounded.

I believe that life is a series of coincidences, and that night, coincidence screwed me over.

I was there with Morgan, my best friend since third grade. She was dating the Senior Class President at the time and it didn't take long before they disappeared, leaving me huddled near the fire with some of the other kids from my school. I felt completely comfortable being there because I've known most of these people since I had moved here when I was five. That's one of the nice things about small towns.

Or so I thought.

When it Rains

I was sitting with my arms wrapped around myself, trying to warm what the fire couldn't, when Drew Heston sat down next to me. My stomach immediately did a somersault; I mean Drew was a senior. Mr. Football, as everyone called him. He was the local hero, the type of guy who would have his own billboard outside of town someday. It didn't hurt that he looked amazing with his short dark hair, light green eyes and broad shoulders.

I had secretly crushed on him since the day I first walked into the doors of my high school. There was something about the way he walked the halls with his head held high that commanded every girl's attention, including mine. I'd never talked to him, but there he was, sitting next to me in front of the fire. I couldn't believe it. Things like that didn't happen to Kate Alexander.

"Hey, Kate, how've you been?" he asked, his eyes burning into the side of my head. I couldn't bring myself to look at him. Just being near him made me lose all comprehension of the English language.

"Fine," I mumbled, biting down on my lower lip. A shiver ran through my body like a freight train as I finally peered up at him.

"Were you at my game tonight?" he asked, bumping my shoulder with his. I could feel the heat coming off his muscular body and it made me blush.

My thoughts drifted back to the third quarter when Drew threw the ball to his star receiver Jackson Reid who, at the time, was surrounded by defenders. My heart raced with excitement as I watched Jackson and three members of the other team jump up to catch the ball at the same time. In the end, Jackson came out victorious because Drew had thrown it right into his hands. It was nothing short of amazing, yet for Drew, it was completely normal.

"You were great," I replied, nervously reaching up to tighten my ponytail. A breeze blew through and a few raindrops fell from the sky. I ran my hands up and down my arms in an attempt to chase the chill from my body, but it didn't help.

"Are you cold?" he asked, scooting his body even closer to mine. The way he was looking at me sent butterflies through my stomach. It wasn't like I was an outcast at school, but I wasn't one of the elite, popular girls that guys like Drew usually spent any of their time on.

"A little. I forgot my jacket at home," I replied, feeling a few more raindrops fall on my cheek.

He stood up and reached for my hand. "Come on. I have an extra sweatshirt in the house you can borrow."

The party was being held at his house since his parents had gone out of town that weekend. I hesitated for a minute before placing my hand in his. I knew of him, but I didn't really know him. It wasn't the first time I'd been to his house, but it was the first time I'd been invited inside. I felt a little uneasy, but I still trusted him. I didn't have any reason not to.

Drew opened the front door, never loosening his grip on my hand as he guided us through the house. My attention was focused on the contemporary paint colors and beautiful cherry wood floors; it barely registered that we were heading upstairs.

I watched as he took a key out of his pocket to unlock one of the doors that lined the second story hallway. He must have noticed the way I was looking at him because his lips turned up on the sides. "I don't like anyone to be in my room but me," he said, pushing the door open.

I nodded, following him inside. Did I feel a little uncomfortable stepping into Drew Heston's bedroom? Yes. Did I think for one moment that I shouldn't be there? No. I'd known him for years and everyone that knew him, thought the world of him.

When he closed the door and locked it, I felt my heart rate pick up. I watched him glance around the room, following his eyes with mine. The walls were a deep navy blue with various football posters covering them. And I'll never forget how it smelled like he had used cologne to cover up the stench of his dirty gym clothes.

Drew remained still, staring at me with glossed over eyes and, suddenly, being there didn't feel right. "Can you find that sweatshirt? I should probably get back outside before Morgan comes looking for me."

"Oh yeah, give me a sec," he said, moving to dig through a drawer in his dresser. I walked to the window at the other end of the room and looked down at the diminishing fire. The rain was falling faster against the glass making it harder to see into the distance, but it looked like everyone had left their spots by the fire. I really needed to hurry up and find Morgan before she left without me.

The house was completely quiet, sending a chill down my spine. I closed my eyes and listened to Drew's footsteps moving closer to me, my heart beating faster every time I heard the rubber soles of his shoes against the floorboards. Everything about being inside his room felt wrong and I knew I needed to escape it. Going to his room was a bad idea . . . and going to that party without Beau was a huge mistake.

As his footsteps continued to get closer, I spun on my heels to head towards the door. I was greeted with dark eyes and a vacant stare. This was not the same Drew that sat next to me by the fire. I wanted to run out of this house and never look back but he was blocking my path. "I'm going to wait outside. It's getting warm in here," I lied, motioning toward his door.

He didn't say a word as he pressed his body to mine, completely closing any gap that remained between us. My

Lisa De Jong

hands were sweaty and my knees felt like they were made of paper. It was as if he was in a trance, and it was scaring the hell out of me.

"Drew."

"It's raining outside, Kate," he said, reaching his hand up to cup my cheek. I stepped back out of his grasp, but he followed me. It wasn't long before my back was against the wall. Even if I wanted to leave, it was too late. His hands rested on the wall behind me, caging me in with his arms. "Mm, you smell so good," he growled, pressing his lips to my neck. I felt helpless.

"Drew, please, just let me go. I need to find Morgan," I cried. My whole body was shaking from a fear unlike anything I'd ever felt before. It was paralyzing, but I was stuck.

He ignored me, running his lips down my jawline. I turned my head to fight, but he followed my movements. "What's the matter, Kate? I see the way you look at me. You want this as much as I do," he said with a husky voice that sent more panic through my already tense body. I used the little bit of strength I had left in me to push on his chest, but he didn't move. Not even an inch.

"Let me go," I pleaded. His right hand came down to grip my hip hard as he roughly pressed his lips to mine. The force of his kiss sent a sharp pain through my mouth, and all that I could taste was the tinge of my blood and the alcohol on his breath.

His hand found the bottom of my shirt and started working the material up my bare stomach. I tried to move my legs forward but he was so much bigger and stronger than me. If anything, my attempts to push him away were only making things worse.

He gripped my wrists tightly and pulled me over to his bed, pushing me flat onto my stomach. I tried to pull my arms loose, but it caused pain to shoot through my wrists. I've never felt more terrified in my whole life. He

v

continued to hold my arms behind my back and pinned my legs down with his knees.

"HELP," I yelled as loud as I could through my panic and tears.

He clamped his hand over my mouth, yanking my head back until my neck ached. "Everyone's outside. No one's going to hear you."

That was it. I was trapped under him, alone with no one to save me. All the fight I had left was drained from my body, and the chances of anyone pulling me out of this hell were getting slimmer by the minute. Tears rolled down my face, soaking his bedspread while I fixated on the raindrops hitting the window. He forced my jeans down so they were left slung around my left ankle. When I heard him working at his belt buckle, I felt like I couldn't breathe anymore. I'd never been exposed like that and it wasn't at all what I wanted. I was saving myself for someone special and Drew was going to take it from me. I gasped for air but I couldn't get any into my lungs. I tried to scream again but no sound came out.

I felt him pressed against my backside and it made me want to throw up. "STOP," I screamed, trying again to free myself from his hold, but he was too strong.

He let out a hushed chuckle from behind. "Are you going to give up?"

"Please, don't," I begged again. It was my last chance and I knew it. He didn't respond and when I heard the sound of foil ripping, I squeezed my eyes shut and said a silent prayer. I wanted it all to be a nightmare I would soon wake up from. I wanted someone to come through that door and stop it from happening. I wanted to be anywhere but there.

Except no one was listening to me that night. I could hear the soft tap of the rain falling on the window, but the rest of the house was completely silent. I used to like the sound of rain but Drew took that from me too.

He pressed into me so quickly that pain erupted through my whole body, sending a deafening scream into the darkness of the room. I squeezed my eyes shut, feeling like I was drowning with no way to get to the surface. I've never felt such intense physical and emotional pain all at once. It was the absolute worst moment of my life.

It still is.

He didn't stop. Not when I screamed. Not when I cried. He kept invading my body with each and every thrust, killing me a little more inside each time. It hurt more to fight it so I remained still, continuing to stare numbly at the droplets that rolled down the window. He grunted as he continued to shred my soul to pieces but I tried my best to block it out. I didn't need to have his words locked into my memory forever when I already had to live with the feel of him inside of me. I knew I'd never be the same after what he did to me.

I'm not sure how long I was in the room, but it felt like an eternity. My whole life flashed before me as I was overcome with grief. For the rest of my life, I would always regret going up to that room with Drew Heston. I could never get that day back or any of the other things he took from me.

The most important thing I lost was my sense of self. It took seventeen years to build my foundation and it took mere minutes to tear it down.

I hate him.

The old Kate is gone . . . and she's never coming back.

And I'll always hate when it rains.

Chapter 1

2 Years Later

I NEVER IMAGINED A DAY WITHOUT LIGHT. A day without hope. A day where I had nothing to look forward to. I used to be a star on the track team, but now I'm only running from myself. I used to dream about becoming a lawyer one day, but now I can't even bring myself to go to college. I used to have lots of friends, but now all I have is Beau . . . and he's leaving for college tomorrow.

Some days I don't even want to go on anymore. What's the point? For a while, people would ask what was wrong with me, but I wouldn't tell them. I wouldn't tell anyone. Why? Who would believe that the town hero raped me? I'm Kate Alexander, the daughter of the never-been-married waitress. The girl who doesn't even know who her father is.

Drew's family has money, so everyone in town thinks they walk on water. They would have turned it all around on me anyway, saying I'd asked for it. I don't know . . . maybe I did. Maybe I did something that made him believe I'd wanted to have sex with him that night. It replays over and over in my head, but I can't make any sense of it.

Nothing makes sense to me anymore.

Living in a small town, and seeing the person who took everything from me walking the halls of our high school, driving down my street, or walking into the diner where I work, had almost killed me. I couldn't eat. I couldn't sleep. I didn't leave my house unless I'd had to, and I'd had more sick days my junior year than I had every other year combined. I was barely living.

I was scared to be alone. I was scared that he would do it again. My once picture perfect view of the world was gone, and all that remained were a bunch of broken pieces that I couldn't glue back together.

When Drew left for college the following summer, I'd taken my first deep breath in almost a year. I started hanging out with Beau again and slowly put on some of the weight I'd lost.

I'm still stuck in that moment two years ago, though. I haven't quite figured out how to move forward. How am I supposed to move on with my life? Am I supposed to pretend that everything is okay when it's not?

I prefer to be alone in my room, listening to music while staring at the ceiling. I can point you to every crack, bump or water stain. I've spent more time staring at it than I have sleeping. I don't like to sleep because when I do I can't control where my mind takes me, and the nightmares are always the same. The flashbacks grip me around the arms and hold me down just like Drew did that night. I want to be free of them. I want them to let me go, but they won't and I can't make them.

I also hate when people ask me if I'm okay. I hate when they ask me what's wrong, or what they can do to make it better. Honestly, I don't think anyone can fix me. I wish they would just stop trying.

My mom is a different story. I think she knows something isn't right, but she doesn't stay at home long enough to learn the truth. I can't blame her, though. She has to work two different jobs to make ends meet; she's working to take care of me just like she has been the last nineteen years, all by herself.

When my grades started to suffer, she'd confronted me about it, but I'd told her that things were getting harder for me and she had let it go. She'd asked why she hadn't seen Morgan around the house lately, and I'd told her that Morgan had a new boyfriend who she spent all her time with. She'd believed that too.

When she asks if I want to go shopping, I say no. When she asks if I want to go out to dinner, I say no. I'm scared that I'll see someone I don't want to see.

It is easier to hide.

And the painful realization that Beau Bennett is moving five hours away from me tomorrow makes me want to curl into a ball and cry until there are no more tears to shed. I've seen him almost every day since we became neighbors when I was five years old, and even though things haven't been the same between us lately, I can't imagine not having him in my life. He means everything to me, even if I can't say it. He's the one person in the world I trust not to hurt me.

He was my dream for so many years.

We played together every day after school throughout elementary. He was just my friend then, of course, because I was going through the whole boys are gross stage, but something changed in middle school. I started to notice things like his beautiful blue eyes, his strong jaw . . . I would sit in class and stare at the back of his head, fantasizing about running my fingers through his shaggy brown hair.

I was going to marry Beau Bennett someday but nothing ever happened between us. I was too scared to make the first move, and he was too busy chasing the pretty girls at school. I used to hope that maybe someday he'd see me like I saw him, but when he finally did, it was too late.

I'm not the same girl anymore. I'll never be her again.

When it Rains

We've had our share of good and bad moments. In fact, the last time Beau and I went anywhere together was our senior prom. Just thinking about it makes me nervous about what today will bring.

Tonight is my Senior Prom. I didn't want to go, but Beau practically begged me to, saying it was something I'd always regret if I didn't. I wanted to tell him there were lots of things I'd regret, but not going to Senior Prom wouldn't be one of them.

In the end, though, Beau's persistence paid off and I agreed to go with him because I know if I don't go, he won't go. I spent some of the money I've earned at the diner on a new dress because I want to look good for Beau. I don't want him to regret choosing me as his date.

When Beau knocks on my door, I'm nervous but a little excited. For one night, I'm going to pretend to be just a normal, happy teenage girl. I take one last look at my long auburn hair in the hallway mirror and smooth down my knee length sapphire blue dress before opening the door. Beau stares down at me with his lips parted, and for a brief moment I wonder if this is really a good idea.

But then he smiles, and all doubt leaves me.

"Are you ready to go?" he asks, holding his hand out to me. He looks amazing in his black suit with a blue tie to match my dress. "Oh wait, I almost forgot." He holds up a small box and opens it to reveal a small corsage made from white lilies, my favorite flower. He carefully slides it over my hand, making sure the flowers are aligned perfectly on my wrist.

"Thank you," I say, slipping my hand in his.

The night is going better than I expected. We spend most of our time on the dance floor, and when we take a break, Beau never leaves my side. A few people stare at me; I assume they're surprised to see me here, but I don't

4

let it get to me. I used to be just another student, but now I feel like I'm constantly on the outside looking in. Tonight, a little piece of me feels as if I'm a part of the world again.

"Do you want to go to the after party?" Beau asks as the lights come on and the principal announces that the last song is playing.

I shake my head. I've already stepped way outside my comfort zone for the night, and I don't want to face all my old friends. I always feel like people are judging me and I hate it.

"Do you want to go hang out by the lake?" he asks, wrapping his arm around my shoulders.

Do I? This is the happiest I've been in almost two years, and I know it won't continue forever. Once I have time to think again, the momentary escape with Beau will be over. Reality always has a way of sucking me in again.

I nod as we get into his truck and roll down the windows. We ride in silence while the wind whips through my hair and country music plays softly on the radio. I wish all moments in life could be like this one. I feel free, safe, and more than anything, I feel a part of the old me creeping into the present.

We pull up by the beach and Beau grabs a fleece blanket from the backseat before jumping out of the truck and coming around to open my door for me. We head toward the lake, placing the blanket down a few feet from the water's edge. It's only May and the air is chilly as we sit next to each other. I inhale the wonderful damp smell the lake provides and enjoy the tranquility it gives me. The breeze blows past us and I begin to shiver.

"Are you cold?" Beau asks.

"Yeah, it's not as warm as I thought it was," I say, wrapping my arms around my folded knees. Beau slips off his suit jacket and places it around my shoulders. It's one

of the things I like most about him; he's always thinking about others before he thinks about himself.

We continue to look over the water's horizon, listening to the leaves rustle with the wind and the soft sounds of the small waves crashing against the beach. It's peaceful here. If life allowed, I would have stayed locked up in this moment forever, especially if it meant I could erase all the others.

"Did you change your mind about college yet?" he asks, breaking the silence.

I haven't changed my mind. I haven't even given it a second thought. It doesn't matter anyway; I don't see much of a future for myself. "No, I'm staying here, at least this year."

"I wish you'd change your mind. You have so much to offer, Kate. You should let the world see it," he says, keeping his eyes on the water.

"I just can't right now," I whisper, swallowing down my emotions.

"Something changed you, and I'm going to keep digging until I find out what that is." His head tilts in my direction and our eyes lock. I want to tell him that the old Kate is never coming back, but we've had that conversation before. He will only ask questions that I don't want to answer.

"I'm sorry," I say, turning my eyes away from him.

My eyelids are getting heavy, so I lie on my back and wrap the jacket tightly around me. I close my eyes and focus on the sound of nature to keep my mind off of other things. When I feel Beau against my side, I open my eyes to see him looking down at me, his head resting in his hand. His face moves closer to mine and I can feel my heart beating hard against my chest. When I feel his warm breath against my mouth, I close my eyes and his lips gently brush against mine. His touch is warm and tender, and I can't help but comb my fingers through his hair. I'm trying to make an old dream come true.

I let myself get lost in him. For a moment, I feel as if we're the only two people in the world and nothing else matters. I feel like there is a small chance I could let go of everything and just be with him like this forever, but when he leans in to me and rests his body on top of mine, panic shoots through my entire body. My mind flashes to Drew and painful memories start to race through my head as I push roughly against his chest. "Stop!" I cry, rolling onto my other side.

"What's wrong? What did I do?" The ache I hear in his voice makes my heart fall a little further into my stomach. This is my fault, not his.

When I felt Beau's body on top of mine, I could see the anger in Drew's eyes and feel the way his fingers dug into my skin. I just want the memories to go away.

"Fuck. Kate, please say something!" Beau says with a strained voice.

I flinch, wrapping my arms around my stomach. "Can you please just take me home?"

I want to tell him. I want to tell someone, but I can't.

He stands in front of me with his hands folded behind his neck. I back away, making sure to put an arms-length distance between us. "Jesus, will you please just tell me what's going on? I can't keep watching you pull further and further away from me."

"Just take me home, Beau," I whisper before walking in the direction of the truck. When I hear him call my name, I stop and turn my neck to look back at him.

"I can't keep doing this shit. Why won't you talk to me? Give me one reason!" he yells, gripping his hair between his fingers.

"You don't want to hear it. Trust me," I cry, covering my mouth with my hand. Just thinking about telling him everything makes the bile rise from my stomach. No one

wants to hear that good little Kate isn't who they think she is. She's been damaged.

"Try me," he says, sounding tired and frustrated. "Nothing you tell me will change the way I feel about you. Nothing."

I shake my head and start walking again.

"Kate come back here!" he shouts. And part of me wants to. Part of me wants to go back to him and wrap my arms around his neck and never let go, but I can't.

I ignore him and climb into the truck, watching him stare toward the water with his hands on his hips. I wanted him so badly at one point in my life, but he deserves so much more than the shell of who I once was. I watch as he picks up a large rock and throws it in the water before wrenching the blanket into a ball and heading toward the truck.

I'm dreading the awkward, silent ride home, and when he kicks his front driver's side tire before climbing in the truck, I know I may have pushed him a little too far this time. He's tried to find out what happened to me many times over the past two years, but this is the first time he's ever kissed me. In a way, I've rejected the one person who I should be holding onto.

He sits in the truck and slams his door shut. I want to look over at him, but I can't bring myself to do it. "I'm sorry," I whisper. I'm not sure if he hears me . . . he doesn't respond.

As he drives me home, he looks lost in his own world, and I know I'm the one who put him there. I want him to be happy, but I'm not the person who can give him that.

He didn't come over to my house for six days afterward. He didn't call or text. I thought I'd finally pushed him too far, but on day seven he knocked on my door, proving why he really is the only guy I can trust.

Since that night, Beau and I have gone back to the way we had been the last two years. I keep him close enough for comfort, but far enough not to let him see inside. Somehow, he can always read me, though, and I both love and hate him for it.

We also haven't been back to the lake since that night. In fact, we haven't gone anywhere. We've either hung out around his house or mine. Maybe it's because I'm afraid of what might happen between us if we're alone. Maybe I'm afraid of what I might tell Beau if he tries hard enough to break down my walls. I'm scared of everything these days.

This may be one of the last days we will have together for a while, so I agreed to go to the lake with him. It holds so many good memories from my past, and I can't help but think that what happened last time could have been a good memory too. I have lots of moments I'd like to hold on to forever, but I'm afraid they will always be overshadowed by that one horrible memory I can't let go of.

Chapter 2

A KNOCK AT THE DOOR IS A WELCOME BREAK. I peek through the window and see the back of Beau's head with all its tousled dark hair and I instantly feel my chest tighten. This is going to be much harder than I'd thought.

I reach for the doorknob and take a deep breath. He turns around as I open the door and gives me the dimple-bearing smile I love so much. My eyes meet his bright blue ones, and I see some of the sadness I feel reflected in them.

This isn't going to be easy on either of us.

"Hey," Beau says, pulling me in for a hug. I breathe in the smell of his soap. Not that I need to; I can close my eyes and remember exactly what he smells like any time I want.

"Hey," I say, pulling back and wrapping my hands around his arms. "Are you all ready to go tomorrow?"

The smile falls from his face. "Everything is ready to go. I wanted to make sure I could spend the rest of my day with you."

I can't decide if I should cry or smile. He's the sweetest, most caring person I've ever met, and for some reason, after everything that's happened between us, he still wants to be around me.

"You look really nice today, by the way," he says, moving his eyes up and down my body. I quickly cross my arms over my chest, very aware that all I have on over my swimsuit is cut off shorts and a white tank. I may be a walking contradiction to the average teenage girl because

I don't like to draw attention to the way I look. If the summer weather allowed it, I would wear nothing but baggy sweats and t-shirts.

Beau, on the other hand, looks carefree, standing in front of me in nothing but black swim trunks and a tight white t-shirt. He's not at all ashamed of who he is.

"I can't believe summer's over already," I say, looking down at my feet. I don't want him to see the tears that are glistening in my eyes whenever I think about living a day without him. He knows me too well, though.

He wraps me in his arms again and kisses my forehead. "I'll come back every weekend if you want me to . . . or you can come visit me. You know I'll do anything for you."

I pull back, shaking my head. "Enjoy the college experience. You don't need to worry about me," I say, whispering the last part. But I don't know if I really want him to listen to me. In fact, I'm pretty sure I don't.

"Come on, let's go," he says, leading me toward his truck. It's an old red beat up Chevy with a loud muffler. In a way, I'm going to miss it too; I always feel better when I hear his truck pulling down our street and into his driveway. It means he isn't that far away if I need him.

I lean my head against the window and try to convince myself that everything will be okay. Just because I don't believe it now, doesn't mean I can't keep trying.

When we arrive at the lake, I put a smile on my face and try to make the best of this last day we have together. The next time I see Beau, he's going to have amazing stories about the things he's done at college and the people he's met . . . the girls he's met.

There's a gnawing feeling in my chest as I watch him set two towels down on the beach. Someday he's going to do this with someone else and he'll be smiling at her like he's smiling at me right now. I don't know why I even let myself think about it because it hurts so damn much.

We sit side by side with our arms resting on our knees and stare out at the blue water. It's quiet now that all of the kids have gone back to school and summer vacations have ended.

I don't come out here often anymore because I'd constantly be looking over my shoulder, jumping at every noise I hear. Today is different, though. When I look at Beau, I feel like everything is going to be okay. He gives me a sense of security; he always has. I can't take my eyes off him as I watch him stand and slide his shirt over his head, revealing his toned stomach.

"You up for a swim today?" he asks, running his hand through his hair.

I look up at the clear blue sky. I shrug. "Why not."

"Hurry up and I'll race you," he teases, resting his hands on his hips.

I roll my eyes and slide out of my clothes, feeling exposed in my one-piece black suit. "Beau, can you just go in before me? Please."

"Come on! I'll let you win," he says, tilting his head to the side.

I move to sit back down on the towel, but he grabs my elbow, halting me in place. "It's just you and me out here. You don't have to be scared."

He quickly lets go of my arm and walks into the water, leaving me standing alone. I watch as his legs gradually disappear under the water before walking in after him. The water is warm and as clear as lake water can be.

He glances back at me when he hears my feet splashing in the water, and I don't miss the grin on his face before he turns back around.

I swim out to him, standing in water that hits right on my shoulders. "Do you remember when we came out here after my mom bought me my first bikini?" I ask, trying to lighten the mood.

"Yeah," he laughs. "I've never seen you turn so red."

"It's not funny, Beau," I say, splashing water at him.

"You screamed so loud, I thought something really bad happened." He shakes his head, trying really hard to control himself. "But then you came out of the water with your hands covering your chest yelling about how you were never coming back to this stupid lake again."

When I came up from diving into the water that day, I realized my bikini top hadn't come up with me. I completely lost it.

"If you were me, you would have been mortified too."

"You were only nine. There wasn't that much to look at," he teases, splashing some water back at me. "And do you remember how long it was before you agreed to come back to the lake with me?"

I playfully smack his shoulder, trying hard not to laugh. "That doesn't matter."

"It was the very next day," he says, holding his hands up in front of his face to avoid getting more water in his eyes.

"I wore a one piece."

"Yeah, the black one with a big pink flower on the front. I remember," he says, lowering his voice.

My heart does this little flip-flop thing it sometimes does when Beau's around. "How do you remember everything?"

"I don't . . . I just remember everything about you," he says, brushing the back of his finger against my cheek.

I swallow, unable to speak as I watch beads of water race down his forehead.

When it's just us, I feel as if we're the only two people in the world. It's actually my idea of perfect. But sometimes, like right now, it feels almost a little too perfect.

"How's your mom?" I ask, turning my attention to the water for a few seconds to break the tension.

He shrugs. "She's already asking when I'm coming back to visit, but I think she'll be okay. It's not like I'm moving across the country. You might have to take care of her for me." A slight smile crosses my lips as I peer down at the diamonds reflecting off of the water. Beau and his mom are close. His dad works a lot of hours managing one of the local factories and Beau's an only child, just like me. I think that's part of the reason we became such good friends.

"Are you going to miss me?" I ask. I instantly regret the words as soon as they slip out of my mouth.

He turns his head to the side before he faces me again with a somber expression on his face. "You really have no idea, do you?"

"I'm sorry, I shouldn't have asked," I reply, shaking my head.

He sighs, running his hand through his damp hair. "That's not what I meant."

I can't remove my eyes from his as I watch his jaw move back and forth like he's having an internal debate about what he should say next. I remain still, rolling my lower lip between my teeth as I wait for him to say something.

"Yes, Kate, I'm going to miss you. I'm so damn in love with you, I can barely stand to spend a few hours apart from you, and now we're going to be miles and hours apart. It sucks. It really fucking sucks," he says, lowering his voice a little more with each word.

I'm shocked. Completely and utterly shocked. I don't see how anyone could love me. I'm not pretty. I'm certainly not that fun to be around, and I've let go of all my dreams. What is there to love about me?

I remove my eyes from his, watching his Adam's apple move up and down as he swallows. When I look back up, his eyes are burning into me, and I know he's waiting for me to react. He just laid his heart out in front of me, and I'm struggling with how I feel about it. This is the moment I dreamt of for years. I was the princess waiting for my prince to come save me from the top of the highest tower. Now, I'm unreachable . . . even for Beau.

I look past him to the line of houses on the other side of the lake in an effort to buy myself a few more seconds. "You're not in love with me. There's a difference between being in love and loving someone. I'll always love you, but I'm not the girl you deserve to be falling in love with. You need someone who can give you everything," I say, swallowing down the lump in my throat. I've waited for Beau Bennett to tell me he loves me for years. He's just too late.

He moves in closer, grabbing my chin gently between his fingertips. "I love you. I think I've loved you since I was five."

"Why are you telling me this now?" I ask pinching my eyes closed to avoid his.

"Look at me," he says, frustration laced in his tone. "I've wanted to tell you for a very long time, but I didn't think you were ready to hear it. I'm leaving tomorrow and I couldn't wait any longer."

"Beau, I—"

He stops me, putting his finger over my lips. "Don't say anything yet," he says, slowly removing his finger. "I can't leave tomorrow without asking you something. I don't care about anyone else. I've tried for years to get you out of my head because you were supposed to be my best friend, but I can't do it, Kate. I want you to give me a chance."

Sadness spills through my chest like a disease. I don't have a problem pushing people away these days, but the guy standing in front of me isn't someone I want to lose. That's exactly what's going to happen when I tell him the truth.

"I can't," I whisper as the first tear rolls down my cheek. I can't give him something that was already taken from me.

"Why? Please help me understand. You shut everyone out of your life. You haven't done much of anything in two years. It's like one day you were happy, carefree Kate, and then the next you were gone. What happened to you? I can't fix it if you don't tell me," he pleads, resting his hands on my shoulders.

He's asked me this a million different times, and a million different ways, but I can't tell him the real reason I'm not myself anymore. I never do, and tomorrow he'll be mad at me for closing up again, and then the next day he'll start to come around. It's what we've always done, but I know it can't be this way forever. "It's just not good timing. You're leaving tomorrow."

"If you ask me to stay, I'll stay," he says, searching my eyes. I'm always worried that he'll find the truth buried in there somewhere, but he hasn't yet. I pray he never will.

I shake my head. "I'm sorry, Beau," I say, my voice cracking a little more with each word. I step out of his grasp and start walking toward the beach, not looking back.

I hate Drew Heston right now. It took him less than ten minutes to ruin my body, but the emotional scars keep cutting deeper. He took away my hope, my dreams, my future, and I'll always hate him for it.

I don't bother drying off before I throw my tank and shorts over my swimsuit. Beau, more than likely, won't talk to me for the rest of the day. We've done this before. I know that he's going to take a few minutes to calm down before he comes out of the water and then walks to his truck without saying a word. He'll drive me home with nothing more than a sideways glance.

Only the other times, he hadn't told me he loved me. I don't know what this means for us going forward. He's done the one thing I was afraid to do when I felt the same way a couple years ago, and I've done the same thing I feared he would do back then. I feel sick to my stomach when I think about what I've done to him. He placed his heart in my hands and I crushed it.

I sit in the truck for several minutes staring out at the water before Beau opens the driver's door and jumps up into his seat. He turns the key in the ignition and puts the truck in reverse. As predicted, he doesn't even say a word as he drives back into town and pulls onto our street. The silence is deafening.

When he pulls into his driveway, he puts his truck into park, but doesn't move to get out. I chance a quick glance to see him staring forward with his jaw clenched. I look away, frustrated with myself for not being able to move forward. I wish there was a way to end the war being fought inside of me right now.

I grab my purse and open the door, carefully stepping down and shutting the door without looking back. I start to walk across his yard to my house when I hear his car door shut. He's mad which means he'll probably walk behind his house and lay on top of the old trampoline. If it's light out, he'll close his eyes to listen to the sounds that surround him, but if it's dark, he'll stare at the stars. He's been doing it since he was ten.

I'm almost to my front steps when I feel a big hand wrap around my upper arm. I flinch. I have a hard time being touched, but I have an even harder time when I don't see it coming.

I spin around, ready to battle, but when I see the sad, dark look on his face, I stop. Nothing I can say or do is going to be worse than what I've already done today. "Are you going to come over and say goodbye to me in the morning?" he asks, defeated. I force a slight smile onto my face. He won't leave tomorrow if he thinks I'm upset with him. Truth is, I'm not upset with him . . . I'm only upset with myself.

"Yes, what time are you leaving?"

"Nine in the morning," he says, swallowing hard. He's staring at my lips like he wants to taste them.

Panic grips my chest tight and I can't pretend anymore. I hate when he looks at me like that. "I'll come over in the morning," I say, wiggling from his grasp. I hear him say my name twice before I get in the house, but I don't turn around. I can't let him complicate things. My life is already a crazy maze that I can't find my way out of.

I'm surprised to see my mom sitting in the living room when I open the door. Sometimes I feel like we're just roommates co-existing in the same space. She works the morning shift at the diner, then comes home to change before working at the local bar and grill in the evening. She rarely has a day off.

She looks up at me, smiling. "Hey, where have you been?"

"I went swimming with Beau. He's leaving tomorrow," I say, looking down at my fingernails.

"I still don't understand why you decided not to go to college. Don't you at least want to enroll in some classes at the community college? Nurses make really good money, you know." I hate having this conversation, and I'm certainly not in the mood to have it now. I don't want to go to college because I don't want to be around other people my age. Besides, college is for people who know what they want and have dreams for the future.

"I'm just taking this year off. I'll save some money, and then I can go next year," I answer, continuing to avoid her eyes. "What are you doing home, anyway? I thought you had to work tonight?"

She looks a little taken back by my question. "I thought you would need me tonight since your best friend is leaving tomorrow."

I'm surprised that she even remembered to be honest. I usually have to remind her of everything, and I haven't brought up Beau's departure once. She seems to know what I'm thinking and points to the calendar next to the computer desk. I'd written down the day he was leaving months ago, silently counting down the days.

I look back at her and relax my shoulders. "Thanks."

"Do you want to order pizza and watch a movie? Beau can come over if he's not busy," she says, patting the spot next to her on the couch.

"I don't think Beau wants to come over tonight," I say, sitting down next to her. I can see her staring at me out of the corner of her eye.

"You know, I always thought the two of you would end up together someday," she says, using her fingertips to move a few pieces of hair out of my eyes.

"He's just a friend." I don't want to talk about Beau and what we have or don't have. I've had enough of that today.

She shakes her head at me and focuses her attention back to the TV. I think my mom has this idea of what real love should be, but I don't think she's ever experienced it. She's dated lots of guys over the years but never stuck with one for long. I don't even know if her idea of the right guy exists.

"Can we just have ice cream?" I ask, breaking the silence. When I was younger, my mom and I used to eat ice cream for supper when I was sick. I think a heart full of excruciating pain qualifies.

She looks at me and smiles. "Yeah, I just bought two cartons of Ben & Jerry's this afternoon. What kind do you want?"

"Did you happen to get Cherry Garcia?"

"Of course, I did," she says, patting my knee.

We sit under the same large blanket, eating from our two large bowls of ice cream. It doesn't take all of my pain away, but I don't feel alone with it. I still can't believe that Beau loves me. For so long, I've wanted him to want me, and maybe he has that whole time. Watching Beau leave tomorrow, especially after everything that happened today, is going to be really hard.

Chapter 3

I DON'T WANT TO WATCH BEAU LEAVE, but I can't let him go without seeing him one more time. I know I can call him whenever I need to, but there's just something about being able to see him that makes me feel so much better.

I'm going to miss him, more than I probably even realize right now. We've gone through all the major phases of our lives together, but I've decided to sit this one out. When I chose not to go to college, I didn't think I would regret the decision, but knowing Beau's leaving without me in exactly twenty-six minutes is filling me with uneasiness. Things never seem to hit me until they are right in front of my face. Just like everything else, I've pretended that Beau will always be by my side, even though I knew he'd be leaving soon. In some ways, it's easier to pretend, but right now all that time spent convincing myself that this day would never come is making my heart ache.

I remember the day I moved into this house as if it was yesterday.

My mom is busy unpacking boxes in the kitchen, and all I seem to do is get in her way, so I decide to walk out to the backyard to swing on the old tire that hangs from the big oak tree. I'm in my own world, a little sad that we've left my old neighborhood and friends. I'm not swinging that high; I'm having enough fun just digging my toes into the dirt. My mom's going to be mad because I'm getting my good tennis shoes dirty, but I don't care.

I'm sick of moving, and I don't care about these stupid shoes.

I see a ball roll past my feet, stopping right in front of me. When I look up, there's a boy in dirty grass stained blue jeans and a navy blue Power Rangers t-shirt. He has longish dark hair and smudges of mud all over his face. When he smiles, I *laugh; he's missing three of his front teeth and looks like one of my mom's Halloween creations.*

"What are you laughing at?" he asks, looking behind his back.

I giggle again. "Nothing."

"That swing isn't safe, you know. See that up there?" he says, pointing at the branch that was hanging on to the trunk by a small piece of wood. "It's going to fall soon. That's what my mom says."

I ignore him, continuing to sway back and forth on the swing. Boys can be so dumb, and I'm only a little bit off of the ground. If I fall, it won't hurt that much.

"What's your name?" he finally asks.

"Kate," I say, shielding the sun from my eyes. "What's yours?"

"Beau. Like a bow and arrow. My dad likes to hunt," he says, smiling again.

I don't know much about hunting, because I don't have a dad to tell me about it. I never have, and it doesn't bother me until other kids talk about their dads.

I climb out of the tire and straighten my shorts. "This town sucks."

Beau shrugs. "I think you might like it here."

And I did. I'd really liked the house and the town, and after a few weeks, I'd really liked Beau.

He's been one of my best friends ever since.

That was the first time he rescued me. That branch did snap a few days later, narrowly missing my head. Beau didn't say I told you so; he just helped me up and went to get my mom. I liked that he didn't end up to being the type of boy who had to be right because I wasn't the type of girl who liked to be wrong.

I hear a car door slam shut outside and look out the window to see Beau staring at my front door. I feel bad about how we left things yesterday. From the expression on his face, I can tell he's conflicted too. Everything feels out of place, and I can't shake the feeling that our relationship will never be the same.

I can't take my eyes off him as he turns towards his door. I need to go out there and say my goodbyes, but I'm not sure where I should even start. Yesterday he told me that he's in love with me, and I pushed him away. Should I just go out there and pretend like nothing happened?

I really screwed this one up.

I throw on a pair of jean shorts and my hooded Iowa Hawkeye sweatshirt. That's where Beau's going to school, and this is my unspoken way of supporting him. I take a few deep breaths and open my front door just as Beau comes out of his house again. Our eyes lock and we both stand motionless. I want to run to him and beg him not to leave, but I don't want to hold him back any more than I already have. I don't want him to know how much him leaving town is hurting me.

He walks toward his truck, placing another box into the back before walking in my direction. I think my heart stops beating for a second; I'm so nervous. He's wearing a grey Hawkeye t-shirt with his faded jeans resting low on his hips. I try to focus on that and not the intense, dark look in his eyes, but those eyes have always been hard for me to avoid.

He pulls me into his arms, burying his nose in my hair. "Good morning," he whispers. I rest my cheek against his chest and close my eyes, listening to the sound of his voice.

"Good morning," I mumble, not bothering to look up at him.

"Kate, I'm really sorry about yesterday. I shouldn't have thrown all that stuff at you right before I leave for school," he says, running his hands up and down my back, "but I meant every word."

This is kind of what I was hoping wouldn't happen. I was hoping we could just forget it all.

"Beau, I care for you, but things are different between us. You're my friend, and I can't handle a relationship with anyone right now," I say, trying to look up at his face, but he's holding me so close to his chest that I can't move.

"I'll wait for you," he says, finally letting me out of his grasp. He takes my face in his cool hands and kisses my forehead. I'm going to miss that too.

"Are you ready to go?" I ask, trying to change the subject. Just asking him causes my chest to tighten.

"I have two more boxes in the house that I have to grab, and then I'm done," he replies, looking back over at his house. I expected to see his mom outside fussing over him, but I haven't seen her once this morning.

I grab his hand and start walking up the steps. He seems hesitant. "Come on, I'll help you grab the last of your boxes."

He smiles, but it's a sad one. "Are you trying to get rid of me?"

I ignore him as I continue up the steps. As soon as I open the front door, I can smell fresh chocolate chip cookies. Mrs. Bennett must be baking.

"Oh hey, Kate, would you like a cookie?" she asks, taking a pan out of the oven.

"No, thanks. I just had breakfast." It wasn't the truth but my stomach is so tied up in knots that I'll be surprised if I can eat anything for the next week.

"Well, I'm going to send some home for you and your mom. Jeff and I don't need to eat them all," she smiles, rolling more dough into balls.

I follow Beau to his bedroom, which looks empty compared to what it was just a few days ago. Most of his Iowa posters are gone, and his charcoal grey comforter is missing from his bed. My eyes fly to the bulletin board that hangs above his desk, and I notice that the pictures of the two of us are also missing.

"I'm going to put all of them up in my room," he says, coming to stand in front of me. I bite my lip to hold back a smile. It makes me feel better knowing that he doesn't want to forget about me.

"Beau, why is your mom baking cookies so early in the morning?" I ask.

He rolls his eyes. "She wants to make sure I have enough to eat at school. I swear, she thinks I'm going to kindergarten all over again." Beau's mom reminds me of one of those sixties sitcom moms; always doing special things for him and his father. I spent a lot of time here growing up. In fact, I think I ate more suppers here than I did at my own house.

"So, where are the boxes you need help with?" I ask, glancing around the room.

"You really are trying to get rid of me," he laughs, pointing towards his closet.

Of course I don't want to get rid of him. I just don't know how long I can hold the tears back. I almost have myself convinced that this is just another day for the two of us, but once reality hits I'm going to be a mess, and the clock is ticking.

I help him out to the truck with the last two boxes and stand silent with my hands tucked into my back pockets. This is the moment I've been dreading.

"Well," I say, staring nervously at my feet, "I guess this is goodbye . . . for now."

He places his hands on my shoulders, gently rubbing his thumbs against my neck. "This is see you later. I could never say goodbye to you. Ever," he says, pressing his lips to my forehead.

My eyes fill with tears that had threatened me all morning. "I'm going to miss you, Beau," I cry, wiping my cheeks with the sleeve of my sweatshirt.

"I'll come home next weekend. I promise."

I shake my head. "No, you have to live your life. Please, don't worry about me. I'll be okay."

"Kate, don't try to push me away," he says, pulling me into his chest.

"I'm not. I'm just letting you go," I cry. The longer Beau holds onto the idea of us, the longer it will take him to find something better. He deserves all the good the world will give him. He deserves the love of someone who can give him everything. I have to let him go so he can find that.

"Stop, Kate. I'm coming back for you every weekend."

"No, listen to me. I think it would be best if we spent some time apart. I need to work on myself, and I want you to worry about other things besides me," I say, feeling his hands grip the back of my sweatshirt a little tighter. I look up at his face to see his eyes are glossed over. This sucks.

"Kate—"

"No, just don't. I'll call you every day, but please, do this for yourself," I plead. This is the hardest freaking thing I've ever had to do. I want Beau to come back every weekend and see me so that I never have to go a day without seeing him, but I'm not going to be selfish. My future was taken from me, and I can't take his too.

"I'm coming back once a month," he says, letting go of the back of my shirt. The front door of his house opens, causing us both to step back. His mom and dad are following him to Iowa City to bring his furniture so it must be time for him to leave.

He walks to the driver's side door without taking another look in my direction. My heart falls into my stomach.

He climbs in and rolls down the window, using his index finger to motion me over to him. I hesitantly step forward, scared to death that he may say something I don't want to hear. When I'm close enough that he can touch me, he cups my cheek in his hand. "I'll play this game by your rules. But, Kate, remember that I can't shut my feelings off just because you tell me to," he says, putting his hand back on his steering wheel.

I stand back and watch him pull out of the driveway, waving as he disappears down the street with his parents following close behind. I want to crumble to the ground and bury my head in my hands, but I run into my empty house instead, not stopping until I'm face down on my bed. My body shakes as I let the tears flow for what seems like hours. For a moment, I regret telling him not to come home every weekend, but Beau can't start moving forward with his life if he's always looking back at me.

I stay in bed for the rest of the day, alternating between staring at the ceiling and crying. It's the same thing I did after I left Drew Heston's house that night. In fact, I stayed like that for days, telling my mom I had the flu. I'd always been a strong girl before, barely shedding a tear over anything, but things have really changed the last two years. I feel like I'm crying more often than not.

I often wonder what would have happened if I'd told someone what Drew did to me that night.

Drew finally stops moving, making a loud grunting sound that makes me sick to my stomach. I'm numb and broken. I feel the sweat from his forehead dripping on my back, and it disgusts me. He crawls off my body and throws my clothes at me before walking out the door. I'm almost too scared to move, but I do it anyway. My whole body aches as I climb out of the bed and pull my underwear back up my legs.

When I see the blood smeared on the inside of my thighs, I start to cry so hard that my vision becomes blurred. It's a reminder of what he took from me and what I can never get back. I pull my jeans on and button them before adjusting my shirt and bra. I don't waste any time before throwing open his bedroom door and glancing down the hall. I don't see or hear anyone around. I just have to find Morgan and get out of here before anyone else sees me.

I'm almost to the stairs when a hand wraps tightly around my arm, pulling me back until I'm pressed against a hard, strong chest. I'm afraid to turn around and see who stands behind me, so I pinch my eyes shut and wait.

"Don't even think about telling anyone about tonight. You wanted it, and they wouldn't believe you anyway."

My body is shaking so much that I can't talk. I just want to go home and try to forget tonight ever happened.

He tightens his grip on my arms, digging his fingers into my skin. "Did you hear me, Kate? No one will believe you," he repeats. Tears are welling up in my eyes because deep down I know he's right.

I nod, waiting for him to let me go. I hate the roughness in his voice. I hate the feel of his hands on me. I fucking hate Drew Heston.

He loosens his grip and pushes me forward causing me to stumble. "Get the fuck out of my house."

I quickly run down the steps and out the front door into the rain, not looking back once. When I find Morgan, she's too drunk to realize that anything is wrong. Her boyfriend drives us home as I slump down in the backseat, letting the tears fall. I feel used and dirty. Why did he choose me?

If Morgan hadn't been drunk that night, she might have noticed how fragile I was. Would I have told her? If my mom had been home that night when I opened the door, would I have told her? If Beau had seen me that night, he would have known.

But there was no one.

Chapter 4

I'M SCHEDULED TO WORK TODAY, and the distraction couldn't be more welcome. After watching Beau drive away yesterday, my heart can't handle another heart-breaking, soul-shattering day like that. Besides, I care about Beau too much, and I never want to see that pained look in his eyes again and know that I was the one who caused it.

I pull on my dark blue jeans and my red Bonnie's Diner t-shirt then look at myself in the mirror. Just as I predicted, my eyes are puffy and red from almost twenty-four hours of marathon crying. I pull my hair into a high ponytail and rub some concealer under my eyes before applying foundation to the rest of my face. The last thing I want is all of my customers asking what's wrong with me. It's easier to act that it's just another day.

When I'm satisfied with how I look, I grab my keys and head out the door. Without even realizing what I'm doing, I stand with my eyes fixated on Beau's house. I wonder what he's doing right now. Does he miss Carrington yet? Does he like his new roommate?

I can't let myself dwell on it, though. It's time to get in the car and face my new normal. It just sucks that my normal keeps getting more and more unpleasant. I once thought I had everything, but ever since that night I've been unhappy and alone. Beau has been my only exception for the past two years and now he's gone.

I'm lost.

I really have no idea where my life goes from here. I want to say it can't get any worse, but I've thought that before and there always seems to be a deeper hole to sink into. Some days I don't even know if I can go on.

What's the point?

When I pull into the parking lot behind the diner, I put the car in park and rest my forehead against the steering wheel. Just thinking about making it through the day alone makes it difficult to breathe. It's like someone is constantly sitting on my chest.

I take a few deep breaths, trying to get some air in my lungs to ease the panic, but I'm struggling to gain control. Sometimes it helps to close my eyes and imagine I'm sitting on the beach looking out onto the lake, but I'm so overwhelmed I can't even bring myself to go there today. Not having control of my emotions is like being in a speeding car without brakes, or like a vice gripping my ribs and squeezing. I feel lost and desperate, and I have no idea when this is all going to stop.

Maybe it never will.

When I'm finally able to feel my hands again, I turn off the ignition and make my way inside. I clock in and wrap my black apron around my waist. It's just before seven and the morning crowd will be filing in soon. Our town only has two restaurants and Bonnie's is the only one open for breakfast. It's usually full of farmers who come in to compare harvest notes or other locals looking to avoid their own kitchens. The work is easy, and a little mundane, but that's all I can handle right now. There are three waitresses each morning, and we each take eight tables. I prefer the tables towards the front window because people tend to chat less when they're staring out at the passersby.

I spot my usual group of retired farmers at the table closest to the door. They love to come in right at seven in the morning and stick around until well after nine. I don't mind them because they can go on and on about the current price of corn and don't ask for much as long as I keep their coffee cups full. There are four of them, and they always order the same thing for breakfast every morning. I can honestly say there are some days I don't speak one word to them for the entire two hours they're here.

"Hey, you, I didn't even see you come in," my mom says, wrapping her arms around my waist. I lean my head on her shoulder, taking in the familiar scent of her perfume. She's been wearing the same kind since I can remember and it always soothes me. It brings me back to a time when everything was okay and all I had to think about was which pink dress to wear that day.

"I was running a little late, so I went straight to my tables," I say, lifting my head to peek out to the dining room to make sure my customers are taken care of. "It's nice and quiet today."

"You could probably go home if you wanted to. We can handle this." She lets go of my waist and begins brewing a fresh pot of coffee.

I ponder the idea of going home, but I know if I do I won't be able to keep myself from feeling. I'd just lock myself in my room and cry until my eyes were swollen. At least when I'm here, I can keep my mind on something else.

"No, I'll stay. I need the money," I say. That's not exactly true. I've been working here for almost three years and I've barely spent a penny.

My mom smiles at me before grabbing the full coffee pot and heading back to the dining room to serve customers. Sometimes I think she's worried that the only reason I didn't attend college was because I couldn't afford it. I hate that she feels that way, but it's easier to let her think that than it is to explain the truth.

Around ten, Ms. Carter comes in for a cinnamon roll and a cup of decaf coffee. She's a widow in her mid-eighties. I don't think she has any family around because she always comes in alone. She's the chattiest of my customers, but I don't mind because she's the sweetest lady on earth and doesn't pry too much into my life.

"You look tired today, Katie girl," she says as I fill her coffee for the second time.

"I didn't sleep well last night," I reply, then quickly change the subject. "You have any plans today?"

"Just bridge club right after this. You should join us on one of your days off," she smiles, taking a sip from her freshly filled coffee cup.

We have this same conversation almost every day. Her memory is fading, but kindness still shines through. Some days, she almost makes me smile. Almost.

"I'm sorry, Ms. Carter, but they don't give me many days off."

"Well, I should get going soon. I don't want to be late, Bev Collins will take my chair and I can't have that," she says, laying a five dollar bill on the table.

"I'll see you tomorrow," I wave as she walks toward the door.

"Of course, dear, unless I have other plans." She exits, taking her time getting down the cement step and onto the sidewalk. I've always wanted to spend more time with her and hear her story, but I'm afraid she'll ask about mine.

I wipe down tables and make sure each one has everything it needs before the lunch crowd comes in. I'm usually able to get through breakfast just fine, but I dread lunch. It brings a different mix into the diner and it's unpredictable.

Almost every day during the summer, kids from my high school came in and found it necessary to sit in my section just to see how miserable they could make my day. I became a joke to them just because I didn't fit in.

I swear to God . . .

For as long as I live I will never do to others as they have done to me.

I see Morgan walk in with a group of her friends. They sit in my section, eyeing me like they know exactly what they're doing. Morgan has been treating me differently since the incident with Drew, but I can't blame her completely. I've changed so much, and she has no idea why because I didn't tell her.

I walk toward them hesitantly, ready to take their orders and get away as fast as I can. "What can I get you guys today?" I ask, keeping my attention on the small notebook I hold in my hand.

"I'll take a cob salad with the dressing on the side," Abby replies. Out of the corner of my eye, I can see a smile spread across her lips.

"You?" I ask, pointing my pen towards Dana.

"What's the soup today?"

"Chicken noodle."

"Okay, I'll take a bowl of that and a side salad," Dana answers, crossing her arms over her chest.

Morgan's the last one to order. I briefly glance down at her, but the second I see her eyes staring up at me from over the menu, I focus mine back on the notebook. "And what can I get you?"

She rolls her eyes slowly, making sure the whole table sees it. "Duh, I'll take the same thing I always get."

"I don't know what you always get," I say, looking up to see Abby and Dana with smirks on their faces. I can feel my bottom lip tremble.

Two years ago, I became Kate Alexander, the loser girl who will never leave Carrington; the girl who will always work in the diner with her mother. I hate how they treat me like something less than them just because I've changed. I guess not being 'just like them' is a crime.

She starts to play with her nails, keeping her eyes off me like I'm nothing. "I want a garden salad with Italian dressing on the side."

"I'll be right back with your order," I mumble as I turn my back to them.

I'm not more than two steps away when a voice behind me stops me. "Kate." I spin on my heels to face her. "You better leave the tomatoes off my salad this time," Morgan smiles, quickly beginning a conversation with the other girls at the table.

As I walk into the kitchen, I hear them whispering and giggling. When I hear them say my name amongst their whispers, tears prick my eyes. How can my best friend turn on me simply because I've changed? When I needed her the most, she wasn't there.

I quietly deliver their food to the table and ask if they need anything else, but they just continue to talk like I don't even exist. When Morgan decides to join in, it feels like someone stuck a knife in my heart and twisted it. I don't like to consider myself resentful, but I always wonder what would've happened if she hadn't left me that night.

The worst was the day Drew and two of his football buddies came in and sat in one of my booths. Drew had been in the diner enough times before and after the incident to know exactly which section was mine. He usually didn't sit in an area where I had to wait on him, though. He would sit and watch me from afar, but on that particular day he decided it was time to cause more trouble for me than he already had.

When it Rains

My whole body tenses the second I see him from across the room. He smiles at me like we're old friends, and I instantly feel sick to my stomach. I know I can't do this. I don't see one day in my future where I will ever be able to face Drew without having the panic and horror of that night hit me.

I walk to the kitchen to find my mom filling a glass with ice water. "Mom, I feel sick. I think I'm going to have to go home," I say, placing my hand over my midsection.

"Oh, sweetie, I'm sorry you're not feeling good, but we're swamped out there. Can you stick it out for a little bit longer?" she asks.

I peek through the window in the door-every table is full and a few people are still waiting inside the door. I'm waging an internal battle with myself when the other waitress on duty comes flying through the door, throwing her notepad on counter.

"It's a zoo. Where are all these people coming from?" she says, placing her hands on her hips.

I close my eyes and take a deep breath. "I'll stay," I say hesitantly. I hate letting people down and can't say no. "Can you take table ten for me, though?"

"Yeah, I can do that," she answers, using the back of her hand to wipe her forehead. The weight of my chest starts to ease up.

When Drew and his posse figure out what I've done, they start taunting me as I walk by. "Hey, Kate, are you going to take our order? I think you already know what I like!" Drew yells as I walk past. Just like that night, I want to run away and never come back, but I can't. This job is the one of the only things I have left that keeps me going.

I continue to serve my customers like Drew isn't even there. It's hard to do, though, when he's forcing himself into my life. Every time I see him, I want to scream and hit him until my fists hurt so much that they go numb. I can feel his eyes on me, but I don't look in his direction even once; I'm not going to give him the gratification. I think it really bothers him that I'm the only girl who doesn't acknowledge his existence.

I've always wondered if I'm the only girl he's ever hurt, or if there might be others. I wouldn't be able to live with the guilt if he did it to another girl after me. It was the one reason I almost came forward, but in the end I knew it wouldn't matter because nobody was going to believe me.

When they lay their cash on the table and start to get up, Drew's eyes briefly lock on mine, and I quickly look away. The sight of him makes me feel dirty. I've never despised something, or someone, so much in my entire life.

Out of the corner of my eye, I see him walking toward me with a disgusting grin on his face. I want to run, but my feet are cemented in the ground and all I can do is stare as he stops in front of me. "I haven't seen you at a party in a while. Don't you want to come out and play again soon?"

I quickly turn and head toward the ladies room, locking the door behind me. A panic attack takes hold of my body, and I work hard to try and regain my composure. Knowing he's only a few feet away intensifies my symptoms as I desperately try to catch my breath. When I'm to the point that I think I might pass out, I crouch down and rest my head in my hands, taking several deep breaths. I've avoided having any conversation with Drew up until this point, and I only have a couple more months to get through before he leaves town. I just need to avoid him for a little while longer, and then maybe I'll be able to move on with my life to some extent. I'm not sure how much time passes in the bathroom before I feel like I can function again, but when I do finally step out, he's gone.

I haven't seen him since. Rumor has it that he left town early for football camp. All my old friends have gone off to college to start the next phase of their lives, but I'm still here trying to decide if my life even has a next phase.

Chapter 5

LATER IN THE DAY, when the diner is empty, the bell above the door dings, alerting my attention to a new customer. I look up and find that my eyes are fixed on the unfamiliar man at the door; they refuse to focus on anything else.

That's the other thing about small towns, when anyone new rides into town, it turns into a breaking news story. And if you stay any longer than a few hours, everyone knows your business. The guy standing near the door in faded blue jeans and a fitted sky blue t-shirt is definitely not from around here. His blonde hair is standing up all over the place like he just rolled out of bed and ran his fingers through it a few times.

His eyes lock on mine, and the corner of his lips turn up on one side causing me to turn around quickly and head to the kitchen out of his view.

After a couple minutes have passed, I look through the small window in the kitchen door and breathe a sigh of relief when I see he's not sitting in my section. I always had a shy demeanor, but what happened with Drew made it much, much worse. I live every day of my life in constant fear somebody will take advantage of me.

Living life that way is like not even living at all.

It's impossible to do my job from the kitchen, so I make an attempt to pull myself together. It's time to face the stranger whether I like it or not. I watch as the tables quickly fill up with the lunch crowd, and I move into autopilot, making sure each of my tables has menus and drinks. Most of the people are regulars, so it doesn't take me long to get their orders and bring them to the kitchen. This may not be my dream job, but I'm sure good at it.

When I deliver my first table their meals, I notice the guy in the blue shirt staring in my direction. This time he's not smiling. Instead, his eyebrows are pulled down as if he's studying me. Our eyes lock and all the chatter in the room seems louder as I stand frozen in the middle of the packed restaurant. I don't know if it's the expression on his face, or the fact that his eyes haven't left mine, but I can't make myself look away.

Someone runs into me from behind, sending me a couple steps forward and breaking the connection I'm having with the stranger. When I look back at him, his gaze is focused out the window. I don't know what just happened between us, but I make my way back to the kitchen before he tries to look my way again. I have no idea why he's having this effect on me.

At this point, I don't even know if it's good or bad.

When I leave work, I notice I have four text messages and two missed calls, all from Beau. Just seeing his name on my screen makes my heart skip as I work to blink the tears away so that I can read his messages.

Beau: How R U?
Beau: R U Working?
Beau: Please text me so I know you're okay . . .
Beau: I miss you.

I miss Beau like crazy but knowing he's thinking of me even when he's five hours away gives me hope that maybe we can come away from this separation with our friendship intact.

He's going to make new friends, I'm sure of that. He's smart, funny, good-looking, and he's not shy at all. I'm not going to let him spend every free second of his day worrying over me anymore. I just hope he doesn't completely forget me.

I should try calling him back, but I can't even think about him right now without crying. I don't want him to worry, so I opt for a text instead.

Kate: I'm good. Just got off work.

I want to tell him I miss him too, but that would be an admission of the truth, and that isn't something I've been very good at lately. And no matter how much I know he wants to hear me say it, I still can't do it.

Truth is, I miss him so much more than I thought I ever would. He's been my only reason to breathe, and even though he still is, it's more difficult because he's so far away. My phone beeps again.

Beau: I was worried about you.
Kate: Don't worry. I'll be ok.

I don't want him to worry about me tomorrow when I don't answer his texts or calls. It's not that I don't want to . . . I just need to put some space between us right now. I know Beau, and if I let it go too long, he'll get in his car and drive right back home just to check on me.

Beau: Call me tonight?

I desperately want to hear the smooth baritone in his voice.

Kate: Having dinner with Mom. Tomorrow?
Beau: Tomorrow then.

Beau's not stupid. He knows my mom and I rarely have dinner together, but he doesn't ask any questions.

I spend the remainder of my evening lying in bed, listening to Coldplay as I fixate my eyes on the ceiling. Maybe it's the soothing sadness of the lyrics, or the sound of Chris Martin's voice, but I can never get enough. I can't stop thinking about what I could have had with Beau. What things would have been like if none of this ever happened to me. I wanted him for so long but didn't think he felt the same way. Now, he wants me, and I can't understand why. Why would anyone want the broken girl I've become? I wait for sleep to take over and put a temporary end to my thoughts.

～～～

The next morning I don't want to go to work. I force myself out of bed and start the shower before grabbing a clean pair of jeans and a Bonnie's t-shirt out of my closet.

When I step in the shower, I let the hot water fall over my face before turning and letting it heat my entire body. I focus on the scalding drops of water as they fall. It's painfully hot, but keeps my mind off the internal pain that I'm rarely able to escape.

The first time I did it was the night Drew raped me. I felt fragile, furious and more than anything, I felt like a disgusting piece of garbage. I didn't think I'd ever be able to clean away his scent or his touch from my body. The minute I walked in my front door, I went straight to the bathroom and turned the water to the hottest setting. At first it made me cringe, but the water made me feel clean and the heat dulled the pain in my heart as it burned my skin.

I haven't been able to stop since.

My morning shift goes by quickly, dealing with many of the regulars. Ms. Carter comes in right as the breakfast crowd is clearing out and takes her usual seat in my section.

"Good morning, Katie girl. Isn't it beautiful outside today?" she asks, glancing out the window. I rarely pay any attention to the weather . . . unless it's raining. Those are my worst days.

I look ahead and see the bright blue sky and nod my head. "Yes, it's nice outside today."

"I can't believe summer is almost over. Won't be long until the snow is flying," she says, looking back up at me.

"Are you having the usual today?"

"I'm too old to change now," she laughs. That actually makes me smile. Her life seems so simple and she's content with it.

I plate a warm cinnamon roll and pour Ms. Carter a cup of coffee and deliver it to her table. I'm feeling better than I did this morning, and I'm even considering going for a run after work, when my mom pops her head through the door.

"You have a new customer in your section," she says with a huge grin on her face.

My mom's not one for throwing out meaningless smiles, so the way she looks at me when she says it has me curious. I open the door to the dining room and stop dead in my tracks.

He's come back.

The guy from lunch yesterday is sitting at one of the smaller tables in my section, watching me with raised eyebrows. My feet feel as if they weigh one-hundred pounds each.

I don't know what it is about him that unnerves me, but the way he stares at me makes me feel like I should know who he is, or that maybe he knows who I am.

I swallow my restraint and move toward him, never taking my eyes off his. As I get closer, I notice they're a unique light-greyish-blue shade that is only highlighted by the navy blue t-shirt he's wearing.

I stop a little bit further back from the table than I usually would and take a deep breath, trying to erase the thoughts going through my head. "Can I get you something to drink?" I finally ask, grabbing for my notepad. I can remember just about anything, but I need something to keep my hands and eyes occupied.

"Good morning to you too," he says, smiling and shaking his head at me. He leans back in his chair, letting one arm fall behind it so that his body is turned toward me.

I can't take it anymore. "Do I know you?" I ask.

"Only if you count the little staring contest we had yesterday," he replies, letting the corners of his mouth turn up a little more. "My name's Asher Hunt."

"And what are you doing here, Asher Hunt?" I feel a little bit of my snarky side take over where my nervousness once lay.

"Well, obviously, I'm hungry. And this is the only place that's open in this town," he says, leaning forward to rest his elbows on the table. I notice a tattoo on the inside of his right arm, but I can't see enough to make out what it is.

"I mean, what brings you to Carrington?" I tap my pen against the notebook, drawing his eyes down to it.

He shrugs. "I'm trying the small town life for a while. You know, figuring out if it really is the simpler way to live."

For a moment, I just look at him, unsure of what to say to that. The truth is, no matter where you live, your life is full of complications. It's not the environment that causes them; it's the people around you, or those who are gone for that matter. But taking one look at his suddenly distant eyes, I know I don't have to tell him that.

I clear my throat. "So what can I get you to drink?"

"I'll take a chocolate shake and a glass of water, please," he replies glancing out the window.

I don't wait for him to look back up at me before heading back to the kitchen to make his shake. I take my time putting the milk and chocolate syrup in before pressing the button to mix. It's so loud that I don't hear my mom approach behind me.

"That guy's kind of cute, don't you think?" she asks, grabbing the ice cream and placing it back in the freezer.

I roll my eyes, grabbing a glass from the shelf to pour the shake into. My mom and I never talk about guys. The only guy I ever let myself think about is Beau. Sure, the guy is okay, but it means nothing to me.

"Hey, what are you girls gossiping about?" Diana asks. Diana is the other waitress that works most mornings.

"Did you see the guy who sat in Kate's section? I saw him in here yesterday too. He's kind of cute. Much better looking than most of the guys in this town," my mom answers. She should know; she's dated quite a few.

Diana peeks through the small window in the kitchen door before looking at my mom and shaking her head. "He's bad news, Lynn. That's Daniel McNally's son, and I've heard the only reason he's in Carrington is to escape some trouble he got into in Chicago."

"But his last name is Hunt," I say, filling a glass with ice for the water.

"That's because his mom left town with him and got remarried shortly after he was born. McNally barely saw him after that," Diana says, handing me two straws. "Just be careful."

"Don't worry. I'm not interested."

I head out toward Asher again, placing his drinks on the table. He appears different from the smiley, cocky guy who sat here just a few minutes ago. His shoulders are drooped, and when he looks up I notice his eyes have lost some of their curiosity.

"Can I get you something to eat?" I ask, trying to avoid looking directly at him. My mom was onto something because he's the first person in a long time who I've actually been a little intrigued by. I need to keep some distance, though, because at the end of the day, all I know is his name.

I blink, realizing that he's been staring at me while I'm lost in thought. "I'll just take an order of French fries," he replies, twirling his straw around in his shake.

By the time his order is up, the place is packed for lunch, and I don't have any more time to chat when I set his fries on the table. In fact, I don't even have time to bring him his check. Diana does it for me because an entire table orders a round of milkshakes that I have to make. By the time I make it back out to the dining room, he's gone.

I deliver my tray of drinks and head over to clean up Asher's table, noticing that he left me a five dollar tip and a note on a napkin.

I'd love to see you smile once in a while.

I stare at the door and take a deep breath, crumpling the napkin into a ball and shoving it into my pocket.

Chapter 6

A COUPLE DAYS LATER, I decide it's time to give Beau a call and see how things are going. He's been at school for almost a whole week and has tried to call me every day, but I haven't answered. We've texted back and forth a few times, but I miss hearing his voice. I think I'm ready to do it without falling apart.

The phone barely rings once before he picks up. "Hello."

Okay, I was wrong, hearing his voice makes me want to cry again.

"Hey," I say, squeezing my eyes shut in an attempt to control my defiant emotions.

"It took you long enough to call me back," he says in his teasing tone. It's almost as if he knows I need him to lighten the mood. Sometimes I think he knows me better than I know myself.

"Sorry, I've been busy at the diner. I miss you, though."

The breath he inhales is so loud that I can hear it through the phone. "Kate, are you sure you don't want me to come home this weekend? I'm done with class at noon tomorrow, so I can be there by supper." There's hope in his voice, but I'm about the let him down again.

"Don't. I have to work all weekend anyway. Besides, I'm sure you have a party or two you can go to instead," I say, trying to talk him out of it without saying no.

"Kate—"

"Please, Beau. I need you to do this for me. Meet new people and enjoy the experience," I plead. I want him to have the things I can't right now, even if it means I have to give up the one person besides my mom who means something to me.

"Next weekend, I'm coming home, and you're not allowed to argue with me about it," he says, sounding serious and a little father-like. I may be wounded, but I can take care of myself.

"So, what have you been up to, college boy?" I ask, resting my head on my pillow.

"Are you changing the subject on me?" His voice is a mixture of amusement and frustration.

"Beau, please."

"Fine," he sighs. "I've been going to class, hitting the gym, studying, eating and sleeping. Nothing much more exciting than what you've been doing, I'm sure."

He's right. I've been working, running, and sitting alone in my bedroom.

And, every now and then, my mind wanders away from Beau and veers toward Asher. I barely know him, and I haven't seen him since he left the note on the napkin, but I can't help but wonder what he's all about.

"How are your classes?"

"They're not hard, but I had two papers assigned to me already this week. You know how much I fucking hate writing papers," he replies.

"Yeah, but you're good at it. I think you just hate them because they're too easy for you," I say, smiling slightly. Beau was one of the smartest kids in our class. He hasn't decided what he wants to be when he "grows up," but he can really do anything he wants.

"I guess I am," he says. If I'm not mistaken, I think I can sense a smile in the tone of his voice. "Look, Kate, I hate to cut this short, but I have a class I need to get to."

I'll talk to you again tomorrow." The last part sounds like more of a question than a statement.

"I work until two, but I'll answer if you call me any time after that."

Talking to Beau actually makes me feel better, rather than sad. I'm looking forward to talking to him again. I'm hoping that with each day, and each phone call, the distance between us will get a little easier to handle. Maybe I can make it without him here.

"You better."

"Bye, Beau."

"Bye, Kate."

Since I have the whole day off, I'm going to run until my legs give out on me. I pull on a pair of gym shorts and a tank top before lacing up my tennis shoes. It's the one thing I still like to do. It's a way for me to clear my mind and let go of some of the pent up anger and stress that has taken residence in my body.

I close the front door and stand on the porch of our small one story house, stretching my legs and arms. Fall will be here soon, and the humidity has already started to dissipate, leaving a tolerable warm September day. Our small town has a few biking trails that are nice for running, but I choose to stay close to the busy streets. There are always lots of people and cars around—the only way I really feel safe.

I take off, letting my feet hit the pavement as I take in the sights and sounds, allowing all my thoughts to come to the forefront. My feet may be moving, but I'm still in the same place, trying to figure out what the future holds for Kate Alexander. I think about my mom and how she had me when she was about my age. I couldn't imagine having a child right now. I think about my dad and what he would have been like. My mom says she only dated him for a couple months, and that he had quite the wild streak.

When it Rains

I think about all the things that have happened in my life, good and bad, but in the end I always end up focusing on the worst. I don't know why I continue to do this to myself. I let it all play out in my head over and over until my legs can no longer carry me. Maybe I'm hoping that if I think about it enough, I won't be able to think of it at all. I know that's not going to happen, but that doesn't mean I have to stop wishing for it.

I always run the same path, but today for some reason, I find myself detouring down Mr. McNally's street. I know I'm just curiously looking for a glimpse of Asher or his life, but I can't stop myself. Whenever there's a puzzle, I want all of the pieces so that I can put it together. Whenever there's a mystery, I want to solve it. It's the main reason I wanted to study law.

Asher is a puzzle to me. Why is he in Carrington? Why does he look at me like he knows me when I've never seen him before? I want to know it all, and I have no idea why. I haven't cared about much of anything in two years. He's different than other guys in Carrington. He has this confident yet mysterious thing about him that I can't stop thinking about. I feel like he wants to know me, but not like he's judging me. He's not comparing me to anything that I used to be.

McNally's house is quiet, but there's an old black Mustang in the driveway that was never there before. I slow my pace just a little to get a better look before speeding off toward home.

I'm only a couple blocks away from my house when it starts to rain. It takes only seconds before my muscles tense and I start to feel dizzy. My legs are so tired, but I push myself as hard as I can to escape the weather. Whenever it rains, it all comes rushing back to me. Every single second of what happened that night flashes through my mind. I can see Drew. I remember the sharp pain he caused inside me, and the rough feel of his light stubble on my face.

My jaw and hands start to tingle by the time I finally reach my front door and run inside. I don't bother taking off my shoes. I go straight to my room and turn the radio on so that it's loud enough to mask the sound of the rain on my window. I lie in bed and let tears fall down my face, soaking my pillow until I can't cry anymore. It should never be okay for someone to spend more time crying than they do smiling.

I remain in my room, listening to music for the remainder of the day, only getting up to take a shower and grab a sandwich from the kitchen. Having a day off work gives me too much time to think and I find myself actually looking forward to tomorrow.

⁓⌣⌣⌣⌐

I'm just finishing up with Ms. Carter when the door opens and Asher walks in. I stop wiping off the table and stand up straight, waiting to see what he's going to do next. He's wearing grey shorts and a black t-shirt that just grazes the top of his shorts and his blonde hair is as unruly as the first day I saw him. But today, he doesn't look confident or sad; he looks unsure as he stands with his hands in his pockets.

He slowly walks toward me, a small smile playing on his lips. I have no idea what he's going to do and it both excites me and scares me.

He stops two feet in front of me. "You look surprised to see me," he says to me confidently.

I can't take the eye contact anymore. It's making me feel crazy things that I haven't felt in forever. "No. I mean, I thought maybe you left town. It only takes a couple hours to see all this place has to offer."

He laughs, leaning in close so I can feel his breath on my ear. "I saw you run by my house yesterday," he whispers. I instantly jump back out of fear. I hate when people get that close to me. The only two people who I allow to touch me are my mom and Beau. I quickly look around the room to make sure no one has seen us, but we're the only two people in the dining room. His eyes follow mine before they meet again. I can't get his amused expression out of my head.

I take a deep breath to regain my composure. "I run every day," I reply, shrugging my shoulders.

"Did you like my car? You seemed to be admiring it," he says, running his teeth over his bottom lip. I'm drawn to them, but I quickly refocus my eyes on his.

"I've never seen a car like that up close before. It's very nice," I say, trying to suppress the warmth I feel on my cheeks.

"It's a 1967 Mustang, fully restored." He smiles. "I worked on it for two years to get it looking that good."

We're both still, locked in some sort of crazy awkward staring contest. I'm waiting for him to say something because I struggle with this social stuff. He obviously doesn't, so I try to leave the ball in his court until I can't take it anymore.

"So, do you want a table?" I finally ask, breaking the uneasy silence.

He smiles. "Yes, it's been a couple days since I've had a milkshake."

"We're open every day you know," I tease.

He looks away before speaking. "I had some stuff I had to take care of. You can't have milkshakes every day." His words are ice cold, and I want to know why, but I quickly drop the subject.

"Well, have a seat and I'll grab one for you," I say, walking toward the kitchen. I don't look back at him, but

I can feel his eyes on me. I rest my palms against the counter and close my eyes. I need to get a grip and leave the guy alone. I'm in no shape to take him on as my project, and he sure as hell isn't ready to deal with all my baggage.

I take my time making his shake before heading back out to the dining room. He's sitting in one of the booths with both arms resting across the back of the bench, eyes fixated on the cars that go by on the street. "Here you go. Do you want anything to eat?"

He glances up at me before leaning forward to twirl his straw in his shake. "Just an order of French fries, please."

I nod, quickly heading toward the kitchen again. His personality feels so hot and cold—it makes me crazy!

We don't say anything to each other when I bring out his fries, but I notice how he dips them in his shake, and it makes me smile. There's no better combination than salty and sweet; I know, because I do the same thing.

When he's done with his fry basket, I bring out his ticket, setting it on the table without saying a word. As I turn toward the kitchen, I feel a large hand grip my forearm.

He must have noticed that I winced because he quickly lets go of me. "I have a question I want to ask you before I go. Would you show me around town sometime? I'm new, and have no idea what there is to do here."

I roll my eyes. "You're kidding me, right? You literally start at one end, drive ten or so blocks, and you're on the other side. There isn't anything to do." There's a little more bite to my voice than what I intend, but I know his game. If he thinks he's going to trick me into something like hanging out with him, he's in for a surprise.

He leans back against the booth, smiling up at me. "What do you do for fun?"

I hesitate. This is the moment I admit that I have no life and don't know the meaning of fun. "I don't. I work, I run, and that's it."

"Well then, I dare you to go to Carrington Days with me tomorrow," he says, cocking his head to the side.

"You can't be serious," I remark. He doesn't seem like the type of guy who would have any fun at our small town festival.

He shakes his head. "Oh, I'm very serious."

My mouth goes dry, and the only thing I want to do is run out the door and never look back. "I don't date," I blurt, immediately regretting the way it came out.

He gives me a better view of his straight white teeth. Maybe he likes to see me squirm, or maybe he likes the challenge. "I'm not asking you for a date. I'm daring you to . . . be my tour guide at Carrington Days."

"Why are you daring me?" I wonder if this is how he always gets girls to do what he wants. He may think he knows me, but he still hasn't figured out that I'm not like other girls.

"You seem like the type of girl who doesn't back down from a challenge," he says, pulling his wallet from his back pocket. "Are you going or not?"

"I work tomorrow." He needs to let this go. There are lots of other girls out there that would love to show him around Carrington Days. Why me?

"So, I'll pick you up at three?" he asks, throwing money on top of his bill. He isn't looking at me, but I can't take my eyes off of him. He's got to be the cockiest guy I've ever met.

"How do you know what time I get off?" Has he been following me? Has he been asking other people about me? If he has, I don't want to know the stories he's been told.

He stands, causing me to step back to regain my personal space. "I know a lot of things. So, three o'clock then? I'll even buy you a funnel cake."

I'm too shocked to speak. No one has ever talked to me like this, and I don't know how I feel about it. He's almost to the door when I find my voice again. "I'll meet you there at three. At the entrance to the carnival."

He nods, confidently walking right out the door.

I don't know what just happened. I wanted to say no, but my heart won out. Only time will tell if this is something I'll regret.

Chapter 7

WORK FLIES BY WAY TOO FAST. We're busy because people from surrounding communities have come over for our town's summer festival. I secretly wish my boss would ask me to pick up an extra shift tonight, but he doesn't. I don't even have Asher's number to call and tell him something came up or that I'm sick and can't make it.

Unfortunately, it looks like I'm going to have to keep my word and meet Asher at the fair.

The whole drive home, I mentally run through all the scenarios on how this afternoon could go. I'm stepping way outside of my comfort zone to do this today, and if I admit that to him, I don't think he'll be surprised. My plan is to tread slowly, and if something goes wrong, I'll just go home. I'm trying not to make this harder than it has to be. It's a public place; there will be plenty of people wandering around.

Who knows? Maybe I'll actually have a little fun. And at the very least, I'm getting some free fair food out of it.

I quickly jump in the shower, because I only have thirty minutes to get ready. I decide on dark skinny jeans and a long green tank I have hanging in my closet but have never worn. I don't have time to dry my hair, so I put some product in it and let the natural waves take over. I'm not one for much make-up, but I apply some moisturizer, a little mascara and a thin layer of lip gloss. I don't care how I look most days, and I'm not going to go out of my way to get all dolled up for a guy I barely know.

My nerves don't boil to the surface until I'm in the car, heading toward the center of town. My stomach is in knots as I drive around, looking for a place to park. I pull into one of the church parking lots and finally find an empty spot. My hand shakes when I reach up to turn the car off.

The thought of just going home runs through my mind again, but something tells me that Asher would be at my house looking for me not long after. It wouldn't be hard to figure out where I live if he doesn't already know. Maybe this should scare me, but something deep down inside tells me he would never hurt me.

Carrington Days is a big festival with carnival rides, entertainment, and plenty of fried food. Later tonight, they'll have a free concert in the park with a beer garden. I haven't been here the last couple years, but I remember coming here as a kid and having a really good time. My mom used to let me go on five rides, and then right before we went home, she would buy us a bag of the warm Tom Thumb donuts. Just thinking about those makes my mouth water. Those are the type of memories I always want to hold onto.

It feels as if a million butterflies have been let loose in my stomach by the time I reach the entrance. I don't see Asher anywhere, so I find an empty spot on the bench and wait. Maybe he'll do me a favor and just not show up.

I recognize many of the families that walk past. If anyone is surprised to actually see me here, no one acts like it. One little girl walks up to me and reaches a hand full of sticky cotton candy in my direction. "No, thank you," I say, smiling as her mom comes up behind her and apologizes. I would love to be that young again; things were so much simpler.

"So you can smile," a deep masculine voice says from behind me. I look over my shoulder; Asher is standing there, grinning at me. He looks tired, but good in his khaki shorts and light blue t-shirt.

"Everyone can smile," I reply hesitantly, standing to face him.

"Yeah, but not everyone does." When I'm about to tell him that everyone without a smile has a reason for it, I realize that's the one thing I don't need him to dig any deeper into.

"So, what do you want to see first?" I ask, nervously biting my lower lip.

He points his thumb behind his shoulder. "Do you want to try the rides?"

"Aren't we a little old for that?" I ask, shifting my weight to one side. It then dawns on me that I have absolutely no idea how old he is. It's never come up, but how could it have come up when I've spent no more than ten minutes with him?

"No one is ever too old for fun," he says, reaching for my hand. I pull both arms across my chest to avoid his touch and he pulls back, running his hand through his hair. "You're not easy to get to know, are you?"

Shrugging, I ask, "How old are you anyway?"

"Answering my questions with questions?" he says, shaking his head. Maybe I'll just piss him off enough that he'll end this whole thing. "I'm twenty-three. How old are you?"

"Nineteen."

"See, that wasn't so hard. A fact for a fact, let's try that once a day and maybe after a week or two, we'll be more comfortable with each other. Now, let's get on one of these rides," he says, grabbing for my hand again. This time I hesitantly let him take it. It feels odd at first, but after several seconds, I relax, letting him lead the way.

Most of the carnival rides are more suited for young children, but Asher insists that we ride the Ferris wheel. I compromise and tell him I will go on it with him if we can head over to the food stands right after. I can smell the warm cinnamon from the donuts, and it's making my stomach growl.

When we're secured into the car, Asher rests his arm behind me. To my surprise, I don't freak out from the contact. There's an honesty to him that makes me want to know him a little bit more. But I know better than to trust too easily . . . it can get me in trouble if I'm not careful.

Every time we go up to the top of the Ferris wheel, I can see the whole town of Carrington. I can see where almost every memory I've ever had took place from up here. There's my old elementary school and the high school as well as my house and the diner. Up here, I feel above it all, like the world can't touch me. But it's only going to last for about three minutes before it all ends and my feet are back on the ground.

When the ride stops, Asher pushes his fingers through the front of my hair. I instantly close my eyes, trying not to draw back. "You had a few pieces of hair out of place," he whispers, tapping the end of my nose with his fingertip.

"Thanks," I say, opening my eyes again.

"So, what do you want to do now?" he asks as we climb out of our seat.

"Donuts," I reply, grabbing for his hand and pulling him toward the food stands. His skin is slightly calloused, and I notice how perfectly his hand fits in mine. It's comfortable.

He laughs before quickly catching up to me. It's turning out to be a pretty good day, and I'm actually glad that I came. Beau's the only person who I usually feel comfortable around, but it's nice to know I haven't completely forgotten how to make friends.

"Have you lived here all your life?" Asher asks. I look in his direction and notice how the corners of his eyes crinkle up against the sunlight. My grandma always said how fine lines were a sign of wisdom. Maybe she was on to something.

"Since I was five," I reply, glancing at the small craft booths as we walk by. There's everything from quilts to flower arrangements, but nothing that peaks my interest.

"Do you ever travel?"

"No, we never had the money to do much of that. Sometimes we go into the city. You?"

"My family usually takes two trips a year. I've been to Europe, Mexico, Costa Rica and over half of the fifty states," he says, squeezing my hand in his. "Carrington might be one of my favorites, though. It has certain things that other places can't offer."

My whole body stiffens. He's moving way too fast; somewhere I'm not ready to go. "It's so peaceful here. Something about it makes me feel untouchable," he continues. I let out the air I've been holding in my lungs and relax back into just enjoying his company.

"What do you like to do for fun? I mean before you decided to enjoy the peace of small town life."

"Up until last year, my life was all about drinking and having a good time. This past year, I've been trying to figure out where my life's actually going," he says, looking over at me with one of the saddest expressions I've ever seen. I want to tell him he doesn't have to pretend for me because I certainly won't be doing it for him.

"And did you get it all figured out?" I ask.

He reaches his hand up to rub the back of his neck. "No, sometimes we don't get to decide our future. Let's just say I'm taking a little break from it all."

I know exactly what he means. One night, one moment, one decision can change the whole path that our future takes. This is one thing I can relate with.

"Do you want to talk about it?"

He shakes his head. "No, let's just have fun today. That's what we came here for, isn't it?" he asks, stopping in front of the donut stand.

"I guess it is," I say, trying to bite back a smile.

The line is long, but it's worth the wait when we finally get to the front and I have the warm bag in my hand. Words can't even express how amazing these donuts taste. I haven't had one in two years, so I'm going to savor every bite today.

We've just started eating our donuts when I notice Morgan and her posse moving in our direction. I drop the donut into the bag and watch them in silence. Asher must have sensed my sudden change in mood because he looks from me to the girls approaching us.

Morgan's eyes stay on me, while the two girls behind her have theirs set on Asher. "Hey, Kate, who's your new friend?" I already want to throw-up on her black wedge sandals. She hasn't paid much attention to me in two years, and now she wants to act like we're friends so that I'll introduce her to Asher?

"If you want to know, why don't you ask him yourself?" I say, surprised that I'm actually standing up to them.

"Geez, Kate, you don't have to be such a bitch," Jenna says from behind Morgan. I can feel my face reddening. I feel a hand press against my lower back and look up to see Asher standing right next to me.

"Wait, are you guys on some kind of date?" Morgan asks, her eyes going wide. She's probably thinking that Asher looks way too good for me.

"Look, why don't you girls move along," Asher says, taking one step forward. His tone scares me, but it doesn't seem to affect them in the slightest.

Morgan steps up, standing so that her breasts almost rub against his chest. "When you're ready to have fun, which you certainly won't have with Kate here, come find us," she purrs. I don't know what happened to her, but she's sure changed from the girl I used to know.

"Not likely," Asher says as he grabs my hand and pulls me away.

As soon as we are away from the crowd, I pull my hand from his and feel the tears collecting in my eyes. Maybe I'm not meant to have any sense of normalcy around here.

I turn and start walking to my car. I've had enough of today; it's just a reminder of why I don't let myself do these kinds of things anymore. The memories always flash back, and the people who knew me before always measure me against the girl I used to be. I'm not her anymore, and I'm not sure if I even liked her when I was. She was naïve and stupid, and her actions are what got me here.

"Kate," I hear behind me. I don't turn around. I don't slow my pace. I just keep going. "Kate, come on, don't be like this."

He eventually catches up to me but he's winded, bending to catch his breath. "Where are you going?"

"Home," I say, unlocking the door.

"Why?" he asks, throwing his arms in the air.

"You saw what happened back there. You shouldn't be wasting your time on me. I just want to go home." My lip quivers as I reach for the handle of the car door and pull it open.

"Running isn't going to solve your problems, you know," he says, leaning against the side of my car.

"No, but it certainly gets me far away from them," I cry, sitting in my driver's seat and pulling the door shut. I just want to go home.

"Kate!" he yells. I pull the car out of park and wait for him to step back.

He slams his hand against the hood of my car, hard enough to make me jump but not to leave a dent. "Fuck," he says under his breath. I don't know if he intended for me to hear it, but I did.

I'm not even out of the parking lot before I feel warm tears roll down my cheeks. I should have never agreed to come here.

This isn't my place anymore.

Neither my mom nor I work on Sundays. I'm not sure how I feel about that today. I need the distraction that work provides, but I don't want to run the risk of seeing Asher. What happened yesterday had nothing to do with him; I realized that while I was lying in bed last night. It had everything to do with my issues, and I wish I could go back and change the way I handled it.

My past has nothing to do with him. My shame and guilt have nothing to do with him. But it all bleeds into every aspect of my life, and this is the reason we can't be friends. I can't let anyone else get hurt because of me. Everyone should stay away from me because, in the end, I know I'll let them down.

I decide to go for a run before my mom gets up and suggests we should go out for breakfast, or traps me into a day of Lifetime movies. The minute my feet start pounding on the pavement, I feel some of the tension leave my body.

I saw Asher as a new beginning, but eventually he'll figure out how I used to be. I think if I could move away from here to a place where no one knows me, I might have a chance at happiness, but I can't do that either. There's a comfort in staying home . . . but there's so much agony too.

I can't decide if I want to stay or run away, but I do know I'm afraid of being alone.

We all build a sense of identity as we grow up. It's shaped by our family, our friends, where we grow up, our talents, our weaknesses, our victories and our mistakes. Hopefully, by the time we reach adulthood, we know who we are.

I was almost there once; I'd been on the cusp of figuring out who I was, but it was all wiped away because someone felt like he needed to steal my power away from me one night.

I need to get it back somehow, or there won't be anything left of me.

When I return home, I take a long, hot shower before being sucked into a movie marathon with my mom. Lucky for me, she's tired from a long week at work and doesn't feel like talking much. Sometimes I wish we had a different relationship so I could tell her everything. I've often played out how I would tell her about Drew in my mind, but it never ends the same. Would she be ashamed of me? Would she tell me how stupid I was for going into the house that night? I just can't bring myself to that point, knowing there is a chance she'll be disappointed in me. I still need her.

It's past eight in the evening when there's a knock at the door. Mom's been asleep on the couch for at least an hour. I run to my room and grab a zip up sweatshirt to cover my cami and cotton pajama shorts before peeking through the side window to see who's at the door.

It's Asher. What's he doing here?

I slowly open the door just enough for him to see me. "Can I talk to you for a minute?" he asks nervously as he leans back against the railing.

I put my index finger over my lips, looking back at my mom to make sure she's still sleeping, and then slip out the front door. "What are you doing here?"

"We didn't do our fact for a fact today," he says, rubbing the back of his neck.

"What?" I ask, dumbfounded. He came all the way over here just to give me a fact.

"My fact for the day: I wanted to come over here as soon as you drove away yesterday. I want to know you. I want to know what it is that made you cry, but more than that, I want to know what I have to do to make you happy again," he says, his voice soft.

I'm taken aback. Why does he care so much? He doesn't know me, but his sights are set on figuring me out. Maybe we're more alike than I thought.

"Why do you care?" I whisper.

He shakes his head. "I don't know. I just can't stop thinking about you." I feel a lump growing in the back of my throat.

"Asher, there are lots of other girls in this town who would be happy to get to know you. Don't waste your time on me," I say, looking down at my hands to avoid his reaction.

He places his finger under my chin, lifting my eyes to his. "I only want to know you." My heart is beating so fast that he can probably see it through my sweatshirt.

"I don't do the whole dating thing," I say, trying to catch my breath.

"I just want to be your friend."

"Why me?"

"Why not you?" he asks, running his thumb across my chin.

"It's not easy for me," I whisper, trying to pull my eyes from his, but the finger he still has under my chin won't let me.

"What do you have to lose?"

He has no idea how much a person can lose by trusting someone, absolutely no idea. But I can't quiet the voice in my head that's telling me to take a chance on Asher . . . I had fun yesterday before my past came crashing down on us.

I nod, hesitantly. "Okay."

"Well then, friend, tomorrow I'm picking you up after work and we're going to do something fun."

"And what's that?" I ask, nervously.

"It's a surprise," he says before starting down the steps.

I watch him walk down the sidewalk without muttering a word. When he reaches his car, I realize I never gave him a fact. "Wait!" I yell.

He stops in front of his car and I move toward him, not wanting the whole neighborhood to hear me. His hands are in the pockets of his jeans as he brushes his tongue along his lower lip. For the first time, I actually sense tension between us, but it's not bad tension. It's just a strong pull that I can't quite explain.

"I never told you my fact," I say, stopping in front of him.

"Oh, yeah. What is it?" he asks, smiling down at me.

I take a deep breath. "I've really needed a friend lately." Just admitting that was a big step for me. I hate when people see my weakness.

He cups my face and lets his thumbs run across the plains of my cheekbones. I close my eyes and feel tenderness in Asher Hunt. There are crazy little things going on in my stomach that I haven't felt in a very long time.

When he pulls back, he just lets go, taking a few steps before walking to the driver's side of his car. "See you tomorrow."

I move back to the sidewalk and wave as he pulls away from the curb. I can't believe that I just let that happen to me.

Chapter 8

I WOKE UP THIS MORNING FEELING . . . different. I'm actually looking forward to something, and that's a new concept for me. Asher shocked me when he stopped by my house last night, but I'm so glad he did. He brings feelings out of me that I haven't felt in a long time. For the first time in two years, I really want to see and feel what it's like to live.

When I got back in the house last night, I had yet another missed call from Beau. On Saturday when he called, I didn't answer because I had just gotten home from the carnival and I knew if he heard my voice at that moment, he'd come straight home.

And last night, I didn't pick up the phone when he called either. I don't know why. I feel guilty because it seems like I might be replacing Beau's absence with Asher and I'm not ready to explain that to Beau.

Work was slow today, but I'm finally heading home to get ready for Asher's surprise. I have no idea what to wear because I have no clue what we're doing. I select a blue maxi dress and pull a thick brown belt on over it to dress it up. He didn't say what time he'd be here exactly, so I quickly tie my hair into a tight knot at the top of my head and put on a little gloss and mascara.

When the doorbell rings, my heart starts to race. When I open the door, the guy standing in front of me looks the same as every other day with his wild, but perfectly in place, blonde hair. He's wearing faded blue jeans and a grey polo shirt which molds nicely to his body.

And I don't miss the way his eyes travel up my body. "Do I look okay?" I ask. "I didn't know what we were doing."

"You look beautiful," he remarks, causing me to briefly look away. Compliments are not something I take very easily. It means that someone is paying attention to me, and it makes me uncomfortable.

"Can you tell me where we're going? I mean, it isn't anywhere private, is it? I like to be around people," I ramble, not giving him a chance to answer.

He rubs the back of his hand up my arm. "Hey, calm down. If it's that important to you, I can tell you."

I nod. "It is."

"You know you can trust me, right?" he asks, tilting his head to the side.

"It's not about you. It's just this thing I have-"

He places his finger over my lips. "It's okay. You don't have to explain. We're going to Omaha to hang out for the rest of the day."

"Really?" I ask. I expected the movies or maybe dinner, but I wasn't expecting a road trip.

"Yeah, I thought it would be nice to do a little exploring and see what there is to do outside of this town."

That makes two of us, I think to myself as he helps me into his Mustang. It's nice and clean inside with pristine leather seats. It's only going to be the two of us in the car, but I trust him. He's done nothing but try to help me since I first met him.

The conversation on the way into the city is light. He asks me why anyone would want to live on a farm, and I tell him that some people like the solitude, which turns into a discussion over the difference between the people and places in both Chicago and Carrington. I've never been to Chicago, but I imagine things are just a little different there.

"Why did you leave?" I ask, sneaking a quick glance in his direction.

He hesitates, running the tip of his tongue across his lower lip. I've noticed he does that a lot. "I'm not ready to share that fact yet."

"What fact will you share today?" I ask.

"Let me see . . . I quit school one semester before getting my engineering degree," he says, surprising me.

"Why did you do that?" I ask. Engineering isn't easy, so to put that much work into it only to quit would be tragic.

He sighs. "That's another thing I'm not ready to share."

"Okay," I say, turning my head to look out my window. I can see the taller buildings that make up downtown and realize we must be getting close.

"It's your turn," he says, bringing my attention back to him.

"Well, my original plan for this year was to go to college and major in Pre-Law," I say, staring straight ahead.

I feel his eyes momentarily look in my direction, but I don't move to meet them. "Why didn't you go?"

"That's not a fact I'm ready to share today," I say, almost mocking him. The corners of his mouth turn up, and I can't help but let mine do the same. I may have met my match with this one.

He asks me if I've been to the zoo and I haven't. I've lived one hour away from one of the top zoos in the country for fourteen years, and I haven't gone there once. He says he's never been either so that's where our adventure begins. I'm relaxed as we walk from exhibit to exhibit. No one knows who I am here, which to me is the best part.

Every once in a while, Asher places his hand on the small of my back or touches my shoulder to get my attention. At first, it makes me feel a little uncomfortable, but the more he does it, the more I begin to relax.

I make a big mistake when I agree to go with him to the reptile gardens. I should have known he was up to something.

"Have you ever held a snake before?" he asks, lifting an eyebrow.

"No, and I never want to," I reply, crinkling my nose up.

"You're going to today," he says, grabbing my hand.

"There's no way you're going to get my finger anywhere close to the skin of a snake, let alone hold it."

He stops, turning to face me. "What are you so afraid of?"

"No one said anything about being afraid," I counter, taking a small step back.

"That's what I thought," he smiles, moving us forward again. My hand is sweating in his when he stops in front of the zookeeper who's handling a snake to entertain a few kids that have gathered around him.

Asher steps up to the man and says something that I can't quite make out over the screams of the children. The zookeeper looks over Asher's shoulder and smiles at me before motioning me over to him. I swear to god I'm going to kill Asher with my bare hands after we leave here.

At first I don't move, but everyone is staring at me, so I feel like I don't have much choice. My stomach turns as I step forward. I glance over my shoulder as I walk past Asher and he winks at me. I roll my eyes and take in the legless reptile that is wrapped around the zookeeper's neck.

"Hi, my name is Mike. That young man over there said you wanted to hold a snake, and this here is a good one to start with." I'm frozen in place; I can't believe I'm actually going to go through with this.

"Now, if you hold out your hands, I'm going to place him in them to start out with. I'll be right here if you need anything." My fear is shooting bullets through my body.

"Hey, if you really don't want to do this, you don't have to," Asher says quietly from behind me.

I look at the kids' excited faces and shake my head. "No, I'm going to do this."

I hold my hands out and wait for Mike to place the snake in my arms. My heart beats rapidly as I try to control my body so that I don't scare the snake. I swallow hard when I feel the scaly skin in my palms.

"Now, let me know when you get used to him, and then I'm going to try something else," Mike says, staring at me intently.

Asher soothingly rubs my upper arm when I start to shake. After I calm down, Mike takes the snake and carefully wraps it around my shoulders. "Hold on to either side of him. He won't hurt you."

I inhale and exhale through my nose, trying to calm my nerves. "You're doing awesome," Asher whispers. I watch the snake slither in my hands and after a couple minutes of calm, I begin to relax. I haven't pushed myself to do anything like this in some time, but it feels good to conquer a fear.

Mike then carefully grabs the snake from around my neck and shakes my hand. "You did great. Don't forget to wash your hands," he grins.

"Thank you," I reply, taking one last look at my new reptile friend.

Asher places his hand on the small of my back and guides me through the crowd. As soon as we're outside again, I wrap my arms around his neck. "Thank you."

"For what?" he asks, wrapping his arms around my lower back.

"For helping me face my fears." I pull back, staring into his bright, smiling eyes.

"That was the goal, but something tells me we still have a few more fears to work through."

"It's going to take more than a snake to work through those," I say, glancing away.

"I know, but I'm going to try." He entwines my fingers with his and leads the way to the next animal exhibit. Sometimes I think he knows exactly what I'm holding inside, but I know paranoia has a grip on me. Even though he scares me, he awakens something within me.

After the zoo, he drives us downtown for dinner at a little pizza place. It's been so long since I've had anything besides the diner, sandwiches or my mom's rare cooking. Right now, anything different would be a treat.

We order a four-cheese pizza and two sodas before heading to a small booth by the window. Besides my daily glimpses of his life, I still know very little about Asher.

"Do you have any siblings?" I ask.

"I have a half-sister. She lives with my mom and step-dad in Chicago," he says, rolling a napkin between his fingers.

"You miss her?"

His eyes shoot up to mine. "Every day."

"I don't have any siblings, so I have no idea what that feels like. Most of my old friends couldn't stand their brothers and sisters, so I was kind of glad I didn't have them."

"My sister is ten years younger, so we don't have much to fight about."

"True. Will you get to see her again soon?" Chicago isn't that far away.

"Look, can we talk about something else for a while?" he asks, sounding slightly irritated. I nod, but I wish he would stop tiptoeing around his past with me, but that would also mean I would have to stop tiptoeing around mine and I'm not ready to start doing that.

The waitress ends the awkwardness, placing our pizza on the table. We eat our first slices in silence, occasionally making eye contact. I usually like the peace, but with Asher I need more. It's like the more I talk to him, the better I feel inside. How has this guy learned so much about me already? I thought I was as translucent as metal, but he sees right through me.

"Have you ever been fishing?" he asks, cutting the silence.

"My grandpa used to take me. I haven't done it since he passed away, though. I think I was ten the last time," I say, pulling some of the cheese back from the second slice of my pizza.

"My dad has a dock out by the lake. Come out there with me tomorrow," he pleads, looking into my green eyes with his blue-grey ones.

The lake is pretty secluded this time of year, but I hesitate. "I don't know."

"Do you work tomorrow?" he asks, leaning his right arm over the back of the booth. I get a better glimpse of his tattoo as his sleeve moves up his arm, revealing a date ending in 2011, two years ago. He notices the path of my eyes and moves his arm down to his side. That must be another thing he's not ready to talk about.

"Yeah, I work until two again," I reply.

"I'll pick you up at 2:30 then," he says, standing up and reaching for my hand. "Come on, let's get you home." I don't argue with him. I think if I can handle a trip out of town, I can probably handle a couple hours of fishing.

The ride back to Carrington is quiet, and it doesn't take long before I drift to sleep with my head resting against my window. When Asher wakes me up shaking my knee, we're already in my driveway, and I can see the light of the living room shining through the curtain. Mom must be home early tonight.

I rub my eyes and reach for the handle, but Asher wraps his hand around my forearm, stopping me. "Wait, Kate. I just wanted to tell you that I had a really good time today. I know I'm not the easiest guy to get to know, but I like hanging out with you."

I turn toward him and watch his gaze float to my lips then back to my eyes. I've seen that look before, and it scares the hell out of me. "I need to go," I say, turning to open the door.

When I make it halfway to the front steps, I turn and see him outside of his car with his forearm resting on the top of the vehicle. Even with only the light from the street lamp, I can see his eyebrows pulled together. It's the same concerned look I saw that first day in the diner.

"I'll see you tomorrow," I reassure him as I start to walk back toward the house again. As soon as I'm inside, I lean against the door and close my eyes.

"Where have you been, Kate? I've been worried sick. Your car was still here, and you don't usually go out at night," my mom says, her voice a mixture of anger and concern. I'm not in the mood to argue with her.

"I was out with a new friend."

"Is it that boy from the diner? You heard what Diana said," she says, putting her hands on her hips.

"We're just friends," I reply as I start walking toward my room. She doesn't spend much time being motherly, but when she does she usually picks the wrong battles. I cried my eyes out for days after I got home from Drew's house that night, but she didn't question my "sickness" even once. I took a shower five or six times that weekend, and she thought I was just doing it to reduce the fever I didn't have. I've been a fraction of my old self for almost two years, but she barely notices. Either she didn't know me too well before, or she doesn't spend enough time with me now.

Or maybe I just haven't changed as much as I thought.

"What do you know about him?" she asks, following close behind me.

"He's really nice and he's fun. Plus, I'm pretty sure that I'm old enough to choose my own friends!" I toss back, opening my door and closing it behind me.

She pounds on the door a couple times, but I don't move to open it. She knows better than to come in here when I have the door closed. It's my space, the only place to reveal my emotions without anyone seeing them.

She finally stops. "Just be careful."

I change into my pajama shorts and a t-shirt before lying in my bed and staring at my favorite spot on the ceiling. There's an old water spot, and if I stare at it just long enough, it looks like a flower in bloom. I've often laid here thinking about how similar humans are to flowers. We start out as seeds before we start to grow and at our peak we bloom. I lived most of my childhood in bloom; everything was beautiful and I had a great outlook. Things weren't always perfect in my life, but to me, it was normal. I was naïve and Drew took advantage of that, blocking all my sunlight until I began to wilt. I've spent hours—days even—trying to figure out what it takes to bring a flower back to life.

I'm still not sure.

The more days that go by, the less hope I have. I've had a few brief moments where a few rays shined through; prom, all the time spent with Beau and my trip with Asher, but the sun always disappears again. The darkness is too powerful.

Chapter 9

WHEN ASHER PULLS UP IN FRONT of my house ten minutes early to take me fishing, I'm not ready. He honks a couple times before I open the front door and wave my hand at him to let him know I need five more minutes.

He jumps out of his truck and runs up to my front door, causing my heart to race. "Can I wait inside?" he asks.

My mind starts to work overtime, and all the little voices that like to speak over me are going off in my head. I haven't been alone in a house with any guy except for Beau since everything that happened. If something were to happen right now, my mom won't be home for at least eight or nine hours and most of my neighbors are at work. No one would hear me if something happened to me.

But I know Asher's different, so I open the door all the way and move back to let him in. I take a few calming breaths and close the door before turning to face him. My stomach feels like I just took a wild roller coaster ride, but I'm going to see this through. It's all about baby steps.

"I just have a few things I have to finish. The remote is on the couch if you want to watch something."

He smiles. "I'm a little early. Take your time."

I take several deep breaths as I head to my bedroom to change out of my pajamas. It's been cloudy and windy all day, so I decide on a pair of black leggings and a long grey off the shoulder sweatshirt. I check my reflection in the mirror and see that my eyes are not as dark and puffy as usual. It turns out I've spent fewer nights with my mind lingering in the past and more thinking of Asher. He makes me look forward to my tomorrows, and he's always pushing me to try new things.

I put my hair up to keep the wind from blowing it into my face, and then quickly brush my teeth before joining Asher in the living room. He looks tired and worn out today. If I left him alone for a few more minutes, he probably would have fallen asleep.

"Are you ready?" I ask, startling him.

He switches the TV off and stretches before standing up and walking in my direction. My breathing begins to accelerate as he moves closer with this intense, burning look in his eyes. As soon as he's within reach, he grabs my hand in his and walks us out the door to his car. I can barely keep up, he's moving so fast. He opens my door and waits for me to climb in before crouching down on the grass so that our eyes are level.

"You need to understand that I'd never hurt you. Every time we're alone or I get too close to you, you look so scared of me, and I can't stand it when you look at me like that, Kate."

He doesn't wait for me to respond. He stands and closes my door, leaving me speechless. I think a lot of people misinterpret my fear for sadness. I'm not a happy girl but the one thing that holds me back more than anything is the feeling that someone or something is out there waiting to cause me pain. I feel like that every single day, and it's exhausting. I can't believe how easily he sees through me. He's learned more about me in one week than anyone else has picked up on in years.

He doesn't bother looking at me when he gets into the car and puts it in drive. I relax, sinking down into my seat as we drive through town toward the lake. It's only a ten-minute walk from my house, but Asher seems to be attached to his car. It would be nice to have in case it rains. *God, please don't let it start raining.*

As we pull up a gravel driveway, I notice Asher's dock is on the opposite side of the lake from the beach that Beau and I frequented as kids. This side is full of houses; some big ones owned by successful business people in the area and some smaller ones used mostly for fishing. It turns out Asher's dad has one of the smaller log cabin type homes out here. It's cute, but I think the deck out back is bigger than the entire house.

Asher turns the car off and turns to face me. "Ready?"

"Yeah." I smile.

It turns out fishing is more relaxing than I ever thought it could be. Instead of being nervous because it's only the two of us, I feel comfortable, and I think I shock both of us when I laugh at Asher's attempt to get me to put my own worm on the hook. The sun may not be out today, but I feel warmth shining through my soul as I'm able to forget everything.

It's quiet out here. Every now and then, we hear birds fly over or the wind blowing through the long grass, but everything else is still. If you come out during the summer, the lake is packed with boats, but today we only see one small fishing boat in the distance.

My bobber goes under water, causing me to scream like a schoolgirl. I don't remember the last time I was this excited about anything. I start to reel it in, but it must be hooked on something because my pole is bending, but the line isn't moving.

Asher steps behind me, wrapping his arms around mine to grip the pole on either side of my hands. I take a few deep breaths to ease the grip on my chest. "Take it easy. We're going to move it a little to the left and try it again," he whispers, his mouth not far from my ear. He guides my hands to the left until we're able to reel the line in. When the hook finally lifts from the water, all that's on it is seaweed.

"So I guess I don't have the first catch of the day," I joke, laughing for the second time today.

"I guess not," he laughs, keeping one hand on the pole and wrapping the other around my waist so that my back is against his chest. I close my eyes, letting myself feel the warmth of his body against mine. His fingers stroke my side, sending butterflies into flight in my stomach.

"That means I still have time to get the first catch," he says, pressing his nose into my hair. I feel safe in his arms, and for a second I imagine myself spending more time wrapped up in them, but I quickly let the thought go. We're just friends, and I can't be anything more than that with anyone right now.

He surprises me by kissing the top of my head before letting me go. I feel cold, wishing I had the courage to ask him to wrap me back up again. He keeps giving me these lasting memories that make me aware of the heartbeat that still exists within me. I haven't had these feelings in so long, and I'm not sure what to do with them.

"I think it's time I tell you my fact for the day," I pause, glancing down at the dock, "I haven't laughed this much in two years."

He stops working on the hook and seems to contemplate what I said. He's probably wondering what happened two years ago, but he doesn't press me. He knows what it's like to have to keep things buried inside.

"I'm glad," he says, returning his attention to the hook. He pulls the last bit of the slimy greens off before putting another worm on the hook and throwing it back in the water for me.

"So what's yours?" I ask, turning to face him. He puts my pole down in a holder at the end of the dock next to his and stares down at me like something is tearing him up inside. He swallows hard, looking up to the sky, then back at me. I want to curl up in his arms and take away his uncertainty, but I can't solve problems that I know nothing about.

His brows are pulled in as he moves closer to me and reaches his hand up to my face. Even if I wanted to, I couldn't look away from him right now. His eyes captivate me and pull me in every time I see them. Right as his hand is about to touch my face, he pulls it back to his side. His eyes move down to my lips before coming back up to meet mine.

"I really want to kiss you . . . but I don't want to scare you away," he whispers.

I step back to get some more space between us so that I can catch my breath. He closes his eyes tight and turns to look out onto the water. My skin tingles and that fluttery feeling is back in my stomach. If he had given me a million chances to guess what he was going to tell me today, I would never have guessed this.

I want to say something, but all my thoughts are fuzzy. He starts reeling in our fishing lines and packs up his tackle box, throwing things inside and closing it shut. I feel horrible, but I still can't say anything. He seems hurt, but not shocked. I'm the one in shock.

He turns around and looks everywhere but at me with his hard eyes. "We should get going. It's getting darker to the west. I think a storm is coming," he says before walking past me to put the poles in the storage shed. My heart sinks past my stomach to my feet. Would I have let him kiss me?

I walk to the car and wait for him, resting my head against the passenger side window. I sneak a glance at him when I hear his door open, but he doesn't look my way. He starts the car and doesn't waste any time before putting it in reverse. His jaw is tense, and he's gripping the steering wheel as if it's his lifeline. I want to apologize, but I have no idea where to start, so I focus back out my window, watching the houses go by until I snap out of my daze and recognize the ones on my own street.

I thought I'd be relieved when he dropped me off, but I feel like crap because I still haven't said a single word to him. If I don't acknowledge it, it will all go away.

He stops in front of my house, putting the car in park, but not saying anything. I unbuckle my seatbelt and put my hand on the door handle, pausing before opening it. "I'm not scared of you," I whisper before opening the door. I don't look back to see his reaction, my heart won't allow it. I don't stop until I'm in my house with my back resting against the front door. Only then do I realize that I did want Asher Hunt to kiss me.

I've been pacing around my room since Asher dropped me off. All I can think about is how I'm going to make this right. The last few times we've been together, he always makes plans with me for the next day before letting me out of his sight, but he didn't make any this time. I should let him come to me when he's ready, but I'm just worried that maybe he never will be.

My phone starts to ring and I quickly move to my dresser not even bothering to see who it is before picking it up. I want to hear Asher's voice again.

"Hello," I say, continuing to pace.

"You finally answered your phone."

Beau.

Shit. Shit. Shit.

I wasn't prepared to explain anything to him tonight.

"Hey," I say, banging my palm against my forehead. I've been stupid to ignore him for this long. All I've done is create an even more awkward conversation.

"Look, Kate, I don't know what's up with you, but when you don't answer my calls, I worry about you. What's going on?" he asks. Beau never beats around the bush, and he always expects the truth from me. I just wish he knew how much further he pushes me away by always expecting something from me. Asher pushes me to do things I wouldn't usually do, but Beau pushes me emotionally. Maybe, subconsciously, I am pushing him away so that I can figure out who I am now.

"I'm sorry. I've had a lot on my mind," I reply. I'm good at giving only half of the truth.

"I'm coming home this weekend," he says, frustration dripping from his voice.

"No. I want you to spend one month just having fun, and then if you want to come see me for a weekend, you can. Maybe I can even come to visit you." The last part isn't likely to happen because too many people from my past go to the same college; people who made my life hell the last two years because I wasn't "me" anymore.

"Dammit, why are you doing this? And what's this shit about if I want to come see you?" he asks, his voice getting angrier.

"You've been with me almost constantly for two years, Beau. At some point, you just have to live your life and let me wallow in mine!" I yell, more than a little frustrated with him.

"I talked to Morgan the other day," he says suddenly.

"What does she have to do with this?" I ask, softly banging my head against the window. He knows how Morgan treated me, and I'm surprised he even gave her the time of day.

"She stopped me in the student center to tell me she saw you last weekend at Carrington Days. She said you looked really good . . . with your new friend," he says, putting extra emphasis on the last word.

I close my eyes tight and turn back to the window, sliding down to the floor. I didn't want him to find out about Asher this way. I don't want him to think he's replaceable because he's not.

"Oh, that was just Asher. He's new in town, and I was showing him around," I reply, resting my forehead against my knees.

"I could barely get you out of the house when I was around, but you're going to Carrington Days with some random new guy?" His voice is full of frustration.

I wince. "He dared me."

He's silent for a few seconds. I try to think of something else besides my lame excuse, but I can't. "You know what, I'm too tired to deal with this today. I'll just text you tomorrow." He doesn't wait for me to reply before hanging up the phone.

I feel like someone just drove a screwdriver through my heart. I don't know why I keep him at arm's length when it's obvious he just wants to be there for me, but I also don't know why he lets me. He just wants what's best for me, but I hate that he keeps sacrificing his own happiness to give it to me. I don't deserve it. I send him a quick text before getting ready for bed.

I'm sorry.

I started the day out with a best friend and a nice guy who I've been having fun getting to know. Now, I'm pretty sure that my best friend isn't talking to me, and that guy who I'd like to know better is probably giving up on me.

Why can't things just go back to the way they used to be?

Chapter 10

I HAVE TODAY OFF, and all I can think about is how I'm going to fix the mess I created yesterday. Beau never responded to my text, but after a day or two, I'm hoping he'll come around and talk to me again.

Asher is a different story. I don't know if he's used to running from things like I do, or if he faces them head on, but I feel as if I'm the one in control of the situation. It's my turn to make a move and decide where we go from here.

After lunch, I take a chance and run to his house to talk to him. I need to let him know that what he said yesterday doesn't affect our friendship, but I can't be any more than that right now.

When I reach his street, I notice his Mustang isn't in the driveway, so I jog past the diner and it isn't there either. The only other place I can think of that he might be is the lake house. I pick up my pace. I need to talk to him and get everything out in the open before I lose the courage to go through with it. The longer run just gives me more time to figure out exactly what I'm going to say.

As I near the residential side of the lake, I can see his car in the driveway, and my heart starts to beat a little harder inside my chest. I'm only minutes away from trying to salvage one of the few good things to have walked into my life.

I slow to a walk as I get closer. I can hear movement from behind the house, so I speed up my pace, anxious to see him again. I hear his voice but my feet halt in place when I see that he's not alone. He's facing my direction, but his eyes are focused on a woman with long blonde hair who stands less than a foot in front of him. He's holding a piece of her golden locks in his hand, running his fingers down the length of it. The worst part . . . he seems to be enjoying himself.

He isn't looking at her like he looks at me, but there's a lightness to his expression that I don't normally see. I don't know who the girl is, but I find myself getting irritated when I see the attention he's giving her.

I can't watch them anymore. I walk backwards a few steps before turning to run back down the driveway.

"Kate, wait!" Asher shouts.

I hear his feet hitting the gravel and I stop, knowing it won't take him long to catch me.

"What are you doing here?" he asks. I can feel him close behind me.

I spin around to face him, trying to come up with a new plan for how I'm going to apologize. His eyes are shooting darts into me, and the light expression he had just a couple minutes ago seems desperate now. I'm only a couple feet away, but I can hear every breath he takes. It reminds me of the way he looked at me on the dock before he told me he wanted to kiss me.

"I came to apologize for the way I acted yesterday," I say, looking behind him to see the blonde looking in our direction. "But I see that you're busy so I'll just leave you two."

I turn to start toward the road again, but he grabs my arm and pulls me back into his chest. "Don't go," he whispers.

I try to move forward, but his arms are wrapped too tightly around me. "Please let go of me!" I yell, trying to free my body from his arms. Being confined instantly makes me tense.

He loosens his grip on me, but continues to hug me close. "Stay."

When it Rains

I squeeze my eyes shut, shaking my head back and forth. "Why? I don't want to be the third wheel."

"Stop! Becca just came over to say hi," he says. I can feel his warm breath against my neck.

"Asher, I'm just going to go. Call me or something," Becca says, walking around us toward the house next door. He lifts one hand in front of us to wave goodbye but doesn't loosen his hold on me.

"It looked like more," I say with a little more edge in my voice than I intended.

"Why does it matter?" he grits through his teeth.

That's one question I don't have an answer to right now. I don't understand why seeing him with someone else affected me so much when the reason I came over here was to tell him I wanted to remain friends.

"I don't know!"

I just can't take it anymore. The last twenty-four hours of frustration and regret catch up to me, and all I can do is fall back into his arms. The last few days, I started to feel more like a person with a beating heart, but now I feel like it's all slipping away from me again. Asher spins me around so that my chest is pressed against his and holds me tight in his strong arms as I let everything pour out of me. Usually, I shut myself down until I'm safely inside my bedroom before I let myself breakdown, but for some reason I'm able to let Asher see it all.

"Will you talk to me?" he asks, carefully rubbing his hands up and down my back.

I shake my head against his chest. Just because I'll let him see me like this, doesn't mean I'm ready to let him hear about the ugly demons that live inside me. He holds me against his body until I've calmed down enough that my body stops shaking.

He takes a step back, but wraps his hands around my elbows to keep me close. "I think now would be a good

88

time to tell you my fact for the day. I've been with my share of girls, but you are by far the most complicated, frustrating one. Yet, for some reason, I can't stop thinking about you."

"I'm not with you," I say, shaking my head.

He swallows, briefly looking away from my eyes. "I know."

For the first time, it hits me. The reason my heart was on fire when I saw him with his fingers in Becca's hair, and the reason I'm so frustrated . . . is the reason I came here today. I want his fingers caressing my hair.

And right now as I stare at his lips, I want to feel those too.

I'm jealous.

"What is Becca to you?" I ask, trying my best to hide the bitterness in my voice.

He glances up at the clear blue sky before his eyes find my face again. "She's lived next door for as long as I can remember. When I was younger and I visited my dad, we used to have lots of fun together. She's just an old friend."

"Do you like her?"

He pinches his eyes shut, shaking his head. "Not the way you think. She came over here, and I thought I could get lost in her . . . to forget you. It didn't work, in case you're wondering."

"You looked pretty content when I walked around the house," I say, shuffling my feet in the gravel until a layer of dust comes up.

"I was just trying to have fun," he says, reaching up to tuck a stray piece of hair behind my ear. He removes his finger slowly, letting it brush behind my ear. I instinctively close my eyes and feel the warm tingle that runs down the length of my body. It's amazing what one little touch can do.

When I open my eyes, I see the difference in the way he looks at me and the way I saw him looking at Becca. He was being playful with her, but when I look into his stormy blue eyes, I see desire, need and pain. He's letting me see things that he isn't showing others. I want to help him with whatever he's hiding. I think maybe we can even help each other.

I lick my lips, noticing how his eyes immediately focus in on them. "I think it's time for me to give you my fact for the day," I say softly, bringing his eyes back up to mine.

"And what's that?"

I pause and take a deep breath. "I want you to kiss me."

The one hand that still remains on my elbow tightens and his eyes flash back and forth between mine. There's an internal struggle inside of him; I can feel it . . . see it.

"Are you sure?" he finally asks.

I nod. "As sure as I've ever been about anything."

"If I kiss you now, there's no going back," he says, swallowing hard.

I hadn't thought past the kiss, but right now I'd do anything to feel his lips on mine. I nod.

He drops my arm, closing the distance between our bodies and putting his hands on either side of my head. When I feel his warm breath against my lips, I know it won't be much longer. And when it finally happens, I close my eyes, letting myself feel his skin on mine and every emotion that flows through my head.

His lips are soft and gentle, barely touching mine at first, but growing more primal when he sucks my bottom lip between his. And when I grip the front of his shirt in my hands, he runs his tongue along my lips, coaxing mine open for him. I follow his lead, letting his tongue tangle with mine. I've only kissed two boys in my whole life if I don't count the one who just took it from me when I pleaded with him not to.

Some kisses are just kisses, but Asher's kiss is the best kind of kiss. It feels like heaven, and I never want to let him go. I feel like I've been living the last two years for this moment . . . for someone to save me. It's a new beginning for me.

He slows his movement before pulling away and ending it with one more soft brush against my lips. I want to grab him and pull him close again, but I'm frozen in place.

"That was so fucking sweet," he says, resting his forehead against mine.

I smile, swaying my body back and forth. He's being modest. That kiss was out of this world.

"Asher, can you help me with the groceries?" I hear a deep male voice yell from behind me.

"Shit," Asher mutters, pulling back from me. I instantly miss the contact. "Yeah, Dad. I'll be there in a second." He looks back down at me with a grin on his face. I know what he's thinking because I'm thinking the same thing. We need to do that again. Soon. "I'll be right back."

The sun shines brightly in the sky, glistening on the dark blue water. I place my hand above my eyes to get a better look at the view. This week has been crazy, but I have a better appreciation for everything around me while a hundred thoughts swim through my head. I do know that I want to explore this with him and see where it takes me. Something about the way he looks at me tells me he's safe. I don't think he would ever intentionally hurt me, but I'm still treading cautiously.

After several minutes have passed, I walk to the front of the house to see if they need my help. There's an old red Ford truck sitting next to Asher's car, but I don't see anyone outside. I walk to the front screen door, but stop when I hear Asher yelling.

"I don't have to tell her!"

"What are you going to do? Just string her along until you can't anymore?" his father shouts.

"It's not like that!" Asher yells.

I have a sinking feeling in my stomach. I shouldn't be eavesdropping on their conversation, but I can't stop myself, not when I think he might say something that will help me piece him together.

"You're just going to end up hurting her. Is that what you want?"

"It's my fucking life. Please just let me live it!" Asher screams.

I hear what sounds like a chair sliding against a hard floor and step back from the door. Was he talking about me? Or Becca? And what does he mean by stringing her along until he can't anymore?

I'm not sure what to do, but I don't feel like I'm welcome company anymore. I'm about ready to turn on my heels and run home when the screen door flies open and Asher steps out. His face is red, and he's in such a hurry that he almost walks right past me. I'm used to dealing with pissed off Beau, but I've never seen Asher like this.

"I'll give you a ride home," he calls from behind. His mood has switched so much that it's almost scary.

I follow him to the Mustang, but stop in front of it instead of moving to the passenger side. "I was going to run back home. Don't worry about it."

"Get in the car," he demands, opening the driver's side door to stand between it and the car. His voice has gone as cold as an Iowa winter, but I don't let it affect me. He's struggling with whatever it is his father thinks he should tell me. I want to know what it is so badly, but I'm not going to push him.

I take a few steps in his direction, holding my right hand out. "Let me have your keys."

"Why?" he asks, crossing his arms over his chest.

"Because you don't look like you should be driving right now," I reply, taking a few steps closer.

He laughs. "And you think I'm going to let you drive my car?" Actually that thought hadn't even crossed my mind. My plan was to convince him to take a walk down by the lake, but now that he mentioned it . . .

"What's so funny about that?" I ask, stopping right in front of him.

"I never let anyone drive my car," he replies. It's like he's daring me to ask again. He should know how I feel about dares by now.

I tilt my head and pull my lower lip between my teeth, not missing the way his lips quirk. "It's only a mile. How much damage can I really do?"

His smile falls and his lips part like he wants to say something.

He shuts the door, dropping his keys in my hand as he walks by. I roll them around on my finger once before opening the driver's door and climbing in. Asher settles into the passenger seat with his elbow resting on the top of the window jam and his head resting against his closed fist.

I start the car and glance down only to see it's a stick shift. I hate driving manuals. They made us do it one day in Driver's Ed, and I thought I was going to die . . . it's a good thing our town doesn't have many stop signs. I feel like I'm an inch tall because I convinced Asher to let me drive and now I don't even know how to put it in gear.

"Umm, Asher, I don't know how to drive stick shift. I mean, I do, but I really don't," I confess, scrunching my nose up at him.

He shakes his head, and the faintest of smiles plays on his lips. "Well, you wanted to drive this thing, so it looks like you're going to get a quick lesson on manual transmissions."

Crap.

"Okay, but if I break your car, it's not my fault. I've warned you," I say, adjusting the rearview mirror.

"First, put it into gear then press on the clutch and the break. Don't take your feet off until I tell you to. Now, carefully remove your foot from the brake and put it on the gas while easing up on the clutch." I do exactly as he instructs, and after two tries we're finally moving forward. "Now, pull up in the yard a little bit and then make a circle toward the road."

The one mile drive took over fifteen minutes, but it was worth it. I don't remember the last time I laughed so hard, even if Asher didn't find my eighteen stalls funny. When he instructs me on how to turn it off and put it in park, I think we both breathe a sigh of relief.

"Thanks for taking my mind off my dad," he states out of the blue. My driving skills must have done the trick.

"I'm glad I could help you for once."

"Do you work tomorrow?" he asks.

"Yeah, my normal seven to two," I reply, turning to face him.

"Maybe I'll come see you," he says, running his tongue across his lower lip. It drives me crazy when he does that.

"I'd like that." I smile, turning to walk toward the front door. I'm ready to put this whole day behind me and see what tomorrow brings.

"Hey, Kate," Asher yells from behind me. I stop, looking back at him.

"Yeah?"

The corners of his mouth turn up; showcasing the smile I've been missing since he walked out of the lake house after talking to his dad. "I just thought you should know that you're the best first kiss I've ever had."

He winks at me before jumping into his driver's seat and disappearing down the street leaving me standing there with my fingertips on my lips. It was my best first kiss too.

Chapter 11

THE NEXT MORNING, I find regret stirring deep inside of me. Not because I kissed Asher, but because of what did or didn't happen afterward. I should have asked him about the things his father said. I should have asked him what was bothering him on the ride back to my house, but I didn't. Maybe I was just scared of the truth, but now I'm lying here in my bed wondering what the truth is and what was going through Asher's mind after. It's making me insane.

I let a mysterious and seemingly complicated guy into my life but trying to figure him out is taking my mind off of all of my own problems. I want to ask him about all of the things that make him tick, but then what if he expects the same from me? And what if I can't handle his demons?

When I was a kid, I couldn't wait to grow up, but now I know it's not all it's cracked up to be.

I've been stuck in time at age seventeen for the past two years. My life didn't end in a literal sense that night . . . I'm still breathing, but time is at a complete standstill. I didn't feel like anything spectacular before, but now I don't even feel ordinary. I don't know where to go from here. It's not that I want to live with my mom and work in a diner forever . . . I just don't see much of a future for myself.

Everything I thought I knew about life has been proven wrong. I can't trust people just because I know their name. I have to learn to stand on my own two feet so that I can take the challenges life presents head on.

How? I'm still trying to figure that out. Sometimes it's easier to live in the misery than to crawl out of it. When I'm with Asher, I want to try. He's holding my hand a little tighter each day as I do things I haven't let myself do in a really long time. It gives me a little strength I didn't have before, and it's giving me a glimpse of what my life could be if I learn to let go of some of my anger and guilt. I owe it to myself to at least try.

When I finally roll out of bed, there's only twenty minutes before I have to be at work. I quickly shower, deciding to let my hair dry into natural waves. I'm out the door in my red Bonnie's shirt and faded blue jeans with five minutes to spare. The air is starting to get a little cooler with each passing day; it won't be long until I'm trading t-shirts for sweaters and a coat.

I take a shower without letting the scalding water turn my skin deep red, and I drive to work without panicking. It's going to be an uphill battle, but I know there will come a day when I can begin to focus on more of the positive things than the negative.

As I walk inside the back door of the diner, I greet the cooks, earning me a curious glance from the two of them. I don't usually talk much unless it's my mom or Diana, keeping to myself makes my life easier, even if it doesn't make it happier.

"What's gotten into you this morning?" my mom asks, coming around the corner.

"Just trying to look at life from a different perspective," I reply, tying my apron behind my back.

She places her hand on my arm, halting my movements. "Look, Kate, I'm sorry for yelling at you the other night. I just don't want you to make the same mistakes I did." Her voice is soft and soothing. I want to tell her it's no big deal; I've probably made some mistakes that she hasn't, but as always, I don't say a word.

"We're just friends. There's no need to worry," I say, smiling as I remember the very second his lips touched mine yesterday. It's a moment I won't soon forget.

"Well, you've changed for the better since meeting him, so he must be doing something right." She smiles, walking away.

As the morning comes to an end, my eyes are glued to the door, waiting for Asher to walk in. He'd said he might come see me, so I've been hanging on to the hope that he will all morning. My stomach clenches a little tighter with each passing minute.

Every time I hear the bell above the door ring, my head turns to see if it's Asher, but he never comes.

When my shift is over, I drive home with all things Asher filling my head; the way he looks when he smiles, his scent, and the way he makes me feel when he's close. I want to see him again so badly, but I'm afraid there's a reason he didn't show up today. And if I'm honest with myself, I'm afraid of the rejection.

As I jump in for a quick shower to wash the smell of French fries and bacon out of my hair, I'm reminded of all the times Beau used to come over after I got off work. He would purposefully move, as close to me as he could get, and inhale more deeply than I ever thought was possible. "Hmm, you smell like bacon," he'd say.

Just thinking about him warms my heart, but it also brings me sadness. I've pushed him away without much of an explanation and all it's done is hurt him. I may not be able to explain everything to him right now, but I need to stop pushing him before he falls over the ledge and I lose him forever. He's been the one constant strength in my life, and I can't afford to let him walk away. I see that now.

My first instinct is to crawl back into bed and waste the afternoon away like I'd usually do, but I know it won't help me. I'll drift off to the same place I always do until I cry my eyes out and fall asleep. Instead, I grab a book from my desk and start to read. Reading is something I used to enjoy when I didn't have another care in the world, but that I haven't taken much time to do it the last couple years. I should have never let it go because it's a nice escape from the real world . . . something I've needed desperately.

I'm into the third chapter when my cell phone rings, drawing my attention away from my book. I can hear the chirping ring, but I can't find it. I notice the bottom of my jeans sticking out from under the bed and pull them out, reaching in the front pocket. The screen shows a number that I don't recognize. "Hello?" I say hesitantly, sitting down on the edge of the bed.

"Kate." The agony I hear on the other side of the phone is enough to make me sick.

"Asher?"

"Yeah, it's me. I just needed to hear your voice."

"How did you get my number?" I ask, hesitantly.

"I called the diner. They wouldn't give it to me at first, but I have my ways," he says, sounding as if he's in emotional or physical pain. It's hard to hear anyone sound like that, but when it's someone I'm really starting to care for it's even worse.

"Are you okay?" I ask.

"No, I'm not okay," he replies. "Everything's so fucked up. The worst part is I probably deserve it."

"What are you talking about? Where are you?" I ask, standing up to pace my room. I don't like the way he sounds and I have to go to him.

"Pete's," he says. He's either drunk or losing it. Maybe a little bit of both.

Lisa De Jong

"I'll be there in ten minutes. Don't go anywhere."
Pete's is the local bar, and where my mom works in the
evenings. I've only been in there a few times to bring my
mom something she forgot before work, or to pick up
some dinner for myself. It's really not the type of place a
girl like me goes alone without good reason.

"Kate, don't. I just . . . I just needed to hear your
voice," he mumbles.

"Don't argue with me," I say, hanging up the phone
before he has time to reply. Now I know how Beau feels
when I'm pushing him away and not taking his help when
he offers it to me. When you care about someone, it's
instinctive to want to help that person, no matter what you
have to do to accomplish it.

I change out of my sweats, slip on a pair of faded
skinny jeans, and then pull a long black t-shirt over my
head, and I'm out the door. I wonder if this has anything
to do with what happened between him and his dad last
night, or if something else happened today. I'm not even
sure he'll tell me when I get there, but if all I am is a
sense of comfort for him, I'm okay with that.

I pull into Pete's parking lot and take note of a group
of three guys standing outside the front door, smoking
cigarettes. When I open my door, I hear them laughing
and joking, sounding every bit as drunk as they probably
are. Normally, I would get back in my car and leave as
fast as I could, but Asher's in there and he needs me.

I step out onto the gravel parking lot and concentrate
on the sound of my tennis shoes grinding into the small
pebbles. It helps me take my mind off the uneasiness that
is spreading like wildfire throughout my body. I keep my
eyes on the door as I count my steps, getting closer and
closer. Only ten or so more steps, I think.

"Hey, beautiful, why don't you stay out here with
us?" one of the men shouts, taking a couple shaky steps
toward me. I keep my head up to avoid looking at him

99

and speed up my pace until my hand is finally on the handle. I pull it back, letting out a deep breath when it swings open. "Hey, where you going?" I hear him yell as I pull the door closed behind me. Never in my life did I think I could get through a situation like that without having a complete meltdown, but I did. My thoughts of Asher are more powerful than my fears.

Pete's is decorated in dark wood furniture, and an outdated hunter green covers the walls. The worst thing about the whole place though is the overwhelming smell of beer and sweat. I hate it. That smell brings back so many memories that I wish I could forget, but I have to stay focused.

My eyes dart around the bar, looking for him between the booths and pool tables, but I don't see him anywhere. My stomach rolls. What if he left before I got here? On the phone he'd sounded really out of it, and there's no way he's in the right frame of mind to drive home. I spot my mom behind the bar; maybe she knows where he has gone. Her eyes grow as big as quarters when she spots me.

"What are you doing here this late?" she asks, wiping her hands on a bar towel.

"Um, actually, I'm looking for Asher. Have you seen him?"

She looks at me curiously. "Who?"

"The guy I've been talking to at the diner. Have you seen him?" I ask, fidgeting with my fingers. She's going to ask me a thousand questions about this later.

Her eyebrows pull in as her head nods toward the bathroom. "He went in there about ten minutes ago."

"Why didn't you call me?" She knows that we've become friends, so I'm pissed that she didn't call me to come help him. Wouldn't she know that I'd want to help him?

"I didn't know you guys were that close. Besides, you really don't need to get in the middle of this stuff," she says, resting her palms on the bar in front of her.

"He needs me." I don't wait for her to reply as I walk toward the hallway that leads to the bathrooms.

A bearded guy with faded blue jeans and a racing t-shirt walks out, still working to fasten his pants. I'm beyond disgusted, but I have to find out if Asher is inside. "Is there a young guy with blonde hair in there?" I ask shyly, standing back against the wall.

His eyes roam the entire length of my body, and he smiles. "Yeah, he's puking his guts out. Someone should teach that boy how to hold his liquor."

"Is anyone else in there?" I tried to look over his shoulder when he had the door open, but the partition blocked my view.

He shakes his head. "Not at the moment."

"Thanks," I say as I push past him, anxious to see Asher.

The moment I walk in, I can hear heaving, followed by a few coughs. I walk toward the two bathroom stalls, noticing it smells so much worse in here than it does in the bar. I can't even imagine how much he drank to make himself this sick. "Asher," I say, pushing the door on the first stall. It's empty. I hear the heaving sound again right as I push on the door of the second stall. There he is, perched over the toilet with his elbows resting on either side.

My stomach clenches as I squat down behind him and hesitantly move my hand to rub small circles on his back. "Do you need some water?" I ask as soon as he stops heaving.

"I asked you not to come here," he grumbles, resting his forehead on his hands. He's stupid to think I'd just leave him here by himself. I may not care about much these days, but I'm not going to let him get in any trouble, or even worse, let him drive home drunk.

"I'm not leaving you here. Are you okay to walk, or do you need a minute?" I ask, continuing to rub his back.

"You're not responsible for me," he whispers. His breathing is hard, and I can feel his heart beating against his back.

"Yeah, but I'm the only one here for you right now," I say, trying to hold back my frustration. The only reason I'm here in this smelly bar is to help him. "Can you get up? I think you should get some fresh air."

"Please, just go wait outside. I'll be out in just a minute." He looks up at me with narrowed eyes, but all I can concentrate on is the pale tone of his skin and the lines of sweat that roll down his forehead.

"I'm not leaving you in here like this." He's crazy if he thinks I'm going to leave him with his head over the toilet.

"Can you just give me some fucking space?" he growls, gripping his hair between his fingers. I hate seeing him like this. He usually seems so strong, but right now he seems so weak.

"I'll wait right outside the stall, but I'm not going anywhere," I warn, standing back up on my feet. He glares up at me one more time before resting his elbows on the toilet seat. I close the stall door behind me to give him some privacy. It's quiet for a few minutes as I wait in the center of the bathroom, careful not to touch anything. When I finally hear the toilet flush, relief washes over me. I'm ready to get out of this bathroom and this bar.

The bathroom door suddenly swings open, making me jump back. One of the guys who was outside enters, causing the hair on my arms to stand up. I hold my breath, hoping he'll just walk by and leave me alone.

"Hey, why didn't you just tell me you were going to meet me in here?" he smiles.

The way he's looking at me makes me sick. It reminds me so much of the way Drew stared at me that night, with hunger in his eyes. My ears start ringing, and it feels like the oxygen is slowly being drained from the air.

He stares down at me with a disgusting grin on his face as his feet move a couple steps forward. I can't hear anything but the raging voices in my head that are telling me to get out of here. The only problem is that my feet are firmly planted in the ground, weighed down too much to take a single step toward the door. I feel a firm hand on my elbow, causing me to jump for the second time. When I glance over my shoulder, I see Asher standing there, looking pale, clammy and concerned, but I've never been more relieved to see anyone in my life.

"Stay the fuck away from her!" Asher shouts, pushing against the guy's chest.

The guy raises his hands in the air and steps back, giving Asher and I some much-needed space. His eyes remain on Asher whose chest is moving up and down. If I didn't know Asher, I'd be scared of him too.

"Let's get out of here," Asher says, placing his hand on the small of my back. I'm not watching where I'm going. I just keep walking in the direction Asher leads me until I feel the crisp fall air against my face. I take several deep breaths until the clamp that's wound tight around my lungs begins to loosen, allowing me to breathe normally again. I'm supposed to be here for Asher, but look at me . . . I'm a mess.

I look up to see him staring down at me with his eyebrows drawn together. "Are you okay?" he asks, softly running the back of his index finger against my cheek.

"No," I admit for the first time out loud. I'm not okay. I haven't been in a long time.

He brings his other hand to my other cheek, holding my head in his hands. "Do you want to talk about it?" he asks, looking down into my eyes through the darkness.

"Not right now," I say, squeezing my eyes shut. He doesn't push anymore as he pulls me close to his body, holding me tight.

Chapter 12

IT WAS FOUR DAYS BEFORE I saw Asher Hunt again.

I tried calling him once after I hadn't heard from him or seen him at the diner, but the call went straight to voicemail. I want to see him so badly, but maybe it's time that I let him come to me. Maybe he just needs a little time to sort through whatever is bugging him. So for four long, grueling days all I do is work, run and even got a little more reading done. I'm starting to realize more and more that if I can keep my mind busy with something, the less I think about all the horribly tainted memories that have taken permanent residence in my head.

When I open my front door to head out for my afternoon run, I'm surprised to see Asher's car parked on the street right in front of my house. He's sitting on the hood of his car in his blue jeans and a long-sleeve black t-shirt hugging his chest. It's hard to know how much you really want someone around until they're missing.

"Hey," he says, standing up with his hands in his pockets.

"Hey." I walk slowly toward him, nervous about what he might have to say.

"What have you been up to?" he asks, letting one side of his mouth turn up. One look at those lips has my pulse rising.

"Just work mostly," I shrug, stopping right in front of him.

He reaches out to me, which catches me off guard. It would be easy to hold a grudge and block him out of my life, but as I stand here looking at him, I know that I can't.

I step into his waiting arms, and he pulls me against his toned body, resting his forehead against mine. "I missed you," he whispers. His warm breath against my skin is enough to drive me crazy. I hate that he can affect me so easily.

"Where have you been?" I ask, using the tip of my tongue to moisten my lower lip.

He shakes his head, his forehead still pressed to mine. "I was trying to keep a little distance."

"Why?" Even on the first day I met him, I was drawn to him. I sensed this connection between us, making it hard to stay away even though I knew I should.

"Because, I'm only going to end up hurting you. Look what happened the other night at Pete's," he says.

"But you didn't hurt me," I respond, pulling back to put some space between us.

"You could have been hurt because of me. It didn't happen this time but what about next time? I would never be able to live with myself if something happened to you because of me," he says, pulling my face back toward him and running his thumb over my lower lip.

"So what are you doing here now then?" I ask.

"I warned you that if you let me kiss you, things would change between us. I can't stop thinking about you."

He kisses along my jawline, inching his way closer and closer to my lips. I can't even remember if I'm supposed to be mad at him right now. Or what I would possibly be upset about. It really doesn't matter. I wanted him to kiss me then, and I want him to kiss me now.

I'm getting more and more attached to him. If he leaves, or decides not to come around again for days, I don't know what I'll do. I need someone around who I can count on and who I can trust. I'm not going to be a convenience for anyone. I never want to feel used again in this lifetime.

He's either with me, or he's not.

There is no in-between.

I push against his chest to break the contact between his lips and my skin. "You can't just disappear for days like that."

"I know," he says, swallowing hard.

The longer I look at him, the more I feel myself caving to what I feel in my heart. The voice inside my head is telling me to protect myself from what could happen if I fall for him and it all falls apart. But the voice inside my heart is yelling at me to never let him go.

"I want to make an exception for you, but I don't know if I can. I won't be able to take it if this ends badly," I say, letting my eyes pierce into his.

He looks up to the sky before focusing back down on me. "I want to be here for you."

"Promise?"

"I can't make promises, Kate. I want to get to know you, and I want to be there for you, but I don't think being your friend is going to work for me anymore. I want to kiss you whenever I want. I want to hold you. I want you to tell me all of your secrets and eventually tell you all of mine. I want you in my life," he says, placing his index finger under my chin.

He stares at my lips for several seconds before drawing his eyes back to mine. "Can I kiss you? I've been thinking about it since the first time we kissed, and honestly, I don't know what I'll do if you say no."

I open my mouth, trying to push for the words I want to say, but I can't. I don't know what to say to that. But right now he's looking at me like I'm the best thing that's ever happened to him.

I think it can only get better from here.

When it Rains

Taking a deep breath, I nod against the finger that still rests under my chin. He looks at me with such intense fervor; almost like I'm the only woman on the planet. As his face moves toward mine, I close my eyes, ready to relish in everything he can give me. He surprises me by softly kissing my eyelids, then moving his lips down to my cheek. His tongue licks the edges of my lips, lingering for a while, playing and nibbling. As his hands move down my back, his tongue presses against the seam of my lips, begging to connect with mine.

I slowly open my eyes and see his looking right at me. It's completely different to kiss with my eyes open than it is to kiss in darkness. When I look at him, I feel like I can see right through him. I'm not thinking about myself for once; I'm only wondering what's going through his mind.

I close my eyes again and let myself feel the warmth he brings to my body as he tangles his tongue with mine. It's the longest kiss I've ever shared with anyone, and I may never be ready for it to end.

He cradles my face in his hands and slows before pulling his lips away from mine. I stare up at him curiously.

"What are you doing right now?" he asks, rubbing his thumbs across my cheekbones.

"I was going to go for a run."

He tilts his head to the side. "I think that can wait until later. Besides, you're too thin as it is."

"I thought guys liked that," I say, crossing my arms over my chest. I know I could stand to gain a few pounds, but no one else is complaining.

"Well, not this guy."

I open my mouth to say something, but he leans in to kiss me instead. "Hang out with me," he whispers against my lips.

"Do you want to come inside and watch a movie?" I ask, pulling back just enough to look him in the eye.

He smiles. "There's nothing I'd rather do."

"What are we doing standing out here then? Let's go inside, and pick out a movie." I walk past him toward the house, glancing back to make sure he's following behind.

As soon as we enter the house, I motion him toward the couch and walk to my bedroom to change my clothes. "Make yourself at home. I'll be right back."

I throw on a pair of dark blue skinny jeans and a grey thermal, taking a couple extra minutes to comb my fingers through my hair and put on a little mascara. I'm not one of those girls who spend hours on her appearance, but Asher doesn't seem to mind.

I leave my room and see him sitting on the couch staring at the blank television screen. When I'm close enough to touch, he reaches for my hand and pulls me down next to him. Once I'm cuddled next to him, he grabs my hand in his and brings it to his lips. "I talked to my sister yesterday."

I look up, noticing how tense he seems. "How did it go?"

"She cried. It made me feel like complete shit," he tells me.

"I don't understand why you can't just go visit her. It would be better for both of you."

He looks down at me for a split second before focusing his attention back to the screen. "I wish it was that easy."

"Why does it have to be so hard?" I ask. He always sounds so sad when he talks about her, and I can't help but wonder what might be going on in his family.

"Maybe I will soon," he says, ignoring my question.

"If you want me to come with you, I can," I offer, pushing some of the stray hair off his forehead.

He reaches for my hand, entwining our fingers together. "It's something I probably need to do by myself."

"Asher, you know if you ever want or need to talk about anything, I'm here," I whisper, focusing on the sadness evident in his crystal blue eyes.

"I know," he says, running the back of his finger across my cheek. "But there are some things you just can't change no matter how much you talk about them."

I swear this guy has read all of my theories on life. That or we're two people with similar souls who just happened to be in the same place at the same time.

"I know exactly what you mean." His face lifts like I've taken a huge weight off of him. He was probably expecting me to push him more, but I can't do that to him when I know it doesn't help me.

"Do you want something to drink?"

"I'll take a glass of water."

"Are you sure you don't want a beer?" I ask, trying to hold back a smile.

He raises his eyebrows, shaking his head. "No, I think I've had enough alcohol for a while."

"I've never been drunk," I shrug.

"Seriously?" he asks, raising his eyebrows even further.

"Yeah, when you're drunk, you don't have control over what you do, or what others may try to do. I like to have control."

"I get what you're saying, but no one ever has complete control over those things, even when they're sober," he says. There's a hint of sadness in his voice as his eyes focus on the blank TV screen. It's the second time tonight that he's said something that makes me think about how I've been living my life for the last two years. The past is always so much clearer than the future.

"Why don't you pick out a movie from the cabinet, and I'll grab the drinks."

I rest my palms on the counter and take a few calming breaths before opening the fridge. My heart is falling so fast that I don't think the rest of me has had time to catch up yet.

When I walk back into the living room, Asher is kneeling in front of the DVD player pressing his thumb to the eject button. "What did you pick?" I ask, setting the glasses on the coffee table.

"I can't get this stupid thing to open. We either have to watch what's in here, or do something else," he says, turning to face me.

"What's in there now?" I ask.

"Steel Magnolias," he replies, crinkling his nose. My mom loves that movie; I swear she watches it at least once a week.

"You've got to be kidding me," I say, biting my thumbnail. I was really looking forward to watching something funny.

I consider the options. I have a small TV and DVD player in my room that I bought when I first got my job, but I don't know if I'm ready to be in my room alone with Asher.

I look down at Asher who's waiting for me to make a decision. I open my mouth to ask him if he wants to watch it in my room, but I can't bring myself to do it. Just thinking about it puts a heavy weight on my chest. He's going to know something's wrong with me. He's going to end up leaving because I can't even enjoy some of the simple things in life.

Strong arms surround me, pulling me close to his familiar scent. "Hey, what's wrong?" he asks, rubbing small circles on my back.

I bury my face in his t-shirt, gripping the bottom of it in my fists. "Everything," I say honestly.

"Do you want to talk about it?"

I shake my head against his chest. The pressure of his arms eases the overwhelming pressure in my chest.

"You don't have to stay with me," I mutter, after a few moments of silence.

"Hey, look at me," he says, using my elbows to pull me away from him. I fix my eyes on the ground, staring at the tips of my black flats. His finger rests under my chin pulling my eyes up to his. "Keep those bright green eyes on me and listen to what I'm about to say," he demands, taking a step in my direction. If I'm breathing right now, I can't tell, but he certainly has my full attention.

"I'm not going to be the guy who's going to leave when things get tough. You've been through some shit, I can see it all over your face, but I want to try to make it better, Kate. You deserve to be happy."

I definitely feel my heart beating now; so fast I can feel it in my neck. He didn't blink once during his mini speech, and I'm pretty sure I didn't either. He's like a tow truck pulling me out of my wreckage.

"I don't think you can make everything better," I admit, honestly.

He cups my face in his hands and moves so that his face is only a few inches from mine. "I'm going to try." His lips brush across mine so quickly that I think I've only imagined it.

"I'm actually pretty tired. Do you mind if we call it a day and try the movie thing some other time?"

He nods, removing his hands from my face. "I'm picking you up at three o'clock tomorrow. We're going fishing."

"Okay," I whisper. I remember the last time we went and how he almost kissed me. Things have certainly changed since then.

"Are you sure you're okay here alone?" His eyes are searching mine for something hidden in their depths.

"I'll be fine." I've been pretending to be for a long time; that's probably not going to change now.

He nods and then leans in to kiss my cheek. His hands travel down my arm as he walks away, until only our fingertips touch. He looks back one more time before breaking the connection.

I miss him the second the door closes.

Chapter 13

"HEY, HONEY, WHERE ARE YOU off to today?" my mom asks, pulling a coffee cup from the cupboard. She gets one night off a week from Pete's, and today is her lucky day.

"Asher's coming to get me soon. We're going fishing," I reply, pulling my hair up into a loose knot at the top of my head.

"Are you being careful?"

"You don't have anything to worry about when I'm with him. He's a nice guy," I say, crossing my arms over my chest.

Her eyes snap to mine. "So is Beau."

Her words are like a slap in the face. Beau is one of the nicest people I've ever known, but it's easier for me to let Asher in. Asher tries to understand me layer by layer while Beau goes straight for the center. Plus, Asher seems to have his own secrets, which helps me not feel so guilty about mine.

"I can't explain it, but being with Asher makes me feel different."

She stares at the ceiling and shakes her head.

"And Beau's the guy who used to come stay with you every time you were sick. He's the guy who took you to prom when you didn't have a date. Don't turn your back on that because you never know when you'll need him again; when he might need you again, Kate. Friends like that are rare."

"Mom—" A knock at the door brings our attention to the door. "Look, I've got to go. We can talk about this again later." I grab my purse and head for the door before my mom has any time to sink her teeth into Asher. I would love for her to get to know him so she can see what I've seen, but it won't work if all she sees in my future is Beau.

"Are you in a hurry?" he asks, after I slam the front door.

I skip down the stairs, only looking back once to make sure my mom isn't following. "I'm just excited to go fishing again." I say, opening the passenger door.

"Are you okay?" he asks, drawing one of his eyebrows up.

"I haven't felt this good in a long time." I turn and smile at him as he turns the ignition. He shakes his head at me and links his hand with mine.

The drive to the lake is short and quiet. I'm trying to center my emotions, and Asher's probably trying to figure out what exactly is going on inside my head. I don't even know if I could answer myself. My mom made me feel like crap for letting someone other than Beau into my life. I love Beau, but Asher's who I need right now.

"Are you going to get out of the car?" Asher asks, interrupting my thoughts.

I look at him. "How long have we been sitting here?"

"Long enough for me to see how cute you are when you're daydreaming." He smiles.

I turn my face so that he won't see the slight blush in my cheeks. Asher Hunt is always keeping me on my toes. "Let's go fish before you start reading my mind." I listen to him laugh as I exit the car and walk toward the lake.

As we approach the lake, he points to an old boat on the side of the dock. "We're taking that today."

"We're actually fishing on a boat this time?" I ask, staring at the beat up fishing boat with nothing but two seats inside.

"Fuck yeah, my dad said we could use it as long as we brought it back in one piece," he replies, placing the fishing poles and tackle box in the boat.

Looking at the boat again, I can't help but laugh. I don't think the boat is even in one piece as it sits tied to the dock. Asher climbs in first, holding his hand out for me to climb in. The way the boat wiggles back and forth when I put my first foot in makes me hesitate, but Asher grabs my hips and lifts me until I'm standing next to him.

"I won't let anything happen to you." He kisses me before turning to untie the knots that hold the boat in place.

I carefully sit down on one of the two seats and watch his muscles flex under his tight grey t-shirt. It's a nice distraction from the pile of lumber we're about to take out into the middle of the water. It's been cloudy and windy all day with temperatures hovering in the sixties. My grandpa used to call this perfect fishing weather, but I fail to see the perfection.

"Ready?" Asher asks, wiping his hands on his jeans.

"Ready as I'll ever be."

He grins at my reluctance and points. "There's a life jacket under each seat, but my job is to make sure you don't need one."

"Have you taken this thing out by yourself before?" I ask, biting nervously on my nail.

"Kate, trust me," he says, giving me a warning look.

"It's not you I have issues with . . . it's the boat."

He shakes his head and turns back to the rope that keeps the boat connected to the dock. Deep down, I know he wouldn't be taking me out on the lake if he couldn't return me to shore in the same condition.

He pushes away from the dock and takes his seat, grabbing the two oars that rest along the side of the boat. *This thing doesn't even have an engine!*

"Do you want me to help you get this thing going?" I ask, watching him as he starts to move his arms back and forth, moving us further and further into the water.

"I got it," he says with a smile, never taking his eyes off me. The way he looks at me makes warmth pool in my stomach. The more I'm around Asher, the more I realize he could really hurt me if things didn't end well between us.

"So, who's going to catch more fish today?"

"I didn't know it was a contest," I reply, tucking some loose strands of my dark hair behind my ears.

"Everything with me is a contest. It's the only way I can motivate myself to do anything," he says, letting his lips turn up on one side.

I sit forward, resting my elbows on my knees so that my body is a little closer to his. "Oh yeah? What other contests do we have going on that I don't know about?"

He stops moving his arms and pulls the oars into the boat. I glance around and notice we are already in the center of the lake; the boat feels so much smaller, and so much more vulnerable out here.

He sits forward and grabs my chin between his index finger and thumb. "We're also going to see who can steal the most kisses today," he growls, brushing his lips against mine, "I already have the lead. And I don't like to lose."

My heart is racing as he sits back in his seat and grabs the oars again. His cocky grin and the way he runs his tongue over his bottom lip before pulling it between his teeth are enough to spin my hormones out of control. He laughs and shakes his head. That boy . . . he knows exactly what he's doing.

"Let's catch some fish. I think this is a good spot," he says, throwing a metal anchor into the water. "My dad says this is the best location, so let's test that theory and see how right he is."

My fears about the boat have started to dwindle; it seems to be okay as long as we don't move too much. Asher doesn't even ask me if I want to put a worm on my own hook this time. He just does it and hands me my pole, loaded with the bobber and all. His hand brushes against mine when I grab for the handle, sending a tingle up my arm. It doesn't get past Asher because a dimple-bearing smile lights up his face as he reaches for his own pole.

"Do you want to make a bet?" he asks out of the blue.

"It depends on what kind of bet you want to make, Mr. Hunt," I smile. He has this way of making me think of nothing but him. I kind of rather like when he takes over that part of me.

"Well, Miss Alexander, I think the person who catches the most fish should get a little prize."

"And what's the prize?" I ask, watching the glimmer in his blue eyes.

"Winner's choice." He shrugs. The smile falls from my face as I think about what he probably wants from me if he wins. I'm not ready for anything more than what I've given him. I don't know if I ever will be.

"Hey, come back to me. What are you thinking about?" he asks, running his thumb across my cheek.

I lean into his touch and take a deep, cleansing breath. "I'm sorry. I just get lost in my thoughts sometimes."

"When I wagered that bet, I didn't mean whatever it is that you're thinking," he whispers, lowering his hand from my face.

"I didn't-"

"Not everyone is out to get you, Kate. I'm not the guy who needs to make bets in order to get something like that from a girl," he says, his eyes searing into mine like a blade.

I glance up at the grey skies to pull my eyes away from him. "You don't know my whole story. You wouldn't understand it even if I told you."

"Even if I don't understand, I can listen," he says, rubbing the back of his neck.

"Then tell me why you're really in Carrington because I don't believe all this simple life bullshit, Asher," I say, not even trying to control my growing temper anymore.

"You know what? Let's forget I mentioned listening, or any of the other shit, and just fish. The person who catches the least amount of fish gets to paddle this boat back to the dock." He doesn't wait for me to reply before turning back to look over the side of the boat. I don't know how he expects me to open up to him if he can't seem to do it himself.

I find my bobber floating above the water and focus my eyes on it. When I finally glance over at him, his shoulders are visibly tense. I'm starting to resent myself because I always turn his sweet gestures and teasing into something it's not.

"Well, it looks like we're both going to lose," I say, breaking the uncomfortable silence.

He turns his head in my direction. "The way this is going, I'd say you're probably right," he says. The serious expression on his face makes me feel as though we may not be referring to the fish anymore.

For a long time, I've made myself believe that it's okay to push all the people who care about me away. I did it to most of my high school friends, although now that I look back on it, I don't think they were ever true friends to begin with. And Beau . . . well, I've had him dangling off the edge of a cliff for over two years, and he's still holding on for dear life.

I still haven't quite figured out where Asher fits in. The only thing I know for sure is that I'm more free and happier when I'm with him than when I'm without him.

Something cold hits my nose like a dagger breaking me from my thoughts. Darker clouds have moved in and I notice pouring rain off in the distance. This is one situation I never envisioned myself being stuck in. I can't even stand being locked away in my room when it rains much less out in the middle of the lake trapped in a small boat that requires paddling to get us from one point to another.

Drops of water start to fall more frequently and it feels as if someone has sucked the air right out of me. My mind takes me back and I feel Drew's repulsive fingers all over my body again. I hear his voice yelling things at me that I'll never forget. I smell him . . . even through the scent of rain and lake water. I pinch my eyes closed, place my hands over my ears and bury my head between my knees, letting my tears mix with the water pooled on the floor of the boat. The rain is falling so hard on my back that I don't realize that a hand is gently moving up and down my spine.

Asher. I almost forgot he was here because all I could sense was Drew.

"You're shaking. Please just tell me what's wrong. Tell me what you need," he pleads, leaning so that his mouth in as close to my hand-covered ear as he can get. I hear his voice, but I'm not really able to process his words. The sound of the pouring rain hitting the lake and boat muffle anything that comes out of his mouth.

"Get me off this boat. Please, I need to go inside," I panic. Nothing is more important to me in that moment than getting out of the rain.

My life is like a top, spinning and spinning until it can't spin anymore and has no other choice but to fall. I have no one to catch me, but how can they when I won't let them?

Asher's hand is still on my back, which means this boat hasn't moved at all. "Asher, please, I need to get off this boat," I cry, "Please." My whole body trembles.

Adrenaline whips through my body and I struggle to grab an oar. There are so many things I should have done differently that night. God, he ruined everything.

"Kate!" I hear Asher yell.

I can't look up. I'm going to be sick soon, and it's all because of the asshole who took my life away.

"Hear me out, Kate. Look at me," he says loudly.

I continue to ignore him. I can't stop myself from shaking, from shutting him out as I feel the rain soaking my body.

"I killed my best friend last year!" I hear Asher yell. "It's all my fucking fault. If I hadn't been so stupid, she'd still be here."

I stop crying when I hear his confession ringing through my ears loud and clear like a tornado siren. I snap out of my daze to look at him. His chin lowers to his chest, and I watch him fight the emotion that wants to come to the surface. My heart twists when I look at him; I've never seen anyone so broken in my life.

"Asher," I say softly, slowly reaching my hand toward him and running his hair between my fingers.

His head snaps up and I react, pulling my fingers away. "She was drunk at a party, and I let her drive home. Who does that? Who lets someone who means so much to them drive home when they can barely walk?" he asks, fisting his hair in his hands.

My heart shatters in my chest as I watch the anguish wash over him. "Why did you let her drive home?"

He flinches, taking a few seconds to collect himself before his eyes shoot up to mine. "I was drunk and stupid. I let her climb into the seat of her little red car and drive away without even putting her seatbelt on. She didn't even make it ten blocks before she slammed head-on into a tree." His hands are still tugging all the hair they can grasp. I want to touch him, but I'm too afraid to move my hand.

"We heard the sirens and decided to go see what was going on." He swallows. Tears are pooling in his eyes, but he's constantly glancing toward the sky to hold them in. "Do you know how horrible it is to pull up to the scene of an accident and realize the person inside the mangled car is your best friend? Megan was the kindest, most caring person I've ever known, and now she's gone."

I've been so wrapped in his story that I forgot about the droplets that are still crashing into my body. I know what it's like to live with guilt and secrets. They weigh you down until you quit fighting them altogether.

I hesitantly rest my hand on his shoulder and give it a gentle squeeze. "If you were both drunk, how is it your fault? You have to forgive yourself."

His head snaps up. "We promised each other that one of us would always stay sober to make sure we both made it home okay. That night, I changed the rules. I had an argument with my mom and step-dad, and I needed to blow off some steam. She had already had a couple drinks when I took my first sip," he says, pinching his eyes shut. "I was so fucking selfish. I believed we were invincible, and I learned the hard way that we're not. Now I'm paying for it."

"Is that why you're in Carrington?" I ask.

He slowly shakes his head no. "That's a story for another day."

He stares at me as I open my mouth to something, but nothing comes out. There's a battle going on inside me. Is Asher the person who I can entrust my secret to? Once it's out, it's not mine to hold onto anymore. It might make me feel better if I have someone to talk to when the memories are pulling me under.

"Kate, please say something. Don't look at me like that. I know what I did was wrong, but I can't do anything about it now. It's too late!" Asher shouts. His worried eyes are burning through me.

My whole body trembles as I try to catch my breath. The sound of the rain is piercing through my ears again. I just want this all to be over.

"I was raped," I murmur, watching his eyes double in size.

"What?" he asks, seemingly shocked by my admission. I pinch my eyes closed, and work to find the words to explain who I am today. It's about time I told someone.

As soon as I open my mouth to speak, he grabs my face in his hands. "I am so sorry."

"What?" I ask, pulling back.

His grip around my face tightens as he pulls me close to him again. "I'm sorry that happened to you. No one should have to go through that." And that's all it takes before I'm sobbing in his arms. "It's okay. I've got you now."

"I should never have gone into his bedroom," I cry, gripping Asher's soaked t-shirt.

He grips my arms and pulls me back to look at him. "It's not your fault. Do you hear me? None of this is your fault."

He holds me tight against his chest as I tell him what happened that night. I tell him about the football game and the bonfire that followed. I explain how I felt when the popular quarterback sat down next to me and focused all his attention on me. I struggle through what happened when we went into Drew's house.

When I tell him about the rain mocking me while Drew held me down, his arms tense up. I thought telling my story would suffocate me, but I feel as if a huge weight has been lifted off my shoulders. He knows everything now and is free to do whatever he wants with it. My secret feels safe with him.

After I've laid my painful secret in his hands, he sits down next to me and pulls me onto his lap, carefully centering us in the seat to keep the boat steady. "Shouldn't we head back to shore?" I ask, wrapping my arms around his neck.

"I have one more thing I have to do first," he whispers, placing his hand at the back of my neck. His eyes focus on my lips as he slowly brings me closer. I watch as water drips from his damp hair and rolls down his face.

When his lips finally touch mine, I close my eyes, trying to focus only on what Asher's doing to me, but he pulls back before I can.

He sweeps my hair to the side and kisses my neck. "You're beautiful," he says in my ear, sending shivers down my spine. I tilt my head and let him place light kisses up and down my throat before he captures my lips.

"From now on . . ."

kiss.

"When it rains . . ."

kiss.

"Think of me."

I swear my heart just melted into a puddle on the ground. It's a moment I'll never forget . . . the moment Asher Hunt kissed my fears away. I've spent two years waiting for the sun, and all I've needed was him.

His warm lips continue to slide over mine as I run my fingers through the hair above his neck. His touch warms my body, even in the cold rain. I instantly miss him when he sits back and smiles at me.

"We should get out of here and dry off before you get sick," he says, brushing his thumb across my lips.

"Thank you," I smile.

"For what?"

"For giving me a reason to smile again," I reply, biting my lower lip.

"I always want you to have something to smile about, pretty girl," he says, tilting his head to the side. He glides his lips over mine one more time, then slides me off his lap.

I watch as he sits back in his seat and pulls the anchor up. He rows us back to shore as I let the sounds of the rain penetrate my ears.

As soon as we're next to the dock, he ties the boat up and jumps up on the platform, reaching his hand out for me. "Let's go find you some dry clothes."

He helps me out and pulls me towards the cabin. "What are you doing?" I squeal.

"Taking care of you."

And he does. Once we're inside, he hands me a pair of his grey sweatpants, some dry socks, and a hooded Chicago Bears sweatshirt. He even lets me take a shower first while he cooks something to eat. It's getting late, and I should go home soon, but I'm not ready for this day to end.

I spend a few minutes staring at myself in the mirror while the shower heats up. My long dark hair is a tangled mess, but my skin has a brilliant glow that I haven't seen in a long time. I smile at myself then peel the wet clothes from my body and step into the shower.

As the warm water washes over my pruned skin, I think about everything that happened today. I can still hear Asher's words in my head, and I feel the need to lock them away somewhere safe.

The fact that Asher trusted me with his secret gives me a sense of importance in his life. It feels like he needs me just as much as I need him.

Once I feel clean, I turn the water off and wrap a towel around my body and another around my hair. The skin on my fingers still feels dry and wrinkled against the towel, but being stuck out there in the rain was well worth it.

A knock at the door makes me jump. "Hey, are you almost done in there? I have tomato soup and grilled cheese."

"I'll be out in a minute," I yell back, quickly pulling my clothes on.

I open the door, and I'm immediately met by Asher. He kisses the tip of my nose before grabbing my hand and leading me to the kitchen. It smells amazing. There's nothing like soup and sandwiches on a cold day.

"Do you want to stay here tonight?" he asks as we sit down at the table.

My whole body tenses. "I don't think that's a good idea."

He tilts his head. "You can have my bed. I'll sleep on the couch," he says, grabbing my hand. "It's pouring rain outside, and I'd feel more comfortable if you were here with me tonight."

I nod, using my free hand to lift a spoonful of soup to my lips. I'm too tired from the emotional ride earlier to argue. Besides, I now feel as if nothing bad can touch me when I'm with Asher.

"Are you doing okay?" he asks, rubbing his thumb across the top of my hand.

"Yeah. Are you?"

"I don't know if it will ever be okay, but I feel better when I'm with you."

"I feel the same way," I admit. I help him clean up dinner and look at the clock; it's already past eight. "I'm going to go let my mom know where I am."

"When you're done, do you want to watch a movie?"

"I'm really tired, and just kind of want to go to bed."

He lowers his head. "Okay, I'll get the couch ready."

I find my purse on the chair next to the door and grab my phone to send my mom a text. She's still at work, and she probably wouldn't even realize I'm gone until morning, but I don't need her sending out a search party to find me.

Kate: I'm staying at Asher's tonight.

I press send and notice I have two missed phone calls from Beau and several texts. I tuck my phone back in my purse, not bothering to listen to his voicemails or read his texts. It can wait until tomorrow. I'm too exhausted to deal with anything else today.

Asher comes around the corner, pointing his thumb toward the bedroom. "It's all set. I left you two pillows. I hope that's enough."

"Thank you," I say, walking toward him. "I appreciate everything you've done for me today." I brush my lips against his cheek before starting toward the bedroom.

I don't get far before he grabs my hand, halting me in place. "I'd do anything for you," he says, running his thumb across the top of my hand.

He smiles and I smile back at him before heading to the empty bedroom and laying my tired body across the bed. I bury my head in the pillow; it smells like the soap in his shower. I love that Asher doesn't drench himself in cologne. He always smells fresh and earthy.

As I settle in, I hear the rain hitting the metal siding outside. Being in the dark room, lying in a bed that isn't mine brings some of the old, heavy feelings back. I realize it will take some time to let go of my fears, but now I know that I don't have to do it alone.

I tiptoe out of the bed just in case Asher is already sleeping. When I turn the corner, I see that he's not. He's staring up at the ceiling with his hands crossed over his chest.

"Asher?" I say softly.

His head snaps in my direction. "Yeah?"

"Will you come lay next to me? It's raining and . . ." My voice trails off. I hate that I sound like a scared little girl.

He quickly stands, stepping in my direction. "Didn't I just tell you that I'd do anything for you?"

He's close enough that our chests are practically touching, and my whole body goes on alert. His mouth is so close that I can feel his breath on my lips. My breathing picks up when his lips descend on mine. I wonder if there will ever be a time when he doesn't have this effect on me.

"Let's go to bed," he whispers, pulling his head back and grabbing my hand.

He doesn't skip a beat as he guides me into the room and closes the door behind him. He turns, gently placing his hands on my hips and drawing me close to him. I close my eyes when he finally touches his lips to mine. They feel like warm cotton candy against my skin. He takes his time licking, nibbling and biting until I can't feel them anymore.

"How was that for a goodnight kiss?" he asks, pulling his bottom lip between his teeth.

"I think you already know," I smile, crawling back into his bed. He doesn't make me wait long before he joins me.

I tuck myself under the nice warm comforter, but I keep my back turned to him. I'm scared of what might happen if I continue to look. I feel movement on his side of the bed followed by a large hand gripping my hip. "Kate, can I hold you? I want to know what it's like to fall asleep with you in my arms."

My gaze is fixed on the window, watching the rain roll down the panes. "I think I'd like that," I whisper. He places one arm beneath my head and the other around my waist. He hugs me close, fitting us together like one. I listen to the rain hitting hard against the window and concentrate on how it feels to be here in Asher's arms. He's my life size security blanket keeping me safe and content. This is exactly what I need to think about when I hear the rain.

"Why did you decide to tell me your secret?" I ask, entwining my fingers with his.

"Because I knew it was the only way I'd get you to tell me yours."

Chapter 14

WAKING UP FROM THE BEST full night's sleep I've had in a long time wrapped in two strong arms is nothing I'll ever complain about. I've been missing out on some of the best things in life. The critical moment that lasted mere minutes of my life bled into years . . . and Asher is the only one who has been able to make the bleeding stop.

Asher's presence is like the moment you open a present, and all that remains is the plain white box and you have no idea what surprises lie inside. I get that anxious, excited feeling in my chest every time I see him.

And if he thought his secret would change how I view him, he was wrong. As a matter of fact, I think I feel even more connected to him. We both have horrible pasts that we're trying to get over, and now we each have someone to do it with.

It always seems like the things I worry about the most never turn out as bad as I think they will. It's the things I don't see coming that throw me right on my ass. I realize the key to living is getting past the things I can't change and putting my energy into the things I can. It's something I wish I could've realized a long time ago.

"Are you awake?"

I break out of my thoughts, turning my head to see Asher's beautiful blues staring back at me. The sun shines brightly through the window making his eyes look even more brilliant than I remembered.

"I guess I am." I smile.

"I'm glad because while you're really cute when you sleep, you're even more breathtaking when you're awake," he says, running the tips of his fingers along my jawline.

"I was just thinking the same thing about you." His slightly too long blonde hair is going every which way, but it suits him, and I can't stop my fingers from combing through it.

"Are you flirting with me, Kate?"

"I don't know the first thing about flirting." My cheeks instantly heat up as I pull my lower lip between my teeth.

"You're cute when you blush," he remarks, adjusting his pillow so that his head is closer to mine. "And everyone can flirt . . . they just have to find someone who inspires them to do it."

"Are you complimenting yourself now?" I ask, trying to hold back a laugh.

He smiles, kissing the corner of my mouth. "Take it however you'd like."

"You're a smooth talker, Asher Hunt." Asher says things that most guys I know wouldn't even think about saying to me.

For several minutes, we lie there as Asher runs the pad of his fingertips across my cheeks, lips and down the sensitive skin under my ears, as if he's memorizing each part. He slowly slides his hand to the back of my neck and pulls me in. When his lips press against mine, I close my eyes and enjoy the tingle he sends throughout my body. His fingers dance up my back and down my bare arm before settling on my hip. Surprisingly, I don't think about what happened before. For the first time since my innocence was stolen away from me, I feel comfortable letting someone else touch me. The way his hand brushes against my skin isn't forceful, or rough . . . it's soothing. It just feels so right, like the way a man should touch a woman.

When he breaks contact, I want to protest. I never thought I'd be able to do this much without running for the nearest exit, but here I am.

And I want more.

My eyes lock on the tattoo on the inside of his arm and I can't stop my fingers from running over it.

"That's the date Megan died. I put it there as a reminder," he says, looking down at my fingers.

"You'll never forget. She's right here," I whisper, resting my hand on his chest.

"Thank you for trusting me with your secret. I'm sorry that happened to you. If I could go back and change it, I would," he says, running his fingers along my collarbone.

"But the thing about the past is that it can't be rewritten. Somehow, I have to learn to deal with it and you have to forgive yourself for what happened to Megan."

"Sometimes it feels like I'm being punished for what happened that night," Asher says softly, just a few inches from my lips.

"What do you mean?" I ask, pulling my head back to look into his eyes.

"I don't know. I guess everything bad that happens afterward seems like God's way of paying me back." He pauses, moving his fingers up to caress my cheek. "But since I've met you, I feel like I've been given a second chance. It's been a long time since I've felt like I was living with something other than regret, and I owe that to you."

"And I owe my happiness to you," I whisper, pressing my lips to his. "You've already opened my eyes to so many things that I wouldn't let myself see before."

"I don't know what I did to deserve moments like these," he says, brushing a few strands of hair from my forehead. I understand his pain because I would be a mess if something ever happened to Beau, but he has to let go of the guilt that he's holding. He can't change what happened . . . no one can. I also realize I'm being a hypocrite because I've spent the last two years holding on to a past I can't change.

"You deserve a lifetime of moments like these," I say, kissing him again. He reaches behind my head to deepen the kiss, paying attention to my lips first, and then pressing his tongue into my mouth. My heart flutters when he slides his hand under my shirt to massage my lower back. I moan as he slows the kiss and pulls my lower lip between his teeth.

When I look into his eyes again, I see lust mixed with concern. "If I ever push you too far and you want to stop, all you have to do is tell me. I'm not the type of guy who takes things from a girl that she doesn't want to give. I'm not him," he says, nuzzling my nose with his. "I need you to remember you always have control. Always."

I lift my head and softly kiss his cheek. "I'd like to continue what we were doing."

"I can manage that," he says, propping his head in his hand. I'm bursting with anticipation as I wait to feel more of his delicious kisses.

Asher doesn't disappoint. He wraps his hand around the back of my head again, tangling his fingers in my hair. I wait anxiously for the explosion that always goes off inside my body when his warm skin first touches mine. He has a way of pulling me out of the deep, dark black hole I thought I'd be lost in forever. With each day spent with him, I get a little closer to the surface and I can finally see the sun poking through.

If I had known life could be like this for me, even after everything that happened, I would have worked a little harder for it. But maybe he's the only one who could bring this transparency back to my life. It's something I wouldn't have found on my own.

"Where do you want me to kiss you first?" he growls, making my heart beat at lightning pace. He's giving me control. For the first time, I'm comfortable enough to take that control.

"My neck, below my ear," I pant, closing my eyes while I wait for him to shower my body with kisses. I've never wanted something more in my entire life.

My breath hitches when his tongue brushes against the delicate skin. When his lips finally press against the same spot, they linger, letting me take in the moment and store it away in my memory.

"Where do you want me now?" he whispers above my ear, sending an electric current from my forehead to my toes.

"My lips. I need to feel your lips."

He teases me, nuzzling his nose against mine before giving me what I really want. When it finally happens, it's like I'm floating on a lone cloud on the clearest of summer days. And when his tongue starts dancing in circles with mine, I feel a ping in my heart and wrap my arms around his neck to bring our bodies closer.

My dream quickly turns to a nightmare, though, when he leans his body over mine, trapping me between him and the mattress. Out of nowhere, all I feel is Drew, and my whole body stiffens.

I don't feel Asher's lips. Instead, I feel that pain that was caused when Drew forced his lips on mine. Suddenly, it's not Asher's body leaning on top of mine, but Drew's weight holding me down. When I feel his hardness press up against my thigh, the moment right before Drew pushed into me that night plays in my mind. I can feel the physical and emotional pain as if it's happening to me right now.

Fear.

"Kate," Asher says shaking my upper arms. I was so consumed by my inner demons that I didn't realize he had stopped kissing me.

"Just get off me," I cry, pressing against his chest. "Now." All my control is gone again, and helplessness is the terrorist messing with all of my happiness.

There's a look of pure horror on Asher's face as he quickly moves to my side. I feel as if I've become some sort of monster. I know I'm not, but there sure as hell is one living inside of me, constantly reminding me why I can't enjoy simple things like having a passionate moment with the incredible guy lying next to me.

Asher carefully pulls away the hair from my tear stained cheeks and lightly runs the back of his finger along the side of my face. "Please tell me what I did wrong," he begs, staring at me with burning intensity, "because I never want to see that look on your face again."

My chest feels like it's being compressed in a clamp, and all I can do to ease the pressure is take a few deep, cleansing breaths. I should be enjoying this. I'm with a guy who is patient and caring, but all I see is the jerk who did this to me. Some things don't work out the way they're supposed to, I get that, but this . . .

This is beyond any punishment that anyone could ever deserve.

"I don't like having anyone on top of me. It brings back too many things I'd like to forget. But it has absolutely nothing to do with you," I tell him, crying. I place my palm against his cheek.

"Are you sure?" he asks, shutting his eyes tight. "Cause that sure didn't sound like nothing." I can feel that my history is going to have a negative effect on him. It's the reason I should have never started this in the first place. Somehow, I'll end up pushing him away and ruin whatever this is between us.

But I'm in too deep to give up to give up on him now.

"You've been nothing but good to me; more than good actually. But if we're going to do this, you have to understand that you're not just getting me. You're also getting my past. I wish that I could bleach out all the bad, but this is who I am."

He runs his fingers through the hair that frames my face. "I want to make things better for you, not worse. I don't want to be a bad memory. I like who you are. I love every fucking thing I see when I look at you."

If my heart could melt, it would be in a puddle at my feet right now. This guy is definitely a Carrington import . . . they just don't breed them like this around here. Well, unless you count Beau. I used to think he was the one who made the world turn on its axis. Maybe I'd still feel that way if things hadn't changed so drastically.

"I like you too," I say, trying to even out my breathing.

"Then we don't have anything to worry about." He brushes some more loose strands of hair away from my eyes.

"Where did I find you?" I ask, giving the hint of a smile.

"Well, I think I technically found you." He smiles.

"You did walk into my territory," I say, grinning from ear to ear.

"There's that smile I want to see more of." He presses a kiss to my forehead, then the tip of my nose, and ends on my lips.

I have to remind myself that I only had a momentary setback, but I'm not going to let it ruin me. I'm not going to let it ruin us. Learning to let go is hard, but Asher's proving to be a great teacher.

"I should probably go home. Mom and I always watch movies on Sunday."

"Do you have to go? I sure wouldn't mind watching movies with you all day," he says lightly kissing my lips.

"I'll take you up on that someday, but today is not that day." I smile.

"Have it your way then. If you change your mind later, you have my number." He winks, unraveling his arms and sitting up in the bed. I instantly miss his warmth.

"I'll grab your clothes from the dryer," he says, standing and stretching his arms above his head.

I certainly wouldn't mind wearing his sweatpants and t-shirt home; they have his woodsy scent all over them and it settles everything inside of me. It amazes me how much I notice about him that I don't notice about anyone else . . . he's a colorful abstract painting that I can't peel my eyes away from.

His room, however, is anything but a work of art. His walls are a sterile white without a single thing hanging on them. There's a small oak desk against the wall opposite the bed, but the only thing that's on it is a notebook. There's a window to the left of the bed with an old ivory curtain covering it, and an old worn dresser on the right side of the bed. While the room is obviously lived in, there isn't anything that gives me a glimpse into Asher's life.

"All clean," Asher says, walking back into the room. He's changed from his sweats into jeans and a navy blue t-shirt, which highlights every muscle on his arms and chest perfectly.

"Thank you."

"No problem. I'll wait for you in the living room so you can get dressed." He kisses the top of my head before exiting the room. I quickly change into my clean clothes and comb my fingers through my hair as the morning's events run through my mind. Now that Asher and I understand each other, it's easier to be honest with him when something happens that triggers a memory.

I'd thought I was just going fishing; in no way did I ever think I would tell Asher about my secret. After he'd told me his, I couldn't hold back anymore. In fact, it just sort of came out as if it was meant to happen that way. And he didn't judge me. He didn't tell me everything I'd done wrong. He'd simply tried to wash away some of my fear by giving me memories that I would remember for the rest of my life. He's erasing some of the hurt and fear from my heart.

I may not be into superheroes, but if I were, Asher would be it for me.

After I'm dressed, I quickly go in the bathroom to fix my ponytail and brush my teeth using my finger and some toothpaste I found in the drawer. When I'm done, I take a few extra minutes to look at myself in the mirror. There's a hint of a change on my face and it looks, and feels, good.

I wish I could feel this way every minute of every day for the rest of my life. But if what happened with Asher is any indication, there will come a day when it rains and everything comes back to haunt me again. When it does, I know that Asher and his warm, soft lips will be strong enough to push it out of my memory.

As soon as I leave the bathroom, I spot Asher sleeping on the couch. He looks so peaceful with his arms crossed over his chest and head resting against the back of the couch. I hate to disturb him, but my mom will have a search party out for me if I miss movie day.

"Asher," I say softly, gently shaking his shoulder.

He doesn't even blink.

"Asher," I repeat, shaking him a little harder this time.

He opens his eyes, taking a few seconds to adjust to the light. "I must have been exhausted. Are you ready to go?" he asks, stretching his arms along the top of the couch.

"You look tired. I can call my mom to come get me if you want to sleep," I offer, rubbing my fingers together. My mom wouldn't be too happy about having to leave the house on a Sunday, but it's only a five minute drive. She can manage.

"I'm sorry. I'm just out of it, I guess," he says, standing in front of me. "But no one is taking you home except me." He brings his lips to mine, sucking on my lower one just long enough to drive my whole body completely insane. He pulls back with a wicked grin on his face. "Plus, if I drive you home, it gives me an excuse to do that one more time."

"Just one more time?"

He closes the distance between us again, placing his large hands over my cheeks. "I'll kiss you as often as you want. All you have to do is ask."

"Kiss me," I whisper, watching his lips shorten the distance to mine.

"Are you asking or are you telling?" he asks. His mouth is so close that his warm breath caresses my lips as our chests touch.

"I'm telling you," I say, swallowing hard.

He moves even closer. I swear I almost feel his lips on mine . . . a mere whisper away. "And what if I don't kiss you right now?" he asks, staring into my eyes so fiercely that I see my eyes reflected in his.

"Then I'll just have to kiss you," I reply, standing on my tip toes to pull his lower lip between mine, much like he had done to me. I'm not sure if it's better to be on the giving or receiving end of this, but either way it feels really good.

"All better now," I smile.

"You're trouble, you know that?" he teases, grasping my hand in his.

"That's one thing I've never been accused of," I say, following behind as he starts toward the door. The crisp fall air pricks my cheeks as soon as we step outside. The sky is clear, and leaves are beginning to settle in the grass in vibrant shades of red, orange and yellow. As I breathe in the change in season, I wish every day was just like this one.

"And what time does movie day usually end?" Asher asks as soon as we're both safe inside the car.

"Whenever we run out of movies to watch," I shrug. I don't think there are many we haven't seen yet.

"There's something I'd really like to do with you tonight." There are all sorts of conclusions I can draw from his comment, but I keep in mind that he only seems to have my best interest in mind. He hasn't shown me anything different since the day I met him.

"And what's that?" I ask, staring at him intently. I get a fluttery feeling in my stomach looking at the half smile that appears on his face.

He rests his arm along the back of the seat and looks back to pull out of the driveway, peering at me through the corner of his eyes. "You're just going to have to come over later to find out."

"I'm not big on surprises," I say, crossing my arms over my chest.

"We're just going to have to change that." He briefly looks toward me again, placing his hand on my knee, before focusing his attention back on the road. He's right. Surprises don't usually bring out good reactions in me, but the guy sitting next to me is full of ones that do.

"You can try." I smile, glancing out the passenger side window. As we pull into town, we pass house after house. Most of the homes are probably about as old as the town, but people have always taken pride in their houses and lawns here. It gives the illusion of one of those perfect Brady Bunch reruns, but what those shows fail to illustrate is the truth of what goes on behind closed doors. It's not full of people who have dinner together every night at six; it's full of people living real lives with real problems. Drew grew up in one of the nicest houses in and around this town, but the beauty of the house doesn't reflect the kind of guy that he is inside.

Some of us are just lucky enough to know the truth.

I'm so lost in thought that I don't realize we've already arrived at my house until the car comes to a stop. It's the small white house with chipped paint and weeds growing in the flowerbeds. Its appearance screams that we don't care, or that we don't have the money to care. I think it's a combination of both, but it certainly doesn't reflect the people we are.

I feel a big, slightly calloused hand wrap around mine. "Hey, what are you thinking about over there?"

"I was thinking about the houses and the people who live inside them." I tell Asher my thoughts as his jaw works back and forth.

When I look over at him, but he quickly recovers, kissing each knuckle on the hand that rests in his. "You can't keep dwelling on the things you can't change," he says, smiling sadly.

"I know that you're right, but it's easier to say than it is to actually do."

"You should talk to someone about what happened to you. Like a counselor or something. You can't keep carrying that kind of secret on your back. It's eating you up inside," he says, squeezing my hand.

He's right, and I know it, but that doesn't mean I'm ready to take that step. "I'll think about it."

"If you ever need to talk again, I'm here for you," he says, bringing my fingers to his lips.

"Thank you . . . for everything."

We sit silently, staring into each other's eyes. I'm realizing that there's so much you can tell about a person from their eyes. I like what I see in Asher's, but I want to strip the pain away.

"So I'll see you tonight then?" he asks, scooting closer to me.

"I guess I can arrange that." I bite my lower lip, waiting for him to make his move. His eyes are zoned in on my lips as he moves even closer. He presses a firm yet lingering kiss on them and I can't resist pulling his hair between my fingers.

He breaks the kiss, resting the top of his forehead against mine. "Do you even realize how special you are?"

"I do when I'm with you," I whisper.

He runs his fingers up and down my arm, sending shivers down my back. "I want you to feel that way all the time, with or without me." I don't like his somber tone, and I hate the mention of ever having to be without him.

"I like being around you too," I say, swallowing hard. Asher opens his mouth to say something, but is interrupted by a knock on the passenger side window.

When I look up, all I see are two pained blue eyes searing holes into my chest.

Chapter 15

I FEEL LIKE I'M ON A MERRY-GO-ROUND that keeps spinning and spinning and won't slow down. I'm sitting next to the man I think I'm falling for, while the man who has always been there for me, stares at me with fiery rage. It's not a comfortable spot to be in.

"Who's that?" Asher asks, leaning in close to get a better look at Beau.

"Um . . . that's my friend, Beau," I answer, trying to control my breathing.

"And why does your friend look like he wants to kill someone right now?"

I'm not stupid; I know exactly why Beau has a murderous look on his face. I told him I wasn't ready for any of the things I'm now doing with Asher, and he just became a witness to the contrary. How do I even explain this? How do I tell him that Asher's different without everything coming out wrong?

It's like I'm in the middle of the road between two lanes of oncoming traffic . . . waiting for someone to come to me. This time, unfortunately, I need to save myself while figuring out how I'm going to do it without hurting either of these men in the process. I wouldn't be able to live with myself if I did—they're the only friends I have left.

"I need to go talk to him," I say, reaching for the door handle. Deep down, I think Asher will be okay, but I have to make Beau understand that this has nothing to do with him.

Asher doesn't let me get too far away before pulling me back toward him. "I want to go with you." His eyes peer into me with almost as much intensity as Beau's. What have I gotten myself into?

"I don't think that's such a good idea." In fact, I think it would be the equivalent of shooting Beau in the heart when he's already on the ground. I did this and I need to be the one to take care of it.

"Please. Just let me meet him and then I'll leave," he pleads, moving his eyes up to Beau again.

I've been with Asher in some way or another for the last few weeks. I've given him some of my trust, and every day he earns a little more of it. I can trust him with this . . . I hope.

"Fine, but please don't cause any trouble. Beau's the only person I have besides you and my mom. I can't afford to lose anyone right now."

"I wouldn't want you to," he whispers, tucking a piece of hair behind my ear.

"Just promise me you won't start anything, even if he tries," I beg, glancing back and forth between his eyes.

"I promise."

"Let's go then," I say, reaching for the door handle again. Beau takes a couple of steps back, giving me enough space to get out.

Everything moves in slow motion as I step onto the curb, watching Beau's nostrils flare when he notices Asher walking around the car. Maybe this wasn't a good idea. I want to merge the old and the new, but this might not be the best time to do it. Maybe I should have explained everything to him first to give him a chance to process everything.

"Who the hell are you?" Beau asks, glaring directly at Asher. His attention then turns back to me, his eyes shooting nails into my heart. "Who the fuck is he, Kate, and what is he doing here?"

"Beau, this is Asher," I hesitantly nod toward Asher who stands to my left.

Beau completely ignores him. "And where the hell have you been? I've been calling and texting you for the last twenty-four hours." He's gritting his teeth trying to control his temper, but it's not working very well.

"She was with me," Asher says, placing a protective hand on my lower back.

Beau doesn't make a move or even give him a second glance. His eyes burn into me as he stands with his hands on his hips. "You told me Asher was your friend, Kate," he says, his Adam's apple pulsing in his throat.

I stand, fidgeting with my fingers as I think of the right thing to say. "Asher was my friend, but things changed and I can't—"

"Can we maybe talk about this without him standing right there? I have some things I need to say to you," Beau says, taking one step closer.

I don't know how to handle this. Life has proven to be so much better when I let people in, but it was so much less complicated when it was just me.

Asher startles me by grabbing my hand and leading me around to the driver's door. I have no idea what he's doing and I'm too lost in the crossfire to ask. He leans back against the car door and cradles my face in his hands. "I'm not leaving you here alone with this guy."

"I need to talk to him for a few minutes. It's just going to make things worse if you stay here," I answer, honestly. When I glance back at Beau, the pained look on his face when our eyes meet guts me. When he breaks the contact, the stabbing pain in my heart feels like it's almost enough to kill me. I turn back to Asher, intent on making things right with both of them.

"Kate—" he starts in an uncertain tone.

"It'll be okay," I say, cutting him short. I place my hands on top of his, feeling his cold hands pressed against my cheek and my fingers.

He nods, looking over his shoulder to get a glimpse of Beau. "If you need anything, call me. I can be here in less than five minutes." He grazes my lips with his before disappearing into the car. Anxiety bubbles over inside me as I think about what Asher must be thinking as he gets ready to leave me, and what Beau must be thinking watching me with Asher. As soon as he drives away, I wrap my arms around myself to chase the cold away. It could be the temperature outside, or the sudden emptiness I feel inside, but I can't quite get rid of it.

When I glance at the front yard again, Beau is no longer standing there. In fact, I don't see him anywhere. There's a lump of pain in the back of my throat as I walk toward the one place I know he escapes to when he needs to think or calm down. It's the same place he went when he was in trouble with his mom or dad when we were younger. It's the same place he went when his grandpa died when we were twelve. It's probably the same place he went every time I tried to push him away the last two years of high school; I just never had the courage to find him those times.

As soon as the trampoline comes into view, I see him lying on his back in the middle of the large black circle. Just watching him lie there motionless makes my stomach churn. There is no way that I'm going to get through the next few minutes without falling apart . . . I can't even imagine what this is doing to him. I'm the one in control, and he has no choice but to live with whatever decision I make, no matter how much it might hurt him. This whole situation makes me want to fall to the ground and beg him to listen. And when I think about what will happen if he won't . . . I can't even put that sort of heartache into words. I knew I loved him before, but seeing him now, in so much agony, I realize how deep that emotion really is.

"Can I join you?" I ask, running my fingers across the metal ring that surrounds the trampoline. It's so quiet that the faint phone ringing at the neighbors' house is the only disturbance.

When he doesn't respond, I slowly crawl onto the trampoline hoping to get his attention. I need him to say something. It really doesn't matter if it's anger that I hear; I just need to know that he's not giving up on our friendship. Silence means nothing, yet it means everything.

I mimic his position, resting my hands under my head and crossing my legs at the ankles. I throw my gaze in every direction besides his, trying to get a grip on my emotions as I try to figure out what to say to make this better. The sun reflecting off of the black fibers provides a little bit of the warmth my body had been missing, but I need the guy lying next to me to fill in the rest. When I finally get the courage to glance over at Beau, all I see is the side of his face. I don't know how much more of his silence I can take. I need to feel him breathe, and I would give anything to hear his voice.

"I didn't want to stay and watch you kiss him again," he says quietly. I'm surprised that he broke the ice first, but his words only drown me further into misery. I didn't even think twice about Beau seeing us when I kissed Asher's cheek, but now that he pointed it out, I feel like an insensitive bitch. He didn't deserve that. He didn't deserve any of it.

"Beau, I'm sorry. I wasn't thinking." I stare at him, trying to read what's going on in his mind right now.

"It really shouldn't matter that much to me. It's not like you were ever mine," he says, pinching his eyes closed.

"I never meant to hurt you. That was the last thing I ever wanted to do and the fact that I have . . . I'm really sorry," I say, feeling a tear roll down the side of my face. "Make me understand, Kate. Why him? Just a few weeks ago you told me you weren't ready for any of that," he says, finally looking at me with his teary eyes. Hearing his pain feels like a bulldozer driving into my heart, over and over again.

"I didn't think I was ready but—"

"Just say it, Kate! You realized it was me you didn't want. Am I not good enough for you?" He's blinking rapidly, but it's not enough to stop the first bit of moisture that falls from his eyes. My heart feels shattered and broken, beyond any sort of repair. There are no words to describe how much I want him . . . it's just not the same sort of want he has for me.

"That's not it at all," I cry, using my sleeve to wipe the warm tears from my cheeks. "Things are different with him . . . it's hard to explain. He's not trying to bring back the girl I was before D—"

I almost said it. I almost laid my secret out for the second person in two days.

He rolls to his side, resting his head on his hand. "Before what, Kate?" I shake my head, turning away from him. "He knows, doesn't he? You told him after only just meeting him, but you can't tell me." He sits up quickly, causing the whole trampoline to shake underneath us. I feel the anger rolling off his back as it hits me right across the face.

"It's not like that. He shared something with me about himself, and then it just sort of came out." I pause, trying to make sense of why it felt okay telling Asher, but not my best friend. Maybe I should just tell him and let things fall where they may. Maybe, if I told him, things would be less strained between us because he'd understand why I'm not who I used to be. But in the end, all I have are a bunch of maybes with no guarantees and I can't risk damaging our friendship any more than it already is. I'm not ready to tell him, not like this, and honestly I don't know if I ever will be.

"Someday, when the time is right, I hope I'll be able to tell you. But I can't right now."

We lie in complete silence, avoiding the other.

"You remember that time we came out here in seventh grade to look at the constellations?" he asks, tilting his neck to look up at the sky.

"Yeah," I say, sitting up next to him. It was a beautiful night and everything was absolutely perfect. It was also the night I realized I was falling for him.

"I wanted to kiss you that night, and every night after, but I didn't because I was scared. Scared that I would blow the one chance I had with you but now . . . Fuck. I don't even get my chance, do I?" His hands cover his face while I try to catch my breath. "Just answer one question for me. If I had kissed you back then, would things be different between us now?"

"I would have never let you go," I cry. My whole body is shaking; having nothing to do with the bitterly cold weather anymore.

"Tell me why we can't be like that now," he says, sitting up next to me. I'm used to the strong, self-assured Beau, but the guy whose shoulders are trembling next to me looks anything but and it's my fault.

"I can't really explain it. Things change. People change."

If Beau and I had been a couple that Friday night, I probably wouldn't have even gone to that bonfire, and I definitely wouldn't have given Drew the time of day. Beau would have been the center of my whole world.

"So where does that leave us?" he asks, just loud enough that I can hear it.

"You're my best friend. I hope you always will be," I whisper, reaching for his hand. He pulls it away before I get close, causing my heart to drop. He's purposely putting distance between us.

"You said it yourself. Sometimes things change. Just remember that you made this choice, not me," he says in a tone so distant he might as well be a million miles away. I watch in silence as he scoots to the edge of the trampoline and slides off. Things can't end like this.

"Beau!" I yell. He halts in place, his shoulders shaking. "You'll always be the first boy I ever loved. I won't forget that. Ever." Big, ugly tears slide down my cheeks.

He slowly turns, giving me a glimpse of his bloodshot eyes. "Up until a few minutes ago, I thought you'd be my last."

My vision blurs as he disappears into his house without giving me another glance.

His parting words vibrate through my ears. He imagined a forever for us, and I just blew apart any hope he had for that kind of future. If I had been able to communicate better, things could have been different between us. Sometimes I feel like life is just a bunch of failed opportunities. I'll always regret the one I lost with Beau. I think we both will.

My heart feels like a piece of glass that's been slammed against a ceramic floor. It's completely and utterly shattered. I've hurt the one person in my life that has always been there for me. Maybe he'll come around again, but the voice in my head is telling me that I might not be able to undo this.

I pushed him too far this time.

"Kate, is that you out there?" My mom is standing between our house and Beau's with her robe and a pair of pajama pants on.

"Yeah, it's me," I reply, climbing down from the trampoline, "I'll be right there, Mom." I'm not quite ready for that interrogation yet.

"Okay, but hurry up. It's already lunch time." Using the sleeves of my sweatshirt, I wipe the tears from my eyes and take several deep breaths, hoping to calm my racing heart. The last thing I feel like doing right now is watching a bunch of romantic movies. They're just full of lies and false hopes.

A part of me wishes I had stayed at Asher's instead of hurrying home this morning. Maybe then, I wouldn't have had to face Beau like this. Then again it was probably inevitable. I couldn't ignore him forever.

I slowly walk toward the house, trying to swallow the tennis ball in my throat. This is going to be a really long day. When my foot reaches the second step, I hear a door slam and glance up to see Beau climbing into his truck. He starts it up, letting the sound of the old muffler fill the neighborhood. His right hand grips the top of the passenger seat and turns his neck to back out of the driveway, but his eyes quickly snap back to penetrate mine. They're still red and swollen, but the rest of his features are completely expressionless.

All I want is to run to him and beg for some understanding. There's so much I wish I could say to him.

"Are you coming in? A new movie is about to start," my mom yells through a small crack she created by opening the door slightly.

"Yeah, I'm coming," I say, turning to take one more look at Beau's truck. As soon as our eyes meet again, he looks out his back window and pulls out of the driveway. I rub my aching chest with the palm of my hand as his truck speeds down our block and disappears out of sight. I let him go today, giving him the closure he needed to move on with his life.

My mom glares up at me with narrowed eyes when I shut the front door. Her lips are pressed together as she scans my face. "Beau was looking for you earlier. He seemed pretty worried," she remarks, focusing her attention back on the TV screen.

"You know, I'm actually not feeling very good. I think I'm just going to go lie down for a while. I wouldn't be very good company today, anyway." I hurry down the hall, slamming my bedroom door behind me. She yells my name a couple times, but I ignore her. I need some peace; some time to clear my mind.

I do love Beau . . . he's not just my past, I want him to be in my present and my future. But not in the same way he envisioned us.

Chapter 16

I WALK TO WORK, letting the fresh air help clear my mind. The colorful leaves rustle in the trees as a strong wind blows through. The town is eerily quiet this early in the morning, aside from an occasional car or truck passing by. It's not quite like a relaxing spot on the beach, but it's the perfect way for me to work through the maze in my head.

When I woke up this morning, the realization that I didn't do anything wrong yesterday hit me. I'd feel better if I knew what Beau was doing right now and if he's okay. It was going to happen sometime, but I hate how it ripped him apart. Just picturing the look on his face when he walked away from me is enough to make me sick to my stomach.

I keep telling myself that it's for the best.

He'll be able to move on now.

One day, I hope that Beau can accept my choice, and we can go back to the way we used to be before feelings were hurt and things got complicated. I love Beau. I really do, but love is a confusing thing and sometimes it's hard to tell the difference between loving someone and being in love. Someone who's lived for sixty years and loved many times probably couldn't even explain it with precision. How do they expect a nineteen year old to figure it out? Instead, I'm relying on the voices in my head, which have pointed me to Asher over and over again. He makes me want things I never wanted before, and I can't ignore that.

I make it to the diner just in time, hurriedly tying my apron and clocking in. It's quieter than normal because the farmers are in mid-harvest, so they're in and out of here before the sun even comes up. I actually find myself missing the familiar chatter and laughter.

"Hey, Kate," Diana yells from behind me.

"Hey. Busy this morning?" I start prep for a fresh pot of coffee and make sure the water pitchers are full.

"It wasn't too bad. I can't wait until these farmers get out of the field, though. I'm not an early morning person, and trying to hold a conversation before the sun rises is not making me a happy camper." She sighs, reaching over my shoulder for a coffee cup. "How've you been?"

I shrug. "Things are going okay." Things would be great if I could hear Beau's voice right now and know that he's going to be okay. Thoughts of Asher also play in my head. What is he thinking after everything that happened when he dropped me off? He's probably confused. As soon as I can, I'm going to clear everything up.

"Your mom said it looked like you had a little spat with Beau. Do you want to talk about it?"

I roll my eyes and spin to face her. "Is there any gossip you two don't share?"

"I'm afraid not," she says, placing a hand on my shoulder. "Let me tell you, though, every woman from thirteen to one-hundred drools over that boy. Be happy that you're the one he chose to fight with." She leaves me standing there, completely stunned. I appreciate Beau, and respect him for the person he is. That's the reason I need to do everything I can to make things right with him, or I'll regret it.

When I push open the metal door that separates the kitchen from the dining room, Asher is sitting in a booth in my section staring out the window. He comes in a lot when I'm working, but it's usually just for lunch. This is the first time he's actually made it here for breakfast.

I texted him last night and told him I wasn't feeling well. Physically I was fine, but emotionally I was a wreck. Looking at him now, I know without a doubt that my heart pulled me in the right direction. There's something about him that makes it impossible for me to stay away.

When I'm just a few feet away, he notices me. I expect to see a grin spread across his face, but instead he draws his brows in as he runs his hand through his hair. I glance around and quickly realize the frown on his face is, in fact, directed at me.

"You're here early this morning," I say, running my sweaty palms across my apron.

"I wanted to make sure you were okay. What happened to you last night?" His voice is flat, making it impossible for me to read him.

I can't look at him in the eye and tell a half truth. Asher makes me want to have a real life, but I feel guilty about everything because Beau means so much to me. I can't say I'm stuck between the two because my heart tells me over and over again that it's Asher I want. But a person can't have that much history with someone like Beau, and not carry them around with them.

I nervously take the seat across from him, clasping my hands on the table. "I needed some time to sort things out."

"I know," he says, leaning across the table. His eyes lower to the napkin he's been ripping into tiny little pieces.

"Then why did you ask?"

"To see if you would tell me the truth," he says, bringing his eyes back to mine. He looks like he didn't sleep much last night, and it weighs heavy on my heart to think that I also caused Asher pain in some way. Causing unnecessary pain is one thing I've become really good at recently.

"It didn't have anything to do with you. I was emotionally drained, and I needed some time to work through everything that was going on in my head. Beau has been my friend for a long time, and I hurt him."

"Just give him some time. He'll come around."

"I hope so." I want to be optimistic, but I need a sign of something better to come before I can move forward. I get glimpses of it, but then it always seems to fade away.

"He loves you, you know," Asher blurts, glaring out the window. It's early and the streets are almost vacant aside from a few cars parked in front of the diner.

"How do you know that?" I ask, curious how he was able to pick that up after meeting Beau for all of five minutes.

"There's a certain way a guy looks at the girl who he can't live without," he says, still not turning his head to look at me.

"And how is that?" I swallow hard. I have no idea where this is going.

His eyes snap to mine, making it impossible for me to move. "Like she's everything he'll ever need."

I couldn't form a word right now if someone sounded the whole thing out for me. Warmth is coursing through my veins like a runaway train as we stare at each other. I wonder if he's feeling it . . . he obviously has felt it at some point in his life or he wouldn't be able to put it into those words.

"And how did you get so wise?" I ask, trying to slow down my heartbeat.

"Living this life does that to you," he says, glancing out the window again before focusing back on me. "Do you love him?"

"Not in the same way he loves me," I say, nervously fidgeting with my fingers. "Look, I don't know what you think happened yesterday, but right now you're the one I want to spend my time with. I haven't felt this way in a long time." I want to reach across the table and wrap his hand in mine, but I'm hesitant because I have no idea what's going through his head right now. It scares me.

"What do you mean?" His question is eager and hopeful.

"I'm happy," I say simply.

"And I hope that you stay that way," he says softly, reaching for my hand. That's the thing about him . . . he's not afraid to do the things that scare me.

"With you, I finally feel like that's possible." I don't miss the downward cast of his eyes or his hand tightening over mine. Maybe I'm moving too fast or revealing too much.

"Hey, Kate, table four is ready to order," Diana yells, walking past our table with a tray full of plates.

I try to pull my hand from Asher's, but he's got a good grip. "I should probably get back to work."

"I need to head into the city today. I won't be back until later."

"What's in the city?" I ask.

"Just some things I have to take care of," he replies, rubbing his thumb across the back of my hand before finally releasing me. I felt so sure about where our relationship was going yesterday, but uncertainty is all that hangs between us right now. It seems like he's pulling away from me.

"So will I see you soon?" I ask, shoving my hands in the pockets on the front of my apron.

"I hope so," he answers, tilting his head to one side. "By the way, can I get a stack of these napkins?" He grabs the napkin he mutilated off the table and hands it to me. I have this weird feeling in my stomach that I may not see him again, and it's eating me up.

"Is something else bothering you?"

"Nothing you need to worry about right now," he replies, resting his palm against my cheek. I want him to open up to me. I want him to need me the way I need him.

I draw in a deep breath and wrap my fingers around his wrist to pull his hand from my cheek, "Asher-"

"Not now," he says, leaning in closer to me. His expression is more relaxed, but uneasiness still rips through me like a tidal wave. I would give anything to know what's going through Asher's head right now. What if I blew my chance to be with him too? Maybe he's decided that I'm not worth the trouble. I close my eyes and say a silent prayer that it's the latter.

I hear someone clear their throat beside me and turn to see my mom standing at my side, nodding toward my waiting table. "Kate."

"I'm going," I snap, standing in front of her. "Can you get Asher some napkins, please?" Asher's hand brushes the back of mine as I walk past him, sending a warm jolt up my arm. I look back to see his cheeks dimple, a sign that maybe everything will be all right. I need more than a sign right now, though. I need a promise because once I give my heart to someone; I don't ever want it back.

I toss the torn napkin in the garbage and quickly walk over to my table.

───～～～───

When I leave work, I'm still upset about the way Asher was acting when he came in earlier. Is he concerned about my relationship with Beau? Did I do something else to irritate him? I just wish I knew because I hate this living in limbo thing.

As I get closer to my car, I see something white under my windshield wiper. People are always leaving notes about babysitting and lawn services on my car. It annoys me because they end up sitting on the floorboard until it's time for my semi-annual cleaning. When I pull the wiper up and grab the paper between my fingers, I realize it's a napkin with Asher's handwriting in the center.

> Be at the lake house by 7 tonight. Wear something warm.

I suddenly feel completely awake after my tiring day because I'll be seeing Asher in just a few hours. I think that's the key to living a fulfilled life; having a reason or purpose. I have that now, and I'm going to hold onto him for as long as I can.

I throw my phone on the bed and pull on my favorite blue jeans and a long-sleeve white t-shirt. I layer a second t-shirt and then pick a thick navy blue cowl neck sweater from my closet and pull my caramel colored pea coat over it.

As I pull into Asher's driveway just a few minutes later, I'm greeted with the smell of burning wood. I used to think it was one of the best smells on earth, right behind fresh baked bread and turkey on Thanksgiving, but the way the last bonfire turned out, I haven't been able to stomach it ever since.

I climb out of my car and head to the backyard to see if I can find Asher. I don't have to wait long because he's sitting in front of a small campfire, using a large stick to move some logs around. The light from the flame illuminates his face, making it obvious the moment he notices me approaching. "Hey, how long have you been standing there?" he asks, showing me his genuine Asher Hunt smile.

"I just got here." I tuck my hands into the front pockets of my jeans and move closer to the fire. It burns bright orange, and the smell of the burnt wood is overwhelming. It reminds me of the moment Drew sat next to me. But I keep telling myself that Asher is here, and he's nothing like Drew. I shouldn't have to fear doing things like this, and if I can take my first step toward ridding myself of that fear with someone like Asher, I need to seize the opportunity.

He places the stick on the ground and strolls toward me, encircling me with his arms. The light of the fire glows in his eyes as he kisses me softly on the lips while he slowly works to release the tension from my body. It's something I miss as soon as his lips leave mine.

"What's all this?" I ask, wrapping my arms around his neck.

"I want to rewrite another memory for you," he whispers against my ear, "I thought we could sit by the fire and maybe roast s'mores."

"Seriously?" I ask. This is literally one of the sweetest things anyone has ever done for me. There must be a manual on how to make Kate Alexander come to life again because Asher never misses a step with me.

"Fuck, I'm freaking you out, aren't I? I thought it would help, like when we went fishing and it started to rain," he says, running the pads of his thumbs across my cheekbones, "You've been a different person since then, and I wanted to bring a little more of that out of you."

"I'm just shocked, that's all." I tilt my head to look up at the night sky and take a deep breath. For the past two years, I've been hiding behind a mask so that no one will recognize all the painful things that are going on inside me. Now, it's time to take the mask off and figure out who I am after riding life's crazy roller coaster. I can't let the one thing I didn't have any control over ruin me forever.

Grabbing my chin between his fingers, he pulls my lips to his, tasting them a little longer this time. When he's done, the taste of mint still lingers, making me crave him all over again.

"I have a blanket set up over there if you want to get comfortable." He points to a red blanket sitting on top of a patch of grass. There's a basket in the middle with marshmallows, graham crackers, chocolate and a black thermos. He really thought of everything.

This moment is perfect.

"How do you always seem to know what I need before I even know?" I ask, resting my cheek on his muscular chest.

"I just know," he says, pulling his arms tighter around me. "I like making you smile. And, if I can get you out of your comfort zone every once and awhile, that's just an added bonus."

"You're amazing, you know that?" I whisper before leaning up to kiss his chin.

"If anyone else said it to me, I wouldn't believe it. It's different when you say it." He brushes a piece of hair from my forehead and releases me. For the first time, I feel the frigid October air against my cheeks; cuddling close on the blanket sounds really good right now.

Once we're seated on the soft fleece blanket, Asher takes out two metal sticks and places marshmallows on them. "You want to do one?" he asks, handing one to me. I hold it over the fire, letting it puff up to get that burnt layer I love so much.

"I haven't had these since I was a kid," I admit, holding it close to my mouth to blow out a small flame.

"Me either." He hands me a graham cracker with two chocolate squares on top. I squeeze my marshmallow between that and another cracker, feeling the gooey goodness on my fingers.

"How did it go in the city?" I ask curiously.

He shrugs, tearing his eyes away from mine. "It wasn't what I hoped for, but I'll figure it out."

"I think you should go back to school," I blurt. "I mean, don't you get bored around here?"

"Carrington isn't that bad," he answers, solemnly.

"Asher—"

"Did I tell you I have one more surprise?" He reaches to pick up a wooden guitar that I hadn't noticed sitting to the side of the blanket. I'm annoyed that he changed the subject on me, but I'm intrigued enough by the guitar to forget about it for a few minutes.

"You play?"

"I can play a little." He smiles, shyly. Asher is usually anything but nervous . . . it's nice to see him a little off balance. He crosses his legs and places the guitar in his lap. "I've been practicing this, but don't throw anything at me if it's not perfect. It's by The Calling; I slowed it down some, and made it more of an acoustic song."

I wrap my arms around my knees and wait patiently for him to begin. He rests his thumb above the strings, closing his eyes as the first note hits the night air and echoes into my ears. His fingers create a beautiful melody as I let the sound submerge me like rushing water.

When his voice blends with the bass of the guitar, it becomes a magical experience. He shifts his attention between me and the hand that rests under the guitar strings, never missing a note. I keep my eyes fixed on him, watching the flames from the fire reflect in his eyes while letting the husky tone of his voice caress my ears.

It's a song about making the best out of our lives and speaking our minds. I've never heard it before, but it's quickly becoming my new favorite song, and when I close my eyes to hear his voice, I'm quickly everything inside me comes alive.

After playing the last note, I stand and kneel down in front of him, not able to resist the need to touch him in some way. He laid his soul out for me, and now I want to feel the beating heart that created it all. He slowly lifts the guitar strap from his shoulder and places it to the side of the blanket again.

"I need to touch you," I say, hesitantly lifting my hand to his chest.

"You can touch me, hold me, you can do whatever you want to me," he breathes, lowering his eyes to my lips. "This night is all about you."

I cover his heart with my hand, feeling his racing heartbeat. I place my other hand over my own chest and notice mine is beating just as fast, but a force inside propels me forward. I've never wanted to taste something as much as I want to taste his lips. I pull his face between my hands, closing the gap between us, covering his mouth with mine. The taste of chocolate and marshmallow lingers, making him taste almost as sweet. I take the initiative and press my tongue between his lips. He doesn't take any coercing, inviting me in for a sensual game of tug of war.

I wrap my arms around his neck and before I know what I'm doing, he's on his back with my legs straddling his hips. This is all about control for me. I'm controlling the pace, the movement, and how far we go . . . it's all up to me. It feels good, freeing really, to let myself take what Asher is giving me. It's the complete opposite of what I went through at Drew's.

My lips break from Asher's, and I move to place light kisses along his cheeks and across his forehead then down his neck. His hands aren't touching me at all as I explore every exposed bit of skin my lips can access. My whole body floods with warmth, which is a completely new sensation for me. The more I touch him, the more I crave his hands on me. In fact, I don't think I can wait another minute to feel his hands slide over my skin.

"I think it's your turn," I state, placing my hands on either side of his head to hold myself up.

"I don't want to push you to do anything you're not ready for," he says, cradling my neck in his hands.

"Asher, I need this," I respond, pulling my lower lip between my teeth. "I want this." It's my declaration of letting go. I'm ready to move forward with my life.

"Are you sure?" he asks, running his thumbs along my jaw.

"Yes, I want you to kiss me and touch me. Don't hold back," I plead, yearning to feel his passion. "I'll tell you when to stop."

He pulls my face back down, pressing my lips to his. It feels amazing, but I want to go further. I pull away from his grasp, remove my legs from his hips, and lie on my back next to him. "What are you doing?"

"Lying down," I answer, feeling my heart beat against my chest. I need to know that I'm capable of doing this with someone. And Asher feels like the one for me.

His eyebrows squeeze together as he slowly turns to his side, pressing his chest against my arm. He rotates a little more, allowing half his body to cover mine. "Are you okay?" he asks, combing his fingers through the hair that's sprawled on the blanket.

"I will be," I reply, trying to focus on his touch and not the weight of his body.

He lowers his face, lining his left eye with my right. "Have you ever had a butterfly kiss?" he whispers, gently grabbing my hip.

I shake my head, noticing how his eyes sparkle in the moonlight.

"Well, we're going to change that right now." He lowers his head a little more, letting our eyelashes brush against each other. The delicate touch is the most romantic thing I've ever felt. He continues with my other eye and repeats the exact same fluttering, causing a giggle to escape my lips.

When he lifts himself up and draws another line between his eyes and my mouth, my lips part, waiting for the fireworks to go off in my stomach. And when there's no space left between our lips, they begin to explode over and over again. He gives me minutes of pure bliss, letting no part of my face go untouched. As his lips press against the sweet spot right below my ear, his palm runs over my breast. There are at least three layers of clothing between us, but my breath is still too difficult to catch.

I almost feel Drew invading me, but I quickly block him out by keeping my eyes focused on the gentle guy who has given me so much. I want this and Drew isn't taking anything more from me. I'm not going to let him write the rest of my story . . . he has already taken enough.

We stay like that until our noses are so cold that they have no feeling left in them. He doesn't move further than a few touches and dozens of warm kisses. He's successfully rewriting my horrible night.

Asher Hunt is bringing the real Kate back.

Chapter 17

I HAVEN'T SEEN OR TALKED to Beau in a couple months. They say time heals all wounds and I hope that's true for us. I miss him but I have hope that one day things will go back to the way they used to be.

Asher says I just need to give him some space, and I hate to admit it but he's usually right.

Asher has taught me a lot of things.

He has taught me that as long as I'm still breathing, my life isn't over and that I shouldn't be so quick to write myself off. I may not have the ability to control everything that happens to me, but I can decide how I react to it. He has taught me that the more risks I take, the less fear I'll feel over time. If I'm too scared to do anything even remotely out of my comfort zone, I'll never be able to live life the way it's meant to be lived.

And he has taught me what love really is.

Love is the most powerful emotion that lives inside us all. And when you have it, it can help diminish all the painful emotions that bury themselves too deep to be seen.

Things are comfortable but exciting between us. He makes me feel protected and secure. He's breaking down all my walls brick by brick, and the more he takes down, the more I welcome him in.

Tonight he invited me to the lake house, claiming he wanted to cook dinner and watch a movie. A couple months ago, I would have told him no. The mere suggestion that I hang out with him alone in a house would have caused instant panic to take over my whole body.

Things are different now.

My hands grip the steering wheel tightly as I drive toward his house. He said he also had a surprise for me tonight, and I have no idea what it could be. Asher can be very mysterious, so I never quite know what he has up his sleeve.

I pull my old Honda into the driveway behind his car and spot him through the front window, diligently working on something in the kitchen. He's never cooked for me, so I've yet to see if he actually has any skills in the kitchen. It can't be any worse than mine.

When Asher sees me through the window, he nods before disappearing from sight. I take the three steps that lead to the front door, and then lift my hand toward the doorknob, only to have it open before I get the chance. Asher is standing there in a black button down rolled to his elbows and faded blue jeans with a huge smile on his face. I love the way he's looking at me. Just seeing him smile at me makes my blood pressure skyrocket.

"Hey," he says, grabbing my hand and pulling me through the door. As soon as it's latched, he wraps his arms tightly behind my back and buries his nose in my hair. "You always smell good," he murmurs.

"It's just shampoo," I say, laughing and wrapping my arms around his neck. As soon as he lifts his face from my hair, I use my arms to pull his lips closer to mine. I've become addicted to his kisses.

That moment we connect is like a million flash bulbs going off in my head. He exposes every part of me, and I can't get enough of it. He makes me things I never thought I would. His kiss is always very sweet at first, but I know how hungry he is for me the second he traces my lips. I give it to him because I need it just as badly. There's nothing about Asher Hunt that I haven't grown to need.

And when he's done, he always places one gentler, lingering kiss on my lips before he steps back and looks at me with so much adoration in his eyes that I never want to break the visual contact. He gives me worth and purpose. I know I'm falling in love with him, but I'm afraid, at least until I know he feels the same way.

"Are you ready to eat?" he asks, pulling me toward the kitchen.

"I'm starving," I reply, following him step for step. The mixture of garlic and cheese hits my nose, making my stomach growl. I worked this morning and didn't have time to grab any lunch, and when I got home I was too nervous about Asher's surprise to even think about eating anything.

The kitchen is a small galley type kitchen, but there is a small table with two chairs at the far end. He has set out two plates and wine glasses filled with ice water. I can't help but smile at the arrangement.

"I hope you like Italian. I worked hard on this lasagna all day," he smiles, waving me toward the table.

"It smells great. What did you put in it?" I ask, taking my seat.

"Well, let me see," he says, walking toward the garbage. He pulls out a red box and starts reading the back of it. "Bleached lasagna, tomato puree . . ."

I laugh until my stomach muscles hurt. "Stouffer's, huh?"

"You didn't really expect me to make a whole lasagna, did you?"

"I didn't know what to expect when you invited me over for dinner, but to be honest, I kind of expected something like frozen lasagna," I joke, watching him roll his eyes at me before turning back toward the stove.

"Hey, I made the garlic toast and a salad too," he says, tilting his head to the side with a teasing grin. I wonder if he even realizes how sexy he is when he gets defensive. I'm tempted to ask him what brand of salad mix and frozen garlic bread he bought, but I leave it alone. His effort is worth more than scratch cooking.

I sit back and take in the view as he pulls everything out of the oven and works to plate our food. The way his brows pull in as he tries to cut the lasagna into perfect squares is one of the cutest things I've ever seen. I know he went to school for engineering, and I think he would have been really good at it because of his attention to detail. Maybe I can actually talk him into going back.

"Here you go. I hope it all tastes okay, but if it doesn't you can blame it on the frozen food manufacturers," he jokes, placing two plates on the table.

"It looks good." I smile. And it is. Everything melts against my taste buds, especially when comparing it to the cold sandwiches I usually indulge in for dinner.

"What did you do after work today?" he asks, sticking half a piece of garlic bread into his mouth.

"Not much. I took a shower, read a few chapters in my book, and then came here. Same old stuff. What about you?" I ask.

"You'll find out later," he says, avoiding meeting my eyes with his. I would give anything to know what the big surprise is right now. I hate surprises.

"After we're done eating?"

"No, I thought I'd clean the kitchen, then we'd watch the movie, and then I'd give it to you," he says, reaching his thumb up to wipe it along the side of my mouth before quickly pulling it away, "You had some sauce there."

"Maybe we could just skip the movie," I suggest, eating the last bite on my plate. I have no idea what I'm doing, but flirting with Asher seems like the most natural thing in the world to me.

"Oh yeah? I can think of a few things I'd like to do more than watch the movie myself. Maybe we can compromise." He leans into me, resting his hand on my thigh.

I blush, taking a few deep breaths to calm my nerves. Asher is not a shy guy, but sometimes his forwardness catches me off guard. We've done some things that I never imagined myself being able to do before I met him. He makes everything feel natural and does it with such gentle kindness that my body has started to enjoy it, rather than cringe from his touch.

"I'll help you clean up so we can work on that compromise," I say, standing up to clear the table.

He grabs my wrist, halting my progress. "Let's leave these for a little bit."

He wraps my hand within his much larger one and pulls me toward the living room. My breath starts to come a little quicker as I walk with shaky knees toward the couch. He seems so serious which is very unlike him. It makes me nervous.

"I'll be right back," he says, disappearing to the back of the house. I wait with my hands pinched between my shaking knees. The whole house is quiet with the exception of the low hum that comes from the refrigerator and Asher's feet padding on the hardwood floors.

When he comes out of his room carrying his guitar, a grin instantly forms on my face. The last time he played for me is still fresh in my mind, and if his surprise is a repeat performance, it's the most welcome surprise I've had in a long time.

"I've wanted to tell you something for a while now, but I wasn't quite sure how to say it, so I learned to play another song for you," he says nervously before sitting beside me on the couch.

I sit silently with my mouth hanging open as he starts to strum on his guitar. At first I don't recognize the song, but the moment he sings the opening words, "Find me here, and speak to me," I recognize it as *Everything* by Lifehouse. I've listened to this song many times—the lyrics and meaning behind them are absolutely beautiful. And when Asher sings them to me, keeping his eyes on mine . . . it leaves me breathless.

During a break in the lyrics, he runs the tip of his tongue against his upper lip and all I can think about is replacing his tongue with mine. His voice is smooth as a rose petal as it vibrates throughout the room. As the song comes to a close, I notice his eyes are glistening, and the tears instantly begin to fall from mine.

He's everything I'll ever want.

I know this for sure.

After he plays the last note, he sets his guitar up against the side of the couch and turns to me, using the pads of his thumbs to wipe the tears from my cheeks. "Thank you," I mouth, placing my hand against his chest.

He leans his head in, placing a chaste kiss on my cheek. "Everything about that song makes me think of you," he whispers, breathing warm air against my ear and sending tingles through my body.

I press my lips to his neck, keeping them still for a few seconds before trailing them down his warm skin. He nuzzles the tip of his nose in my hair, and then lifts his head to get a better look at the needful expression on my face. He skims his fingertips along my jawline, causing my eyes to pinch shut so that all I have left to concentrate on is the way his fingers feel on me. When he moves down the back of my neck and draws me in close to him, I can feel my pulse in my throat as I anticipate his kiss.

When his lips connect with mine, everything happens a little slower than usual for us. His lips are speaking love to mine, just like the song did. He adjusts his body, moving his knee between my legs so that the fronts of our bodies are connected. I'm so caught up in the moment and the ambiance of his kiss, that I don't realize my back is positioned comfortably on the cushions of the couch until his chest is pressed firmly against mine. We've done this before, worshipping each other with lips and fingers without having to remove any clothes. Tonight, though . . . tonight everything feels different. This feels completely different.

I reach my shaky hands up and slowly work to unbutton his shirt. Asher stops moving and rests his weight on his elbows as he looks down at me. His eyebrows are drawn up, leaving creases on his forehead. He knows everything about my past . . . my worries, and my shame. He knows that taking our relationship to the next step won't be easy for me. He has seen the paralyzing pain and regret that lives inside of me every day. He has held my hand as I've tried to walk out of the darkness the last couple months. In fact, I'd still be buried deep inside my own misery if it wasn't for him.

The palms of his hands rest on the top of my head as he uses his fingertips to trace small circles into my scalp. I unfasten the last button and run my hands across his chest, sliding them over his shoulders and pushing his shirt down his biceps. He leans in and kisses across my jawline.

When he breaks the contact, he sits up on his knees and pulls me up to face him. His eyes flash back and forth between mine. I know what he's searching for . . . it's the same thing I've been looking for.

Reassurance.

I'm at a fork in the road; I can choose to experience everything I intended to in life, or allow myself to be held down by Drew for yet another night. I can't keep letting Drew take over my life. Not when Asher has the ability to make things right for me again.

I nod, holding my arms above my head. His face instantly lights up as he pulls my shirt up, exposing the white lace bra I'm wearing underneath. The way he looks at me with those dusty blue eyes makes my heart melt. It's a far cry from the monstrous expression I saw on

Drew's face that night. This is my opportunity to burn that out of my mind.

I'm ready.

The backs of his hands trail up the length of my arms then he uses the tips of his fingers to trace my collarbone. His movements are slow as his eyes to gauge my comfort level. Every time he removes his fingers from my stomach or any other exposed part of my skin, I crave more.

"Make love to me." My voice is low because I'm trying to suppress all the nerves that are coming to the surface.

His eyes grow wide, but he quickly recovers. "I'm going to do more than that, Kate. I'm going to kiss every inch of your skin, and when I'm done you're going to feel it right here," he whispers, placing his hand over my exposed chest.

I rest my forehead against his, swallowing some of the emotion that threatens to spill tears from my eyes. "Make me forget. I want to feel your hands on my skin. I want to hear your voice in my head over and over, saying words I want to remember instead of ones I want to forget. I want you to touch everything inside of me . . . every part of me."

He presses his lips to mine and slowly lowers me back down to the couch, never taking his eyes off me. "Trust me. When I'm done with you, all you'll think about is me." He leans in to kiss me again. This time his lips linger a little longer, working to calm my nerves. "And I want you to remember that I will never take anything from you that you don't want to give. You have all the control."

I close my eyes and breathe in as much air as my lungs will hold. It's time to let the last unlivable memory be rewritten.

I feel his hands sliding up my stomach, and I open my eyes again to see him staring down at me with a burning intensity. There is no more lingering doubt. The path between us is clear, and I want this. I really want this with Asher, and I can't imagine sharing this moment with anyone else.

"If you want to stop at any time, just tell me. I don't want you to regret this." My body starts to relax before I even realize what's happening. "Come," he says, standing and reaching for both of my hands. When I'm up on my feet, he wraps his arms around me and rests his hands on my lower back.

I nod and he wraps my hand in his, walking us toward the bedroom. As soon as we cross the threshold, he shuts the door and stands behind me with his hands on my hips. He brushes my hair to the side, letting his fingers linger on my skin and sending a tingling sensation throughout my whole body. I feel feather soft kisses along the back of my neck and across my shoulders. Asher uses his lips to caress my back while his hands cover my breasts and the pads of his thumbs run over my nipples. Relaxing into him, I let him hold me up as my body floods with want.

He moves his hands back to my hips, using them to turn me around so that we're face to face again. I can't stop myself from kissing him as his fingers work at the button on my jeans. He slowly pulls them down my legs without losing the connection I've created with our lips.

The pure agony I felt that night when Drew pulled my pants down surfaces again in my chest, but I easily push it away. I step out of my jeans and work the zipper down on his. His hands cup my face as he places sensual kisses on every feature: my cheeks, nose, right above my eyes and ending with my lips. "You're so beautiful, Kate.

So fucking beautiful," he says against my lips before pressing into them again.

His fingers make quick work of the clasp on my bra as I grasp his wild blond hair between my fingers. After he moves my bra slowly down my arms, he walks me backward until the back of my knees hit the edge of the bed. I sit, scooting myself back on my hands and feet until my back rests against the headboard. The way his eyes glow as he crawls up my body makes my heart expand in my chest. His body is perfect; muscular but not too large, and the way his hair sweeps forward across his forehead begs me to run my fingers through it.

He spends several minutes using his mouth to cover every inch of my skin, just like he promised, before nuzzling his nose into my neck. Every time he touches the spot below my ear, shivers run down my spine.

He grasps the edges of my panties between his fingers and slides them down my legs as I feel my breath quicken. Every move he makes is done out of love. He's not just going to have sex with me. He's not going to take anything from me that I don't want to give him. He's going to make love to me, sweet and slow, paying attention to every part of my body.

When his lips softly caress the inside of my thighs, I close my eyes to concentrate completely on his touch. My eyes shoot open as soon as his mouth leaves my skin, and I watch as he sits back, pulling his jeans and boxer briefs down. I ball my hands tightly into fists and swallow the lump that's formed in the back of my throat.

I stay still as he reaches into the drawer next to the bed and pulls out a condom. When I hear the familiar sound of foil ripping, I close my eyes and take a deep breath. As I slowly open my eyes again, I'm met by his warm blues.

"Are you okay?" he whispers, leaning over to kiss my chin.

I nod, brushing a strand of hair from his forehead. "More than okay."

I'm really going to do this. I'm going to have sex with Asher.

He may not be the first guy to be inside of me, but he will be the first guy whose body I've ever wanted to be connected to. This is how I imagined losing my virginity would be like.

He covers my body with his, letting me feel how much he wants this. His face hovers right above mine, and I can see his eyes illuminated by the soft moonlight. "I'll erase everything he left inside you," he whispers against my lips, sliding his hand between our chests, covering my rapidly beating heart.

When his hand moves down my stomach and stops between my legs, I take a deep breath. "Relax," he says, brushing his lips against mine, "I'm going to take care of you." He slowly slips one finger inside of me then two and my whole body tenses up again, but after a few gentle motions, I begin to relax.

Everything he is doing to me feels so right.

A tear rolls down the side of my face as he removes his finger and slowly guides himself into my body. He fills me a little bit at a time, letting me adjust to him. I take several deep breaths and turn my head to the side, trying to concentrate on anything but the old memories that I'm trying to leave behind.

"Keep your eyes on me," he says, using his index finger to turn my face back toward him. He moves slowly, never taking more control than I'm willing to give him. It's a dance of give and take; pleasure and healing.

"Are you okay?" he asks, stopping to cradle my head in his hands.

One look up at his concerned eyes and the question becomes easy to answer. "Yes," I whisper, pulling his face down to mine. I need him to relax and feel this moment with me. This is the most emotionally packed experience that I've ever been through; one blissful experience replacing a haunting memory.

He remains still, never taking his eyes off of me. He slowly starts to move again as his lips brush against mine. There's a little discomfort from the newness of him and my inexperience, but after several slow, soothing movements it eases, allowing me to completely focus on him. I try to read his gorgeous expression, letting the thoughts take away the control that the old, painful memories want to gain.

His body never leaves its place on top of mine. He keeps his pace controlled and barely blinks as his eyes bore into my soul. He looks at me like he wants and needs me, like no matter what I do or what's been done to me; he'll be here for me. He looks at me like he'll never get enough.

His hand reaches between our connected bodies again. "I want you to feel this, Kate. I want to feel you feeling it," he growls, gently stroking my sensitive, aroused flesh. What he's doing to me feels so good. It's chasing the tension from my body. I'm walking closer and closer to the edge of a cliff that I actually want to jump off of . . . and the next time he pushes himself into me, I do. It's like nothing I've ever experienced before. I feel weightless as my body clenches around his.

Asher quickens his pace and his own breathing picks up. Just as I'm recovering from my fall, his body tenses above mine as I watch his lips part. "Kate." His breathing is labored when he slides down next to my body, cradling my head in his hands and laying his head between my breasts.

I'm relishing in the moment, running my fingertips up and down his back. If all things could be like this, there would never be anything to forget. I never want to be without Asher. I feel like he was sent here to awaken my soul, but he chose not to stop there.

He awakened everything.

His head lifts to place a firm, lingering kiss on my lips. When he pulls back, he rolls his lower lip between his teeth and all I can think about is kissing him again. I wrap my hands behind his neck and bring his mouth back down to mine. "Your kisses are amazing," I whisper, smiling up at him.

"No, this whole night has been amazing," he says. "More than amazing actually."

"Thank you," I whisper.

"I'm the one that should be thanking you. You are so fucking beautiful."

"Your body isn't half bad either," I respond, kissing him one more time.

"Will you stay with me tonight?" he asks, rubbing the pad of his thumb against my forehead.

"I'd stay with you every night if you asked me to." He rolls onto his back and cradles me against his chest.

I could definitely fall asleep like this every night.

Chapter 18

WAKING UP WRAPPED IN ASHER'S arms is like waking up on a cloud where nothing can hurt me. I slept better than I have in over two years. There was no lying in bed and over-thinking anything. No nightmares. It was just the two of us.

The whole night has been like a dream to me, and I'm hesitant to open my eyes; I can still feel the steady rhythm of Asher's chest rising and falling under my cheek. I reach down and entwine his fingers with mine, causing his arms to grip me a little tighter. Life should always be made of mornings like this.

"Hey, what are you doing up so early?" he asks in his rough, deep morning voice.

"It's almost noon," I reply, pressing a light kiss to his chest.

"Don't you have to work today?"

"Well, if I did, I would be in some trouble now, wouldn't I?" I tease, resting my chin against his chest.

"Yeah, you would. And Kate isn't one to get herself in trouble, now is she?"

The room goes quiet as I focus on the light stubble that's starting to show on his chin. I've gotten myself into trouble before . . . more than enough trouble. The worst kind of trouble.

"I'm sorry. I didn't mean it like that."

"I know. I just hate that my mind wants to go there all the time," I say, trying to get my mouth to turn up in the corners. Asher would never intentionally hurt me. Not physically. Not emotionally. I seek peace in that every single day.

"Hey, focus on me. Not all of that," he whispers, cradling my face in his left hand.

"I'm trying," I say, leaning into his touch.

"Maybe I can help you with that," he says, flipping me onto my back. Our bodies are still naked from last night's activities, and when he rests his hips on mine, desire runs through my veins from the contact. I've had a taste of what being with Asher is like, and now I'm addicted. I don't think I'll ever get enough of him and the way his skin feels against mine.

First, he makes love to me slowly with his hands, running them from ankle to thigh. His fingertips trail my skin, paying special attention to the sensitive area between my legs, not halting until they've lapped circles around my belly button. When his lips touch the base of my neck, I wrap my arms around his shoulders and pull his chest against mine. I don't think he realizes that I'm the lucky one in this situation. I'm the one who was saved by a man who blew into my life like a storm.

He starts to roll off me, but I grab his arm, halting him in place. "Where are you going?"

"I need to grab something out of the drawer," he smiles, running his thumb over my cheekbone.

"I'm on the pill," I blurt, keeping hold of his arm.

The smile falls from his face but his eyes never leave mine. "Are you sure?"

"I'm sure."

I ease my grip on his arm, and he rests his hands on my hips as he slowly eases into me. This time I focus on the feel of him, the way he fills me so completely. When he kisses down my jawline, I take the opportunity to shut my eyes and let the sensations take over. It's the most incredible feeling in the world, and, this time my body works toward the edge of that cliff all on its own. My back arches as my body clenches around him.

"Open your eyes. I need to see your eyes," he says, trailing his fingers between my breasts. When I open them, I see the shaded blue in his eyes staring down at me.

"Asher . . ."

"Kate," he groans, thrusting into me a little bit harder.

"I love you," I breathe as he lets himself go inside of me. His body convulses over and over before going completely still. I wonder if I've said it too soon but in the moment, being lost in him, that's exactly what I feel. I've felt it for a long time but held it all in, too scared to say it out loud.

"Kate," he says, opening and closing his mouth a couple times, trying to catch his breath.

I shake my head, nervously looking at the ceiling. "You don't have to say anything. I just needed you to know."

"You have a very large piece of my heart. I've never felt this way about anyone, so I don't want you to think that I don't care about you just because I can't say it right now." His fingers stroke my cheeks and I instinctively close my eyes. Asher isn't the first guy I've loved, but I know how confusing those feelings can be. When you open your heart to love, you're also exposing it to pain. Pain from love is the worst kind of agony. I felt it when I broke Beau's heart, and I hope I never have to go down that road again.

"It's okay," I say, trying to hide the disappointment from my voice. His words mean a lot to me, but they don't erase the negative feelings that are boiling over the surface.

"I like you a lot. Like a whole lot," he teases, rubbing his nose against mine.

"I guess I like you a lot too," I tease back, letting my fingers curl into his hair. His blonde locks are way more out of control than they usually are after a night of sleep and two love sessions between the sheets. It suits his wild, uncontrollable side.

"I need to use the restroom. Don't go anywhere," he says, walking his firm naked backside toward the hallway.

I rest my hands behind my head and stare up at the popcorn ceiling that covers the old lake house. It's nothing like my water stained one back home, but it gives me something new to focus on. Instead of drifting to the usual thoughts, I replay the events of last night and this morning. Everything feels just as good as it can possibly be right now.

New ceiling.

New memories.

New me.

I hear the front door slam, and it jolts me away from my new internal paradise. "Asher, are you here?" a deep male voice yells.

Asher comes flying out of the bathroom and opens one of his dresser drawers, pulling out a pair of grey sweat pants and quickly putting them on. "Stay here. I'll be back in a few minutes." He walks toward the door turning back to me as soon as his hand covers the knob. "You might want to put some clothes on . . . just in case."

He doesn't give me a second to ask him any questions. He just walks out of his bedroom door, quietly shutting it behind him. I nervously pull on my clothes from the night before and tiptoe to the bathroom, combing my fingers through my tousled hair.

When I open the bathroom door, I hear Asher yelling. I know I shouldn't eavesdrop, but I can't help it, I hate hearing him so upset.

I close the door until it's only open a crack and lean my ear against it. "Will you just back off! This is my life! Not yours!" Asher yells. The pain in his voice is palpable.

Everything inside is screaming at me to run out there and comfort him, but I know he can take care of things himself. I've seen him do it before.

"It's her life too. You haven't even told her yet, have you?" his father yells back. I recognize his voice from the couple of times I've met him; he is not happy.

"I can't. I just want to fucking be with her. Telling her would ruin everything," Asher replies so quietly that I can barely hear him. My lungs feel like they are being crushed inside my chest. This is déjà vu of the first conversation I heard between him and his dad, and this time I don't think I'm going to be able to just sit back and pretend I'm not hearing this. Asher will probably see the worry on my face the minute he looks at me.

"It's going to hurt her even more if you wait. Is that what you want, Asher?"

"You didn't give a shit about me when I was growing up! Now you choose to start caring about what I'm doing with my life?" Asher screams. I hear loud footsteps on the hardwood floors and quickly shut the door, leaning my back against it.

My heart pounds fast against my ribs as my mind races, trying to figure out what to do next. Should I stay in here and pretend I didn't hear a thing? Should I walk into his room and confront him about whatever this secret is he's keeping?

When I hear his bedroom door slam, I jump and squeeze my eyes shut. Maybe this isn't the right time to confront him. Maybe I should wait until tomorrow after he's had time to cool down.

I haven't learned everything there is to know about Asher, and when I think about what could be worse than carrying the guilt of Megan's death around with him every day, I feel sick to my stomach. I slowly open the bathroom door and glance down both sides of the hallway to make sure no one is around before I cross the hall to

Asher's room. As I open the door, I see him sitting on the side of his bed with his elbows resting on his knees and his forehead tucked into his hands. He looks absolutely destroyed.

I close the door waiting for him to look up and acknowledge me, but it doesn't happen. I've allowed him to be there for me time and time again, and it bothers me that he won't let me help him through this when he obviously needs me too.

I sit beside him on the bed and hesitantly massage his back. He turns to me with sad, red eyes and winces before letting his shoulders relax. He doesn't want me to see him like this, he never does, but I'm not going to leave him. "Do you want to talk about it?"

He shakes his head in sad silence without even looking at me. I sit equally as quiet as I wrestle with the range of emotions that are going through me. I want to be there for him, but I can't escape the sinking feeling in my stomach that whatever he's keeping from me could shatter my world into a million pieces. A voice inside of my head is yelling for me to run before he has a chance to tell me . . . maybe it would be better if I just didn't know. Is it possible that he has someone else in his life that he isn't telling me about? Is he planning on leaving soon? Everything I come up with in my mind scares me to death, and I need some time to sort it all out in my head.

"I'm going to head home. My mom is probably worried about me," I announce, standing up in front of him.

I wait, but all I'm given is utter silence; deafening silence that makes my anxiety grows even more. I pinch my eyes shut and turn to move toward the door.

His hand envelopes mine, stopping me in my tracks. "Kate," he whispers.

"Yeah?" My voice is meek, just a hair above a whisper.

"Thank you for last night. It meant as much to me as it did to you," he says, smiling sadly as he stands in front of me. He lifts my chin with his finger and presses his lips to mine. Whenever Asher kisses me, I feel warmth and contentment working through my whole body, but this time . . . it simply feels like goodbye. His lips linger on mine like a storm cloud on a rainy day. He pulls away, and then leans toward me one more time, running his nose along my neck to breathe me in. When he lifts his head, I start walking toward the door again, leaving my hand clasped in his until they can no longer touch, then slip out of the room, letting a few tears fall from my eyes. How can one of the best nights of my life end so abruptly like this?

As I move through the house, I spot his dad sitting on the couch in the same position Asher was in on the bed. There are two wounded men in this house, and somehow I'm the cause of it all. The more I think about it, the more it upsets me because I feel like I've been dragged into something that has nothing to do with me, but also everything to do with me.

My drive home is quiet with the exception of all of the uncontrollable sobs that roar through my entire body. As I pull into the driveway, the tears blur my vision before pouring down my face. I lost myself. I lost Beau. And now I feel like I'm losing Asher too. The world is always working in the opposite direction from where I am.

If only I could figure out what I'm being punished for.

When I walk through the front door of my house, I know without a shadow of a doubt that my day is not going to get any better. My mom shoots up from her chair at the kitchen table and practically runs toward me, gripping my wrists in her hands. "Dammit, Kate, you can't do stuff like this to me! Where have you been? I tried to call you. I texted you at least twenty times!" she yells, swinging my arms out to get a better look at me. Her swollen eyes are like a sword to my heart. I don't want to hurt my mom. She doesn't deserve my anger because she isn't the cause of it.

"I was with Asher," I whisper, focusing on the empty coffee pot that sits on the table in front of her chair. If I look at her somber expression much longer, I'm going to lose it.

"Well, next time you decide to stay out all night, can you at least have the decency to call me and let me know that you're all right?"

"I don't think there will ever be a next time," I mumble as my lower lip starts to tremble.

She places her palm against my cheek, forcing me to look at her. "Did he hurt you?"

"No. It's been a rough morning, that's all." She lets go of me and tucks some loose hair behind my ear. "I'm going to go to my room now. I'm really tired."

She nods, lowering her hands to her side as I walk by. I'm halfway down the hall when she yells behind me, "By the way, don't forget it's Beau's birthday. Maybe if you give him a call, he can make you feel better."

I keep walking, not because I don't care, but because I'm close to completely falling apart. I want to disappear behind my closed door for days. I want to lie on my back and stare at the familiar stains on my ceiling and replay how Asher made me feel last night and this morning.

Ever since Asher walked into my life, he's been living in the forever space in my head. I've known since that day in the rain that I always want him in my life. I want him to walk with me through all the bad days because no one can hold my hand like he can. I don't want to live another day without hearing the sound of his voice.

It feels like he's letting me go, but maybe if I don't allow him to walk out of my life, I'll be able to hold onto him that much longer. Maybe the negative voices in my head are simply filling it with lies and misunderstanding. Could it really be that simple?

And Beau . . . I completely spaced out that today was his birthday.

I don't know who I've become.

Some days I like the girl staring back at me in the mirror, but today I want to start all over again.

Without even thinking about it, I pull out my phone and attempt to call Beau for the first time in two months. He asked for space, and I gave it to him, but today I just need to hear his voice.

"Hello," he says, in a whispered tone.

"Beau?" The sound of his voice only reminds me how much I've missed him. A thousand I miss you's couldn't even express how much I've missed having him in my life.

"What do you need Kate?"

"I called to wish you happy birthday," I reply, trying to control the tremor in my voice. I had this delusion in my head that he might be at least a little happy to hear from me, but he sounds anything but.

"Thanks," he sighs, letting his voice trail off.

"What have you been up to?" I ask, trying to pull him back to a place that used to be normal for us.

"Just a minute." I wait, listening to his footsteps on the other end of the line. "I have to take this call. I'll be out in just a few minutes, Jess." His voice is muffled, but I can still make out every word.

"Who are you talking to?" I ask before I realize the words have even come out of my mouth.

I hear him let out a deep breath through the phone. "Jessica."

"Is she a friend?" I don't know why it matters to me. It shouldn't matter to me.

"Something like that," he says quietly, like he's scared for me to hear it. A part of me wants to know more, but the other part of me would rather live in oblivion. Beau is free to do whatever he wants. I have Asher now.

At least I hope I still do.

"How is everything going at U of I?" I ask, desperate to change the subject.

"It's fine," he says, sounding like he'd rather be anywhere than on the phone with me.

I wait for him to add something else, but he never does. "Is this how things are going to be between us now? I miss you."

"I—"

"Beau, are you about ready to go? We have reservations at seven." A sweet, cheery female voice yells, sounding closer with every word. This is definitely one of the worst days of my life. Why does it feel like everything is falling apart?

"I'll let you go. It was nice hearing your voice," I say, trying to control my emotions.

"Kate, wait—"

"That's the one and only Kate? Tell her Jessica says hi," the sugary sweet voice breathes as she begins making a kissing sound into the receiver.

I hang up. I can't listen to any more. I deserve it . . . I knew Beau loved me and I made him feel like he wasn't good enough. There isn't anything I wouldn't do to have him in my life again, but it doesn't sound like he's ready to move forward with our friendship.

After revisiting the events of the day over and over in my head, I'm able to calm myself down. Asher just needed space this morning, and I guess Beau needs it too. That's all it is. I start the shower and grab a towel from the hallway closet before stepping in and letting the warm water spray over my body.

All I can do is wait and see what tomorrow brings.

Chapter 19

I DIDN'T HEAR ANYTHING FROM Asher last night, but I hadn't tried to reach him either. It's the first evening we've spent apart for weeks and I hated every minute of it, especially after spending the whole night before wrapped in his arms.

I thought about calling in sick and running to his house to talk to him, but something held me back. I'm going to try to be patient and see how well it pays off.

I clock in, noticing my mom standing near the door to the dining room eyeing me with a concerned expression on her face. Maybe I should have called in sick and spent the day wrapped under the quilt in my all-too-familiar room. I don't want any pity today.

"Are you feeling better this morning?" she asks, walking in my direction.

"I'm fine. I think I just needed some sleep," I reply, tying my apron around my waist.

She narrows her eyes at me. "If you need to talk about anything, I'm always here for you," she says, squeezing my shoulder.

I nod. "Thanks, Mom."

She gives my shoulder one more squeeze before disappearing into the dining room. I wonder if she ever sees me as a disappointment; her daughter with so much potential who held herself back in this small town to waitress instead of going to college. Knowing her, she's probably resigned to letting me find my own way. One day, I might wake up with a dream that's bigger than this.

I serve table after table, feeling like that girl who used to work here before she was swept off her feet by Asher Hunt. It's stupid really, and I realize that when a certain blonde haired, blue-eyed guy walks in with a sexy, knowing smirk on his face. His hands are stuffed in the pockets of his faded blue jeans. The second our eyes lock, he starts moving in my direction, the smile falling off his face.

"What's wrong?" he asks, running his thumb across my forehead.

I blink away the shock that he's actually standing in front of me. "Nothing, I just didn't expect to see you today. I was worried."

"About yesterday . . ." he starts before I place my finger over his lips.

"Not here. Can we talk after I get off work?"

He looks around, lifting his eyebrows as he scans the packed diner. "I guess you are kind of busy right now. Can I come over after your shift?"

"Yes, you know when I'm off." I smile, teasing him about his stalker tendencies. "Do you want something to eat while you're here? You haven't had a milkshake in a while."

"No, I'm going to head back home, but I wanted to leave you with this," he says, reaching into the pocket of his black, puffy coat and pulling out a folded napkin. "I'll see you later." He kisses my cheek and stuffs the napkin into my apron pocket before walking out almost as fast as he arrived.

I grin and find that I have an extra bounce in my step as I finish my shift. I'd give anything for it to be a slow day so that I could go home early and wrap myself around the man I've fallen head over heels for.

After the last table in my section leaves, I complete the task of rolling the silverware and punch out. As I'm getting into my car, the white napkin Asher handed me earlier falls out of my pocket, landing at my feet. I'd forgotten about it, but now that it's in front of me, I can't stop myself from opening it.

I'm sorry I made you leave my house yesterday without a smile on your face. I'll never let that happen again.
Asher

The snow started to fall earlier today as the start of a winter storm moved in. These kinds of days make me want to throw my sweats on and curl up on the couch with hot chocolate and a good book. Maybe I can talk Asher into movie day on the couch.

I throw on grey sweats and tie my hair into a ponytail while I wait for him. I'm always eager to see him, but since we were together a couple nights ago, I feel even more connected to him. I gave him the last piece of me I had to give, and he took it with so much care . . . I'll never forget the look in his eyes as we became one. I'll never forget the gentle way his hands and lips floated over my entire body. It was exactly how I envisioned my first time would be.

The exhaustion of the last twenty-four hours gets to me, so I let myself drift off to sleep. When I wake up, it's half past four and Asher isn't here yet. He's never late when we have plans. I pull my phone out of my purse and check for a text, but there isn't one. I dial his number, but he doesn't answer that either.

I don't have his dad's number, so I can't call him. Maybe he had car problems on the way and is stranded somewhere. He doesn't have the best car for driving on the snow covered, icy roads.

After a few minutes of worrying and wondering what I can do, I grab my coat and car keys and head out the door. I'm not going to be able to concentrate on anything else until I find him anyway. I carefully maneuver my car through the snowy streets, taking the same path he would take to get to my house. When I turn down his street, I see his car still parked in the driveway. At least he's not stuck somewhere alongside the road.

I park on the street in front of his house and walk carefully up the ice-covered driveway. The steps leading up to the front door haven't been shoveled, so I take extra care with them before knocking hard on the glass door. When no one answers, I bang louder, stepping back and waiting for the door to open. But again, no one answers.

Something is telling me that I need to get inside. I look both ways down the street to make sure no one is watching, and then try the handle on the glass door. Surprisingly, it opens. Why is it unlocked? Once inside the living room, I hear nothing but the tick of the old wooden clock that rests on the entertainment center.

"Asher!" I yell. Again, nothing but the sound of the clock passes through the room. I step closer to his bedroom, my heart pounding a little faster with each step. Goosebumps prickle the back of my neck and down my arms as I turn the corner down the hallway. I hear water running in the bathroom, so I softly tap my knuckles against the door and wait for a reply, but there is none.

I carefully turn the knob and slowly push the door open. The water is pouring out of the faucet, but no one stands in front of it. I push the door open a little further and find Asher, hunched over the toilet with his elbows resting on the seat.

"Asher." Just as I say his name, he begins to heave over the toilet again. I kneel down behind him and place my hand on his back, just to let him know I'm here for him. "It's okay," I whisper over and over, trying to soothe him.

When his body finally gives him a break, he grabs a tissue from the box that sits to his side, wiping tears from his eyes. I quickly grab a washcloth and wet it with water so that I can wipe the sweat from his forehead. He leans into my hand, letting me take care of him for once.

"How did you get in here? My dad didn't let you in, did he?" he finally asks, sounding annoyed.

"No, I knocked but no one answered so I let myself in. You weren't answering your phone. What's going on?" I ask, running my fingers up his neck into his wild blonde hair.

"I really don't want you to see me like this. Why don't you go back home and I'll call you when I'm feeling better."

"How long have you been like this?" I ask, avoiding his comments. He's crazy if he thinks I'm just going to leave him.

"For a few hours. I think I have the flu or something," he says, placing his hand over his stomach.

"Will you let me stay and take care of you?"

"You should really go home. I'm not very good company right now," he replies, resting the back of his head against the bathroom cabinet.

"I'm staying," I say, grabbing the washcloth to put cool water on it again.

"I'll make you a deal. Wait outside while I take a shower, and when I'm done you can tuck me in. I think I just need to sleep it off anyway," he says, slowly standing to face me. He looks horrible; his skin is white and clammy, his eyes are bloodshot, and the hair that lines his face is drenched in sweat.

I lightly dab the washcloth across his forehead and cheeks again. "Do you need help getting in the shower?"

"Any other time I'd take you up on that, but I just want to get in and get out. Why don't you wait in my room and I'll be right out."

"Okay, but leave the door unlocked in case you need me," I say, running my fingers along his cheek. I've needed Asher so much, and now he definitely needs me.

I pace around his room, waiting for him to get out of the shower. If I'm lucky, I'll be able to talk him into letting me stay here, at least until his dad gets home. I hate the thought of him being alone when he's obviously very sick. He's strong, I know that, but sometimes even strong people need someone to take care of them.

I've been in his room at the lake house several times, but this is only the second time I've been in the bedroom at his dad's house. It's very plain which I guess I'd expect since he hasn't been here long and wasn't here much before. The one thing that catches my eye is the photo of him with his mom and sister that sits on the table beside his bed. His mom has chin length blonde hair and vibrant blue eyes, while his sister has a head of red curls. They're standing outside with their arms wrapped around each other, looking happy and carefree. I can't imagine leaving that behind. He obviously cares deeply for them if he has this picture right next to his bed. I wish I understood why he won't talk about them more.

The bathroom door opens, startling my attention away from the photo. Asher walks in with black sweat pants and a long sleeved grey t-shirt. He still looks pale, but he's washed away the other remnants of sickness. His blonde hair is wet and spiked going in every which way.

"Ready for bed?" I ask, giving him a small smile.

"Yeah, bed sounds nice right now," he replies, walking to me slowly. He rests his hands on my hips and kisses my cheek. "Thank you."

"You'd do the same for me."

"I'd do anything for you," he whispers against my ear.

I pull back his hunter green comforter and wait for him to crawl in. "Let me stay with you for a while, please. At least until your dad gets home."

He nods once and scoots to the side of his bed. I didn't necessarily mean I wanted to take half of his bed, but if that's what he's offering I'm not going to say no. As soon as I'm tucked in next to him, he presses his body to mine and folds himself around me. It's not long before we are both drifting off to sleep.

When I wake up from my nap, I'm still snuggled tight next to Asher. I don't want to wake him, so I slowly loosen his grip and slide off the side of the bed. He looks so peaceful, and I can't help but softly place a kiss on his forehead before I leave.

As I am walking out, I see his dad sitting at the dining room table. His head is turned toward me, and his lips are pressed together in a pensive line. He opens his mouth but then quickly closes it again.

"Asher wasn't feeling good, but he's sleeping now," I tell him as I fidget with the rings on my fingers.

He nods and turns his attention back to the sandwich in front of him. I watch as he places his head in his hands; his shoulders began to shake.

"Are you okay?" I ask hesitantly, not sure if he knows I'm still standing here.

He startles, looking up at me with wistful eyes. "I'll be fine. I just have a lot on my mind." He uses the back of his hands to wipe his eyes.

"If you need anything, call me." As I show myself out the door, I feel guilty . . . maybe I should stay and make sure they're okay. Maybe I should have asked Daniel what is going on between them.

It takes me awhile to get the ice scraped off my car. When I finally get home, I crawl into bed and try to read, but all I can think about is Asher. My mind keeps drifting to him until I can't keep my eyes open any longer.

～～～

I haven't heard from Asher at all since I left him in bed. I did text him during to see if he is feeling better, but I've heard nothing back. I can't shake this feeling inside . . . the feeling that something is really wrong.

After I start my car to warm it up, I pull out my phone and dial his number. It rings several times before a voice that doesn't sound quite like Asher picks it up. "Hello."

"Asher? Are you okay?"

"No, this is his dad." Why would his dad be answering his phone?

"Is Asher there? I just wanted to ask how he's feeling," I ask, nervously biting my lip.

I hear him sigh heavily, and the phone goes silent for several seconds before he speaks again. "Kate, Asher's in the hospital," he says softly.

"What? Why didn't you call me?" Panic shoots through me like a rocket as I grip the steering wheel tight with my free hand.

"I'm sorry. It was a rough morning and knowing my son, he probably doesn't want you to see him this way."

"I don't care if he wants me there or not. I'll be there in fifteen minutes."

"I can't stop you," he sighs, "but, Kate, you need to be prepared. He's not in very good shape."

I close my eyes tight and pull in all the air that I can through my nose. "I'll be there soon."

I drive home and change as quickly as I can before hopping back in the car. Please just let him be all right.

Chapter 20

THE SECOND THE HOSPITAL DOORS OPEN, I'm greeted by the sterile hospital smell I despise and the white floors that I hate so much. I was here when I broke my arm in the third grade, and then again when I had to have my appendix out right after sixth grade. It's not a place I associate with happiness, and it's certainly not a place I like to visit if I don't have to, but Asher needs me. I walk up to the small reception desk that sits right in front of the door and wait for the receptionist to acknowledge my presence.

"Can I help you?" she finally asks, looking up at me with an annoyed expression.

"Yeah, I'm looking for Asher Hunt," I say, tapping my fingers on the top of her desk.

"Are you family?"

"No, well kind of. I'm his girlfriend."

"Name?"

"Kate Alexander."

She types something in the computer and shakes her head. "I'm sorry Miss Alexander, but you're not on this visitors' list."

"His father knows I'm coming. I just spoke to him on the phone." My voice is loud, but I could care less right now.

She presses her lips together in a straight line and leans in closer to me. "Take a seat and I'll see what I can do."

"Thank you."

I sit on the edge of the seat closest to her desk and nervously play with the strap on my purse. The waiting area is small with an irritating talk show playing on the TV screen in the corner, but I could care less about normal things like mindless television because all I can think about is Asher. Another couple is waiting in the chairs opposite me with their hands clasped together. They both look nervous, and I wonder who they're waiting for.

I keep my eyes on the door, hoping that Asher or his father will walk through it so we can all put this behind us. If I don't see him soon, I'm going to go crazy. The door swings open, and a nurse dressed in blue scrubs walks through it. I hold my breath, praying for her to come talk to me, but she breezes past and heads to the emergency room.

"Miss Alexander," the receptionist calls. I immediately jump up from my chair and take the two steps to her desk. "You can go in. He's in room 112 down that hall."

I don't waste any time thanking her as I take off down the long hallway. When I reach the door, I peek through the small window and see Asher's dad with his back to me. He's looking down at his son whose head is turned in the opposite direction. Asher looks so tired and sad; I want to burst into the room and throw my arms around him, but I carefully open the door so that I don't disturb anything that's going on between them.

"You tell her or I will," Daniel demands right as the door closes.

Asher's eyes shoot to me, and his father spins around. "I'm sorry, I didn't mean to interrupt. Do you want me to wait outside?" I ask, nervously. The hospital alone is enough to terrify me, but when it's mixed with the tension in this room, it's hard to stomach.

"No, I was just getting ready to leave. I need to go take care of a few things at home, and then I'll be back," Daniel says, turning back toward his son. "I think Asher has something he needs to talk to you about anyway."

Asher shakes his head in disapproval and turns to face the lone window in the room. Daniel stops next to me and pats my shoulder before exiting the room. I have an empty feeling in my stomach as I watch Asher. I still have no idea why he's here, but it's becoming apparent that whatever it is, it's big.

I gradually move closer to the bed, grabbing his hand in mine as soon as it's within reach. "How are you doing?" I ask, stroking the back of his hand with my thumb.

He doesn't say anything. He doesn't turn to me. He doesn't hold my hand tighter in his. I hold my breath, waiting for a little piece of anything from him so that I can start to put the puzzle together and stop my stomach from sinking any further into the pit. I want him to fall into me and let me make it all better. He's done it for me over and over again.

He shakes his head, closing his eyes tightly before focusing them on me again. "You mean everything to me," he finally replies. Just looking at him makes my eyes well up with tears. I've seen pain time and time again, but Asher's living in agony. "Please don't cry," he says, running his thumb along my cheek.

"You're scaring me. What's wrong?" I ask, wiping a couple tears from my cheeks. He ignores my question and turns his head to look out the window once again. "Will you please just talk to me?"

"I can't—"

"Asher, whatever it is, please just tell me," I plead, wrapping his hand in mine again.

He stays silent, shaking his head back and forth as tears pool in his eyes. He looks so broken . . . beautiful, yet broken. The more I press him, the more I see it. Have I been too buried in my own problems to see his?

"Please," I plead again.

"I have cancer," he blurts.

I swallow, trying to turn his words into something else. I couldn't have heard him right. This can't be happening. Not now, not to him.

"You what?"

He faces me and I can see the tears falling from his eyes. I hate seeing him like this. I absolutely hate it. "I'm dying, Kate. I have cancer."

"You're joking, right? Please tell me you're playing a joke on me." I hear myself asking through the ringing in my ears.

He shakes his head, and I take a couple steps back. My whole body trembles uncontrollably as my emotions spill over. I must be standing in the middle of someone else's life . . . this must be a nightmare. I can't lose him.

"No . . . no . . . no . . . this can't be happening," I sob, feeling my knees getting weaker and weaker.

"Don't cry. Watching you is tearing me apart. I didn't mean to hurt you," he cries, reaching for my hand. "I'm so sorry. I know I should have told you sooner."

I fall forward, letting my elbows rest on the bed as my hands tangle in my hair.

I can't move.

I can't think.

I can't breathe.

When I finally feel like I can speak again, I don't know what to say. What are you supposed to say to someone who just told you they're dying? There aren't any words that will make it better. I stare at his sad eyes as I play his words over and over in my head.

I stand up next to the bed again and lightly brush my trembling hand against his cheek. This time he leans into me instead of looking away. "They have treatments and medicines you can try, right?"

He swallows. "There's nothing more they can do for me. I have leukemia and I've tried everything they've suggested, but nothing seems to work."

"You can at least try, can't you? Did you get a second opinion? There has to be something they can do."

"I've tried everything, Kate. All they do is make me sick and prolong the inevitable. I went into the city yesterday to try a new drug and look what it did to me. I don't want to live like this . . ."

"But what if one of those treatments could cure you? I need you, Asher," I cry, placing my palms on the edge of his hospital bed to hold myself up.

"Do you think I want to leave you? I want to live the life I have left . . . with you. I don't want to spend it here." He rests his hand on top of mine and I look up to see tears streaming down his face.

"How long have you known?"

He glances to the window and then back to me. "Almost a year," he says hesitantly.

If he said anything after that, I didn't hear it. I thought I knew what pain was, but nothing has ever felt like this. This is excruciating, mind-numbing, heart-aching type of torture. It vibrates through my body, taking anger and confusion right along with it.

He's known for almost a year, and I only met him a few months ago. He let me fall for him when he knew he was dying. He let me fall for him when he knew he wasn't going to be my forever. Why would he do that? Why would he let me fall in love with him if he knew he would be leaving me soon?

"Why didn't you tell me?" I cry, placing my hand over my mouth.

"What did you want me to say? Hi, my name is Asher and I have cancer. I didn't want you to feel sorry for me. Then I got to know you, and I just couldn't bring myself to tell you. I didn't want to see you looking at me like you are right now," he says, his voice trailing off to hide the emotion that seems to be bubbling up inside of him.

I'm so lost right now. I'm torn between yelling at him and comforting him. I hate this! Once again my world has been flipped upside down, and this time there's nothing I can do to fix it.

I feel like I'm going to be sick. This is too much for me right now. It's selfish for me to be thinking about myself, but I can't help it. Asher knew, and he'd kept it from me. I run to the door and leave the room without saying a word. I can't look back. I just can't. I stop the first nurse I see by stepping toward her as she walks down the hall.

"Where's the bathroom?" I ask, all but hyperventilating.

"Go to the end of the hall and take a right."

I cover my mouth and try navigating the halls through my blurry eyes. "Are you okay?" I hear a nurse ask, but I keep moving until I'm shut inside the bathroom and the door is locked behind me. I crouch down in front of the toilet, emptying my stomach over and over again. Maybe this is just a bad dream that I'll wake up from soon. I can't lose him. I just can't. I'm scared of what life will be like without him.

When I'm done, I scoot so that my back is against the wall and fold my knees into my chest. There's an insistent squeeze compressing my heart. My head hurts so bad that it's blinding me.

Cancer. Asher has cancer. I never wanted to hear anyone I love say that word. And Asher . . . he's too young. He has so much left to accomplish, but he's not going to get the chance. Maybe if I pray for a miracle one will come. Maybe if I close my eyes this will all be over.

It's the worst type of nightmare.

The initial shock is starting to wear off, and I know Asher's going to need me. He's been there for me over and over again, helping me escape a lot of my fears. Cancer is a scary thing to face, but death . . . I can't even imagine.

I wipe my eyes and stand up, bracing myself against the wall. I use a long piece of toilet paper to wipe around my eyes, and then rinse my mouth out with water from the faucet. When I look at my reflection in the mirror, all I see is the sad, lost girl I've suddenly become again. I thought I had my life all figured out until just a few minutes ago when the words Asher and dying were used in the same sentence. I spent the past few months building this tower out of blocks only to have cancer come and knock it down.

Why?

Why Asher?

I can't believe this is happening. Not now. Not to him.

I blot around my mouth with a paper towel and pull the door open. I have no idea how long I was in there, and I feel like a zombie as I walk back to Asher's room. Someone says something to me, but I ignore them. I just want to get back to him; feel his skin on my skin and his heart beating against my palm.

I place my hand on the door handle and take a few deep breaths before opening the door to Asher's room. I'm trying hard not to cry, but when I open the door I can't control it. He's facing the window with tears glistening on the sides of his cheeks. I can't get a hold of myself, not that I even want to try at this point. My anger has all been replaced with heartache, which is the most painful emotion to deal with.

I clasp his right hand between my hands and stare down at the guy who I thought would be my forever. Now I know that he might not even get a chance at forever, and that's the biggest lump I've ever had to swallow.

He wipes his tears before looking up at me. He cringes as he takes in my red splotchy face. "Please don't cry. I hate seeing you cry."

"Is it okay if I touch you?" I ask, trying to see where all the tubes are connected. I don't know why but I need to touch him, to make sure he still exists the way I remember him.

"Everything hurts, but you're the only one who can make it better," he says, moving to the side of the bed and patting the space beside him. "Don't be scared. The only place I have anything is my arm." He lifts it up, showing me the IV that's inserted in the top of his hand.

I cautiously sit on the edge of the bed, lifting one leg at a time and moving back to rest my head next to his on the pillow. I'm reluctant to get too close, but there isn't one thing on this planet that could keep me away from him right now.

"Why did they admit you today?" I ask. I didn't think about it before, but he's been sick for months. Why are they just putting him in the hospital now?

"I was dehydrated. They want me here for twenty-four hours of observation and to get some fluids back into my system. I have a morphine supply. How can I go wrong with that?" I lift my head and glare at him; I hate that he's trying to make a joke out of it. There isn't anything about this whole situation that makes me want to smile, let alone laugh.

"Does it hurt?" I ask, skimming my fingertips over his gown covered chest and stomach.

"It's been hurting. It hurt way before I even knew I was sick," he states. There's an ache in my throat as I listen to him. He's been dealing with this the whole time he was walking me through my problems. I must have seemed so selfish because I didn't even notice that anything was wrong with him.

"I wish you would have told me sooner."

He pulls me closer with his free arm and kisses the top of my head. "This is my punishment for letting Megan die. Some days, I feel like I deserve it."

I snap my head up and look down at his somber eyes. "Listen to me," I demand, holding his cheeks in my hands. "You didn't let Megan die. She made a choice that night too, Asher, and you have to let it go."

He pinches his eyes closed and shakes his head the best he can with his face cradled in my hands. "You don't deserve this. Nobody ever deserves this. Do you hear me?" I ask, trying to bury my frustration.

"If it's not my fault, then whose fault is it? There's a reason for everything, and I'm the reason she's not at college right now," he cries. I want to wipe away all his tears and guilt. He's an amazing man who shouldn't have to carry this around with him.

"You need to stop blaming yourself. It will eat you up inside, and it won't bring her back."

"You don't think I know that? It doesn't make it any easier, though," he says, looking up at the ceiling.

"Asher, you saved me. Every day I've been with you, you've shown me a new piece of myself that I thought I lost. You can't forget that," I beg, moving my face closer to his.

"You're stronger than you think," he says, pulling my forehead down to his.

"It's because of you," I whisper.

He's having trouble keeping his eyes open and soon, I hear his breathing even out, and feel the steady rise and fall of his chest.

I try to sleep, but I can't. I don't want to waste a single second with him. They say everything happens for a reason. I don't see any reason for this. I don't want to think about what happens when he's gone. I grip his gown in my fist and bury my nose close to his neck, trying to smell him through the bleached out hospital scent.

I can't.

That's all it takes for the tears to prick my eyes again.

When Asher's father came back to the hospital that night I learned about the cancer, Asher was still sleeping. I had a few questions I don't feel comfortable asking Asher, so I pulled a small notebook and pen out of my purse and quickly jotted down the question that was bothering me the most.

How much longer does he have?

I passed it to Daniel and watched as his eyes closed tight after reading it. When he opened them again, he looked at me with one of the saddest sets of eyes I'd ever seen. He took the pen from my hand and jotted something down before handing it back to me.

Not 100% sure. Probably a few weeks. The cancer has replaced the normal blood cells making him very weak

I stared at his handwriting, reading the message over and over again. For what reason, I don't know. I didn't want to believe it, but the more I read it, the more I realized that I had no other choice.

I know there is always hope, but after the last few days I'm not that optimistic. They let him come home late the next day, but he is so weak that we've spent the last two days lying in his bed, alternating between sleeping and watching movies. Neither of us has mentioned anything about his sickness, or what is going to happen in the future. It's nice to pretend for a while.

I've talked to my boss about having a few weeks off, and he groaned until I told him why. Not only do I want to spend time with Asher, but if I went to work, I probably wouldn't be very useful. There are too many things going through my head.

This morning when I woke up in Asher's bed, he wasn't beside me. I start to panic because he rarely ever gets out of bed without a little assistance from me or his dad. I check the bathroom first, but it's dark and the door is wide open. I hear music coming from the front of the house, and as I round the corner I see Asher sitting with the guitar on his lap. I remember all the times he has played for me and it brings tears to my eyes. I never want to give this up. His voice is soothing and beautiful . . . I can't imagine a day when I don't hear it.

He notices me and immediately stops playing.

"Don't stop for me, I love when you play."

"Did I wake you?" he asks, setting his guitar down against the couch.

"No, you weren't there when I woke up, so I came looking for you," I reply, sitting down next to him. I lace my fingers with his and rest my head against his shoulder.

"Do you want to do something today? I don't think I can spend another day lying in that bed." He wraps his arm behind my back and pulls me close. His arms aren't quite as strong as they used to be because he has lost so much weight and spent most of his days stuck in bed.

"What do you want to do?" I ask, resting my head against his shoulder.

"Dance with me," he whispers, brushing his fingers through my hair.

"Here?" I ask, lifting my head to face him. He looks very serious.

"It's something we've never had the chance to do together and all I can think about is doing everything with you." For the first time in a few days, I'm reminded that we may not have much time left together. There are so many things Asher will never get to experience, and I feel like I've been punched in the stomach every time I think about it. There are bad people in this world that get to live a whole life and Asher, a man filled with so much good, is having his cut far too short. Life just doesn't make sense; it's maddening. Everyone should get to experience a life filled with love, marriage and kids. Everyone should get to choose a career and live out their dream.

"I would do anything you ask me to right now. Anything," I say, trying to hold back the tears that threaten to fall. This will probably be the only time I ever get to dance with Asher Hunt. I can't decide if it's better to know that or not.

He slowly stands, reaching out for my hand. "Kate, may I have this dance?"

I place my hand in his, and he leads me back into his bedroom, stopping to turn on his iPod. I take several cleansing breaths, trying to calm the nervous energy that's flowing through my body.

Cross That Line by Joshua Radin starts to play as Asher spins around to face me. He has a soft expression on his face when he reaches his hand to touch my face and skims his thumb over my cheekbone. I tilt my head to kiss the palm of his hand, then close my eyes and lose myself in the soft feel of his fingertips as they lightly skim my jawline. When he wraps his arms around my lower back, it feels like the most natural thing in the world as we sway back and forth. I follow his lead and wrap my arms around his neck, resting my cheek against his chest.

My body is completely in tune to Asher's as I listen to the beautiful lyrics sink into my soul. This has to be one of the single most memorable moments of my life. It's serene. It's as if we're the only two people on the planet and nothing can hurt us. It's like the whole world is spinning in slow motion.

When I was a little girl, I believed in fairy tales and one of the dreams I had was someday dancing alongside my prince. Asher's that guy for me. He's my dream and my wish come true. He's my prince.

"I love this song."

"It's one of my favorites," he admits, tightening his grip on me a little more.

The song switches to *18th Floor Balcony* by Blue October, and I lift my head to look in his eyes. There's so much sadness, adoration and pain within them. I want to kiss it all away, but this illness is one thing that love can't fix.

"What are you thinking right now?" I ask.

He cups my face in his hands. "That I wish we could freeze time and stay in this moment forever. You?"

"I was thinking that this is the best first dance I've ever had."

"You mean everything in this world to me. You know that right?" he says softly against my lips.

I nod, closing the little bit of distance between us to press my lips to his. I let them linger there, pressed as tightly to his as I can manage. When I break away, I rest my forehead against his and continue to dance until the song ends. It was probably the best dance I've ever shared, but it was probably our last too.

Chapter 21

THE LAST FEW WEEKS I've thought a lot about what my life will be like without Asher around. It's a mirror that I never want to have to look into . . . I'm not ready to lose him. It's not something I even want to contemplate, so how am I going to deal with the reality of it all? I feel like I'm in a constant state of sadness, which isn't how I want to remember the time we have left together.

The worst part is that I think Asher senses it. I've thought a lot about what I'd want right now if the roles were reversed and it's almost impossible to get a clear picture. That picture should never even be painted for someone so young. I'm struggling to keep a positive outlook, but I don't want his last days to be all about what's going to happen; I want it to be about today. I think we both need that.

It's time for us to make memories worth keeping.

We spend time putting up the Christmas tree since the holiday is a week from tomorrow. Asher seems to be getting weaker by the day, so he sits on the floor and hands me ornaments. I'm just happy to spend time with him.

"I hate that you have to do it all yourself," he says sadly, handing me a bright red glass ornament.

I grab it from him and hang it toward the top of the tree. "All that matters to me is that we're together. This is actually the best Christmas I've had in a long time. I can't remember the last time my mom and I even took the time to put up the tree and decorate it." I smile, standing back to admire it.

"This has been the best Christmas for me too . . . even with everything that's happening," he says, returning my smile.

We end our decorating project by putting popcorn on a string to wrap around the tree. It's something my mom and I always did when I was a kid because we didn't have money to go buy all the fancy decorations. I remember doing that more than I remember any gift I received.

And I want to have that memory with Asher.

After we're finished, we watch one of his favorite comedies on Netflix, laughing harder than either of us has in weeks. Laughter really is the best medicine; it makes us both forget the things that have been bringing us down; at least temporarily.

Now, we're both lying in bed listening to Asher's iPod playing softly through the speakers. The small lamp on his bedside table illuminates the room with a soft orange light. We're just talking, but I like spending every second I'm not sleeping, looking at him. I want to engrave everything about him into my mind: the feel of his lips, the unique shade of his eyes, and the silky texture of his hair when it slips between my fingers. I'm scared that one day I'll wake up and I won't be able to remember him.

"Where do you think we would be five years from now?" he asks, slipping his hand under my shirt to run his fingers over my bare stomach.

I jerk my head back on the pillow to get a better look at him. He looks completely serious, but I'm not sure I want to play this game. "What?"

"Just for tonight, I want to pretend that we're a normal couple making plans for our future. That's what normal couples do isn't it?" he asks, letting a small smile touch his lips.

"Asher, I don't—"

"Please, just help me forget for a little while," he pleads, moving his face closer to mine. I used to play house all the time when I was younger, but this is different. Whatever we envision can never be. But if this is what he needs right now, I'll give it to him. I'll walk over burning coals to feel his heart beat against my palm for the rest of my life.

Unless there's a miracle on the horizon, all I'm going to have five years from now is the memory of our game of pretend. I'll have memories of the one Christmas we shared. There will always be the trip to the zoo, the time we went fishing, the night we sat next to the fire and the first time we made love, but I won't get to relive them . . . not with Asher.

"Okay." I bite my lip and let myself be carried away in the dream. "I think we'd be living somewhere far from here. I know you'd get tired of this place after a while, and I'm only here because I'm scared to start over. I'm not sure where we'd go, though. Where would you want to live?" I ask, trying to get lost in the moment.

"Hmmm," he says, glancing toward the ceiling. "I've always wanted to live in Colorado. We could hike, fish, and go rafting. Maybe we could get a small house in one of the small mountain communities. It would be like Carrington, but with so much more to do."

I lay my head on his shoulder, resting my hand over his heart. "That sounds nice. What would you be doing?"

"Well, besides reminding my girl every day that she's the most beautiful, person in the world, I would probably finish my engineering degree and get a job in the field. What about you?" he asks, resting his arm on my shoulders.

"I don't know." I shrug. "Maybe I'd go to law school, or I've even thought it would be nice to own a little coffee shop somewhere. Your little Colorado town sounds like the perfect place," I continue, gripping the front of his t-shirt in my hand. Pretending isn't as easy as I thought, but at least I can see a future now. I didn't care about tomorrow much less five years from now . . . until I met Asher.

"How about ten years?" he asks, running his fingers up and down my arm.

"I've thought about having kids, but I'm not sure yet. It's too early to tell. I know I'd at least have a dog."

"I want kids. I didn't really have my dad growing up, so I want to be that for someone," he says softly. My stomach twists itself up into a knot. There are so many things that people take for granted that the beautiful man in front of me will never get to do . . . simple things that everyone should get the chance to experience.

"I just want to be happy. It doesn't matter if it's just you and me, or if we have five kids. I want to feel at peace with where I am," I reply. My eyes start to well up with tears as I picture Asher and me sitting on our front porch, drinking coffee while we watch our kids play. That vision, when done with a man like Asher, is every girl's dream.

He pulls back and cups my chin, lifting my eyes to meet his. "I need you to promise me something." I nod, choking back tears before he continues. "When I'm gone, I need you to move on. Just because I won't be here—" he stops, squeezing his eyes shut and choking back the hurricane of emotion that he wears all over his face. "I need to know that you can do these things without me. You can't let your life end when mine does," he says, his voice cracking a little more with every word.

"Asher—"

He covers my mouth with his finger. "I need to know that you'll do everything you just told me you wanted to do and more. And, I don't want you to do it for me. I need you to do it for you."

214

Right now, I can't even think about loving another man in this way. How can I find someone better when I've already had the best? Knowing that Asher is sick, and that I can't save him when he needs me the most is eating me up inside. It's coursing through my body like acid. Who is going to want me when I feel so broken and damaged?

I'm getting the chance at a future, and I can't let it be wasted. Not when Asher is struggling for every passing minute.

"I promise," I whisper.

"There's one more thing I'd make sure to be doing five or ten years from now. I'd slowly make love to you every single night and after I was done, I'd hold you until you drifted to sleep. And when the sun came up, I'd make sure to do it all over again because that's what a girl like you deserves . . . a man who adores you. All of you."

"I'd never want you to stop making love to me," I whisper, choking back my tears.

"I would do this first." He leans over me, kissing down the side of my neck. Familiar chills race down my back whenever he touches me there. Wrapping my hand around the back of his head, I let his long, soft hair fall between my fingers.

He pulls back, touching his warm lips to mine and lightly running his tongue across the light arch. "But I'd always come back to these," he says against my lips.

I never ever want to let him go. If I could, I'd freeze this moment with his body close to mine, lips brushing against each other like silk and the sexy tone of his voice playing in my ears. This is exactly what I'd put in my memory box.

"I need to be close to you," he growls, kissing the tip of my nose. "I'm going to make love to you." My voice won't let me respond as he rolls me onto my back and rests his body on top of mine. Not long ago this position would have scared me straight out of this room, but when Asher does it, I crave it. He has a way of touching me that eases away the trepidation, filling my body with passion instead. I arch my back, allowing him to pull my t-shirt up to expose my stomach. He inches his hand from my hipbone to my breasts, then follows close behind it with his mouth.

We haven't done anything like this since the morning at the lake house. Asher's been too weak, and even though I'd do anything to have that with him again, I didn't want to push him. I've been holding onto that one night, and being able to recreate it would mean everything, but knowing this could be the last time hurts my heart.

"Come here . . . these clothes are in my way," he says, pulling me up by my arms and lifting my shirt over my head, quickly unclasping my bra. He runs his palms over my nipples, causing my breathing to quicken. I had resigned to the fact that I'd never feel him inside of me again, but it's about to happen, and I couldn't be more eager. Cupping my face in his hands, he kisses me like I've never been kissed. He starts gentle, and then his lips press harder into mine, almost like he can't get close enough. The contact is warm before it smolders but he gradually slows it down, kissing the corners of my mouth. It's loving, passionate, and intense . . . it's everything a kiss should be.

It's everything Asher is.

I'll always remember the look on his face when his eyes meet mine. There is just enough light in the room to give me a glimpse into what he's feeling, and all the emotions he's experiencing melt into my heart. Seeing him suffer—the person who I owe everything to—is worst type of pain I've ever experienced. He's drowning, and there's absolutely nothing I can do to save him.

"You're so fucking perfect. Don't let anyone make you feel like anything less," he whispers, pressing his lips to the tip of my chin. His hands cup my backside, leaving not a single inch between our bodies as his mouth skims my throat. I want to feel him moving inside me, but I need this too. I want to feel him everywhere.

He slips his fingers into the waistband of my pants and slides them down my legs without removing his mouth from my skin. His clothes soon follow, leaving nothing between us. I wrap my legs tight around his waist and grip his hair in my hands as his tongue traces my left nipple then my right, sending a warm tingle to my core and proving once again that Asher is my sun.

When I feel him at my entrance, I close my eyes, waiting for that one moment when the fireworks explode and my body lights up. I feel his warm hand cradle my cheek as his thumb caresses my lips. "Look at me, Kate," he quietly demands.

I open my eyes and see the pain etched all over his face. I wish I had something magical to wash it all away. "Are you okay?" I ask, running my fingers across his strong jaw.

"No," he whispers, leaning down to place a feather-like kiss to my lips. "I shouldn't ever have to let you go."

Tears form in my eyes making it harder to keep my focus on him. This is so incredibly unfair, I think as I try to swallow the pain at the back of my throat. "You don't have to. No matter if we're together or apart, I'm always with you. I'm alive because of you," I cry, placing my palm to his chest.

"You don't live because of me. You live because you let me love you. You made the choice to breathe all on your own . . . I just helped you find the strength to inhale."

"What did you just say?" I ask, taking a calming breath.

"You don't live because of me."

"No, before that," I say, wrapping my hands behind his neck.

"I love you," he whispers. He slowly guides himself into me, never taking his eyes away from mine. "I was prepared to leave this Earth until I met you, and now I don't want to be anywhere but here with you. I love you so damn much, Kate."

"I love you too," I whisper, feeling my heart clench tightly in my chest.

He pulls out slowly before gliding into me again. A marriage of emotions rips through my body as we move together. I feel like Asher is burning a never-ending scar inside of me, and my heart is spiraling into a deep, dark abyss. This is the single most beautiful, painful experience I've ever had.

Our bodies connect while he kisses along my jawline and runs his hands along the back of my thighs. He's the only lover I've ever had and each one after will only be compared to him.

My fingers touch every part of him that can be reached. I memorize all of the ridges of his spine, the muscle definition in his arms, the stubble along his jaw, but they always end up tangled in his hair.

Whenever you lose someone you love, you have those lingering regrets. You wish you could hug them or kiss them or talk to them . . . I don't want those regrets. I want to do everything with him tonight, no matter how much it hurts me inside because this may be my last chance.

The idea of no tomorrow only makes me grip his hair tighter, never wanting to let go.

"I love it when you do that." His voice shakes, giving me a small window into what he's feeling. He rests his hands along the top of my head and grazes my lips with his before raining kisses along my cheeks and nose. He doesn't say much about what he's going through, but it's got to be tearing him into pieces. How could it not?

His motions slow as his forehead rests on mine. When his chest suddenly vibrates against my chest, and his warm tears fall on my face, it literally hurts to breathe. Maybe this is too much.

"Please don't cry," I beg, cradling his head in my hands. I feel like such a hypocrite because my own tears are now mixing with his.

"This just feels like goodbye, and I'm not ready. I'm not fucking ready," he says, pinching his eyes closed. He's still buried deep inside of me, but our bodies remain still.

I want to help him but I don't know how.

I want to take his pain away, but I can't.

"It's not goodbye. This is what matters. Right here. Right now," I reply, brushing my thumbs across the tears.

"I love you . . . I'm not ready . . . I'm not ready to be without you."

His words are choking me so tight that it's impossible to get oxygen into my lungs. Cancer is holding us both hostages.

"You'll never be without me because you'll always be right here," I say, clutching my chest. "Always," I say softly, pressing against his chest to roll him onto his back. I straddle his hips, slowly taking all of him inside me again.

"You're here with me. Always. Whenever I close my eyes, all I see is you," I whisper, pressing a light kiss to his eyelids.

"When my heart beats, it's beating because of you. Even if you're not touching me, I'll feel you," I cry, trailing kisses across his chest.

"But right now, we're both here, in this bed," I whisper. We're touching, breathing and feeling. I want to stay here, in this moment, and pretend that nothing else matters because right now, when I feel him inside of me, nothing else does.

He nods, eyeing me carefully as I lift myself up slowly then slide back down, not taking a single second of this experience for granted. I repeat the motion several times as his hands circle my breasts. My eyes stare into his blues, neither of us blinking as the pressure builds in my core, lighting a smoldering fire inside of me.

I leave everything else behind, and focus solely on the life that's in front of me. From the soft expression on his face, and the affectionate feel of his fingers along my stomach and thighs, I know he's doing the same.

When my body reaches its peak right as Asher's does, and it's like I'm floating on the highest cloud. Nothing can reach me . . . nothing can reach us. But then the full impact of this moment hits me, my warm tears now dampening his chest.

"I'm so sorry." He sits up, wrapping his arms around my waist.

"For what?"

"For letting you fall in love with me when I knew this would happen," he mumbles, kissing the spot between my breasts.

I use my hands to pull his face up to mine. "I'll never regret you."

He kisses me gently, softly, sweetly . . . whispering my name over and over.

"You're everything to me," he whispers against my lips.

I wrap my arms around his neck, holding him like I'll never have to let him go.

Chapter 22

Asher

WHEN I WAS IN HIGH SCHOOL and college, I thought I had all the time in the world. I didn't care too much about what I did or who it would affect. I was being reckless until one bad decision changed everything.

After Megan died, I tried to move on, but I always felt like what happened to her was somehow my fault. And when the doctor announced that I had cancer, I tuned out everything he said after that. I was in shock.

Then it hit me.

Maybe I deserved this.

This was my punishment for not being there when my friend needed me. I'm the reason she's not here anymore. And I had accepted that until I fell hard for Kate. I questioned myself every single time I walked into that diner, but something was pulling me toward her and I couldn't fight it.

Now as I lie here holding her in my arms, I'm glad she's with me, but pissed off she's going to have to spend any part of her life without me . . . and soon. This isn't going to be fair to her, but cancer is the one thing in my life I have no fucking control over.

"Are you awake?" Kate asks, resting her chin on my chest.

I run my hand up her back until I feel her soft hair between my fingers. "I've been up for a while. I was just about to take my meds."

"Are you feeling okay? Do you need me to call the doctor?" she asks, shooting up to a sitting position.

"I'm okay," I lie, carefully moving to sit up next to her.

"Are you sure? Do you want some water or anything?"

I nuzzle my nose against her cheek, moving down to kiss the delicate spot below her ear. "No, just stay here with me," I whisper against her neck.

"I'm not going anywhere," she says, leaning into me so that her hair falls against my shoulder. Continuing to kiss down her neck, I breathe in the sweet smell of her skin. I'd give anything to remember that smell . . . I never realized how much there is to love about a person until I met Kate.

I slowly brush the hair away from her shoulder to give myself access to her collarbone and shower her soft skin with more affection. The first time I saw her, I was drawn to the unique color of her hair and the way it contrasted with her eyes. Then after staring into those gorgeous emerald green eyes, I realized that there was something different about this girl. I had to know her, whether I was here for two more weeks or two years . . . somehow I knew it would be worth it.

I lightly run my tongue along the center of her neck, stopping to kiss her chin and each corner of her lips. "I love you," I whisper, finally capturing her lips.

A sharp pain suddenly rips through my body, causing me to lean forward and bury my head between my knees.

"Asher! Are you okay? Should I call someone?" Kate asks in a panic, putting her hand on my shoulder.

I shake my head, trying my best to speak through the overwhelmingly excruciating pain. "Just water . . . and a pain pill."

"I'll be right back," she says, hurrying out of the room. The time I have left shouldn't have to be overshadowed with all of this misery. I should be able to sit in bed with my girl and do the things that normal couples do.

But I can't.

Cancer is a motherfucking bitch . . . and there's no cure for the kind that's growing inside me every day.

Why has my life finally become so perfect when all I have left is a date with my maker? Kate will be the last person I'll ever kiss. She'll be the last woman I'll ever make love to . . . the only woman I'll make love to. She gives me purpose in a world that I didn't think had one for me. She gives me the chance at a life I never thought I would have, even if it has to end way before it should.

"Here you go," she says softly as she enters the room again.

"Thanks." I take two pills from her hands and pop them in my mouth. I follow it with a few sips of water and lay my head back on the pillow.

"Better?" she asks, lying beside me.

"It will be," I reply honestly, splaying my hand on her stomach.

Sometimes my body hurts so bad that I just want to get all of this over with, but then I take one look into Kate's eyes and I regain my will to live. I'd give anything to have forever with her.

Her forever . . . not mine.

"Do you need me to get you anything else?" she asks, placing her hesitant hand on my chest.

"I'm okay; let's just stay right where we are." Lying here with her feels good. Besides, I don't have the energy to do anything else.

Last night I wanted to make love to her. It's hard to look at her every day and feel this connection but not be as close to her as I can be. I've had sex with lots of girls, but she's different. She's the one.

Today, I'm paying for it. I knew I didn't have the physical or emotional strength to be with her last night, but I did it anyway. She's my addiction. I can't give her up.

"Do you want me to put a movie in?"

"Let's stay like this a little while longer," I whisper.

"Okay, let's talk then. Who was your first girlfriend?" she asks, moving her head closer to mine.

I laugh just thinking about it. "Her name was Lana Richards. I was fourteen, and she was fifteen."

"How long did it last?"

"Maybe two weeks." I smile, thinking about the day she threw her French fries at my head in the cafeteria.

"It must've been pretty serious," Kate laughs, tracing small circles on my bare chest.

"All the names she called me that day were definitely serious. What about you? Who was your first boyfriend?"

The smile falls from her beautiful face, leaving the sad expression I used to see so often when I first met her. "I never had one," she whispers, freezing her fingers in place. "You're my first."

My chest aches hearing her admit that. She lost so much time because of one asshole, and I'd do just about anything to give those years back to her. I know I can't, but at least I can give her hope for a future.

Placing my finger under her chin, I bring her green eyes back to mine. "I'm glad I got to be your first, but I want you to promise me that I won't be your last."

"Asher—"

"Don't," I say, placing my finger over her lips. "I don't want you to argue with me over this one. I need to know that you'll be all right. I need to know that you're happy."

"I can't even think about that now. Don't you get that? I love you so freaking much . . . I can't see past you, Asher," she says, closing her eyes. "I can't."

"You're special, Kate. Someone is going to see it just like I do," I say softly, running my thumb across her cheekbone. "I don't want to leave until I know you can live without me. And when I say live, I mean smiling. I just want you to be happy."

"Stop. Please, just stop," she mumbles, covering her face with her hands.

Using the little bit of strength I have left, I pull her toward me and hold her close to my chest. I hate seeing her like this, knowing that I've caused it. No one should ever have to talk to their girlfriend about this shit. It hurts so fucking much, but I push through it because I know she needs my strength.

I don't want her to feel guilty. I don't want her to think her life ends after me. She did that once and lost so much because of it.

"I'm sorry. Not because of what I said, but because I had to say it," I say, combing my fingers through her hair.

"Can we talk about something else? Please."

I use the hand resting behind hers to pull her closer to me, feeling her warm breath mix with mine. "Loving you is easy, but it makes this so much harder."

Her warm lips graze mine over and over again. "I love you."

I hold her close to my chest, and I feel the weight of my eyelids getting heavier and heavier. I don't want to close my eyes. I hate falling asleep because I'm missing so much of the time I have left with this girl, but control is something I have very little of now.

It's preparing me for what's to come.

I want her to be okay . . . it's what I pray for every time I feel myself drifting. I pray to wake up and see her beautiful face one more time. I pray for a miracle, but the more I think about it, the more I realize I was already given one.

Kate.

Chapter 23

THE FIRST THING THAT CATCHES my eye as I pull down my street is Beau's old beat-up Chevy. I haven't spoken to him since I learned Asher's sick. Not because I don't want to but because I haven't had time for anyone else.

Asher and I have been spending every moment together, but once in a while when he's sleeping, I leave to run a few errands. I hate every minute of it the time we spend apart. I'm always afraid I'm going to miss one of the rare moments he's awake, or that he'll take a turn for the worse and I won't be there for him.

As I stop in my driveway, I remember the relief I used to feel every time I saw Beau was home. I feel a little bit of it right now. I'm half expecting him to come out the front door like he used to but he doesn't.

Those days are gone.

When I walk into my house, it's overwhelmingly quiet. My mom's spot at the kitchen table is empty, and the television is off.

I quickly throw a few items into my duffle bag, not paying any attention to whether they match. I take a couple minutes to leave my mom a note apologizing for all the dirty clothes I left in the laundry room and head back out the door.

The cold air hits my face as I run down my steps toward my car. With any luck, it'll still be warmed up from the drive over here.

"Kate!" I hear a familiar voice yell from behind me.

I halt in place, hesitant to turn around and face him.

"Kate!" This time, I can tell he's closer.

Taking a deep breath, I turn and look at the man I didn't even know I missed so much until this moment. "Hey, what are you doing home?"

"Winter break," he replies, running his fingers through his hair, "I was hoping I'd see you."

"I'm sorry I can't stick around. I have a lot going on right now," I say, nervously adjusting the strap on my bag.

Beau closes the space between us and lifts the heavy bag from my shoulder, carefully sliding it down my arm and placing it over his own shoulder. "I know. Your mom told me about Asher. I . . . don't know what to say. Do you want to talk about it?"

"No," I answer, shaking my head.

He nods, glancing toward the street then back to me. "If you need anything, I'm here for you."

"Thank you. That means a lot," I say, folding my arms across my body to keep warm. "How long are you home for?"

"Until next Sunday. Look, if you have time, we could get a pizza or something before I go back. Just to catch up."

"I'm sorry, but I don't think I'm going to be able to. I don't like to leave him," I answer, digging my shoes into the light dusting of snow on the ground.

"Do you want me to put this in your car?" he asks, lifting the strap of my bag up from his shoulder. "I have something in my house for you. I'll just give it to you now."

Before I even have time to reply, he opens the back door of my car and throws the bag in then opens the driver's door and starts the engine.

"Wait in the car. It's too cold for you to be standing out here," he says as he climbs out and holds the door open for me.

I slide into the seat. I don't have the energy or the time to argue with him. "You didn't have to get me anything. I didn't—"

He shuts my door and quickly disappears into his house. I feel horrible because I didn't buy him a present. I haven't had time to think of anyone but Asher.

I lean forward and grip my steering wheel tight as I watch him step outside with a small rectangular box in his hand. Things aren't as easy between us as they used to be.

He opens the passenger side door and climbs in. "Here. Open it."

I hesitantly grab the package from his hand and run my fingers over the red ribbon before untying it. I rip the paper, revealing a white box. I carefully lift the lid and peel back the thin foam that covers the top.

What it reveals takes my breath away.

"Do you like it?"

I run my fingers along the smooth wood corners and feel tears building in my eyes. "It's beautiful. Where did you get it?"

"I've had it for a while. I have one I keep in my room to remind me of home and I thought you might like it too. You know, to remind you of better days," he says quietly, never taking his eyes off the picture, "It's our spot."

It's a picture of the lake, taken from the spot on the beach where we usually sit and stare out onto the water.

"Thank you," I whisper, trying to hold back my tears.

"Now you can go there whenever you need to," he says, brushing his thumb under my eye, "I didn't mean to make you cry."

"I feel bad that I didn't get you anything."

"Don't worry about it. I know you've been busy."

The way he's looking at me right now makes me want to wrap my arms around him, but I need to go . . . Asher needs me. "I should probably go in case Asher wakes up."

As soon as the words leave my mouth, he turns his head to stare out the window. "Well, call me if you need me," he says, turning back to me. "I miss you, Kate."

I nod, unable to speak as I watch him get out of the car and walk away.

⌒‿‿‿⌒

I wish I could take Asher's place . . . I think it would be easier to die than to live without him. He means so much to me . . . he is the architect of the person I've become these last few months. I don't want to live this life without him. I don't want to spend a single night without him.

I was living in this horrible nightmare, and he gave me reason to dream again. How am I going to dream when he's gone?

Why does God always have to take the best? That's certainly what he's taking from me.

He's taking the best thing that has ever happened to me.

"Do you need any more pain medicine?" I ask, holding his hand in mine. He's had a morphine IV for the last couple of weeks. He's so weak that he's been confined to the bed. There are no more fishing trips. No more trips to the diner.

He nods, closing his eyes again. He's so thin and pale, but what's dimmed the most is the light behind his smile. I miss it.

It's been four weeks since we last made love . . . on the night we planned the future we will never have together. Every day, his spirit fades a little more, right along with his strength. Each day he sleeps a little more than the day before.

Today, he's been asleep all day.

I lie next to him and watch the life being drained from his body. A little bit of his soul is slipping away with it. He's fading away from me, and soon I won't be able to touch him with my hands, or feel his warm skin against mine. I want to savor him. Forever.

"Come lay up here with me," he mumbles, I listen to every word he says because I know the day he says his last words is going to be a knife to my heart.

"Are you sure you're up for that?" I ask, hesitantly. I don't want to hurt him any more than he already hurts.

"You're the only thing that makes me feel alive. Now get up here," he demands, never opening his eyes once.

"Fine, but remember you asked," I reply, kicking my slippers off. I crawl under the warm comforter and snuggle up to his side. His body is always ice cold now, but I have no problem warming him up.

"What's the date today?"

"January 14."

"I want to go outside and look at the stars," he says, wrapping his arm around my back.

"It's twelve degrees outside, Asher," I say, using my pinky to trace circles on his chest.

"Do you think they have stars in heaven?"

"What?"

"Do you think there are stars in heaven?" he pauses, swallowing so hard that I can hear it. "I was just thinking about what it would be like to look up and never see them. It's kind of what connects the world, you know? It doesn't matter if we're here, or halfway across the world . . . we all see stars. Someday soon I'm not going to see them anymore, Kate."

A tear falls from my eye, but I quickly wipe it away with the sleeve of my sweater. I've tried to be so strong for him, but when he says stuff like that it knocks me down like a hurricane.

"Asher—"

"Don't." He tilts my chin up, making me look straight into his eyes. "I don't want you to tell me that there's still hope. I don't want you to tell me that everything will be okay," he says sadly, his eyes filling with tears. "I'm dying. This is me dying."

I pull up on my knees so that my face is only a few inches above his, cradling his cheeks in my hands. "We're both here right now. I don't want to think about what tomorrow might bring, or the next day. This isn't a game of pretend. It's living in the moment, and it's how I want to spend every last hour, minute and second we have left together."

A tear escapes his eye, and I kiss it away. If I could kiss it all away, I would. Cancer is a darkness that is spreading through his body . . . killing him slowly . . . robbing him of light, and all I can do is sit back and watch, praying for the miracle that will probably never come.

He falls asleep not long after. It comes easy for him, but I can't bring myself to do it. I'm afraid I'll miss something if I fall asleep, but most of all I'm afraid that when I wake up, I won't feel his heart beating against my palm. I don't think I'll ever be ready for that moment.

I slowly get out of bed to call my mom and ask her for a favor. She has been really understanding through all of this, never questioning my decision to spend every waking minute with Asher.

A short while later, there's a soft knock on the bedroom door. I carefully climb out from under the covers and slide my slippers back on. I open the door a few inches and see Daniel standing there with his arm resting against the door jam. "Hey, Kate, your mom is in the living room. She says she brought something for you," he announces, stepping back so I can come out of the room.

"Thanks." Asher's dad has been so lost. When I first started staying here, we would all eat dinner together with little bits of conversation here and there. Now, Asher doesn't eat, and the two of them rarely talk. His dad checks on him every morning before work, once after work, and once before he goes to bed. I want to help them mend their relationship before it's too late, but both are too stubborn to make the first move.

My mom stands behind the couch, looking at the old photos of Asher and his father. The distance between the two of them is even more evident in pictures; they end when Asher is really young and pick up just a few months ago when he moved back to Carrington.

"Thanks for doing this for me," I say, pulling her into a hug. It's little things like this that show me how much she cares for me. She would do anything for me.

"It's not a problem. Anything you need, Kate," she replies, squeezing me tight.

"Thank you." I breathe in her perfume and my eyes tear up. Going through this with Asher makes me appreciate the people I have around me, especially my mom. Even through all of our struggles, I know how much she loves me and how much I love her.

"How's Asher doing?" she asks, pulling back to look at me and my tear stained cheeks. Her eyebrows draw close together as she grabs my head in her hands. "Oh, sweetie, I wish I could take all this pain away, for both of you. I love you so much, and seeing you like this breaks my heart."

"I just feel so helpless. I wish I could do more for him," I cry, squeezing my eyes shut.

"You're stronger than you know, Kate. I am so proud to call you my daughter," she says, lightly kissing my cheek.

"I love you, Mom, in case I don't tell you enough."

"I love you, too."

Three words have never been so powerful.

"I should probably get back to Asher before he wakes up. I want to surprise him with that," I say, glancing at the cardboard box on the coffee table.

"Do you want me to stay?" she asks, gently squeezing my upper arm.

I shake my head. "No, I'll be okay."

"Call me if you need anything," she says soothingly, wrapping her arms around me for another hug.

"I will." I walk her to the door, feeling the weight in my chest getting heavier. I want her here with me. She walks down the snowy path, looking back once to give me a heart-warming smile. It's that smile that makes me feel like I'm at home. It's that smile I'm going to need to see a lot more of really soon.

When I walk back into the bedroom, Asher is talking on his cell phone. "I miss you too," he says, sadly into the receiver. "Can you put mom back on?"

I quietly close the door behind me and set the box my mom brought on the dresser. Asher spots me and pats the area next to him on the bed. "Hey, Mom, I just called to see how things were going?" I watch as he nods and closes his eyes. "Mom, please don't cry. I don't like it either, but she can't see me like this."

He shakes his head, pinching his nose between his fingers. "I'm sorry. I just can't." He's silent for a while, focusing his attention out the window. I would do anything to make this better for him. It's hard to watch the person you love fall apart in front of your eyes. "Okay, I'll talk to you later. I love you," he says before tossing the phone on his nightstand. I give him a few minutes of silence to sort through the things that are going through his head before I crawl into bed next to him and wrap my arms around his thin waist.

We both quietly drift off to sleep. When I finally stir, it's dark outside, and Asher's eyes are still closed next to me. I carefully pull my arms from his waist and place my hand over his heart. It's the same way I verify that he's still sleeping every time I allow myself to fall asleep. I roll out of bed to open the box my mom brought over earlier. I'm hoping the item inside will make him happy, even if just for a few minutes.

I pull the turtle shaped figure out of the box and set it on the nightstand before plugging it in. It does exactly what I hoped it would do. Now I just have to wait for him to wake up and see it.

I turn it off and walk out to the kitchen to get something to drink. I'm not surprised to see Daniel sitting at the table staring off into space.

He startles when he hears my feet walking across the hardwood floors. "Hey, how's Asher doing tonight?"

"He's sleeping," I answer, smiling sadly. Sleeping is what makes Asher feel the most comfortable, but I miss doing simple things like talking to him.

"Asher's mom called earlier. She and his sister are coming to visit tomorrow," he says, rubbing his temples with his fingertips. "I know he doesn't want his sister to see him like this, but I think he'll regret it if he doesn't."

I nod. "Do you think we should tell him?"

"No!" he exclaims, shaking his head. "He'll only argue about it. It's not worth it."

"Do you know what time they're getting in?"

"Around lunchtime."

"Okay." I grab a glass out of the cupboard and fill it with water. When I turn around again, Asher's dad has his face buried in his hands. I stand next to him and hesitantly place my hand on his shoulder. "Are you okay?"

"No," he cries, banging his hand against the table. "No parent should have to watch their child die. I'm supposed to be long gone before him, goddammit."

My own eyes start to burn with tears. "It's not fair, Daniel, but we have to focus on the time he has left."

"He was so miserable before he met you. Thank you for being there for him. I think these have been some of the best months of his life, even with the cancer," he admits, sadly. "I haven't always been there for him, but it wasn't because I didn't want to be."

"Maybe you should talk to him. Tell him that you love him."

He closes his eyes tight and shakes his head. "I don't know if he wants to hear it."

"He needs to hear it," I say softly as I watch him open his eyes again.

He nods, showing me the saddest smile I've ever seen.

"I'm going to go see if he's awake," I announce, patting his shoulder.

He rests his hand on mine. "Thank you for everything."

I squeeze his shoulder and walk to Asher's bedroom, anxious to give him his surprise. As I open the door, I see him propped up on his pillow, staring out at the dark night sky. "How was your nap?"

"About the same as the other three I've taken today," he teases, trying to make light out of his situation.

"I have a surprise for you," I smile, slowly walking toward the window.

"And what's that?" he asks, letting the corner of his mouth turn up.

I close the curtain to block out the street lights and head toward the bed. "Close your eyes," I instruct, reaching for the on switch for the turtle. As soon as his eyes close, I turn it on and curl next to him on the bed. "Okay, you can open them now."

His eyes flutter open, and his hand instantly goes to his chest. "How did you do this?" he asks in an emotion-rich voice.

I point to the turtle on the nightstand. "The turtle projects constellations on the ceiling. I wanted you to see the stars."

He pulls me into a hug, holding me as tight as he can manage against his chest. "You're so fucking amazing."

"It's all because of you," I say, feeling his heartbeat against my cheek. I see the big dipper and the small dipper . . . it really is like being outside on a blanket, staring at the night sky.

"Come here." I lift my head and watch the stars glisten in his eyes right before he pulls my lips down to his. He grazes them before kissing each corner of my lips.

It's a beautiful moment that can be written into my fairy tale.

⁓∽

The next morning I have a hard time concentrating on anything because I'm afraid of how Asher will react to seeing his mom and sister. Daniel has left, saying it isn't a good idea for them to be in the same house, which leaves me to pick up the pieces if anything goes wrong.

Just after noon, the doorbell rings. Asher wakes, and glances at the time on his alarm clock. "Are you expecting anyone?"

I hesitate, not sure how to answer that. "Yes, but it's a surprise. Stay here and I'll be right back."

"Kate, why can't you tell me?"

"I'll be right back." Taking several deep breaths, I walk to the front door, leaving my hand on the knob a few seconds before actually turning it. As soon as I do, I'm greeted by two sad smiles.

"You must be Asher's mom and sister," I say, reaching my hand out to greet them.

"Yes, call me Anna," the older blonde responds. "And this is Aubrey." The younger girl looks strikingly like Asher. She's beautiful with blonde wavy hair and the same shade of blue eyes that Asher has.

"I'm Kate. Come in," I say, gesturing them inside.

I want to talk to them and get to know them better, but I can tell they are crawling out of their skin, just waiting to see Asher. "Follow me," I instruct, leading them through the living room and down the hall. Again I hesitate before opening the door. This is either going to be really good or really bad.

Thankfully, Asher's still awake when I push the door open, and the moment he sees them in the doorway, his eyes start tearing up.

"What are they doing here?" he asks looking up at me. Panic runs through me. Maybe this wasn't a good idea. I watch as the room falls completely silent. I take a glance at Anna who has black tears running down her face. This isn't how I imagined this reunion going.

After seconds pass, Aubrey runs to him, resting her upper body on his. Asher seems upset at first, but when he looks at his sister, he melts and wraps his arms around her. Anna stays back for a little bit, but then walks toward her son with her hand over her mouth. She's falling into pieces, and sadly I know exactly how she feels. It does hurt . . . so much.

I stay long enough to see her grab his hand in both of hers before sneaking out to give them their space. I'm glad they're getting this moment, and from the look on Asher's face, I think he's happy to have it too.

I sit quietly on the couch, listening to the tick-tock of the grandfather clock. It feels like hours pass, but it's only because I'm anxious to know what's going on in there. I pray we've made the right decision.

When the bedroom door opens, I stand up and watch the girls leave Asher's room. Anna comes toward me, wrapping her arms around me. "Thank you for letting us come. We all needed that."

"I would do anything to help him."

She lets go of me, resting her hands on my upper arms. "I know, and I'll never be able to thank you enough for that. Take care of yourself, Kate, and please notify me of any changes," she says, reaching into her purse to grab me a business card.

"Thanks, I will," I reply, taking the card from her hand. I jot my cell phone number on a card and hand it to her.

She wraps her arms around me for one more hug before walking out the door. It hits me that this may be the last time she sees Asher alive. Just the thought of it sends a shooting pain through my chest.

As I walk into Asher's room, I'm surprised to see his anger replaced by contentment. He looks . . . appreciative.

He pats the bed beside him. "Thank you," he whispers as I crawl in next to him.

Chapter 24

"KATE, HE'S NOT DOING WELL. I'm sorry, but I don't think he's going to make it much longer. He'll be lucky to get through the night," Mary, Asher's nurse, announces with thick concern in her eyes. She's been sweet through this entire ordeal, reminding me a lot of my grandma with her constant hugging and reassuring words. There have been days I've wanted to cry, but somehow found the strength to hold it in, not wanting Asher to see me fall apart. But the second Mary pulls me into her arms; I can't be that strong girl anymore. She's not just taking care of Asher . . . she's guarding my own sanity under lock and key.

"Isn't there something else you can do for him?" I ask, not able to hide how much my heart is begging for more time. No amount of hugging can soothe me right now.

She reaches up, running her hand over my hair. "No, I'm afraid not. I'm sorry. At this point, it's all about managing the pain."

The floor falls from under me as reality begins to set in. Whether you love someone for ten thousand minutes or ten thousand days . . . no matter how much you prepare yourself for the inevitable, thinking about it will never bruise you as much as hearing the truth.

It rings over and over in my ears as if she said it loud and slow. I want her to take it all back, or tell me this has been a bad dream, but I know it's not. I'm not going to wake up from this. I can't hide from it. I can't ignore it.

This is my life.

This is Asher's life.

Asher was admitted into the hospital last week with pneumonia. His immune system is so weak that he's been unable to fight it. It's like I'm watching an hourglass, holding my breath and hoping that last bit of sand doesn't slip through. It's a race against time that I've wagered inside myself . . . one that I can't win.

I need Asher.

He gives me strength and courage. He gave me my life back. But no matter what I do, I can't seem to give him back his own. I'd take my last breath if it meant he would never have to take his.

I love him.

I know I will love him forever and always.

Anna has been staying in town since he was admitted into the hospital. From the little time we've spent together, I've enjoyed watching her relationship with Asher. It's just hard watching the sadness in her eyes every time she comes in to see him.

I slide into bed next to him and cuddle up against his side. He's so thin and frail. Every once in a while, I run my fingers through his hair or trace hearts on his chest to remind him that I'm close. I stare at him for hours straight, trying to memorize every feature on his face. I often hold his hand in mine and close my eyes, letting myself feel his soft warm skin.

I recall the first day he walked into the diner and caught my attention. I remember the second time he came in and left me the first napkin note. I remember the first time we talked, the first time he made me laugh, the first time we kissed.

I will never forget him.

There was one day we talked about death. I didn't know he had cancer then, but now, looking back, it was all a foreshadowing.

We're sitting on the edge of the dock, looking out onto the water. We aren't fishing; today is simply about relaxing and enjoying our time together.

"It's beautiful out here. I could spend the rest of my life waking up to this every day," I remark, resting my head against his shoulder.

"Do you ever think about death? I mean, what do you think it's like?" Asher asks, wrapping his arm behind my back.

It's something I haven't thought much about. I don't think it's something that anyone likes to think about.

"I don't know. I guess I've always hoped it will just be another life." I pause, trying to collect my thoughts. "I hope it's just like waking up in another place."

"Me too," he replies, kissing the side of my head.

"We have a lot of time before we have to think about that, though. We're not going anywhere. There's too much life ahead of us."

"Yeah," he whispers, turning his face away from mine.

I should have seen it that day, but I was too involved in the things that were going on around me.

I'll miss his voice. I'll miss the peaceful feeling that looking into his eyes gives me. But most of all, I'll miss the comfort of knowing that when the sun rises in the morning, Asher will still be lying next to me.

We tend to regret our yesterdays, live in our todays and forget about our tomorrows, but I'm trying to cherish them all. I say a prayer every night before I let myself drift to sleep nestled against Asher. I pray that there will be a tomorrow. I pray for strength; not just for me, but for Asher too. Every night, I pray for hope because I'm not ready to say goodbye. I want to wake up and see Asher walking around again with that glowing smile on his face again.

"Kate?" Asher mutters, coming out of a deep sleep. It's good to hear his voice for the first time today. I close my eyes and take it in like it's my favorite song. I memorize the tone, tightly holding onto the way he says my name.

"Are you okay?" I ask, touching my finger to his chin.

He wraps his arm around my back, trying his best to pull me closer with the little strength he has left. "I just wanted to make sure you were still here."

"I'm not leaving you," I whisper, lightly pressing my lips to his.

"Is it warm enough to look at the stars outside tonight?" he asks, breathing loudly. He's been confused and disoriented at times when he's awake.

"Not tonight," I answer, resting my head back against the pillow. I trace my fingertip on his chest, making little hearts and spelling out, "I love you."

"I must have fallen asleep during the movie?" he asks, trying hard to swallow.

"Yeah, you did," I say, playing along. It's easier that way.

"I had a dream about you," he says slowly, trying to catch his breath.

"Yeah?"

He nods slightly. "You looked so pretty like always, and you were coming toward me in a white dress." He stops, taking a few seconds to take several deep breaths. "The closer you got to me, the more you cried. And when you were close enough, I grabbed your hand." He pauses. I can feel how hard his chest is moving up and down under my hand.

"It's okay. You should just try to get some more rest." I want to hear everything that he has to say, but it's draining him a little more with every word. My heart aches, wanting to hold on to him for as long as I can.

He moves his body just enough to face me, exhausting all of his energy with one simple movement. "Just listen to me," he whispers, resting his palm against my cheek. "After the minister said a prayer, I told you how beautiful you were." He stops again, closing his eyes this time.

"Asher—"

"No, please," he whispers, opening his eyes for me again. "I told you that every star in the sky was made for you, and they were, Kate. You light up my world even in my darkest moments."

Tears stream down my face as I watch the tears roll down his. This shouldn't have to happen this way. This moment should be in a church, in front of our family and friends. But because of one stupid six-letter word, these words are being said in bed . . . on the night I will probably lose my soul-mate.

He inhales a deep breath and touches his palm to my cheek. "I told you that I loved you over and over again because I do, Kate." He stops, struggling to breathe. I wish I could do it for him. I wish I could give him my strength. "I love you so much, and the thought of leaving you alone is killing me more than cancer ever could."

He gasps for air and all I can do is watch as I continue to stroke his cheek.

"I need to know that you're going to be okay." His breathing is heavy and he's struggling for every word. "I need to know that you'll think about the good times we shared, and never settle for anything less than how you felt in those moments."

"I will," I cry, kissing the tip of his nose.

"You deserve it all, with or without me," he whispers against my lips.

The tears aren't streaming anymore; they're running down my face. Asher tries to wipe them away, but gives up when he realizes it's pointless.

"I wish I could have this moment, and the one after that, but this is what God's given us," he struggles. He's so pale . . . so weak. "I want to hold you. Please don't leave me," he cries, burying his face in my shirt.

"I would never leave you," I cry, holding him close to me, "Never." I hate this so much, but I need to push through it for him. There is so much I want to say to him.

"You gave me my life back. You cared about me enough to push past my demons. You made me want to be with you every minute of the day because you made me feel things that no one else could. And whether you're lying beside me or living in my memories, I will love you. Forever. Always."

He draws in a few deep breaths through his sobs. He's struggling for his next breath and every time he gets it, I hope it won't be his last.

I'm
Not
Ready . . .

He slowly drifts off to sleep with his cheek pressed against my shoulder. I hear every breath he takes as I lie silently, eager to hear the next. After a while, I count them and as every hour passes, I start to sense more and more of a struggle. That hourglass is running low, but I can't turn it over . . . life doesn't work that way.

His mom and dad come in the room every now and then to check on him. They don't say much, but I can tell by the broken look on their faces that it's ripping them apart inside. Neither seems to know what to say, but they sit beside the bed watching Asher. Asher opens his eyes every once in a while, and they share a few knowing *glances.* He knows they care, or they wouldn't be here when things are so tough.

Asher starts to stir beside me again, and I lift my head up to look into his mesmerizing blue eyes in case it's the last time he can ever open them. The light behind them is gone, but the same unique crystal blue remains. A tear slips from my cheek and falls on his lips but I kiss it away, tasting the salty liquid. I linger there for several seconds, not wanting the moment to ever end. When I sit back up, his eyes are closed and his breathing is labored.

His body has been going through so much, and his spirit has been broken for days. It's to the point where I know that this is what's best for him. A person can only suffer for so long before the agony starts to strip them of who they are.

I can't physically or emotionally do this for much longer.

His dad, who sits in the chair on the side of the bed, notices too. He crumbles, covering his face with his hands. I've never seen a man more broken. It's sad that it took this to bring them back together and that they didn't have time to mend all the issues between them. He scoots closer to the bed and wraps Asher's hand in both of his.

I wish I was strong enough for all of us, but I'm not.

I lay my cheek next to Asher's on the pillow, letting my tears soak through the cotton underneath me. This would forever be etched in my mind.

Asher inhales a deep breath. "When it rains, Kate. Remember me." His voice is so low, but every word registers with me. It's his goodbye. I know it is. He's struggling to breathe as I rest my cheek against his shoulder.

"I love you, Asher," I whisper, running my fingers through his hair. He doesn't move, but my pleas continue, hoping he can hear me. "I'm so glad that you found me. You're the best thing that ever happened to me. I'll always remember you." I sob, moving a little closer.

"You'll always be in my heart," I whisper right next to his ear, hoping he can hear me.

His breathing slows even more. I grip his t-shirt with my fist and pinch my eyes shut, letting his usual scent fill me. I run my fingertips over his facial features, memorizing each and every one of them. If I can't have him here forever, I'm going to cement everything about him into my mind so that it's with me whenever I need it.

"You mean everything to me," I whisper.

Daniel cries out from the chair on the other side of the bed. He'd been so quiet; I forgot he was even here. "He's gone, Kate."

I lift my head and look down at the man whose soul is connected to mine. He's turning paler, and when I put my hand over the heart that saved me, I feel nothing. He's gone. The man who brought me back to life just lost his.

Time stands still.

I feel lost, like I'm not actually in my own body.

I've known for a while that this day would come, but I never let it seep into my heart enough to truly feel it. Reality has hit me hard and knocked me out.

"I'm going to make some calls," Daniel says, barely able to get the words out.

I don't even glance in her direction. I keep my eyes locked on Asher. I think I love him more now than I did when I woke up this morning. He looks peaceful, like he has the countless other times I've watched him sleep, but this time is different.

I'll never get to see his eyes again.

I'm still breathing, blood is still pumping through my body, but the rest of me . . . empty. Without Asher, I'm having a hard time seeing what's in front of me. I don't know where to go from here. I do know that I owe it to him not to fall back into my old pattern of self-loathing. My way of keeping his memory alive is to live my life. I have a chance to do things that he will never get to experience.

"I'm going to go fishing next summer," I cry, letting my head fall back on the pillow. "And I'm going to try French fries dipped in ice cream."

I run my fingers through his hair, feeling the silky texture one more time. "And, when I have s'mores, I'll make an extra one for you. When I hear our favorite songs, I'll dance for you. I'll do anything for you. I'll do it all for you."

I press my lips to his one last time before burying my face in his t-shirt.

~~~~~

It could have been two minutes later, or two hours later, when Daniel comes in and says something about taking Asher away. I don't move as two hands gently pull me away from him. I watch as they cover him with a white sheet and take him from the room.

I sit quietly on the chair in the corner, bouncing my leg up and down as I watch the world move in slow motion around me. These are people who don't know me, who didn't know Asher. Most of them look sad, but they don't feel what I feel right now. They haven't just said goodbye to someone they love.

This is the loneliest, saddest place I've ever been.

I would give my life for one more dance, one more fishing trip . . . one more chance to make love, maybe under the stars this time. It's amazing how many times in life I've said, "I want to do that someday," not thinking that someday might never come. I will never take someday for granted again.

I've held him for the last time.

I've kissed him for the last time.

But I'll think about him always and love him forever.

Chapter 25

WHEN I WALK INTO ASHER'S HOUSE sometime later, my eyes are locked on his bedroom door. Maybe if I stare at it long enough, he'll come walking through it, and this will all have been a terrible misunderstanding. But it's all a delusion; a big hopeless delusion.

Tears flow from my eyes. I don't even bother wiping them away because they will just continue to dampen my cheeks. I don't have the energy or the strength to care. I'm emotionally and physically numb.

After they took Asher away, his mom left. She wants to fly home and get Aubrey so we can all plan the funeral. I'm not exactly sure how it happened, but I ended up going home with Daniel.

As I stare at the plain walls, I pray again for the nightmare to end, but deep down inside, I know it's an impossible dream. I would give up everything to have him back. Everything.

Daniel sits next to me, but I can't bring myself to look at his face. He's the only other person in this town who knew Asher. And now, we're the only two people in this town who are mourning the loss of him. He may be the only person who can understand what I'm going through right now. It gives us a bond that will connect us forever.

Biting down on my lip, I eye his brown leather shoes as he stands and walks through the living room. As soon as he disappears from sight, I hear crying; deep, painful, screeches. I break down all over again. I wish I was strong enough to comfort him right now, but I can't even do anything for my own broken, tortured heart. Instead, it makes me feel the extreme gravity of the situation.

Asher's never coming back.

Life's not fair. Life's often complicated, leaving us to deal with things that we shouldn't have to. Life can make you smile one day, only to leave you broken into tiny little pieces the next.

I wrap my arms around my legs and rest my chin on my knees. I cry uncontrollably as I close my eyes and picture his face.

Asher's dad must have called my mom because she walked into the house not long after. As soon as I saw her, I fell apart. I've never needed my mom more. She quickly moves toward me and pulls me into her arms.

"I'm so sorry," she says, resting her head on mine. "I'm so, so sorry."

I can't form words as I grip her green knit sweater in my hands and bury my face into the fabric.

"He's not in pain anymore," she says, running her fingers through my hair. We remain in the same place, embraced in each other's arms for several minutes. I'm trying to process everything that happened today while she gives me a soft place to land.

"We're going to get through this," she whispers against my ear.

"I love you," I say, burying my face in her sweater. I want to make sure she knows it, today more than ever. I will never take someone who I love for granted again.

She steps back, holding my face in her hands. "I've loved you since the day the doctor told me I was pregnant. And, every day that love grows stronger, especially when I see the kind, caring woman you've become."

We stay in the middle of the living room, holding each other a little longer. After my body stops trembling, my mom wipes my face with a tissue and helps me sit back down on the couch. "I'm going to go see if Daniel needs anything, and then I'm going to take you home."

I nod, unable to speak through the constant sniffles that remain. When she disappears into the kitchen, I take the opportunity to sneak off into Asher's room one last time. I'm not expecting the rush of emotions that hit me as soon as I open the door. The room holds so many memories, and as they flash through my mind, I lean my back against the wall and sink to the ground. Tears well up in my eyes as I glance around the room. It's where we shared our first and only dance. It's where we made love for the first time and the last. It's where we talked about the future we would never get to see together. It's where I learned what happiness is. It's where I learned that life is meant to be lived.

God, I'm going to miss Asher. I'm going to miss him so much.

"Kate, where are you?" my mom asks from the hallway. I stand and grab the bag of clothes I had left there before answering her back.

"I'm in Asher's room," I reply back, sitting down on the edge of his bed. I notice his guitar resting against his dresser and more beautiful memories come back to me. I'm going to miss that too.

"Hey, what are you doing in here?" she asks, opening the door. She takes one look at me and sits down, wrapping me tight in her arms again. "Hey, it's going to be okay. I know it hurts right now, and if there were anything I could do to make it better, I would. I hate to see you going through this."

Daniel walks in, resting his shoulder against the door jam. His eyes look sad and bloodshot. I can hear him talking to my mom, but their voices are muffled by my grief. It's hard to concentrate on anything but what I've just lost.

Tears pour down my face as I watch Daniel talk to my mom, recognizing every feature that he and Asher share. They have the same defined cheekbones, the same perfectly pouty lips and the same shade of blue in their eyes.

I never want to forget him.

"I'm glad he met you, Kate," Daniel says, wiping a tear from under his eye. He leaves the room without saying another word.

I glance around, trying to see through my blurred eyes. One of his worn t-shirts sticks out from under the bed. Scooping it up, I bring it to my nose to take in the familiar scent. Until it wears off, I plan on falling asleep with it next to me every night.

"I think I'm ready to go," I whisper, standing with my back to the wall.

"Okay, I'm going to drive you home."

"No, I can drive. Besides, I need a few minutes to myself."

She stands in front of me and closes her arms around me again. "Don't argue with me. You're in no shape to drive yourself."

There's no point in arguing with her. I don't have the strength, and I know she's right. "Fine."

"I love you, Kate," she says, kissing my forehead.

"I love you, too."

She leaves the room, leaving me alone to say my goodbye. I take one more look at the familiar ivory curtains and see rain pelting the windows.

I really need Asher right now.

⌒‿‿⌒

It's like I'm floating in the air, watching everyone else go about their lives while mine feels like it's at a standstill. Strangers smile when I don't think they should be. How can someone be so happy when I'm so lost? This whole experience has made me more cognizant of everything around me.

I hate when I walk up to someone and they ask, "How are you today?" How am I supposed to answer that? Do people just expect for everyone to be okay all the time? I'm sure they don't want to hear about how my heart has been torn from my chest and thrown against the wall.

They wouldn't understand.

I help Daniel plan the funeral. He asked me if Asher mentioned anything about how he wanted his funeral to be. We spent more time planning our future than we did planning his death, but it was going to be hard to explain that to his dad. Instead, I helped him pick out the perfect music to be played, and the perfect verses to be read. Asher's life was short but it wasn't without meaning. I want to make sure every second of his memorial means something to his past.

Everyone agrees that Carrington is the best place for Asher to be buried. It's where his roots are. It's going to be the second worst day of my life when I have to watch him being lowered into the ground tomorrow. It will be the last time I can be that close to him.

Nothing can prepare me for that.

Asher's mom drove back to Carrington with his sister, and they've been in town ever since. We've been spending time together, remembering times with Asher and helping Daniel pack up some of his things.

"Do you mind if I take a couple things?" I ask Daniel, that afternoon. I already took a few things the other day, but I feel like no matter how much I take, it will never be enough to bring me closer to him.

"Take what you want. I think he would want you to have his things anyway. He really loved you," he says, handing me an empty box.

The first thing that draws my attention is the turtle I had given him not long ago. That night was so special to both of us, and every time I look at the stars, I think of him. I walk over and pick it up, reaching behind the nightstand to unplug it, then carefully tuck it into my overnight bag.

"Do you need help?" my mom asks, walking up behind me.

"No, I need to do this," I cry, wiping my eyes with the back of my sleeves. "Just give me a few minutes." She backs away, resting her shoulder against the door jam.

Next, I spot his iPod resting on the doc station and carefully remove it, tucking it into my purse. Music was such a big part of us, and there are songs on it that remind me of some of the happiest moments we shared.

Hopefully having these little pieces of Asher will help me. Every day is difficult and comes with new challenges, but surrounding myself with people who are going through the same thing helps.

Watching Aubrey makes me think of Asher. I like seeing the little bits of what I love about Asher in her. I see him in her smile, her eyes, the way she tries to take care of her mom, and even with the warm hugs she gives Daniel.

"Kate, do you want to go get something to eat with me?" Aubrey asks.

The last thing I really feel like doing is eating, but one look at her and I can't tell her no. Asher would have wanted this.

"We can do that," I reply, smoothing my hand over her silky blonde hair. It feels just like Asher's did.

"Where do you want to go? Do you have a Starbucks here?"

That makes the corners of my mouth turn up slightly. "No, the only place that's open right now is Bonnie's, but extize

they have good milkshakes. And if it's coffee you really want, I happen to know it's always fresh."

"Sounds good to me, but it's a little cold for milkshakes, don't you think?" she asks, lifting one of her eyebrows.

"It's never too cold for ice cream."

I take one last look around the room before we pull on our coats and head to my car. It's too cold to be walking around Carrington today. We ride the ten or so blocks in silence, listening to some old country song on the radio. Whenever I hear it, I think of Beau. I selfishly wish he was here with me right now. Just being able to see his face would make me feel better.

Without Beau or Asher . . . well, I'm not quite sure where I belong.

We pull into the familiar parking lot and head into the restaurant. Aubrey seems amazed by the décor of the small diner. It looks like something straight out of the fifties or sixties with the red booths and checkered laminate flooring. I've been there so many times that it's nothing special to me, but I can see how it would amaze a big city girl.

"Are the cinnamon rolls good?" she asks, looking up from her menu.

"I think so, but they are the only ones I've ever had, so I have nothing to compare them to."

"What are you getting?"

I watch her eyes scan the menu before looking back down to mine.

"I think I'm going to have a milkshake and French fries," I say, remembering the way Asher always dipped his French fries in his milkshake.

"That's Asher's favorite. He used to take me out for fries and milkshakes after school," she says sadly.

"It was. That's what he used to order when I first met him." I look up at the door and remember the feeling that washed over me the day he walked in here. He was a stranger then, but I knew that he would become so much more. It's hard to explain, but it's like our souls were meant to be together.

"He really liked you," she tells me.

"Yeah, I really liked him, too," I reply, smiling back at her. I don't know if she understands the deep concept of love. I'm not even sure if I understood it until just a few months ago.

"I miss him already," she says, her eyes welling with tears.

This little girl is breaking what's left of my wounded heart.

"I miss him too," I say softly, resting my elbows on the table so, "but he'll always be right here with us. When you need him, a piece of him will always be with you."

A single tear falls from my eyes as I process my own words. Tomorrow, when we're at Asher's funeral saying goodbye, it's won't necessarily be goodbye. He will always be the reason I breathe to live my life and not just to live. He's the person who showed me that there is a way to get past everything that ever held me down.

He gave me a second chance.

Chapter 26

I'VE KNOWN THIS DAY WOULD COME, but it doesn't make it any easier. Physical pain is bothersome, but emotional pain is suffocating. It's like someone has their hands wrapped around my neck, squeezing as tight as they can. I can't breathe. I can't think straight. I just want Asher back. I don't want to stare down at his lifeless body in a mahogany casket; he doesn't even look like himself. I want him back, holding me and telling me how much he loves me.

Yet, here I am. Standing in front of the rectangle box. I run my hand along the silk fabric that lines the inside as tears run down my cheeks. I recognize some of his features, but others look nothing like how I remember. His skin is pale, and without being able to see his eyes, he's barely recognizable. I'm afraid to walk away because I know I'll never see him again.

He's going to become just a memory, someone I can only look at in a picture. It's a reality that hits me like a cement block. It's hard to stand, so I'm grateful when two hands grip my shoulders, helping to support my weak body. When I turn my head, I see my mom crying right along with me. She removes her hands and wraps her arms around my waist. Her warm, comfortable closeness soothes me and gives me the permission I need to let out every ounce of grief I have left inside.

"Everything's going to be okay. We'll get through this," she whispers, squeezing her arms a little tighter.

"I miss him, Mom," I cry, placing my arms over hers. "Why did he have to go? I loved him." My knees are weak, but her strength holds me up.

"He's always going to be right here with us, Kate."

If I pinch my eyes closed tight, I can see him. I've memorized everything about the last few months.

I can only hope I'll never forget.

He'll always be with me in some way.

"Let's just go over here so that the others can say their goodbyes," she says, running her hands up and down my upper arms. When I open my eyes again, I take several deep breaths in order to gain enough composure to walk back to my seat, but I can't stop myself from looking down at him one last time

"I don't know if I can do this," I sob, gripping the edge of the casket.

She rests her hands on my shoulders, gently squeezing them. "Let's go take a seat," she says softly, dropping her hands from my shoulders to grab my hand. When I turn to follow her, I'm met with blue eyes I haven't seen in months. They're dark, yet unsure. My first instinct is to run toward them, but then I remember everything that happened between us the last year and I hesitate.

I haven't seen him since Christmas and even then, it was only for a few minutes. But now, even after everything, looking at him blankets my heart with warmth. He's been a reminder of all the good things in my life for so long.

Staring at him from across the church, those feelings wash over me again.

I need Beau. If I ever thought I didn't, I was kidding myself. He's been there for me from the beginning. He never let me go, even after what happened the last time we spoke.

I drop my mom's hand and take a couple hesitant steps toward where he's leaning against the wall at the back of the church. When he doesn't move, I continue to walk to him.

Besides mom, he's all I have left.

"I'll save you a seat," I hear my mom say a few feet behind me. When I'm only a couple steps away, he reaches out and pulls me into his waiting arms. I completely fall apart. I don't know what I ever did to deserve a guy like him in my life.

"I'm sorry. I came as soon as I heard," he whispers in my ear. "I'm so, so sorry."

"I miss him," I cry as I pull back to look him in the eyes. "I've missed you."

Beau pulls me against his chest again, running his fingers through my hair. "It's going to be okay. Everything is going to be okay."

We stay like that for a long time, locked in each other's embrace.

"Why didn't you call me when he was in the hospital? I would have come right away," he whispers near my ear.

I shut my eyes tight, battling the overwhelming emotions that are brewing inside of me. I'm unable to form words, and after a few minutes he pulls back, releasing my hands from his shirt. "Don't go. Please stay here with me," I beg, desperate to have him close to me for as long as I can.

"I'm going to sit in the back. You should join your mom up front," he replies, lifting his thumb to wipe tears from under my eyes.

"Beau—"

"Kate, the service is about to start," my mom says from behind me.

I hold one finger up, signaling that I need a minute, but music starts to play over the sound system, halting me in place. Our eyes lock briefly before Beau turns and walks toward the back of the church. There are so many things I want to say to him, but today isn't really the day for any of that. It can't wait long, though.

I know tomorrow is never a guarantee.

After I take my seat, I close my eyes and listen to the music that fills the room. It's a song I've listened to many times in the last few days. I picked it just for Asher. It's a song that I know he loved and one that meant a lot to him.

It now means everything to me.

Hallelujah by Jeff Buckley plays as a slide show displaying Asher's life from birth to just a few months before he died appears on the large projector screen. It's so hard to watch, but this is part of my goodbye. Asher lived so much life before I even met him and watching it flash before my eyes helps me to understand.

He was a happy baby with curly blond hair and dimples visible through his constant smile. He loved his Power Ranger PJ's as a young kid, and lost most of his curls by the time his mom took his picture on the first day of Kindergarten. He loved baseball, football and building towers out of Legos. When the photo of him holding Aubrey for the first time in the hospital pops up, I can't watch anymore. He loved that little girl so much; it's evident in his wide smile and excited eyes. Now, he's not going to be able to see her grow up.

I want to run somewhere far, far away where death doesn't exist. Everyone should be able to live a full life. He should be able to get married, have kids, and live out his dreams of a happily ever after.

I wanted him to be my happily ever after.

My mom grabs for my hand, giving me the will to look up again. There's so much that I never got to see, and now he's not even here to tell me about it.

The next photo is of him and a pretty girl with long blonde hair and piercing green eyes. He's got his arm wrapped around her, and they're both dressed up. Homecoming 2007 it reads at the bottom. The next few photos are also of them, followed by him alone on the day of his high school graduation. The girl must have been Megan; the friend he lost way too soon. The reason he thought he was being punished.

The next three photos bring back memories of us. For the first time, I see from afar how he looked at me, always leaning his body into mine. For the first time, I saw my smile brighten a little more in each photo. The first is the two of us at the zoo, riding the carousel. I thought it was childish, but by the time it stopped, I couldn't wipe the smile from my face. The second is from the night Asher made a bonfire for me. He had insisted that we take a photo when we both had marshmallow stuck to our lips. It was so much fun . . . more fun than I'd had in a really long time. The third one was taken the last time we went fishing. I don't remember seeing anyone take the photo, but Asher is looking up at me while I stand to reel my pole in. By the look on his face, you would think nothing else in this world mattered. He loved me then . . . I can see it.

And the last one is a picture of Asher sitting on the couch playing his guitar for me. It reminds me of the night he made love to me for the first time and showed me what things could be like if I just let go.

The rest of the service is a blur. I'm in a field of memories, too caught up in what was and what can never be again. I hear talking coming from the front of the church, but I don't actually listen to the words. Music plays a few separate times, but I couldn't tell you what the songs actually were. And when everyone stands and exits the church, I stay motionless. This is it.

He's gone.

My mom crouches in front of me, grabbing my hands in hers. "I know this is hard, but are you ready to go?

Asher's family invited us to ride to the cemetery with them, and they'll be leaving soon."

I'm not ready, but that really doesn't matter right now.

I nod, taking a fresh tissue from my mom's hand. I cry, leaning my head back against the church pew. After closing my eyes and taking a deep breath, I stand up straight and start making my way out of the church. As soon as I open the door, Beau is standing with his back to me, staring at the busy street.

"Beau," I sniffle, watching as he turns to face me.

He walks toward me and cups my face in his hands while gently caressing my cheekbones with his thumbs. He opens his mouth twice without saying anything . . . I've never seen him look more conflicted.

"I need to go. The car is waiting for me," I say, nervously looking out to the street.

He quickly lets go of me, running his fingers through his hair. He cut it since the last time I saw him, and it makes him look older. The longer I look at him, the more he feels like a different person. We're both different people now.

He looks away from me, burning a bigger hole into my damaged heart. "I need to get back to school. I just wanted to make sure you were okay." He stops, his eyes meeting mine briefly before looking away again. "If you need anything, please call me."

I watch him walk down a few steps, my heart squeezing more as he gets further and further away from me. I don't want him to go. "Beau!" I shout.

"Yeah?" he says, turning to face me again.

"Can you stay for the burial?" I ask, looking to the side of the church to hide my tears.

He doesn't move. He doesn't say a word.

"Please, I can't do it without you," I plead.

He stares at me for a few seconds before walking toward me. My heart pounds against my chest with the anticipation that he will say yes and the thought that he may say no. "I can't, Kate. I should really get back to school," he pauses, taking a deep breath.

Shock, surprise, confusion . . . they all run through my veins. Why would he come here if he had no intention of staying?

"You just got here. Why did you come if you can't stay?" I whisper, nervously fidgeting with my fingers.

Using his index finger, he tilts my eyes to his. "I needed to make sure you were okay."

"Why?"

"Because I care about you," he says, eyeing me intently.

"Then why won't you stay?" I ask, swallowing hard. I need him, but I feel like I've lost my right to beg.

"I just can't," he says, running his fingertips along my jawline. "You love him . . . that's written all over your face. Kate, I would do anything to be able to wipe that away. But I—"

"Beau, please. Please stay with me."

He sighs as he tilts his head to the sky. My heart pounds as I watch him pinch his eyes closed. When he looks back down without making eye contact, I already know his answer. "It looks like your mom is waiting for you," he says, pointing to my mom who waits next to her car. "I'm sorry, Kate."

I step back, avoiding his eyes. This isn't the time or place to have this conversation. "I should probably get going then."

"I'll talk to you later," he says, tucking his hands into his pocket. He steps toward me, quickly kissing my forehead. When he pulls back, he runs his thumb along the crest of my cheek. "I love you."

I stand still, watching as his figure fades away. Things have been different between us. I'd do anything to go back to what we used to be, but right now we're two confused strangers.

The ride to the burial is quiet. Aubrey rests her head against my shoulder and I lean into her, placing my head against hers. I think about what we're about to do . . . it completely consumes me.

Asher's parents and my mom remain quiet, glancing out the front window. It's peaceful, but it almost gives me too much time to think. My heart needs a break.

When we pull into the cemetery, Aubrey grips one of my hands tightly as my mom grips the other. No one is ready to move because each step forward is one step closer to goodbye.

A lump forms in my throat as we stop in front of the casket. This is it. It's the end of another chapter . . . the best chapter of my life. My knees weaken as the priest starts to say a final prayer. His voice vibrates through my ears, but I couldn't repeat a word he is saying. There are some moments in life we all have to face, even though we don't want to. This is one of those moments.

This will always be that moment for me.

My mom places her arm behind my back to hold me as the tears roll down my face. Aubrey squeezes my hand tightly, but I don't care. Someone could shoot a bullet through my heart right now and I wouldn't notice.

Asher's casket lowers into the ground as the priest finishes his prayer, "when we meet again."

When I can't see it anymore, when I know without a shadow of doubt that I will never see him again in this life, I fall to my knees. Never in my life have I felt so numb.

Asher was the ground beneath my feet, the air that filled my lungs, and the sun that shined above my head. He saved me from drowning. I'd been held under water for four minutes and fifty-nine seconds when I met him. I was one second away from fading.

I bury my face in my hands as I gasp for air. I just want him back. I would do anything, and give up everything, just to have him back.

Two thin arms embrace me, pulling me into a familiar chest. "Oh, it's going to be okay," my mom whispers. "Everything is going to be okay."

"No, it won't be okay! It won't. Why couldn't it have been me?" I yell hysterically, falling into her.

"Don't say that," she cries. She does her best to comfort me by running her hands along my back, but nothing can break through the sorrow I feel right now.

My body trembles against hers as my tears soak her shirt. "I want him back. I just want him back," I cry, fisting her shirt in my hands.

"If there was any way to do that, I would."

"I love him so much," I sob, not paying any attention to anything around me. "Why?" I scream, laying my head on her knees.

"I don't know," she says softly, running her fingers through my hair.

Neither of us moves. I'm paralyzed by the fear of being alone and the sadness that I can't seem to get a grasp on.

When all my energy is exhausted, I stare straight ahead at the dirt that now covers Asher's grave. I keep my eyes focused as person after person drops a handful of dirt onto the mahogany wood. I know it's typical, but I can't do it. It would make me feel like I'm burying him and while that's exactly what we're here for, I can't.

I carefully raise myself up, not bothering to wipe the moisture from my cheeks. There's one last thing I have to do before we leave. I grab the bouquet of flowers from the ground and walk a few feet to his grave. One by one, I take out five flowers, holding them all tightly in my hand as I decide which one to place first.

I separate the blue salvia, running the soft petals across my lips. "I'll think of you forever," I whisper as I place it on his grave.

Next, I grab the aloe. It's not something that normally would be placed on the grave, but it means healing, protection and affection . . . three things Asher showed me. "Thank you," I whisper, setting it next to the first flower.

I place the stem of the daisy between my fingers and inhale the fresh scent. The daisy is a symbol of hope. "Because of you, I can recognize the good moments. And because of you, there are good moments."

Only two items remain, I lay rosemary, the symbol of remembrance, down first. "You'll always live in my heart."

And then I'm left with one red rose . . . the flower that means the most to me. "I love you." It's the hardest flower to let go of, but the one I know I will still feel strongly inside after I do. I carefully place it in the center, lightly running my fingertips over the dirt.

Looking down, I see forever, gratitude, hope, remembrance and love.

I see the time I spent with Asher.

"Kate."

I close my eyes, taking a deep breath before turning around. Daniel stands in front of me with a large yellow envelope in his hands. "I know this might not be the best time to give this to you, but Asher wanted you to have this."

"What is it?" I ask, glancing between him and the envelope. There's something written on the front, but it's hard to make out with my watery eyes.

He shakes his head. "I don't know. He gave it to me a few weeks ago and asked that I give it to you after he's gone."

"Thank you." I take the envelope from his hand and stand up.

"If you need anything, don't be afraid to ask," he says, focusing his eyes on the fresh dirt that stands out from the rest of the landscape.

"You too," I reply sadly. He pats my shoulder as he walks past and the only people who remain are my mom and me.

"Are you ready to go?"

I am.

But I'm not.

It feels like I'm leaving him alone.

"Yeah," I cry. "Can you just give me one more minute?"

She nods, kissing my cheek before walking toward the car. As soon as I know she's out of earshot, I crouch down and kiss the pads on my fingers before resting them on top of Asher's grave. "All the stars shine for you, Asher."

~~~

As soon I'm home, and my bedroom door closes behind me, I open the envelope that Daniel handed me. My hands shake uncontrollably; today has drained all the strength from my body, but this can't wait. I cautiously pull the contents out, scared of what I might find . . . what it might make me feel.

The first thing I pull out is a note written on white paper. I recognize Asher's handwriting right away, and my heart skips a beat. At least for a second, I feel like he's right here with me. I inhale a deep breath and start to read.

Kate,

A few months ago, I was living a life so empty that nothing could fill it. Then I met

266

you, a girl so beautiful yet so lost. I tried so hard to stay away, but obviously I lost the battle. I wanted to help you get where you were going, even if I couldn't stay with you throughout the whole journey.

You're amazing, and I want you to remember that every day. I know there are days when you just want to give up, but you're strong, Kate. You can get through this.

The first time I saw you, I wanted to take away the sadness in your eyes. I questioned myself over and over because I knew the time I had left was not going to allow us forever and you deserve a forever. There was a voice inside me that said you would be better off if I walked toward you instead of walking away. I'm glad I listened because I love your smile and everyone should see it.

I didn't know the girl you were before your struggle, but I probably would have liked her too. The struggle isn't worth your last breath. Never forget to breathe.

If you close your eyes, you'll be able to see me, no matter where you are. Always remember the way we danced, the way it felt when we kissed, and how good it felt to live and love. I left a couple things in this envelope to help you with that. Please don't use them to dwell on the past. Use them to remember how good things can be. You deserve the world. The best parts of the world.

When it Rains

You're the best thing that ever happened to me. I lived more in the last few months than I did all the months before them. I want you to take these lessons and live for me, Kate.

When it rains, think of me. I'll be your umbrella, Kate. I'll be your barrier from the storm, when life gets too heavy. Don't let the storm wash you away. Allow it to nourish new life.

You're strong. You're beautiful. You're everything. Never forget these things and don't let anyone tell you differently.

Love,
The guy who's still smiling because of you...

Fresh tears stream down my face. How is it even possible to cry anymore? Everything he said hit me deep. I could never ever regret him. How can I regret someone who knew how to glue all of the pieces of me back together?

And rain . . . the only thing I think about when it rains these days are his kisses. Anything that happened before has been washed away by new kinder storms.

Next, I reach inside and pull out a small box that rattles when I shake it. My fingers tremble as I open the lid and what I see causes an excruciating tightness in my chest. Running my fingers along the silver chain, I can't take my eyes off the tiny umbrella or the blue glass crystal raindrop that hangs under it. It's gorgeous. I unclasp it and place it around my neck before returning my attention to the envelope.

I pull Asher's iPod off my dresser and place the small buds in my ears. As soon as I settle into my bed, I hit play. Asher's voice begins to sing *Everything* by

268

Lifehouse, and when I close my eyes, I can see him on the couch playing for me. Pressing the charm of my new necklace between my fingers, I slowly drift to sleep with the beautiful words filling my ears.

Chapter 27

IT HAS BEEN FIFTEEN DAYS OF EMPTINESS.

It has been 360 hours of loneliness.

It has been 21,600 minutes of missing him, but I'm still ten times more alive than I was in the days before I met him.

Today is the first time I've gone to work in two months. I never left Asher's side in his last few weeks, and I've spent the last two trying to figure out what to do without him. This feels like a turning point for me . . . I can either choose to move forward, or fall back into the place I was in after Drew raped me.

As I step into the diner, the smell of fried food instantly hits me and I'm immediately reminded of memories with Asher. I miss the days of watching the door, waiting for him to come in.

They always say you don't know what you have until it's gone, but I figured out a long time ago that Asher was special. Now I have an angel watching over me.

My mom walks into the kitchen where I'm standing, staring into space. If she was in a hurry before, she doesn't show it now. Her green eyes are warm as a sympathetic smile touches her lips.

"Are you sure you're ready for this?" she asks, wiping her hands on her apron. Having her here with me makes this so much easier. She hasn't been my rock . . . she's been my whole world.

I take a deep breath. I'm ready.

"Yes," I reply, returning her smile. "It's nice to get out of the house for once. I'm actually starting to resent the paint color on my walls."

"You can paint them, you know."

"I don't think that will be necessary," I say, shrugging my shoulders.

"Well, I need to get back up front, but let me know if you need a break today," she says, wrapping her thin arms around me. Over and over the last few months, I've realized that she's my home. It doesn't matter where we are or what we have as long as we have each other. We're where we need to be.

"I'll be okay," I whisper, pulling her closer to me.

"Okay, I know the others are excited to see you too." She lets go of me and walks out, looking back one more time before closing the door. I take one more deep breath and clock in. It's one foot in front of the other from here on out. It's the only way I'm going to get through this.

The first thing I see when I walk in the dining room is my regular group of farmers. I never thought that I'd miss them, but I did. It's interesting how people can become such a big part of your life before you even start to realize it.

And the best part . . . they smile as soon as they see me walking toward them. This is just going to be another day as long as I let it be.

"Hey, Kate, we haven't seen you around here in forever. What have you been up to?" one of them asks as they all eye me intently.

"I've been . . . helping a friend," I admit lightly, biting my lip to hold back any emotions that threaten when I think of Asher. Even though I'm learning to deal with it a little more each day, it's hard to verbalize. For some reason, it makes it more real.

"Well, we're glad you're back. I like your mom and all, but you're my favorite waitress."

A smile spreads across my face.

This is my home too.

After the early morning rush ends, Ms. Carter comes in and takes her normal seat. When I bring out her cinnamon roll and cup of decaf, she smiles.

"Hey, Ms. Carter, I've missed you. How's bridge club?" I ask, trying to continue with my normal routine.

She reaches for my hand and pulls me closer to the table. "You don't have to pretend for me," she says quietly.

I glance around the restaurant making sure that no one else heard her. "I'm not." I don't think I'm pretending; I'm just holding stuff in. To me, there is a difference.

"Have you even let yourself cry?"

"Every day," I reply honestly. I've tried not to close myself off this time. I know better than that.

"Sit down," she says, pointing to the seat across from her.

I shake my head, glancing around nervously. "I can't. I'm working."

I stand motionless as she waves my mom over. What is she up to?

"Can Kate take a break for a few minutes? I have something I need to talk to her about," Ms. Carter says, not looking in my direction even once.

My mom eyes me curiously before turning her attention back to Ms. Carter. "I suppose I can handle things for a few minutes." She pats me on the shoulder before walking away. "I'll yell if I need you."

I nod, sliding into the empty seat. The booths are normally comfortable, but right now I feel like I'm sitting on a wooden board. I've known this woman for years, but up until a few minutes ago I thought she was just a nice woman who didn't notice much.

I think all my thoughts and conceptions are about to be proven wrong.

"Don't worry, Kate, I'm not going to ask you to go to bridge with me again." She pauses, taking a sip from her coffee cup. "I just want to make sure you're okay."

I sigh, resting my crossed arms on the table. "I'm going to be fine. I just need some time to find my new normal."

"Who's helping you with that?" she asks, taking another sip from her coffee cup.

"My mom is when I let her. Other than that it's just me," I admit sadly, stealing a quick glance out the window. It's so hard to talk about my feelings.

She reaches into her purse and pulls out a plastic bag filled with what looks like napkins from the diner.

She pulls out the top one and places it front on me. At first I don't believe what my eyes are seeing. It's Asher's handwriting on a napkin like I've seen many times before.

My eyes gloss over, making the print impossible to read. "Where did you get this?" I ask, feeling the first tear roll down my cheek.

Her hand covers mine, and I look up to see her eyes are glossed over too. "There was this young man who gave them to me one day when I came in for my coffee. I didn't know who he was at the time, but after spending a few minutes with him, I knew one thing." She stops, smiling sadly. "He loved the beautiful girl who I come to this diner to see every morning."

Rolling the tiny raindrop that hangs from my neck between my fingers, I wait for her to continue.

"You didn't think I came in here every day for this crap they call coffee, did you? Seriously, they need to put some more grounds in before they brew it." She tilts her head to the side, regaining her serious expression. "I'd noticed how much you'd changed the last few months. One day as I was leaving the diner, he was walking in, so

I stopped to thank him. I'd seen you with him a few times and put two and two together."

I shake my head, feeling my lips tremble. "But why the napkins? I don't get it."

She nods, squeezing my hand tighter. "A couple months ago he stopped by the diner, but you weren't working. The boy was a mess, so I asked him if he'd like to sit and have coffee with me, and he surprisingly agreed. It took a very long time for him to gain any composure when I asked him what was wrong. Anyway, we talked for almost an hour about Carrington, and when I mentioned that I came here every day just to see you, he looked so broken up. He asked if I could keep a secret, and reached into his coat pocket and handed me this bag. He said there would come a day when you would need these, and he wouldn't be here to give them to you."

She laughs sadly, glancing at the full dining room. "I scolded him. I told him if he even thought about leaving you, I'd come find him. He got really quiet and told me he didn't have a choice. He said he'd never leave you if he had a choice." A tear rolls out of the corner of her eye.

"Wait, when was this?" I ask, leaning as far over the table as my body will let me.

"It was the day before he was admitted to the hospital."

Out of habit, my eyes focus up to the ceiling. He knew he was getting sicker. He knew his days were growing fewer and fewer, but he was still thinking about me.

"I figured now that you're back at work, you might be ready for these," she cries, handing me the bag. "You're supposed to read the one I took out first."

My attention goes back to the paper napkin that sits right in front of me on the table. I carefully pick it up, running it between my fingers.

There's a napkin in here for each day I knew you. When you need me, take one out, and I'll be right there talking to you.
Missing you, each and every day.
Love, Asher

I wipe the rapid flowing tears from my eyes and look across the table to see Ms. Carter doing the same thing. "Thank you," I mouth.

"Oh, Katie girl, I'm here if you need me. You know, I lost my husband to cancer, too."

"It doesn't feel quite fair," I say, wiping my eyes.

"I know, but I bet you don't regret one minute you spent with him."

I never will. When I think of him and the memories we created together, it washes the paralyzing sadness that coats my heart away. "Never," I whisper.

"Well, I should probably get going. I have to go play bridge, but I'm thinking about making a change to bingo. I'm getting tired of all the politics that go on in my bridge club," she says, standing next to the table.

She reaches into her purse, but I stop her by placing my hand in the air. "I got this one. Besides, you didn't even touch your cinnamon roll."

"Yeah, those aren't that good either," she replies, scrunching her nose up as she looks at the untouched roll.

"You don't have to keep coming in here if you don't like the food."

"As long as I get to see you, I'll keep coming in," she says, running her thumb across my cheek. "Take care, sweet girl."

For several minutes after she leaves, I stare at Asher's handwriting. Even though he's not here, he's still the most amazing person I've ever known. He always seems to know what I need, even when he isn't here.

As I stand up, I notice my mom standing in the corner with her hand over her chest. Her forehead wrinkles as she watches me and as soon as she sees me moving, she motions to the kitchen before disappearing behind the door.

My knees feel so weak from everything that I have a hard time just putting one foot in front of the other. The diner is still pretty empty, but any minute now it will start filling up with the lunch crowd, and I don't want to have any part in that.

I thought I was ready, but I've been knocked on my ass again.

My mom pulls me into her arms as soon as I walk into the kitchen. "Are you okay? What did Ms. Carter say?"

I press my cheek to her shoulder, breathing in her familiar perfume. "Asher left her these to give me," I reply, holding up the baggie.

"Oh my god," she whispers, resting her head on top of mine.

I stand blanketed in the warmth her body provides. This doesn't feel like it should be my life.

Pulling back, I force her to loosen her grip. "Will you guys be okay if I go home? I need to be alone."

She lovingly brushes the hair away from my eyes with her fingers, "Are you sure you should be alone right now?"

"Please," I plead, anxious to get home and read through more of Asher's notes.

Her thumbs run along my cheekbones before I'm pulled into her arms again. "Go home, but I want you to call me if you need anything. Do you hear me?"

"I'll be okay," I whisper.

She lets go of me, rubbing her hand along the back of her neck. "I worry about you."

I take a few steps toward her and kiss her cheek. "That's what moms are supposed to do."

As I take my apron off and walk out of the diner, I can feel her eyes on my back. I hated all those times she was hovering over me when I was younger, but now it means something totally different.

At every stop sign on the way home, I glance down at the bag of notes that sit on the passenger seat. It's almost like I'm driving somewhere to meet him after not seeing him for a long time. If only I could make all of my perceptions a reality.

When I'm safely in the privacy of my room, I quickly change and crawl under my comforter with the little pieces of Asher I hold in my hand.

I tell myself before reading the first one that I'm only going to read five each day and then when I've read them all, I'll just start again.

My whole body shakes as I pull out the first one, closing my eyes and taking a deep breath before reading.

Your strength is inspiring.

This one makes a small smile spread across my face. I've never considered myself a strong person. In fact, I've always seen myself as weak, especially the last couple years. But now, looking at myself through Asher's eyes, I understand what he sees. It took strength just to remain here.

I pull out the next one, feeling a little more relaxed than I was with the first.

My lasagna recipe . . .
Stouffers from the freezer aisle.

For the first time in weeks, I really, truly laugh. He always had a way of bringing that side out of me.

I miss those green eyes. I hope they're still as bright and vibrant as they were the last time I saw them.

Any remaining hint of the smile I just had is gone. I have a hard time picturing my own eyes in that way, but he always mentioned when they were shining.

If you go fishing, make sure to take my pole.

That's one thing that I don't know if I'm ready to do without him. One of the memories that will live in the forefront of my mind is when he kissed me in the rain.

I love you. I'm truly, madly, deeply in love with you. Don't forget that there are other people around you who love you too. Don't shut them out.

Time passes as I lay there letting my emotions pour out of me. It's tempting to read another note, but I'm not done processing the ones I've just read. Asher always knew how to mix some humor into life, and he achieved a perfect balance today.

"Kate," my mom says, startling me.

Turning my head, I see her standing in my doorway. She came home for me. She walks slowly in my direction, almost like she's afraid of how I'm going to react, then surprises me by lying down behind me and cradling me next to her body. I've messed up so many times. There's so much heartache that I could have saved myself if I had just opened up to her. It's always easier to see things more clearly when you're looking back.

"What's bothering you? Please talk to me," she says, running her fingers through my hair.

I remember how much weight was lifted when I told Asher about the one thing that haunts me . . . the one thing that holds me back. I turn around to face her and say the one thing I've been scared to say for years.

"I was raped," I cry.

She stops, and I feel her fingers tremble against my scalp. "What did you just say?"

"A couple years ago, someone raped me. He held me down and raped me." Sickness coursed through my veins as I relive the whole thing for her. I leave out a few of the details, but in the end when the big secret is washed away, I feel better. One more brick has been lifted from my chest.

And when I'm done, when the cloud has been lifted, she grips me tight against her chest and cries with me. I've thought about this day over and over again, and now that it's done, I regret not doing it sooner.

She's showing me love. Sweet, selfless, undying love.

I love her fifty million times to the moon and back.

"It's not your fault," she murmurs.

"I know that now."

Chapter 28

I'VE NEVER BEEN MORE EXCITED to see winter melt away than I was this particular spring. I'm taking it one day at a time. I've learned that I can't bury the past away; it just makes it worse.

The day I lost Asher is still hard to think about, but I do allow myself to go there from time to time. That's another reason I welcome spring . . . I can lie outside and look at the stars. Every time I do, it feels like he's lying right beside me. If I let my mind go, I can feel him holding my hand, and sometimes I think I feel his fingers brushing through my hair.

I miss him.

The last one hundred and six days I've thought about him one hundred and six times. I've read all his notes at least ten times over, re-reading some of my favorites every day. I don't know if that'll ever get old.

I crawl onto the middle of Beau's old trampoline, stopping in the center to glance up at the clear night sky. It's so much better than the turtle I've been lighting in my room night after night. It reminds me of the campfire Asher and I had last fall. I can almost taste the chocolate and marshmallow stuck on his lips. If I close my eyes, the whole night replays like a film, taking me back to a happier time.

After living a few minutes in sweet memories, I hear a familiar sound in the distance. One I haven't heard in months. The one I've wanted to hear every day since he left for college.

I stay still, waiting to hear the door of his truck squeak. Once it does, it's so tempting to get up and run over and jump into his arms, but it doesn't feel like they're waiting for me anymore. It feels like I've lost that privilege.

Two guys.

Two loves.

Both gone.

I pushed one away and lost the other forever.

Regret fills me. Sadness consumes me.

I bite my lower lip when I hear him slam his door shut and wait silently to hear the sound of his front screen door closing, but it doesn't. Taking a deep, pained breath and closing my eyes, I listen to the sound of shoes rustling in the grass. After many loud, thumping heartbeats, I open them again to see him standing at my feet, watching me silently.

The moonlight reflects on his skin, reminding me just how beautiful he is. Even without the light, I know what's inside of him, and that's the best part. He's the complete package.

"What are you doing out here by yourself?" he asks with the deep husky voice I've missed so much. I used to spend nights replaying how it sounded when he said my name.

"Looking at the stars," I reply, feeling a thickness in my throat. "What are you doing home?"

"I took my last test earlier and I was pretty anxious to get out of the dorms," he says, running his fingers through his brown hair. It's grown out again from the last time I saw him at the funeral. "Can I join you?"

His voice is unsure, but I'm not. I've missed him.

"I thought you'd never ask," I joke, patting the space next to me.

"I'm sorry I haven't called. Things have been crazy," Beau says as he settles in beside me.

"It's okay."

"What have you been up to?" he asks, tucking his hands behind his head.

Sadness floods my chest as I think of all the times I wanted to call Beau, but couldn't gather the courage. I swallow, trying to get a grip on my emotions. I've tried to be better at not holding things in and keeping them to myself, but this was really the only exception.

"Working and reading mostly. I'm thinking about throwing something else in the mix soon."

He laughs, and I feel his hand brush against mine. The tingle it sends running down my back is confusing, so I push it back not wanting to feel something that can never be. I'm not ready to deal with those emotions yet.

"There's always school. You're too smart to stay here."

"Maybe." I shrug. "All I know right now is there has to be more to life than the diner. But honestly, I couldn't have made it through the last few months without that place and the people who come in every day. They're like family now, you know?"

I turn my head to face him for the first time and see him flinch. I know he knows I'm looking at him, but he avoids my eyes.

"I'm sorry I left that day at the funeral. It's weird, you know? Trying to console the person you love while she's mourning the person she loves." He shakes his head, still avoiding any eye contact with me. "I don't know if I was giving you what I thought you deserved, or just being selfish, but when I look back now, I wish I had done things differently."

My heart plummets. Where did things go so wrong? When I try to look back and figure it all out, it always points to Drew, but when I really think about it, it was all me. I didn't deal with things in the best way. I didn't let anyone help me . . . how could they if they didn't even know.

"You didn't do anything wrong. I was selfish to think you'd just drop everything to stay with me," I admit, using the sleeve of my sweatshirt to dab my eyes.

He entwines his fingers with mine, and I swear holding hands has never felt this good. It's a reassurance that there is still a chance for us, for our friendship. "I wanted to be there for you. I wanted to hold you so fucking bad and never let you go, but I couldn't be that guy anymore."

"What guy?" I ask, my chest rising and falling more with every passing second. Why does he do this to me?

"The guy who isn't good enough and would always come second. For some reason, I thought we had it. I fucking felt it, but when it came down to it, I was wrong." He pauses, letting his eyes catch mine for the first time. "When you told me you weren't ready for us, it almost killed me, but I thought it just wasn't our time, that you needed your space."

"Beau—"

"No, let me finish," he interrupts, shifting so that his whole body is facing me. "There was hope for us. When I looked at you, I didn't see the girl I wanted to share my first kiss with, I saw the girl I wanted to share every kiss with. It might sound stupid, but I saw forever in us, Kate. The morning I saw you in the car with Asher, I felt like someone was fucking stabbing me. I never want to feel that way again."

Ironic, since it feels like he's the one choking me right now. Guilt is an all-consuming reaction to things we regret. While I know without a doubt that I wasn't ready for Beau then, I never wanted to hurt him.

"I'm sorry. I hope I can explain it all someday. I know it won't make it all right, but maybe you'll understand. I never ever wanted to hurt you. That was the last thing I ever wanted to do."

"I think I knew that," he says.

I stare back at the sky, identifying constellations to keep my mind busy. I'm glad we had this opportunity to talk and shorten the space between us, but it's also drudging up some things I haven't thought about in a long time.

"Are you home for the whole summer?" I ask.

He lets go of my hand and sits up, rubbing his hand along his forehead. "Yeah, I'm going to work with my dad."

I nod, focusing my eyes on his broad, toned back.

"I better get to bed. I have to work tomorrow," he says, sliding off the edge of the trampoline.

"Beau."

He stops but doesn't turn around. "Yeah?"

"Can we hang out this summer? Like we used to?"

"I don't know," he says, walking away.

Maybe I should have stopped him . . . but I didn't.

⁓⌣⌣⌣⸽

"I'm glad you decided to come in today. How have you been?" Dr. Karcher asks as she rests her clipboard on her lap.

I came once a couple years ago at my mom's urging, but I left without saying much more than my name. I wasn't ready, but then one of Asher's napkin notes pushed me here. I'd held it in my hand, reading it over and over for days before finally deciding to come. Even now, I roll the paper between my fingers, reciting the words in my head.

Talk to someone. If you hold everything in, it will keep you from being the person you could be.

He's right. I've missed out on so many things, and that stops now. Drew is no longer going to be my reason for making any decisions. This is my life, and I'm taking control back.

I still haven't decided how much I want to tell her. I've been here a few other times, but I always close up and end up having to leave early.

She can't turn back time and completely erase the rape.

She can't bring Asher back.

How is she supposed to fix me?

"I'm just taking it one day at a time right now," I reply, trying to get comfortable in my chair.

"What's a normal day like for you?"

I glance at the ceiling, trying to configure what a day is really like. I live it without thinking about it much. "I go to work most mornings. And when I get off after lunch, I usually go for a run. The rest of my day is spent reading or watching TV with my mom when she's home."

"How is your relationship with your mom?" She leans in closer, tapping her pen against her chin.

"It's better than it was. She works a lot, and for a while we just weren't communicating like we should. We're working on that."

"Has your relationship always been a challenge?" What do any of these questions have to do with why I'm here?

"No, I started to pull away when I was sixteen," I answer.

"And why was that do you think?"

"I think it was a combination of growing up and pulling away. I pulled away from almost everyone," I admit, resting my elbow against the side of the chair. I don't know if the chair is uncomfortable, or if it's just being here that makes it feel that way.

"What caused you to pull away?" she asks, tilting her head. Dr. Karcher has an interesting look about her with frizzy brown curls and glasses that are slightly too large for her narrow frame.

I focus my eyes on the diplomas that hang on the wall. There are at least six of them, but they don't impress me. It's all just paper to me until I see something come out of this.

"Something happened a few years ago, and I just couldn't find a way to deal with it." I stop, lifting my legs up in the chair so that I can wrap my arms around them. "Why should anyone else have to deal with them?"

"And when you think about it now, how do you feel?"

This I have to think about before answering. It's definitely less painful to think about than it once was, but it still affects so much of my life. It holds me back and threatens me.

"It still hurts. It will always hurt, but the ache gets easier to deal with as the days pass."

"And what are you doing to deal with it?"

"Trying to face some of my fears head on," I answer honestly.

"Let's talk about that . . ."

For an hour, we go back and forth, playing a game of tug of war with our words. I tell her about my childhood. I tell her about growing up without a dad when everyone else around me had one. I tell her about Beau and how close we were growing up. And when we get to the point where she asks me why it all changed, I have to make a decision. Am I going to tell her why things are so different for me now, or is that something I should save for another time?

"Why aren't you and Beau as close as you used to be?" she asks, leaning forward in her chair.

I tuck my hands between my knees and lock my eyes on the bookcase on the right side of the room. I know she's not going to tell anyone, but she's still very much a stranger to me. Something about it just doesn't feel right yet. "Kate, your secrets are safe with me. Let me help you," she says quietly, twirling her watch on her wrist.

"How much time do we have?" I ask nervously. Maybe our session is almost done, and I can just leave and decide what I want to do later . . . if I actually decide to come back.

"You're my last appointment today. Take as much time as you need."

Another fork in my road . . . another moment where a decision can change everything.

So I talk. I tell her about the night my life changed, and when I call myself naïve, she stops me and tells me it wasn't my fault. I know that's true, but I also know I could have changed the way things ended that night by not going into that house and not trusting Drew.

"Do you ever think you've overcompensated? Are you pushing everything and everyone away because of this one twisted guy?"

I shrug. "Sometimes. I pushed Beau away, and he's the nicest, most honest person I know. I didn't feel normal and couldn't grasp why anyone would want to hang out with me."

"Have you ever loved someone who's changed? Did you still love them after?" After thinking about it, I realize most people in my life have changed. We all change.

"Yeah," I whisper, feeling the tears building in my eyes.

"Why would Beau be any different?"

"I don't know," I say, shaking my head. "I don't know. Maybe it was all me."

"Why do you say that?"

"I don't think I deserve him anymore," I cry, puncturing my own heart by saying the words.

"And what happened to make you feel that way?" she asks, setting her notebook on the small table in front of her. My whole body aches as I relive the moment that changed my life.

"I was raped," I sob, curling my legs into my body.

"How was that your fault?"

I cover my face with my hands and rest my elbows on my knees. This is draining me completely.

"Kate, you can talk to me," she whispers, running her hand up and down my back.

"I didn't do anything to deserve it! Okay? I was there because my friends were there. I just wanted to talk and have a good time." I run my sleeve across my eyes. "He tricked me. He robbed me."

"And why would Beau think any less of you?"

I internalize her words, and when I'm done, it's a slap in the face. I was wrong. I've been wrong for almost three years, and it's time to fix it.

Chapter 29

Beau

"CAN WE TALK?" Kate asks.

The last thing I expected today was to have her knocking on my door. But she did, and now she's standing right in front of me, looking up at me with those big green eyes I love so fucking much. Every time I look at her, I'm reminded of why this girl owns my fucking heart and why I can't get her out of my head.

After I left for college, I tried to tear my heart away from her. It's been almost a year, but I haven't been able to let her go. Not with how deep she's twisted inside of me. I've tried, Lord knows I've tried, but I don't think I can ever get her completely out of my head. I love her.

"Do you want to come in?" I ask, looking past her to the quiet street we've lived on for almost fifteen years.

She eyes me nervously, biting her lower lip. It drives me crazy every time she does that. "Actually, I was hoping we could go out to the lake," she pauses, clasping her fingers in front of her. "We haven't gone there at all this summer."

I hesitate because every time we've gone to the lake it has ended badly. I don't know what it is, but that place no longer holds the good memories it did when we were younger. The last time we were there, I laid my whole heart out for her, and I'm pretty sure it's still there, buried in the sand. "I should stay home and work on packing my stuff. I leave for school again in a few days."

"You're leaving already? School doesn't start for weeks," she blurts, sadness lining her eyes.

"Yeah, I got an apartment with a couple other guys. They're letting us move in August first because it's been empty all summer."

"Oh," she says, looking down at the ground. "I'll let you pack then. I just thought that maybe—"

She starts to back away, but I stop her. "Kate, wait," I say quickly, running my fingers through my hair. The way she's looking at me, you'd think I just ran over her puppy. I hate seeing that look on her face. "Give me ten minutes to change."

She nods and I feel relief as I watch her face relax.

Every time I look at her, I remember the day she moved next door. My mom saw her first and told me to go introduce myself. I thought it was stupid because I hated girls, but I've never regretted it. All of my best memories involve Kate . . . and some of my worst.

I've stuck by her even when she has tried to push me away. I love her, and I've tried to tell and show her over and over again, but nothing works.

The day I left her at the funeral hurt. I wanted to stay with her, but she was grieving over someone else. Her eyes once sparkled when she looked at me, the same type of sparkle I saw that day when she was with Asher in his car. I saw that look on her face many times up until a couple of years ago and then she changed.

The glimmer in her eyes was gone.

And I had no idea what changed.

I throw on a pair of swim trunks and a shirt before making my way back down the stairs. There's an unsettled feeling in my stomach. If she didn't mean so much to me, I'd walk right out there and tell her I don't have time to deal with this today.

Instead, I open the front door, getting a glimpse of Kate sitting on my front steps. "Ready to go?" I ask, slamming the old screen door shut.

She turns around, and if I didn't know better, I'd swear her whole body is shaking. I don't know why she's so nervous. Sure we haven't seen each other much this summer, mostly because I've been avoiding her, but we've hung out thousands of times. Things shouldn't be this way. It's not how it was meant to be, or how I wanted it to be.

"I'm ready."

I walk past her, making my way to the truck. Jumping in, I refuse to look back at her. When she's ready, she'll come on her own. I keep myself busy, rolling the windows down and turning on the radio. Hey Pretty Girl by Kip Moore is playing. It's funny how it's everything I wanted to say to Kate for so long, but waited until it was too late.

This is all that's left of us. We're two people who aren't happy when we're apart, but can't seem to get things right when we're together.

The door of the old Chevy creaks open and I watch out of the corner of my eye as she climbs in. After she slams her door shut, she rests her head against the back of the seat and holds her fingers outside the window like I've watched her do many times before. I like that she's the only girl I know who doesn't mind the wind blowing through her hair. It's when she looks her best.

"What do you want to do at the lake?" I ask, pulling out of the driveway.

"I thought we could talk. Summer's almost over, and I've barely seen you," she says shyly, fidgeting with string on her shorts.

"What do you want to talk about?"

"Can we wait until we get to the lake? I'm not ready yet," she says, her voice cracking slightly.

"You're scaring me, Kate." I steal a quick glance in her direction to see her head resting against the window. She looks absolutely miserable, and I swear to God I'm not leaving here until I find out what's causing it.

"I'm sorry. We'll talk when we get there. I need a few more minutes," she replies, wiping her finger under her eye.

Instinctually, my hand covers her knee, and to my surprise she doesn't flinch like she normally does. It's like I'm driving into a long, dark cave without any headlights. Why the hell does it feel like I'm not going to like where this is going?

As we pull into the parking lot near the lake, I notice the tears sliding down her cheeks. "Kate," I whisper, reaching for her hand.

She pulls it back and opens the door, getting out before I have a chance to say anything else. I'm frozen, watching her run toward the lake. It's surprising that she's not stopping or hesitating; there are lots of families out here today, and usually she would just hang behind and watch.

She runs to where the water meets the sand, kicking her sandals off and running her toes through the water. I stay back to give her a couple minutes to calm down. I don't know what's gotten her so upset, but we're not leaving here today until I find out.

"Are you ready to talk?" I ask, standing beside her.

"Can we go sit over there? I want us to be alone," she says, pointing to the small dock to the left of the beach.

I grab her hand without replying and walk us away from the crowd. "You're really fucking scaring me, Kate. As soon as we get over there, I need you to tell me."

Her body goes stiff beside me, and I regret the harshness that bled through my voice. This is obviously not easy for her, and I'm not helping the situation.

"I'm sorry," I whisper, running my thumb over the top of her hand. I pull her closer to my side in an attempt to calm her.

She sits down on the edge of the dock first, dangling her feet over the side. Taking my shoes off, I take the spot beside her and let my own feet fall into the water.

"Kate, tell me, what's going on?"

"It's about Drew," she whispers, running the lake water between her toes.

"Drew? Drew Heston?"

"Yeah," she says, looking up at me with tear-filled eyes.

"What about him?" I ask, thinking that something happened to him. Not that I care. The guy is a total douche who thinks the sun sets on his freaking schedule. Every single football game throughout my high school career, I prayed that someone would tackle him and put him out for the season. It never happened, but picturing it sure as fuck helped.

Kate's quiet and I hate it. Her silence always kills me, but when she reaches up with her shaky hand to tuck a piece of hair behind her ear, I want to pull her into my arms. "Kate."

She sucks in a deep breath, tilting her head back to look at the sky. I've never seen anyone look so lost and in pain. I feel sick just watching her.

The next thing she says is so quiet that I can barely hear her, but it nearly kills me when she says it. "He raped me."

My whole face heats as I watch her chest rapidly moving up and down. I want her to tell me I heard her wrong, or that it came out wrong, but of course that's not going to happen. Kate wouldn't make this shit up.

I swear I'll kill that bastard. I'll strangle him with my bare fucking hands. I swear to god, I'll do it for her.

"What did you just say? When?" I choke, gripping the wood board with my fingers. The old wood is ripping into my skin, but I don't care. Every muscle in my body is screaming for me to go after that asshole . . . but Kate needs me more.

"It was almost three years ago, at his house after a football game." She stops, looking over at me. Her tear-stained cheeks are like a sword in the heart to me.

No woman in this world deserves to be touched when she doesn't want to be. And when I think about it happening to *my* Kate, it rips me into a million little tiny pieces.

When I regain my composure, all I'm left with are questions. "How? We always went to those things together."

Her lips part, then close again. "You weren't there that night."

"What do you mean I wasn't there? I was always there." I panic, feeling an overwhelming pressure building in my chest.

Kate shakes her head, her sad eyes burning into me. "It was a Friday that you were grounded. I went with Morgan, and she left me by the fire alone. Drew came and started talking to me, and after a while it got really cold and started to rain." She stops, wrapping her arms around her legs.

"What happened?" I ask, feeling my own emotions bubbling up inside me. I can't escape the feeling that this was somehow my fault. I should have been there for her.

"He offered to get me a sweatshirt, so I followed him into his house to get it. I didn't think much of it. It was just Drew, you know?" she cries, covering her eyes with her hand. I reach my arms out to pull her close, but she pulls away. I want to hold her and tell her how sorry I am that the one time she needed me, I wasn't there.

I sit back with my hands resting on the dock again. "You don't have to tell me the rest—"

"No, I need to. Just let me get it out," she interrupts, taking a few deep breaths. "At first, everything was fine. And then nothing felt right. The house was completely quiet, and he was staring at me."

She shakes her head as tears roll down her face. Honestly, I don't know if I can handle hearing the rest, but she seems determined. A lump forms in my throat when I think about how much courage it must have taken for her to get to this point after all this time.

"Before I knew it, he had me pinned to the wall and then I was on a bed. His whole body was on top of me, and I couldn't get him off, Beau. I tried, but he was too strong," she sobs.

I reach out again and this time she lets me cradle her in my arms. Her head rests against my chest as I pull her tight against me. I'd do anything to go back in time and make this go away. I hate so much that it happened, but I also hate that she didn't tell me about it sooner. I could have been there for her.

It all makes sense now. When I think back to the last few years and how she had changed. She'd changed a lot. She went from being the girl who smiled every time she saw me, to being the girl who never smiled at all. She went from being the girl who had a lifetime of hopes and dreams, to the girl who struggled just to get through a day in school.

She quit being my girl, and now I understand why.

Her tears bring me back to where we are now. "Why didn't you tell me?" I ask, running my hand up and down her back.

"I didn't tell anyone. I couldn't. I didn't think anyone would believe me and—" she pauses, pulling back to look at me with her swollen red eyes.

"What is it?" I ask, brushing the hair off her face.

"He threatened me. I was so scared, Beau. He's a Heston, and I'm just me. Do you know what it feels like to walk around with this? It sucks. Every day for two years . . . I was here, but I was just getting by. Asher changed all that, but then he left too. I don't deserve this."

I carefully grip her upper arms, making sure her eyes are locked on mine. "You did nothing to deserve this. Do you hear me? Nothing," I say, cupping her face in my hands. I don't want to admit it, but Asher being in her life has helped her. As much as I hated seeing him with her, I loved seeing her with brightness in her eyes again.

Love is unselfish; that's how I know what I feel for Kate is the real thing.

She falls back into me as I continue to brush my fingers through her hair. Minutes tick by, but she hasn't moved once. One side of me wants to ask her a million questions while the other side just wants to hold her.

She laughs sadly, looking right up into my eyes. "I loved you for so long, you know? Your name was the one I wrote in the hearts on my notebook all through middle school. I thought my life would end just like this . . . with you."

My breath catches, savoring the words I've wanted to hear for so long. Words I'd given up on a long time ago. "It can still end that way," I say, running my thumbs along her jawline.

"No it can't. You know where you're going, and I'm just the girl who will hold you back."

"Kate—"

"No, listen to me. I loved you for so long, but it was never the right time for us. Then someone broke me, literally tearing my beliefs apart . . . my dreams, my life. I didn't think I'd ever recover. I didn't think I'd ever have a chance to be normal again. Asher gave me a second chance, and then his life was taken too soon," she says, breaking down again when she mentions him. "Now I don't know what I'm supposed to do with my life. I don't know what the future holds for me, and I can't take you along for the ride until I get it all figured out."

My heart beats rapidly as I rest my forehead against hers. For years, I've looked for any excuse to touch her skin. "You can't do everything alone. Let me help you. Let me be there for you."

She brushes her lips against mine, catching me completely off guard. "I need to figure out who I am first."

Cupping her face in my hands again, I press my lips to her forehead. I always said I'd wait for her, but there have been a few times I wanted to give up on the whole idea of love. After what she told me today, I know I can't give up on her just yet. She's not replaceable, not in my eyes.

"I love you," I whisper, kissing the tip of her nose. "And I'll give you the time you need. I'll still be waiting for you."

"I can't make any promises."

"I'm not asking you to. I'm asking for you to remember me when you're ready to move on," I say, wrapping my hands around the back of her neck.

"Where did I ever find you?" She smiles, brushing a few more fallen tears from her cheeks.

"In your backyard," I reply, smiling back at her.

"Thank you," she says, moving to sit next to me again.

"For what?" I ask, throwing a rock out into the water.

"For hearing me."

"Always. I just wish I would have heard you sooner," I say, grabbing her hand in mine.

"I wish I could have told you, but everything seems easier when you're looking back on it."

There are lots of things I'd like to go back and change, but falling in love with Kate Alexander is not one of those things.

Chapter 30

Five Weeks Later

Taking risks isn't something I'm good at, but today I'm hoping that all changes. Yesterday was my last day at the diner, and today will be the last day I wake up in my bed under this roof.

I'm actually going to college, and it's scary as hell.

My mom won't be there to hold me in her arms when I need her, but for the first time in a long time I feel as if I'm strong enough to stand on my own.

"You all ready to go?" she asks, carrying the last tote out to my car.

"Yeah, I think so."

"Are you sure you don't want me to drive you? I feel like I should at least drop you off," she says, trying her best to close my over-packed trunk.

"I'll be fine. It's only a few hours away."

I watch as she finally succeeds, facing me with a triumphant look on her face. It falls away quickly as she wraps her arms around my neck, pulling me as close to her as I can possibly get. "I'm going to miss you."

"I'm going to miss you too, Mom," I say, encircling her small waist in my arms.

"I know I haven't been home as much as I should be, but I'm going to miss you. Who's going to watch movies with me while eating Ben & Jerry's?" she asks with a lightness in her voice that I don't often get to hear.

"I'll come home as many weekends as I can, not that it matters. You have someone else to share your ice cream with now," I reply, looking over her shoulder to see Daniel watching us from our front porch. I'm not exactly sure how it happened, but they've been dating for a couple months now. I'm happy for them because they're both so good for one another. They truly deserve that kind of happiness.

"Now, don't come home every weekend. I want you to enjoy the things that I didn't get to enjoy when I was your age. This is your time," she whispers, kissing the side of my head.

"I love you, Mom."

"I love you too." She steps back, gripping my upper arms. Her eyes are teary, but she wears a satisfied smile. She makes me feel like I'm going to accomplish something, even if I'm unsure of it myself.

"Well, I better get going. I don't want to drive in the dark," I say, glancing up at the bright summer sky. I know it's going to be a clear night . . . perfect for watching the stars.

My fingers run along the silver chain that hangs around my neck until I feel the little umbrella. I never take it off . . . I don't think I ever will.

I can't leave without saying goodbye to Daniel. He's become a part of my family, and my mom and I are pretty much all he has. I'm ready to shake his hand, but he pulls me into a hug instead.

"I'm proud of you. We all are."

"Thank you, for everything," I whisper, nodding toward my mom.

He smiles, focusing his attention behind me. "She's an amazing woman."

"That she is," I agree, stepping back. "I better get going. Take care of her for me?"

"I will," he says, tucking his hands into his front pockets.

When I stand in front of my mom one last time, I'm a mixture of sadness and excitement all wrapped into one. I remember some kids from high school being absolutely through the moon at the prospect of having their freedom in college. I'm excited to get some space, there's no doubt about that, but I'm also terrified of what's going to happen once I'm dependent on myself and myself alone.

If things work out the way I want them to, I won't have to be alone for long.

I give my mom one more hug and climb into my car. As I pull away from the house, I wave my hand in the rearview mirror to make it visible to them. A year ago, I would have felt guilty about leaving her, but she's in good hands . . . and she's happier than I've ever seen her.

When I'm cruising down the highway, I turn on the iPod and let the soft, familiar voice fill my head. After Beau left to go back to college, I spent many afternoons alone in my room thinking, and many nights out on the old trampoline looking at the stars.

I want to go to school to become a youth counselor and help other young girls who may have gone through the same thing I did with Drew. Living a meaningful life is important to me. It's not about money or prestige. It's about helping as many people as I can through my experience and education.

I'm not just doing it for myself . . . it's my gift to Asher; a way to honor the man who gave so much back to me.

I've stumbled over and over again, but I'm still on my feet.

There's hope.

I also realize that there's a difference between soul mates and true love. Looking at the surface, they are similar, but when I dug deep down inside, I found they were different.

I found my soul mate. Asher understood all the complexities that made me who I was. We had an instant connection, and over time it grew into something so deep, strong and meaningful that it will stick with me forever. He brought me a sense of peace and happiness. He made me aware of the beauty in life, and for that I will forever be thankful.

I found my true love. Beau has been there for me over and over again, through good times and bad. He would give up his world for me, and I would do the same for him. He would give up everything just to know I was okay as he has proven time and time again. When I am with him, there is no possibility of an end for us.

Is one type of love better than the other? I don't know, but I'm lucky enough to have found them both. I'm lucky that Asher opened my eyes again because if I had never met him, I probably never would have realized how much I really do love Beau.

It's easy to look at it now and see I've always belonged to Beau in some way or another. I spent hours watching him out my window this summer, doing everything from mowing his yard to washing his truck. There was even one day where I watched him help the older lady who lives across the street plant her flowers. He's perfect.

Everything he does amazes me. I fall in love with him every day, and he doesn't even have to say a word. We have a bond that's unbreakable, and that is why I'm taking this chance now.

Apart, we're only half of what we are when we're together. He completes me, and I'm ready to feel whole again.

The drive is long and boring. I pass miles and miles of cornfields before finally pulling into Iowa City. I should go check in with my new roommate, but I can't wait any longer to see him. We've spoken a few times on the phone, but he's been giving me time to think and decide what it is I want out of life.

Now, I feel like I have it figured out. Excitement washes over me when I think of what he's going to say when I tell him. We've both been waiting for so long, but I hold the key and I'm about to unlock our future.

I park in front of his apartment and take a few deep breaths, trying to calm my nerves. This is the beginning of yet another journey for me.

The sun heats my face as I walk up the sidewalk to the old brick building and take the steps to his floor. When I asked his mom for his address, she grinned. I think she knows. I think she's always known.

Butterflies go crazy in my stomach as I find his door and raise my hand to knock. I've never been so nervous in my whole life. I'm about to knock again when the door swings open. A tall blonde with big blue eyes stares back at me.

"Is Beau here?" I ask, trying to see into the apartment.

Her eyes roam up and down my body before landing back on mine. The grin on her face sounds alarm bells in my head. "He just got out of the shower. Would you like me to go get him?" she asks, running her tongue over her teeth.

I feel sick to my stomach. Maybe I waited too long?

"Umm, no, I'll just call him later," I say softly, taking a few steps back.

"Are you sure you don't want me to go get him?" she asks, leaning against the doorframe.

"Yeah, thanks though," I say, walking steadily down the hall to the stairs.

Disbelief washes over me. Before he left, I was under the impression that he would wait for me a little while longer. I knew it wasn't fair to make him wait forever, but five weeks . . . why did he give up so quickly?

I can't stop the tears from running down my cheeks. I've wanted him for so long that he's become my living dream, and now it's obvious that he's going to stay that way. I have many regrets, but if I never get a second chance, this will be my ultimate regret.

I love him.

I make my way out the door and down the sidewalk to the street. I left him behind, and now he's over me.

"Kate! Wait!" a familiar voice yells from behind me, stopping me in my tracks.

I don't want to turn around and let him see the tears. He shouldn't feel sorry for moving on when I'm the one who waited so long to realize what he means to me.

"Look at me," he whispers, so close that I feel the heat of his chest against my back.

"I can't. I need to go."

He stands behind me and presses his hand to my stomach. It feels so right. "Why did you come if you weren't going to stay?"

"Beau, please," I cry, leaning my head back against his shoulder, allowing the water droplets from his bare chest to soak into my shirt.

"Talk to me," he demands.

I could tell him the truth, but I decide to go with a half-truth. "I'm here for school. I signed up for some classes."

"Why are you crying?" he asks, moving around me to get a better look at my face. He has nothing on but a pair of black athletic shorts and droplets of water are rolling out of his hair.

He's everything I've always wanted, and I'm too late. I don't want to hear it, but he asked me to always be honest.

"I came for you."

His eyes move back and forth between mine. "Then why didn't you stay?"

Pinching my eyes shut, I use the back of my hand to wipe my cheeks. "When your girlfriend answered the door . . . I realized I was too late. I didn't need to hear you say it."

He places his finger under my chin. "Open your eyes."

I hesitate, not wanting to see him when he tells me I'm right. "Kate, I'm only going to ask you one more time. Open. Your. Eyes. Please."

This time I do, and when I look at him I see the old playfulness I'm used to. I want to run and pretend that this never happened. I want to run back to a time when he was there, telling me how much he loves me and never let him go.

His face comes closer to mine until his lips are a whisper above mine. "You got it all wrong, beautiful."

"What?" I ask.

"Rachel is my roommate's girlfriend," he says, a hint of a smile playing on his lips.

I stop, rolling his words around in my head. " I don't get it. She was looking at me like—"

"She was looking at you like that because she knows you're my Kate. Everyone in that apartment, or who has ever been in that apartment, knows who you are." He smiles.

"She's not—"

"No," he says, shaking his head slowly and cupping my face in his hands. "I've been waiting for you."

His lips brush against mine, causing my heart to pound against my chest. When he breaks contact, his thumb runs against my lower lip.

"I'm here," I whisper, leaning into his touch.

"That's good because I can't wait any longer," he says, lifting me up in his arms. His lips press against mine, this time lingering a little longer.

It's exactly the moment my dream became a reality.

Beau is my light, my stars, my sun . . . he gives me hope.

He's where my new life begins.

Epilogue

One Year Later

I'VE LEARNED THREE THINGS IN MY LIFE.

First, I can't keep things locked inside. They will eventually eat me up until there is nothing left, and life is too short to live in solitude. One of the things Asher taught me is that every day should be worth at least one smile.

Second, I should never take anyone or anything for granted. It's easy to assume that when someone walks into our life they will always be there. But I know that one day, one moment, one ounce of bad luck can change everything. I lost Asher way too soon. He had the most beautiful soul, and without him I don't know how long it would have taken me to find myself again. I'm never going to be the girl I was, but right now, I'm the person I want to be. I'm content with who I am and where my life is going.

Third, love is a powerful emotion. It has the ability to get you through anything. But you have to let it.

For the past year, Beau and I have learned that over and over again. We're also learning that you fight with the ones you love more than the ones you don't . . . but I wouldn't have it any other way.

"Hey, are you ready to go?" he whispers in my ear, wrapping his arms around me from behind.

"Yep, let me grab the cooler, and I'll meet you outside."

He kisses my cheek when I look over my shoulder and loosens his grip, resting his hands on my hips. "Don't take too long, beautiful. I can't wait to see you in that new blue bikini."

"Beau."

"Yeah?"

"The quicker you let go of me, the quicker we can make that happen," I smile, attempting to take a step forward, but he pulls me back into him.

"One more kiss," he says, spinning me around to face him. He wastes no time pressing his lips to mine. He starts slowly, gently pulling my lower lip between his teeth. I moan with the tingle it sends shooting down my spine. Every kiss is a first kiss with Beau Bennett. Yet this time, when I'm expecting more, he pulls back. "Hurry up. We'll finish that when we get to the lake."

I bite my lower lip, knowing it will make him crazy. He deserves it for leaving me hanging like that. When he tries to grab for me again, I step back. "Go wait in the truck."

He winks at me, melting my heart like butter. "You better hurry," he growls, playfully smacking my ass before walking backwards toward the door.

This is our last time at the lake for the summer before we have to return to school. It's our place, and it always will be. We've talked about moving back here after school and maybe buying a house by the lake, but I think it's a little too early to plan that far ahead in the future. It's definitely a place we'll always come to visit.

When I walk into the kitchen to grab the cooler, I catch my mom and Daniel locked in an embrace. Sometimes they're almost too cute. They have spent every minute this way since they got married. I smile, realizing how similar mine and Beau's relationship is to theirs.

"Beau and I are heading out to the lake. Are we still grilling tonight?" I ask, stopping at the door.

"Of course. We invited Beau's parents over too since it's your last night home," my mom replies, resting her head on Daniel's chest.

"Sounds good. We'll see you later," I say, waving with my free hand before opening the door.

Beau is sitting in his truck with his arm hanging out the window and country music blaring through the stereo. His smile widens when he sees me, and everything feels right.

I'm going to marry that boy someday. Not tomorrow, not next year, but someday. He's my forever.

"It's about time," he says as I climb into the truck.

"Beau."

"Yes, beautiful?"

"Just drive," I smile, sticking my hands out the window to feel the warm summer air. The ride is quiet except for the sounds of country twang and wooden guitars that blare through his speakers. Music has become a symbol of the different periods in my life. I still have the iPod Asher left me, and I listen to it often. I'll always miss his voice . . . it's a reminder of all the things he's given me.

A couple months after Beau and I officially started dating, I told him about it and all the other good memories I have of Asher. I wasn't sure how he'd react, but he understood. I'm sure he wishes he could have been the one to save me, but I think he's grateful to have me back no matter what road I took to get there.

As we pull into the parking lot, I notice that the beach is pretty empty for this time of year. Crowds don't bother me like they used to, but being here alone with Beau sounds like a little slice of heaven.

"What are you waiting for?" Beau asks, running his thumb along my cheekbone.

"I was just thinking about how much I love this place." I smile, looking over at the love of my life.

"It holds a lot of memories," he says, tucking a few strands of loose hair behind my ear.

"That is does. So let's go make new ones." I give him my best seductive grin. Anyone else might laugh at it, but Beau gets it.

We waited months before we had sex. It was good because it allowed us to rekindle our emotional bond. Our love is so strong, and nothing could destroy it now. We worked for fifteen years to get to this point, and nothing is going to come between us.

I jump out of the truck and wait for Beau to grab the cooler from the back. We make our way to "our spot"—a little clearing in the tall grass—and lay down an old flannel blanket. I decide to play with Beau a little bit and slowly pull my shirt over my head. His eyes double in size as he takes in my new bikini top, and he watches as I unbutton my shorts and let them slide down my legs. I absolutely love when he looks at me like that.

"Come here," he demands, holding out his left hand.

I do as he asks, but I walk to him slowly, enjoying the anticipation. When I'm close enough that he can touch me, he grabs my hand and presses my body against his. He skips the 'slow' this time and presses his tongue into my mouth. Wrapping my arms around his neck, I feel every part of him, inside and out. His touch is warmer than the sun on my skin, and it's easy to get lost in him.

He's my true love and my best friend.

As his mouth and tongue continue to dance with mine, his hands run up and down my back. Everything he does, he does carefully, but the second I pull his hair between my fingers, he gets the hint and runs his thumbs over my nipples.

A few miraculous raindrops fall from the sky and land on my head. When I look up, I see a lone storm cloud over our heads. A laugh escapes my lips as I finger the umbrella around my neck.

"Thank you," I mouth before letting my eyes connect with Beau's again.

He picks me up off the ground and spins me around, kissing me again with his warm lips while the rain pours down.

"I love you so fucking much," he says, resting his forehead against mine.

"I love you too," I say, pulling him in for another kiss.

When it rains think of me. I look up, letting the rain hit my face and smile.

Every two minutes, someone in the U.S. is sexually assaulted and 44% of victims are under the age of 18.

If you have been a victim of sexual abuse, you are not alone. You can contact the Rape, Abuse, Incest National Network at www.rainn.org or 1-800-656-HOPE.

Acknowledgements

FIRST, I WANT TO THANK MY FAMILY for putting up with my crazy hours and lack of home-cooked meals over the last few months. I couldn't do this without the support I receive from my husband and my amazing, understanding children.

To my critique partner Mireya, you continue to push me when I just want to give up. You lift me up when I'm feeling down, and I'm grateful to have you in my life. You'll always be the other half of my crazy.

To Jessica, words cannot express how much your friendship means to me. Thank you so much for everything you did to help me get When It Rains to where it is. I could say how much I appreciate you one thousand times over and it still wouldn't be enough.

To Jennifer, thank you for your editing expertise. You are the queen of turning a good sentence into a great sentence.

To my amazing beta readers: Amy B., Amy C., Melissa, Christine, Mint, Jennifer and Deanna, thank you! When It Rains would not be where it is without your feedback.

I would also like to thank Angie at Angie's Dreamy Reads for putting together my blog tour and Christine at Shh Mom's Reading for helping with the cover reveal.

And last but not least, I'd like to thank all the fans and bloggers who have supported me throughout my writing journey. I wouldn't be where I am today without you!

About the Author

LISA DE JONG IS A WIFE, mother and full-time number cruncher who lives in the Midwest. Her writing process involves insane amounts of coffee and many nights of very little sleep but she wouldn't change a thing. She also enjoys reading, football and music.

Twitter: @LisaDeJongBooks
Email: lisadejongwrites@gmail.com
www.lisadejongbooks@blogspot.com

Coming Soon . . .
Always Imperfect (Imperfect #1)—December 2013
Sometimes Imperfect (Imperfect #2)—February 2014
This Love Thing—Early 2014
Once Again—Spring 2014

Arsen

A broken love story
By Mia Asher

Prologue

Broken.

I'm lost.

I'm drifting away . . .

Drowning in a sea of sorrow and pain as waves of regret keep pulling me down where an undertow of resentment won't let me break free.

Maybe I should just give up?

As I stare blankly into Dr. Pajaree's beautiful dark eyes, listening to her prognosis in her pragmatic, yet friendly voice, I can't help wondering where the magic has gone? Is real life contaminating our fairy tale romance with all its ugliness?

Yes.

Maybe.

"It's better known as habitual abortion . . . recurrent pregnancy loss . . . RPL . . . three or more pregnancies that end in misca . . ."

With my arms tightly wrapped around my stomach, I rock back and forth as I try to listen to what she's saying, her words drifting in and out of my consciousness.

I know I should be paying more attention because she's explaining to me why I'm not woman enough, why I can't keep a baby in my body long enough to be able to hold it in my arms, but all I want to do is shake off the cold blanket of numbness that enfolds me.

It's not working. I'm still so very cold, so very dead inside. Feeling Ben's strong arm wrap around my shoulders stops the manic rocking, but even his warm embrace can't help me get rid of this helplessness threatening to take over.

I wonder why doctors wear white coats. It's such an ugly color.

Sterile.

Ben gives my shoulder a supportive squeeze, waking me from my drunken-like stupor.

"Tell us what to do, where to go, who to see . . . it doesn't matter. We will do it, Dr. Pajaree. No matter what the cost is," Ben says, not letting go of me. Focusing my gaze on Dr. Pajaree's face once more, I listen to her next words.

"Yes, Ben." Dr. Pajaree looks at Ben with understanding in her eyes for a moment, then turns in my direction. "Cathy, since this is your third miscarriage I think it's time we ran some tests on both of you. I'm talking about parental chromosome testing, blood tests for thrombophilia, thyroid function, ovarian function . . . if we can identify the cause for RPL, then we can look at treatment options."

"E-Excuse me. I need to use the ladies' room. Sorry."

The chair makes a horrible screeching sound as I forcefully push it backwards and leave the room, but I don't care. Running to the bathroom, I lock myself inside and stand in front of the sink. I notice a sheen of sweat covering my forehead and my entire body seems to be shaking slightly.

Swallowing hard, I close my eyes as I try to compose myself.

I can't have another panic attack.

I can't.

"Cathy! Open the door, Cathy! Please, let me in," Ben pleads as he bangs on the door.

"Please, Cathy. Open the door." There's a hint of desperation in his voice.

Not wanting to draw more attention to us, I open the door and let Ben in. As soon as he walks through, he enfolds me in an air robbing, soul crushing hug and buries his face in the curve of my neck.

"Babe, please . . . don't give up. It will be okay. I promise you, I'll leave no stone unturned. There's no place in the world where I won't take you, there's nothing I won't do until we have a child to call our own. I promise you, Cathy." Tightening his grip around me and pulling me closer to him, he roughly whispers, "For you I will do anything. Anything."

As I return his embrace, I believe the earnest prayer he's chanting in my ear, and I believe his words with my whole heart, but even Ben can't stop the numbness settling around me, settling around my heart.

I can feel myself withdrawing from him.

From his love.

From my marriage.

And there's nothing I can do to stop it.

Nothing.

Chapter 1

"Babe, can you pick up the dry cleaning today? I may be running late. Amy needs me to go to the airport and pick up the new guy."

My husband lifts his brown eyes from the newspaper he's holding, and smiles the same smile that robbed me of my breath the first time I met him eleven years ago.

It doesn't rob me of my breath anymore.

Sometimes it feels as if I am living with a man who I don't know. A man whose face seems familiar but remains a stranger.

Sometimes I feel like the normalcy of our lives will drive me insane.

"Sure, no big deal. Just remind me who this new guy is?" He puts the newspaper down on the table and runs his hand through his short black hair. Looking at my husband now as his lips touch the rim of the coffee mug, I realize how handsome he really is. The realization that I seem to have forgotten what he looks like, truly looks like, hits me like a running bull in Pamplona.

Am I so desensitized to him that I have forgotten how his maple-brown eyes shine like the brightest gemstone when he looks at you straight on? How his gaze is as penetrating as the tip of the needle when it pierces your skin? I seem to have forgotten that when he smiles a little dimple appears on his left cheek. That dimple is taunting me, begging me to kiss it, but I don't. I really don't have time to be sitting here, admiring my husband. I have to get to work.

"Cathy? Are you listening to me?" He's waving his large hand in front of my eyes, trying to get my attention back. I snap out of my reverie, refocusing on his face and his mouth. He's speaking to me, but all I hear is the annoying electric buzzing of the landscaper working outside in our garden.

Buzz—Buzz—Buzz—Buzz

Trying to clear my thoughts, I shake my head. "Sorry, babe. The landscaper is distracting me. What were you saying?"

Tenderly smiling at me, Ben says, "Your boss, Cathy. You said Amy wants you to go to the airport and pick someone up tonight?"

"Oh, yes. I'm not sure who the guy is, but apparently he's coming with his son and wife. I think he's going to take over the company. I don't know. Anyway, I've got to run."

Standing up, I make my way to my husband and bend down to kiss him on the cheek. As I'm straightening, Ben grabs the back of my neck and guides my face back to kiss him on the lips. Startled, I don't immediately kiss him back until I feel his tongue trying to make its way inside my mouth. I open my lips to welcome him in, and we begin to kiss earnestly. His tongue tangles with mine as I feel his hand sneaking up under my skirt, making its way to my core. When his thumb hooks under the edge of my panties and moves them aside, his middle finger enters me and I break the kiss.

I straighten my body completely and look down at Ben who just grins widely at me. His lips look moist from our kiss, and I can't help laughing out loud when he smiles at me like that. I think he has two speeds-horny or tired.

"Seriously, Ben? I have to get to work." I turn around, but Ben's hands grab my waist from behind and pull me back to sit on his lap.

Oh, my . . .

He laughs in my ear as he nudges my ass with his huge erection, "Can't help myself around you, Cathy. You're just so damn sexy in the morning. Come on, it will be a quickie." His tongue is inside my ear, tracing its contours while his hand goes back to work under my skirt.

"Ben, stop it. I have to get to work. I'm already late . . . as . . . it . . . is . . ."

"Yes, baby?" he huskily whispers in my ear.

Oh, those fingers of his . . .

Recognizing what is going on, and what I don't want to happen, I push his hands off my body, and stand up. As I look down the length of my body trying to smooth my skirt free of wrinkles, and pacify the rapid beating of my heart, I notice that my hands are shaking. After taking a few calming breaths, I look up to see him watching me with a raw and naked hunger as he brings the finger that was just inside me to his mouth and sucks it.

Hard.

Ben pulls his finger out and his tongue follows behind, tracing the lingering flavor of my body on his lips. I feel a powerful shot of heat surge straight where his hand was not too long ago.

When Ben realizes that I'm not moving, he chuckles then grabs me by the hand, pulling me forward and lifting me until I'm straddling his hips.

"Babe, I've missed you," he says roughly.

As he leans down to nuzzle my neck, I sense some sort of desperation growing within me. I do want him. I want him to take the lead, make everything go away. His hands close around my wrists, moving them to wrap around his neck, then he grabs my ass, pushing me against his erection.

"I need you, babe. So fucking much," he says before he lets go of me and begins to slowly unbutton my silk shirt, pulling down my bra and exposing my breasts to him. Without breaking the kiss, I let go of his neck and unbuckle his belt, unzip his dress pants and pull down his boxer briefs. I take his hard erection in my hand and begin stroking him, feeling the strength of his dick in my fingers.

"Enough," he says roughly as he puts a hand over mine, stopping me. "Let me."

I nod, allowing him to do whatever he wants to me. We become frantic, our need for each other vibrating through our bodies, and we barely have time to lift my skirt and slide my panties to the side until he pushes forward.

"Fuck, you're wet." We both look down to where our bodies are connected and watch as he begins to pull out of me. There's nothing more sensual than watching your lover's arousal as it leaves your warmth covered with your body's reaction to his touch. Covered in want.

Connected as we are, I'm overcome by this feeling of wanting to be owned by Ben. To drive him mad with desire.

"No more talking, Ben." I pull his head down towards mine and kiss him once more, letting the rhythm of his thrusts set the pace of our lovemaking

After I reach my release, Ben allows himself to do the same.

"Jesus Christ," he mutters.

Breathing heavily, with our arms still around each other, my legs wrapped around his waist, and our bodies cooling off, we look at each other and smile. Whatever desperation I sensed in me before has dissipated.

For now.

"Damn, wife, if that's what you call breakfast," he grips my hips, "I think I may never skip it again." He smirks.

"Better than coffee?" I ask, blushing.

Ben throws his head back and laughs. He cups my cheeks, and makes me stare at him until I lose my way in his brown eyes.

"Yes, so much better than coffee," he caresses my lower lip with his thumb. "I love your smile, wife. Even after all these years it can go straight to my . . ." he nudges me gently, still inside me, "and my heart." He leans down and plants a soft kiss on my smiling lips. "I love you, babe."

"I love you, too. I guess we need to take another shower before work." I untangle my legs from his waist, our bodies disconnecting, and get off his lap. Wrapping my shirt around my bare chest, I make my way to our bedroom with Ben following close behind.

When my hands land on my empty stomach, I shut down the voice inside my head, reminding me of the overwhelming emptiness spreading inside me like a black hole, sucking all the happiness around me.

The voice telling me that everything remains the same.

Or not.

Made in the USA
Charleston, SC
12 December 2014